A GENT FROM BEAR CREEK

LECTOR HOUSE PUBLIC DOMAIN WORKS

HAPPY READING!

A GENT FROM BEAR CREEK

ROBERT E. HOWARD

ISBN: 978-93-5342-033-8

First Published: -

LECTOR HOUSE LLP
E-MAIL: lectorpublishing@gmail.com

A GENT FROM BEAR CREEK

BY

ROBERT E. HOWARD

CONTENTS

CHAPTER I

STRIPED SHIRTS AND BUSTED HEARTS

If Joel Braxton hadn't drawed a knife whilst I was beating his head agen a spruce log, I reckon I wouldn't of had that quarrel with Glory McGraw, and things might of turned out different to what they did. Pap's always said the Braxtons was no-account folks, and I allow he's right. First thing I knowed Jim Garfield hollered: "Look out, Breck, the yaller hound's got a knife!" Then I felt a kind of sting and looked down and seen Joel had cut a big gash in my buckskin shirt and scratched my hide trying to get at my innards.

I let go of his ears and taken the knife away from him and throwed it into a blackjack thicket, and throwed him after it. They warn't no use in him belly-aching like he done just because they happened to be a tree in his way. I dunno how he expects to get throwed into a blackjack thicket without getting some hide knocked off.

But I am a good-natured man, and I was a easy-going youngster, even then. I paid no heed to Joel's bloodthirsty threats whilst his brother and Jim Garfield and the others was pulling him out of the bresh and dousing him in the creek to wash the blood off. I got on to my mule Alexander and headed for Old Man McGraw's cabin where I was started to when I let myself be beguiled into stopping with them idjits.

The McGraws is the only folks on Bear Creek besides the Reynoldses and the Braxtons which ain't no kin to me one way or another, and I'd been sweet on Glory McGraw ever since I was big enough to wear britches. She was the tallest, finest, purtiest gal in the Humbolt Mountains, which is covering considerable territory. They warn't a gal on Bear Creek, not even my own sisters, which could swing a axe like her, or fry a b'ar steak as tasty, or make hominy as good, and they warn't nobody, man nor woman, which could outrun her, less'n it was me.

As I come up the trail that led up to the McGraw cabin, I seen her, just scooping a pail of water out of the creek. The cabin was just out of sight on the other side of a clump of alders. She turned around and seen me, and stood there with the pail dripping in her hand, and her sleeves rolled up, and her arms and throat and bare feet was as white as anything you ever seen, and her eyes was the same color as the sky, and her hair looked like gold dust when the sun hit it.

I taken off my coonskin cap, and said: "Good mornin', Glory, how're you-all this mornin'?"

"Joe got kicked right severe by pap's sorrel mare yesterday," she says. "Just knocked some hide off, though. Outside of that we're all doin' fine. Air you glued to that mule?"

"No'm," I says, and clumb down, and says: "Lemme tote yore pail, Glory."

She started to hand it to me, and then she frowned and p'inted at my shirt, and says: "You been fightin' agen."

"Nobody but Joel Braxton," I said. "'Twarn't nothin'. He said moskeeters in the Injun Territory was bigger'n what they be in Texas."

"What you know about it?" says she. "You ain't never been to Texas."

"Well, he ain't never been to the Injun Territory neither," I said. "'Taint the moskeeters. It's the principle of the thing. My folks all come from Texas, and no Braxton can slander the State around me."

"You fight too much," she said. "Who licked?"

"Why, me, of course," I said. "I always do, don't I?"

This harmless statement seemed to irritate her.

"I reckon you think nobody on Bear Creek can lick you," she sneered.

"Well," I says truthfully, "nobody ain't, up to now--outside of pap."

"You ain't never fit none of my brothers," she snapped.

"That's why," I said. "I've took quite a lot of sass offa them ganglin' mavericks jest because they was yore brothers and I didn't want to hurt 'em."

Gals is funny about some things. She got mad and jerked the pail out of my hand, and says: "Oh, is that so? Well, lemme tell you right now, Breckinridge Elkins, the littlest one of my brothers can lick you like a balky hoss, and if you ever lay a finger on one of 'em, I'll fix you! And furthermore and besides, they's a gent up to the cabin right now which could pull his shootin' iron and decorate yore whole carcass with lead polka-dots whilst you was fumblin' for yore old cap- and-ball pistol!"

"I don't claim to be no gunfighter," I says mildly. "But I bet he cain't sling iron fast as my cousin Jack Gordon."

"You and yore cousins!" says she plenty scornful. "This feller is sech a gent as you never drempt existed! He's a cowpuncher from the Wild River Country, and he's ridin' through to Chawed Ear and he stopped at our cabin for dinner. If you could see him, you wouldn't never brag no more. You with that old mule and them moccasins and buckskin clothes!"

"Well, gosh, Glory!" I says plumb bewildered. "What's the matter with buckskin? I like it better'n homespun."

"Hah!" sneered she. "You oughta see Mr. Snake River Wilkinson! He ain't wearin' neither buckskins nor homespun. Store-bought clothes! I never seen such elegance. Star top boots, and gold-mounted spurs! And a red neckcloth--he said silk. I dunno. I never seen nothin' like it before. And a shirt all red and green and yaller and beautiful! And a white Stetson hat! And a pearl-handled six-shooter! And the finest hoss and riggin's you ever seen, you big dummox!"

"Aw, well, gosh!" I said, getting irritated. "If this here Mister Wilkinson is so blame gorgeous, whyn't you marry him?"

I ought not to said it. Her eyes flashed blue sparks.

"I will!" she gritted. "You think a fine gentleman like him wouldn't marry me, hey? I'll show you! I'll marry him right now!"

And impulsively shattering her water bucket over my head she turned and run up the trail.

"Glory, wait!" I hollered, but by the time I got the water out of my eyes and the oak splinters out of my hair she was gone.

Alexander was gone too. He taken off down the creek when Glory started yelling at me, because he was a smart mule in his dumb way, and could tell when thunder-showers was brewing. I run him for a mile before I caught him, and then I got onto him and headed for the McGraw cabin agen. Glory was mad enough to do anything she thought would worry me, and they warn't nothing would worry me more'n for her to marry some dern cowpuncher from the river country. She was plumb wrong when she thought I thought he wouldn't have her. Any man which would pass up a chance to get hitched with Glory McGraw would be a dern fool, I don't care what color his shirt was.

My heart sunk into my moccasins as I approached the alder clump where we'd had our row. I figgered she'd stretched things a little talking about Mr. Wilkinson's elegance, because whoever heard of a shirt with three colors into it, or gold-mounted spurs? Still, he was bound to be rich and wonderful from what she said, and what chance did I have? All the clothes I had was what I had on, and I hadn't never even seen a store-bought shirt, much less owned one. I didn't know whether to fall down in the trail and have a good bawl, or go get my rifle-gun and lay for Mr. Wilkinson.

Then, jest as I got back to where I'd saw Glory last, here she come again, running like a scairt deer, with her eyes all wide and her mouth open.

"Breckinridge!" she panted. "Oh, Breckinridge! I've played hell now!"

"What you mean?" I said.

"Well," says she, "that there cowpuncher Mister Wilkinson had been castin' eyes at me ever since he arriv at our cabin, but I hadn't give him no encouragement. But you made me so mad awhile ago, I went back to the cabin, and I marched right up to him, and I says: 'Mister Wilkinson, did you ever think about gittin' married?' He grabbed me by the hand and he says, says he: 'Gal, I been thinkin' about it ever since I seen you choppin' wood outside the cabin as I rode by. Fact is, that's why I stopped here.' I was so plumb flabbergasted I didn't know what to say, and the first thing I knowed, him and pap was makin' arrangements for the weddin'!"

"Aw, gosh!" I said.

She started wringing her hands.

"I don't want to marry Mister Wilkinson!" she hollered. "I don't love him! He turnt my head with his elegant manners and striped shirt! What'll I do? Pap's sot on me marryin' the feller!"

"Well, I'll put a stop to that," I says. "No dem cowcountry dude can come into the Humbolts and steal my gal. Air they all up to the cabin now?"

"They're arguin' about the weddin' gift," says Glory. "Pap thinks Mister Wilkinson oughta give him a hundred dollars. Mister Wilkinson offered him his Winchester instead of the cash. Be keerful, Breckinridge! Pap don't like you much, and Mister Wilkinson has got a awful mean eye, and his scabbard-end tied to his laig."

"I'll be plumb diplomatic," I promised, and got onto my mule Alexander and reched down and lifted Glory on behind me, and we rode up the path till we come to within maybe a hundred foot of the cabin door. I seen a fine white hoss tied in front of the cabin, and the saddle and bridle was the most elegant I ever seen. The silverwork shone when the sun hit it. We got off and I tied Alexander, and Glory hid behind a white oak. She warn't scairt of nobody but her old man, but he shore had her number.

"Be keerful, Breckinridge," she begged. "Don't make pap or Mister Wilkinson mad. Be tactful and meek."

So I said I would, and went up to the door. I could hear Miz McGraw and the other gals cooking dinner in the back room, and I could hear Old Man McGraw talking loud in the front room.

"'Taint enough!" says he. "I oughta have the Winchester and ten dollars. I tell you, Wilkinson, it's cheap enough for a gal like Glory! It plumb busts my heart strings to let her go, and nothin' but greenbacks is goin' to soothe the sting!"

"The Winchester and five bucks," says a hard voice which I reckoned was Mister Wilkinson. "It's a prime gun, I tell you. Ain't another'n like it in these mountains."

"Well," begun Old Man McGraw in a covetous voice, and jest then I come in through the door, ducking my head to keep from knocking it agen the lintel-log.

Old Man McGraw was setting there, tugging at his black beard, and them long gangling boys of his'n, Joe and Bill and John, was there gawking as usual, and there on a bench nigh the empty fireplace sot Mister Wilkinson in all his glory. I batted my eyes. I never seen such splendor in all my born days. Glory had told the truth about everything: the white Stetson with the fancy leather band, and the boots and gold-mounted spurs, and the shirt. The shirt nigh knocked my eyes out. I hadn't never dreamed nothing could be so beautiful--all big broad stripes of red and yaller and green! I seen his gun, too, a pearl-handled Colt .45 in a black leather scabbard which was wore plumb smooth and the end tied down to his laig with a rawhide thong. I could tell he hadn't never wore a glove on his right hand, neither, by the brownness of it. He had the hardest, blackest eyes I ever seen. They looked right through me.

I was very embarrassed, being quite young then, but I pulled myself together and says very polite: "Howdy, Mister McGraw."

"Who's this young grizzly?" demanded Mister Wilkinson suspiciously.

"Git out of here, Elkins," requested Old Man McGraw angrily. "We're talkin' over private business. You git!"

"I know what kind of business you-all are talkin' over," I retorted, getting irritated. But I remembered Glory said be diplomatic, so I said: "I come here to tell you the weddin's off! Glory ain't goin' to marry Mister Wilkinson. She's goin' to marry me, and anybody which comes between us had better be able to rassle cougars and whup grizzlies bare-handed!"

"Why, you--" begun Mister Wilkinson in a blood-thirsty voice, as he riz onto his feet like a painter fixing to go into action.

"Git outa here!" bellered Old Man McGraw jumping up and grabbing the iron poker. "What I does with my datter ain't none of yore business! Mister Wilkinson here is makin' me a present of his prime Winchester and five dollars in hard money! What could you offer me, you mountain of beef and ignorance?"

"A bust in the snoot, you old tightwad," I replied heatedly, but still remembering to be diplomatic. They warn't no use in offending him, and I was determined to talk quiet and tranquil, in spite of his insults. So I said: "A man which would sell his datter for five dollars and a gun ought to be et alive by the buzzards! You try to marry Glory to Mister Wilkinson and see what happens to you, sudden and onpleasant!"

"Why, you--!" says Old Man McGraw, swinging up his poker. "I'll bust yore fool skull like a egg!"

"Lemme handle him," snarled Mister Wilkinson. "Git outa the way and gimme a clean shot at him. Lissen here, you jack-eared mountain- mule, air you goin' out of here perpendicular, or does you prefer to go horizontal?"

"Open the ball whenever you feels lucky, you stripe-bellied polecat!" I retorted courteously, and he give a snarl and went for his gun, but I got mine out first and shot it out of his hand along with one of his fingers before he could pull his trigger.

He give a howl and staggered back agen the wall, glaring wildly at me, and at the blood dripping off his hand, and I stuck my old cap- and-ball .44 back in the scabbard and said: "You may be accounted a fast gunslinger down in the low country, but yo're tolerable slow on the draw to be foolin' around Bear Creek. You better go on home now, and--"

It was at this moment that Old Man McGraw hit me over the head with his poker. He swung it with both hands as hard as he could, and if I hadn't had on my coonskin cap I bet it would have skint my head some. As it was it knocked me to my knees, me being off-guard that way, and his three boys run in and started beating me with chairs and benches and a table laig. Well, I didn't want to hurt none of Glory's kin, but I had bit my tongue when the old man hit me with his poker, and that always did irritate me. Anyway, I seen they warn't no use arguing with them fool boys. They was out for blood--mine, to be exact.

So I riz up and taken Joe by the neck and crotch and throwed him through a winder as gentle as I could, but I forgot about the hickory- wood bars which was nailed acrost it to keep the bears out. He took 'em along with him, and that was how he got skint up like he did. I heard Glory let out a scream outside, and would have hollered out to let her know I was all right and for her not to worry about me, but just as I opened my mouth to do it, John jammed the butt-end of a table laig into it.

Sech treatment would try the patience of a saint, still and all I didn't really intend to hit John as hard as I did. How was I to know a tap like I give him would knock him through the door and dislocate his jawbone?

Old Man McGraw was dancing around trying to get another whack at me with his bent poker without hitting Bill which was hammering me over the head with a chair, but Mister Wilkinson warn't taking no part in the fray. He was backed up agen a wall with a wild look on his face. I reckon he warn't used to Bear Creek squabbles.

I taken the chair away from Bill and busted it over his head jest to kinda cool him off a little, and jest then Old Man McGraw made another swipe at me with his poker, but I ducked and grabbed him, and Bill stooped over to pick up a bowie knife which had fell out of somebody's boot. His back was towards me so I planted my moccasin in the seat of his britches with considerable force and he shot head-first through the door with a despairing howl. Somebody else screamed too, that sounded like Glory. I didn't know at the time I that she was running up to the door and was knocked down by Bill as he catapulted into the yard.

I couldn't see what was going on outside, and Old Man McGraw was chawing my thumb and feeling for my eye, so I throwed him after John and Bill, and he's a liar when he said I aimed him at that rain-barrel a-purpose. I didn't even know they was one there till I heard the crash as his head went through the staves.

I turned around to have some more words with Mister Wilkinson, but he jumped through the winder I'd throwed Joe through, and when I tried to foller him, I couldn't get my shoulders through. So I run out at the door and Glory met me just as I hit the yard and she give me a slap in the face that sounded like a beaver hitting a mud bank with his tail.

"Why, Glory!" I says, dumbfounded, because her blue eyes was blazing, and her yaller hair was nigh standing on end. She was so mad she was crying and that's the first time I ever knowed she _could_ cry. "What's the matter? What've _I_ did?"

"What have you did?" she raged, doing a kind of a war-dance on her bare feet. "You outlaw! You murderer! You jack-eared son of a spotted tail skunk! Look what you done!" She p'inted at her old man dazedly pulling his head out of the rooins of the rain-barrel, and her brothers laying around the yard in various positions, bleeding freely and groaning loudly. "You tried to murder my family!" says she, shaking her fists under my nose. "You throwed Bill onto me on purpose!"

"I didn't neither!" I exclaimed, shocked and scandalized. "You know I wouldn't hurt a hair of yore head, Glory! Why, all I done, I done it for you--"

"You didn't have to mutilate my pap and my brothers!" she wept furiously. Ain't that just like a gal? What could I done but what I did? She hollered: "If you really loved me you wouldn't of hurt 'em! You jest done it for meanness! I told you to be ca'm and gentle! Whyn't you do it? Shet up! Don't talk to me! Well, whyn't you say somethin'? Ain't you got no tongue?"

"I handled 'em easy as I could!" I roared, badgered beyond endurance. "It warn't my fault. If they'd had any sense, they wouldn't--"

"Don't you dare slander my folks!" she yelped. "What you done to Mister Wilkinson?"

The aforesaid gent jest then come limping around the corner of the cabin, and started for his hoss, and Glory run to him and grabbed his arm, and said: "If you still want to marry me, stranger, it's a go! I'll ride off with you right now!"

He looked at me and shuddered, and jerked his arm away.

"Do I look like a dern fool?" he inquired with some heat. "I advises you to marry that young grizzly there, for the sake of public safety, if nothin' else! Marry you when _he_ wants you? No, thank you! I'm leavin' a valuable finger as a sooverneer of my sojourn, but I figger it's a cheap price! After watchin' that human tornado in action, I calculate a finger ain't nothin' to bother about! _Adios!_ If I ever come within a hundred miles of Bear Creek again it'll be because I've gone plumb loco!"

And with that he forked his critter and took off up the trail like the devil was after him.

"Now look what you done!" wept Glory. "Now he won't never marry me!"

"But I thought you didn't want to marry him!" I says, plumb bewildered.

She turned on me like a catamount.

"I didn't!" she shrieked. "I wouldn't marry him if he was the last man on earth! But I demands the right to say yes or no for myself! I don't aim to be bossed around by no hillbilly on a mangy mule!"

"Alexander ain't mangy," I said. "Besides, I warn't, tryin' to boss you around, Glory. I war just fixin' it so yore pap wouldn't make you marry Mister Wilkinson. Bein' as we aims to marry ourselves--"

"Who said we aimed to?" she hollered. "Me marry you, after you beat up my pap and my brothers like you done? You think yo're the best man on Bear Creek! Ha! You with yore buckskin britches and old cap- and-ball pistol and coonskin cap! Me marry you? Git on yore mangy mule and git before I takes a shotgun to you!"

"All right!" I roared, getting mad at last. "All right, if that's the way you want to ack! You ain't the only gal in these mountains! They's plenty of gals which would be glad to have me callin' on 'em."

"Who, for a instance?" she sneered.

"Ellen Reynolds, for instance!" I bellered. "That's who!"

"All right!" says she, trembling with rage. "Go and spark that stuck-up hussy on yore mangy mule with yore old moccasins and cap-and- ball gun! See if I care!"

"I aim to!" I assured her bitterly. "And I won't be on no mule, neither. I'll be on the best hoss in the Humbolts, and I'll have me some boots on to my feet, and a silver mounted saddle and bridle, and a pistol that shoots store-bought ca'tridges, too! You wait and see!"

"Where you think you'll git 'em?" she sneered.

"Well, I will!" I bellered, seeing red. "You said I thought I was the best man on Bear Creek! Well, by golly, I am, and I aim to prove it! I'm glad you gimme the gate! If you hadn't I'd of married you and settled down in a cabin up the creek somewheres and never done nothin' nor seen nothin' nor been nothin' but yore husband! Now I'm goin' to plumb bust this State wide open from one end to the other'n, and folks is goin' to know about me all over everywheres!"

"Heh! heh! heh!" she laughed bitterly.

"I'll show you!" I promised her wrathfully, as I forked my mule, and headed down the trail with her laughter ringing in my ears. I kicked Alexander most vicious in the ribs, and he give a bray of astonishment and lit a shuck for home. A instant later the alder clump hid the McGraw cabin from view and Glory McGraw and my boyhood dreams was out of sight behind me.

CHAPTER II

MOUNTAIN MAN

"I'LL SHOW her!" I promised the world at large, as I rode through the bresh as hard as Alexander could run. "I'll go out into the world and make a name for myself, by golly! She'll see. Whoa, Alexander!"

Because I'd jest seen a bee-tree I'd located the day before. My busted heart needed something to soothe it, and I figgered fame and fortune could wait a little whilst I drowned my woes in honey.

I was up to my ears in this beverage when I heard my old man calling: "Breckinridge! Oh, Breckinridge! Whar air you? I see you now. You don't need to climb that tree. I ain't goin' to larrup you."

He come up and said: "Breckinridge, ain't that a bee settin' on to yore ear?"

I reched up, and sure enough, it was. Come to think about it, I had felt kind of like something was stinging me somewheres.

"I swan, Breckinridge," says pap, "I never seen a hide like yore'n not even amongst the Elkinses. Lissen to me now: old Buffalo Rogers jest come through on his way back from Tomahawk, and the postmaster there said they was a letter for me, from Mississippi. He wouldn't give it to nobody but me or some of my folks. I dunno who'd be writin' me from Mississippi; last time I was there was when I was fightin' the Yankees. But anyway, that letter is got to be got. Me and yore maw have decided yo're to go git it."

"Clean to Tomahawk?" I said. "Gee whiz, Pap!"

"Well," he says, combing his beard with his fingers, "yo're growed in size, if not in years. It's time you seen somethin' of the world. You ain't never been more'n thirty miles away from the cabin you was born in. Yore brother Garfield ain't able to go on account of that b'ar he tangled with, and Buckner is busy skinnin' the b'ar. You been to whar the trail goin' to Tomahawk passes. All you got to do is foller it and turn to the right whar it forks. The left goes on to Perdition."

"Great!" I says. "This is whar I begins to see the world!" And I added to myself: "This is whar I begins to show Glory McGraw I'm a man of importance, by golly!"

Well, next morning before good daylight I was off, riding my mule Alexander, with a dollar pap gimme stuck in the bottom of my pistol scabbard. Pap rode with me a few miles and give me advice.

"Be keerful how you spend that dollar I give you," he said. "Don't gamble. Drink in reason. Half a gallon of corn juice is enough for any man. Don't be techy- -but don't forgit that yore pap was once the rough-and-tumble champeen of Gonzales County, Texas. And whilst yo're feelin' for the other feller's eye, don't be keerless and let him chaw yore ear off. And don't resist no officer."

"What's them, Pap?" I inquired.

"Down in the settlements," he explained, "they has men which their job is to keep the peace. I don't take no stock in law myself, but them city folks is different from us. You do what they says, and if they says give up yore gun, even, why you up and do it!"

I was shocked, and meditated a while, and then says: "How can I tell which is them?"

"They'll have a silver star stuck onto their shirt," he says, so I said I'd do like he told me. He then reined around and went back up the mountains, and I rode on down the path.

Well, I camped late that night where the path come out onto the Tomahawk trail, and the next morning I rode on down the trail, feeling like I was a long way from home. It was purty hot, and I hadn't went far till I passed a stream and decided I'd take a swim. So I tied Alexander to a cottonwood, and hung my buckskins close by, but I taken my gun belt with my cap-and-ball .44 and hung it on a willer limb reching out over the water. They was thick bushes all around the stream.

Well, I div deep, and as I come up, I had a feeling like somebody had hit me over the head with a club. I looked up, and there was a Injun holding on to a limb with one hand and leaning out over the water with a club in the other hand.

He yelled and swung at me again, but I div, and he missed, and I come up right under the limb where my gun was hung. I reched up and grabbed it and let _bam_ at him just as he dived into the bushes, and he let out a squall and grabbed the seat of his pants. Next minute I heard a horse running, and glimpsed him tearing away through the bresh on a pinto mustang, setting his hoss like it was a red-hot stove, and dern him, he had my clothes in one hand! I was so upsot by this that I missed him clean, and jumping out, I charged through the bushes and saplings, but he was already out of sight. I knowed it warn't likely he was with a war-party--just a dern thieving Piute--but what a fix I was in! He'd even stole my moccasins.

I couldn't go home, in that shape, without the letter, and admit I missed a Injun twice. Pap would larrup the tar out of me. And if I went on, what if I met some women, in the valley settlements? I don't reckon they ever was a young'un half as bashful as what I was in them days. Cold sweat busted out all over me. I thought, here I started out to see the world and show Glory McGraw I was a man among men, and here I am with no more clothes than a jackrabbit. At last, in desperation, I buckled on my belt and started down the trail towards Tomahawk. I was about ready to commit murder to get me some pants.

I was glad the Injun didn't steal Alexander, but the going was so rough I had to walk and lead him, because I kept to the thick bresh alongside the trail. He had a tough time getting through the bushes, and the thorns scratched him so he hollered, and ever' now and then I had to lift him over jagged rocks. It was tough on Alexander, but I was too bashful to travel in the open trail without no clothes on.

After I'd gone maybe a mile I heard somebody in the trail ahead of me, and peeking through the bushes, I seen a most pecooliar sight. It was a man on foot, going the same direction as me, and he had on what I instinctly guessed was city clothes. They warn't buckskin nor homespun, nor yet like the duds Mister Wilkinson had on, but they were very beautiful, with big checks and stripes all over 'em. He had on a round hat with a narrer brim, and shoes like I hadn't never seen before, being neither boots nor moccasins. He was dusty, and he cussed considerable as he limped along. Ahead of him I seen the trail made a hoss-shoe bend, so I cut straight across and got ahead of him, and as he come along, I come out of the bresh and throwed down on him with my cap-and-ball.

He throwed up his hands and hollered: "Don't shoot!"

"I don't want to, mister," I said, "but I got to have clothes!"

He shook his head like he couldn't believe I was so, and he said: "You ain't the color of a Injun, but--what kind of people live in these hills, anyway?"

"Most of 'em's Democrats," I said. "But I ain't got no time to talk politics. You climb out of them riggin's."

"My God!" he wailed. "My horse threw me off and ran away, and I've bin walkin' for hours, expecting to get scalped by Injuns any minute, and now a naked lunatic on a mule demands my clothes! It's too dern much!"

"I cain't argy, mister," I said; "somebody's liable to come up the trail any minute. Hustle!" So saying I shot his hat off to encourage him.

He give a howl and shucked his duds in a hurry.

"My underclothes, too?" he demanded, shivering though it was very hot.

"Is that what them things is?" I demanded, shocked. "I never heard of a man wearin' such womanish things. The country is goin' to the dogs, just like pap says. You better git goin'. Take my mule. When I git to where I can git some regular clothes, we'll swap back."

He clumb onto Alexander kind of dubious, and says to me, despairful: "Will you tell me one thing--how do I get to Tomahawk?"

"Take the next turn to the right," I said, "and--"

Jest then Alexander turned his head and seen them underclothes on his back, and he give a loud and ringing bray and sot sail down the trail at full speed with the stranger hanging on with both hands. Before they was out of sight they come to where the trail forked, and Alexander taken the left branch instead of the right, and vanished amongst the ridges.

I put on the clothes, and they scratched my hide something fierce. I thinks, well, I got store-bought clothes quicker'n I hoped to. But I didn't think much of 'em. The coat split down the back, and the pants was too short, but the shoes was the wust; they pinched all over. I throwed away the socks, having never wore none, but put on what was left of the hat.

I went on down the trail, and taken the right-hand fork, and in a mile or so I come out on a flat, and heard hosses running. The next thing a mob of men on hosses bust into view. One of 'em yelled: "There he is!" and they all come for me full tilt. Instantly I decided that the stranger had got to Tomahawk after all, somehow, and had sot his friends onto me for stealing his clothes.

So I left the trail and took out across the sage grass, and they all charged after me, yelling stop. Well, them dern shoes pinched my feet so bad I couldn't make much speed, so after I had run maybe a quarter of a mile I perceived that the hosses were beginning to gain on me. So I wheeled with my cap-and-ball in my hand, but I was going so fast, when I turned, them dern shoes slipped and I went over backwards into a cactus bed just as I pulled the trigger. So I only knocked the hat off of the first hossman. He yelled and pulled up his hoss, right over me nearly, and as I drawed another bead on him, I seen he had a bright shiny star on to his shirt. I dropped my gun and stuck up my hands.

They swarmed around me--cowboys, from their looks. The man with the star got off his hoss and picked up my gun and cussed.

"What did you lead us this chase through this heat and shoot at me for?" he demanded.

"I didn't know you was a officer," I said.

"Hell, McVey," said one of 'em, "you know how jumpy tenderfeet is. Likely he thought we was Santry's outlaws. Where's yore hoss?"

"I ain't got none," I said.

"Got away from you, hey?" said McVey. "Well, climb up behind Kirby here, and let's git goin'."

To my surprise, the sheriff stuck my gun back in the scabbard, and so I clumb up behind Kirby, and away we went. Kirby kept telling me not to fall off, and it made me mad, but I said nothing. After an hour or so we come to a bunch of houses they said was Tomahawk. I got panicky when I seen all them houses, and would have jumped down and run for the mountains, only I knowed they'd catch me, with them dern pinchy shoes on.

I hadn't never seen such houses before. They was made out of boards, mostly, and some was two stories high. To the north-west and west the hills riz up a few hundred yards from the backs of the houses, and on the other sides there was plains, with bresh and timber on them.

"You boys ride into town and tell the folks that the shebang starts soon," said McVey. "Me and Kirby and Richards will take him to the ring."

I could see people milling around in the streets, and I never had no idee they was that many folks in the world. The sheriff and the other two fellers rode around the north end of the town and stopped at a old barn and told me to get off. So I did, and we went in and they had a kind of room fixed up in there with benches and a lot of towels and water buckets, and the sheriff said: "This ain't much of a dressin' room, but it'll have to do. Us boys don't know much about this game, but we'll second you as good as we can. One thing--the other feller ain't got no manager nor seconds neither. How do you feel?"

"Fine," I said, "but I'm kind of hungry."

"Go git him somethin', Richards," said the sheriff.

"I didn't think they et just before a bout," said Richards.

"Aw, I reckon he knows what he's doin'," said McVey. "Gwan."

So Richards pulled out, and the sheriff and Kirby walked around me like I was a prize bull, and felt my muscles, and the sheriff said: "By golly, if size means anything, our dough is as good as in our britches right now!"

I pulled my dollar out of my scabbard and said I would pay for my keep, and they haw-hawed and slapped me on the back and said I was a great joker. Then Richards come back with a platter of grub, with a lot of men wearing boots and guns and whiskers, and they stomped in and gawped at me, and McVey said: "Look him over, boys! Tomahawk stands or falls with him today!"

They started walking around me like him and Kirby done, and I was embarrassed and et three or four pounds of beef and a quart of mashed pertaters, and a big hunk of white bread, and drunk about a gallon of water, because I was purty thirsty. Then they all gaped like they was surprised about something, and one of 'em said: "How come he didn't arrive on the stagecoach yesterday?"

"Well," said the sheriff, "the driver told me he was so drunk they left him at Bisney, and come on with his luggage, which is over there in the corner. They got a hoss and left it there with instructions for him to ride on to Tomahawk as soon as he sobered up. Me and the boys got nervous today when he didn't show up, so we went out lookin' for him, and met him hoofin' it down the trail."

"I bet them Perdition _hombres_ starts somethin'," said Kirby. "Ain't a one of 'em showed up yet. They're settin' over at Perdition soakin' up bad licker and broodin' on their wrongs. They shore wanted this show staged over there. They claimed that since Tomahawk was furnishin' one-half of the attraction, and Gunstock the other half, the razee ought to be throwed at Perdition."

"Nothin' to it," said McVey. "It laid between Tomahawk and Gunstock, and we throwed a coin and won it. If Perdition wants trouble she can git it. Is the boys r'arin' to go?"

"Is they!" says Richards. "Every bar in Tomahawk is crowded with hombres full of licker and civic pride. They're bettin' their shirts, and they has been nine fights already. Everybody in Gunstock's here."

"Well, le's git goin'," says McVey, getting nervous. "The quicker it's over, the less blood there's likely to be spilt."

The first thing I knowed, they had laid hold of me and was pulling my clothes off, so it dawned on me that I must be under arrest for stealing that stranger's clothes. Kirby dug into the baggage which was in one corner of the stall, and dragged out a funny looking pair of pants; I know now they was white silk. I put 'em on because I didn't have nothing else to put on, and they fitted me like my skin. Richards tied a American flag around my waist, and they put some spiked shoes onto my feet.

I let 'em do like they wanted to, remembering what pap said about not resisting no officer. Whilst so employed I begun to hear a noise outside, like a lot of people whooping and cheering. Purty soon in come a skinny old gink with whiskers and two guns on, and he hollered: "Lissen here, Mac, dern it, a big shipment of gold is down there waitin' to be took off by the evenin' stage, and the whole blame town is deserted on account of this dern foolishness. Suppose Comanche Santry and his gang gits wind of it?"

"Well," said McVey, "I'll send Kirby here to help you guard it."

"You will like hell," says Kirby. "I'll resign as deputy first. I got every cent of my dough on this scrap, and I aim to see it."

"Well, send somebody!" says the old codger. "I got enough to do runnin' my store, and the stage stand, and the post office, without--"

He left, mumbling in his whiskers, and I said: "Who's that?"

"Aw," said Kirby, "that's old man Brenton that runs the store down at the other end of town, on the east side of the street. The post office is in there, too."

"I got to see him," I says. "There's a letter--"

Just then another man come surging in and hollered: "Hey, is yore man ready? Folks is gittin' impatient!"

"All right," says McVey, throwing over me a thing he called a bathrobe. Him and Kirby and Richards picked up towels and buckets and things, and we went out the oppersite door from what we come in, and they was a big crowd of people there, and they whooped and shot off their pistols. I would have bolted back into the barn, only they grabbed me and said it was all right. We pushed through the crowd, and I never seen so many boots and pistols in my life, and we come to a square corral made out of four posts sot in the ground, and ropes stretched between. They called this a ring and told me to get in. I done so, and they had turf packed down so the ground was level as a floor and hard and solid. They told me to set down on a stool in one corner, and I did, and wrapped my robe around me like a Injun.

Then everybody yelled, and some men, from Gunstock, McVey said, clumb through the ropes on the other side. One of 'em was dressed like I was, and I never seen such a funny-looking human. His ears looked like cabbages, and his nose was plumb flat, and his head was shaved and looked right smart like a bullet. He sot down in a oppersite corner.

Then a feller got up and waved his arms, and hollered: "Gents, you all know the occasion of this here suspicious event. Mister Bat O'Tool, happenin' to be pas-sin' through Gunstock, consented to fight anybody which would meet him. Tomahawk riz to the occasion by sendin' all the way to Denver to procure the services of Mister Bruiser McGoorty, formerly of San Francisco!"

He p'inted at me, and everybody cheered and shot off their pistols, and I was embarrassed and bust out in a cold sweat.

"This fight," said the feller, "will be fit accordin' to London Prize Ring Rules, same as in a champeenship go. Bare fists, round ends when one of 'em's knocked down or throwed down. Fight lasts till one or t'other ain't able to come up to the scratch when time's called. I, Yucca Blaine, have been selected as referee because, bein' from Chawed Ear, I got no prejudices either way. Air you all ready? Time!"

McVey hauled me off my stool and pulled off my bathrobe and pushed me out into the ring. I nearly died with embarrassment, but I seen the feller they called O'Tool didn't have on no more clothes than me. He approached and held out his hand like he wanted to shake hands, so I held out mine. We shook hands, and then without no warning he hit me a awful lick on the jaw with his left. It was like being kicked by a mule. The first part of me which hit the turf was the back of my head. O'Tool stalked back to his corner, and the Gunstock boys was dancing and hugging each other, and the Tomahawk fellers was growling in their whiskers and fumbling with their guns and bowie knives.

McVey and his deperties rushed into the ring before I could get up and dragged me to my corner and began pouring water on me.

"Air you hurt much?" yelled McVey.

"How can a man's fist hurt anybody?" I ast. "I wouldn't of fell down, only I was caught off-guard. I didn't know he was goin' to hit me. I never played no game like this here'n before."

McVey dropped the towel he was beating me in the face with, and turned pale. "Ain't you Bruiser McGoorty of San Francisco?" he hollered.

"Naw," I said. "I'm Breckinridge Elkins, from up in the Humbolt Mountains. I come here to git a letter for pap."

"But the stagecoach driver described them clothes--" he begun wildly.

"A Injun stole my clothes," I explained, "so I taken some off'n a stranger. Maybe that was Mister McGoorty."

"What's the matter?" ast Kirby, coming up with another bucket of water. "Time's about ready to be called."

"We're sunk!" bawled McVey. "This ain't McGoorty! This is a derned hillbilly which murdered McGoorty and stole his clothes!"

"We're rooint!" exclaimed Richards, aghast. "Everybody's bet their dough without even seein' our man, they was that full of trust and civic pride. We cain't call it off now. Tomahawk is rooint! What'll we do?"

"He's goin' to git in there and fight his derndest," said McVey, pulling his gun and jamming it into my back. "We'll hang him after the fight."

"But he cain't box!" wailed Richards.

"No matter," said McVey; "the fair name of our town is at stake; Tomahawk promised to supply a fighter to fight O'Tool, and--"

"Oh!" I said, suddenly seeing light. "This here is a fight then, ain't it?"

McVey give a low moan, and Kirby reched for his gun, but just then the referee hollered time, and I jumped up and run at O'Tool. If a fight was all they wanted, I was satisfied. All that talk about rules, and the yelling of the crowd and all had had me so confused I hadn't knowed what it was all about. I hit at O'Tool and he ducked and hit me in the belly and on the nose and in the eye and on the ear. The blood spurted, and the crowd hollered, and he looked plumb dumbfounded and gritted betwixt his teeth: "Are you human? Why don't you fall?"

I spit out a mouthful of blood and got my hands on him and started chawing his ear, and he squalled like a catamount. Yucca run in and tried to pull me loose and I give him a slap under the ear and he turned a somersault into the ropes.

"Yore man's fightin' foul!" he squalled, and Kirby said: "Yo're crazy! Do you see this gun? You holler 'foul' just once more, and it'll go off!"

Meanwhile O'Tool had broke loose from me and caved in his knuckles on my jaw, and I come for him again, because I was beginning to lose my temper. He gasped: "If you want to make an alley-fight out of it, all right. I wasn't raised in Five Points for nothing!" He then rammed his knee into my groin, and groped for my eye, but I got his thumb in my teeth and begun masticating it, and the way he howled was a caution.

By this time the crowd was crazy, and I throwed O'Tool and begun to stomp him, when somebody let bang at me from the crowd and the bullet cut my silk belt and my pants started to fall down.

I grabbed 'em with both hands, and O'Tool riz up and rushed at me, bloody and bellering, and I didn't dare let go my pants to defend myself. I whirled and bent over and lashed out backwards with my right heel like a mule, and I caught him under the chin. He done a cartwheel in the air, his head hit the turf, and he bounced on over and landed on his back with his knees hooked over the lower rope. There warn't no question about him being out. The only question was, was he dead?

A roar of "Foul!" went up from the Gunstock men, and guns bristled all around the ring.

The Tomahawk men was cheering and yelling that I'd won fair and square, and the Gunstock men was cussing and threatening me, when somebody hollered: "Leave it to the referee!"

"Sure," said Kirby. "He knows our man won fair, and if he don't say so, I'll blow his head off!"

"That's a lie!" bellered a Gunstock man. "He knows it war a foul, and if he says it warn't, I'll kyarve his gizzard with this here bowie knife!"

At them words Yucca fainted, and then a clatter of hoofs sounded above the din, and out of the timber that hid the trail from the east a gang of hossmen rode at a run. Everybody yelled: "Look out, here comes them Perdition illegitimates!"

Instantly a hundred guns covered 'em, and McVey demanded: "Come ye in peace or in war?"

"We come to unmask a fraud!" roared a big man with a red bandanner around his neck. "McGoorty, come forth!"

A familiar figger, now dressed in cowboy togs, pushed forward on my mule. "There he is!" this figger yelled, p'inting a accusing finger at me. "That's the desperado that robbed me! Them's my tights he's got on!"

"What is this?" roared the crowd.

"A cussed fake!" bellered the man with the red bandanner. "This here is Bruiser McGoorty!"

"Then who's he?" somebody bawled, p'inting at me.

"I'm Breckinridge Elkins and I can lick any man here!" I roared, getting mad. I brandished my fists in defiance, but my britches started sliding down again, so I had to shut up and grab 'em.

"Aha!" the man with the red bandanner howled like a hyener. "He admits it! I dunno what the idee is, but these Tomahawk polecats has double-crossed somebody! I trusts that you jackasses from Gunstock realizes the blackness and hellishness of their hearts! This man McGoorty rode into Perdition a few hours ago in his unmentionables, astraddle of that there mule, and told us how he'd been held up and robbed and put on the wrong road. You skunks was too proud to stage this fight in Perdition, but we ain't the men to see justice scorned with impunity! We brought McGoorty here to show you that you was bein' gypped by Tomahawk! That man ain't no prize fighter; he's a highway robber!"

"These Tomahawk coyotes has framed us!" squalled a Gunstock man, going for his gun.

"Yo're a liar!" roared Richards, bending a .45 barrel over his head.

The next instant guns was crashing, knives was gleaming, and men was yelling blue murder. The Gunstock braves turned frothing on the Tomahawk warriors, and the men from Perdition, yelping with glee, pulled their guns, and begun fanning the crowd indiscriminately, which give back their fire. McGoorty give a howl and fell down on Alexander's neck, gripping around it with both arms, and Alexander departed in a cloud of dust and gun-smoke.

I grabbed my gunbelt, which McVey had hung over the post in my corner, and I headed for cover, holding onto my britches whilst the bullets hummed around me as thick as bees. I wanted to take to the bresh, but I remembered that blamed letter, so I headed for town. Behind me there riz a roar of banging guns and yelling men. Jest as I got to the backs of the row of buildings which lined the street, I run head on into something soft. It was McGoorty, trying to escape on Alexander. He had hold of jest one rein, and Alexander, evidently having rounded one end of the town, was traveling in a circle and heading back where he started from.

I was going so fast I couldn't stop, and I run right over Alexander and all three of us went down in a heap. I jumped up, afeared Alexander was kilt or crippled, but he scrambled up snorting and trembling, and then McGoorty weaved up, making funny noises. I poked my cap-and-ball into his belly.

"Off with them pants!" I hollered.

"My God!" he screamed. "_Again?_ This is getting to be a habit!"

"Hustle!" I bellered. "You can have these scandals I got on now."

He shucked his britches and grabbed them tights and run like he was afeared I'd want his underwear too. I jerked on the pants, forked Alexander and headed for the south end of town. I kept behind the houses, though the town seemed to be deserted, and purty soon I come to the store where Kirby had told me old man Brenton kept the post office. Guns was barking there, and across the street I seen men ducking in and out behind a old shack, and shooting.

I tied Alexander to a corner of the store and went in the back door. Up in the front part I seen old man Brenton kneeling behind some barrels with a .45-90, and he was shooting at the fellers in the shack acrost the street. Every now and then a slug would hum through the door and comb his whiskers, and he would cuss worse'n pap did that time he sot down in a b'ar trap.

I went up to him and tapped him on the shoulder and he give a squall and flopped over and let go _bam!_ right in my face and singed off my eyebrows. And the fellers acrost the street hollered and started shooting at both of us.

I'd grabbed the barrel of his Winchester, and he was cussing and jerking at it with one hand and feeling in his boot for a knife with the other'n, and I said: "Mister Brenton, if you ain't too busy, I wish you'd gimme that there letter which come for pap."

"Don't never come up behind me like that again!" he squalled. "I thought you was one of them dern outlaws! Look out! Duck, you blame fool!"

I let go of his gun, and he taken a shot at a head which was aiming around the corner of the shack, and the head let out a squall and disappeared.

"Who is them fellers?" I ast.

"Comanche Santry and his bunch, from up in the hills," snarled old man Brenton, jerking the lever of his Winchester. "They come after that gold. A hell of a sheriff McVey is; never sent me nobody. And them fools over at the ring are makin' so much noise they'll never hear the shootin' over here. Look out, here they come!"

Six or seven men rushed out from behind the shack and run acrost the street, shooting as they come. I seen I'd never get my letter as long as all this fighting was going on, so I unslung my old cap-and- ball and let _bam_ at them three times, and three of them outlaws fell acrost each other in the street, and the rest turned around and run back behind the shack.

"Good work, boy!" yelled old man Brenton. "If I ever--oh, Judas Iscariot, we're blowed up now!"

Something was pushed around the corner of the shack and come rolling down towards us, the shack being on higher ground than what the store was. It was a keg, with a burning fuse which whirled as the keg revolved and looked like a wheel of fire.

"What's in that there kaig?" I ast.

"Blastin' powder!" screamed old man Brenton, scrambling up. "Run, you dern fool! It's comin' right into the door!"

He was so scairt he forgot all about the fellers acrost the street, and one of 'em caught him in the thigh with a buffalo rifle, and he plunked down again, howling blue murder. I stepped over him to the door--that's when I got that slug in my hip--and the keg hit my laigs and stopped, so I picked it up and heaved it back acrost the street. It hadn't no more'n hit the shack when _bam!_ it exploded and the shack went up in smoke. When it stopped raining pieces of wood and metal, they warn't no sign to show any outlaws had ever hid behind where that shack had been.

"I wouldn't believe it if I hadn't saw it myself," old man Brenton moaned faintly.

"Air you hurt bad, Mister Brenton?" I ast.

"I'm dyin'," he groaned.

"Well, before you die, Mister Brenton," I says, "would you mind givin' me that there letter for pap?"

"What's yore pap's name?" he ast.

"Roarin' Bill Elkins, of Bear Creek," I said.

He warn't as bad hurt as he thought. He reched up and got hold of a leather bag and fumbled in it and pulled out a envelope. "I remember tellin' old Buffalo Rogers I had a letter for Bill Elkins," he said, fingering it over. Then he said: "Hey, wait! This ain't for yore pap. My sight is gittin' bad. I read it wrong the first time. This here is for Bill _Elston_ that lives between here and Perdition."

I want to spike a rumor which says I tried to murder old man Brenton and tore down his store for spite. I've done told how he got his laig broke, and the rest was accidental. When I realized that I had went through all that embarrassment for nothing, I was so mad and disgusted I turned and run out of the back door, and I forgot to open the door and that's how it got tore off the hinges.

I then jumped on to Alexander and forgot to ontie him loose from the store. I kicked him in the ribs, and he bolted and tore loose that corner of the building and that's how come the roof to fall in. Old man Brenton inside was scairt and started yelling bloody murder, and about that time a mob of men come up to investigate the explosion which had stopped the three-cornered battle between Perdition, Tomahawk and Gunstock, and they thought I was the cause of everything, and they all started shooting at me as I rode off.

Then was when I got that charge of buckshot in my back.

I went out of Tomahawk and up the hill trail so fast I bet me and Alexander looked like a streak; and I says to myself it looks like making a name for myself in the world is going to be tougher than I thought, because it's evident that civilization is full of snares for a boy which ain't reched his full growth and strength.

CHAPTER III
MEET CAP'N KIDD

I DIDN'T pull up Alexander till I was plumb out of sight of Tomahawk. Then I slowed down and taken stock of myself, and my spirits was right down in my spiked shoes which still had some of Mister O'Tool's hide stuck onto the spikes. Here I'd started forth into the world to show Glory McGraw what a he-bearcat I was, and now look at me. Here I was without even no clothes but them derned spiked shoes which pinched my feet, and a pair of britches some cow-puncher had wore the seat out of and patched with buckskin. I still had my gunbelt and the dollar pap gimme, but no place to spend it. I likewise had a goodly amount of lead under my hide.

"By golly!" I says, shaking my fists at the universe at large. "I ain't goin' to go back to Bear Creek like this, and have Glory McGraw laughin' at me! I'll head for the Wild River settlements and git me a job punchin' cows till I got money enough to buy me store-bought boots and a hoss!"

I then pulled out my bowie knife which was in a scabbard on my gunbelt, and started digging the slug out of my hip, and the buckshot out of my back. Them buckshot was kinda hard to get to, but I done it. I hadn't never held a job of punching cows, but I'd had plenty experience roping wild bulls up in the Humbolts. Them bulls wanders off the lower ranges into the mountains and grows most amazing big and mean. Me and Alexander had had plenty experience with them, and I had me a lariat which would hold any steer that ever bellered. It was still tied to my saddle, and I was glad none of them cowpunchers hadn't stole it. Maybe they didn't know it was a lariat. I'd made it myself, especial, and used it to rope them bulls and also cougars and grizzlies which infests the Humbolts. It was made out of buffalo hide, ninety foot long and half again as thick and heavy as the average lariat, and the honda was a half-pound chunk of iron beat into shape with a sledge hammer. I reckoned I was qualified for a _vaquero_ even if I didn't have no cowboy clothes and was riding a mule.

So I headed acrost the mountains for the cowcountry. They warn't no trail the way I taken, but I knowed the direction Wild River lay in, and that was enough for me. I knowed if I kept going that way I'd hit it after awhile. Meanwhile, they was plenty of grass in the draws and along the creeks to keep Alexander fat and sleek, and plenty of squirrels and rabbits for me to knock over with rocks. I camped that night away up in the high ranges and cooked me nine or ten squirrels over a fire and et 'em, and while that warn't much of a supper for a appertite like mine, still

I figgered next day I'd stumble on to a b'ar or maybe a steer which had wandered offa the ranges.

Next morning before sunup I was on Alexander and moving on, without no breakfast, because it looked like they warn't no rabbits nor nothing near abouts, and I rode all morning without sighting nothing. It was a high range, and nothing alive there but a buzzard I seen onst, but late in the afternoon I crossed a backbone and come down into a whopping big plateau about the size of a county, with springs and streams and grass growing stirrup-high along 'em, and clumps of cottonwood, and spruce, and pine thick up on the hillsides. They was canyons and cliffs, and mountains along the rim, and altogether it was as fine a country as I ever seen, but it didn't look like nobody lived there, and for all I know I was the first white man that ever come into it. But they was more soon, as I'll relate.

Well, I noticed something funny as I come down the ridge that separated the bare hills from the plateau. First I met a wildcat. He come lipping along at a right smart clip, and he didn't stop. He just gimme a wicked look sidewise and kept right on up the slope. Next thing I met a lobo wolf, and after that I counted nine more wolves, and they was all heading west, up the slopes. Then Alexander give a snort and started trembling, and a cougar slid out of a blackjack thicket and snarled at us over his shoulder as he went past at a long lope. All them varmints was heading for the dry bare country I'd just left, and I wondered why they was leaving a good range like this one to go into that dern no-account country.

It worried Alexander too, because he smelt of the air and brayed kind of plain-tively. I pulled him up and smelt the air too, because critters run like that before a forest fire, but I couldn't smell no smoke, nor see none. So I rode on down the slopes and started across the flats, and as I went I seen more bobcats, and wolves, and painters, and they was all heading west, and they warn't lingering none, nei-ther. They warn't no doubt that them critters was pulling their freight because they was scairt of something, and it warn't humans, because they didn't 'pear to be scairt of me a mite. They just swerved around me and kept trailing. After I'd gone a few miles I met a herd of wild hosses, with the stallion herding 'em. He was a big mean-looking cuss, but he looked scairt as bad as any of the critters I'd saw.

The sun was getting low, and I was getting awful hungry as I come into a open spot with a creek on one side running through clumps of willers and cottonwoods, and on the other side I could see some big cliffs looming up over the tops of the trees. And whilst I was hesitating, wondering if I ought to keep looking for eatable critters, or try to worry along on a wildcat or a wolf, a big grizzly come lumbering out of a clump of spruces and headed west. When he seen me and Alexander he stopped and snarled like he was mad about something, and then the first thing I knowed he was charging us. So I pulled my .44 and shot him through the head, and got off and onsaddled Alexander and turnt him loose in grass stirrup-high, and skun the b'ar. Then I cut me off some steaks and started a fire and begun re-ducing my appertite. That warn't no small job, because I hadn't had nothing to eat since the night before.

Well, while I was eating I heard hosses and looked up and seen six men riding towards me from the east. One was as big as me, but the other ones warn't but about six foot tall apiece. They was cowpunchers, by their look, and the biggest man was dressed plumb as elegant as Mister Wilkinson was, only his shirt was jest only one color. But he had on fancy boots and a white Stetson and a ivory- butted Colt, and what looked like the butt of a sawed-off shotgun jutted out of his saddle-scabbard. He was dark and had awful mean eyes, and a jaw which it looked like he could bite the spokes out of a wagon wheel if he wanted to.

He started talking to me in Piute, but before I could say anything, one of the others said: "Aw, that ain't no Injun, Donovan, his eyes ain't the right color."

"I see that, now," says Donovan. "But I shore thought he was a Injun when I first rode up and seen them old ragged britches and his sunburnt hide. Who the devil air you?"

"I'm Breckinridge Elkins, from Bear Creek," I says, awed by his magnificence.

"Well," says he, "I'm Wild Bill Donovan, which name is heard with fear and tremblin' from Powder River to the Rio Grande. Just now I'm lookin' for a wild stallion. Have you seen sech?"

"I seen a bay stallion headin' west with his herd," I said.

"'Twarn't him," says Donovan. "This here one's a pinto, the biggest, meanest hoss in the world. He come down from the Humbolts when he was a colt, but he's roamed the West from Border to Border. He's so mean he ain't never got him a herd of his own. He takes mares away from other stallions, and then drifts on alone just for pure cussedness. When he comes into a country all other varmints takes to the tall timber."

"You mean the wolves and painters and b'ars I seen headin' for the high ridges was runnin' away from this here stallion?" I says.

"Exactly," says Donovan. "He crossed the eastern ridge sometime durin' the night, and the critters that was wise high-tailed it. We warn't far behind him; we come over the ridge a few hours ago, but we lost his trail somewhere on this side."

"You chasin' him?" I ast.

"Ha!" snarled Donovan with a kind of vicious laugh. "The man don't live what can chase Cap'n Kidd! We're just follerin' him. We been follerin' him for five hundred miles, keepin' outa sight, and hopin' to catch him off guard or somethin'. We got to have some kind of a big advantage before we closes in, or even shows ourselves. We're right fond of life! That devil has kilt more men than any other ten hosses on this continent."

"What you call him?" I says.

"Cap'n Kidd," says Donovan. "Cap'n Kidd was a big pirate long time ago. This here hoss is like him in lots of ways, particularly in regard to morals. But I'll git him, if I have to foller him to the Gulf and back. Wild Bill Donovan always gits what he wants, be it money, woman, or hoss! Now lissen here, you range-country hobo: we're a-siftin' north from here, to see if we cain't pick up Cap'n Kidd's sign. If you see a pinto stallion bigger'n you ever dreamed a hoss could be, or come onto his tracks, you drop whatever yo're doin' and pull out and look for us, and tell me about it. You keep lookin' till you find us, too. If you don't you'll regret it, you hear me?"

"Yessir," I said. "Did you gents come through the Wild River country?"

"Maybe we did and maybe we didn't," he says with haughty grandeur. "What business is that of yore'n, I'd like to know?"

"Not any," I says. "But I was aimin' to go there and see if I could git me a job punchin' cows."

At that he throwed back his head and laughed long and loud, and all the other fellers laughed too, and I was embarrassed.

"You git a job punchin' cows?" roared Donovan. "With them britches and shoes, and not even no shirt, and that there ignorant-lookin' mule I see gobblin' grass over by the creek? Haw! haw! haw! haw! You better stay up here in the mountains whar you belong and live on roots and nuts and jackrabbits like the other Piutes, red or white! Any self- respectin' rancher would take a shotgun to you if you was to ast him for a job. Haw! haw! haw!" he says, and rode off still laughing.

I was that embarrassed I bust out into a sweat. Alexander was a good mule, but he did look kind of funny in the face. But he was the only critter I'd ever found which could carry my weight very many miles without giving plumb out. He was awful strong and tough, even if he was kind of dumb and pot-bellied. I begun to get kind of mad, but Donovan and his men was already gone, and the stars was beginning to blink out. So I cooked me some more b'ar steaks and et 'em, and the land sounded awful still, not a wolf howling nor a cougar squalling. They was all west of the ridge. This critter Cap'n Kidd sure had the country to hisself, as far as the meat-eating critters was consarned.

I hobbled Alexander close by and fixed me a bed with some boughs and his saddle blanket, and went to sleep. I was woke up shortly after midnight by Alexander trying to get in bed with me.

I sot up in irritation and prepared to bust him in the snoot, when I heard what had scairt him. I never heard such a noise. My hair stood straight up. It was a stallion neighing, but I never heard no hoss critter neigh like that. I bet you could of heard it for fifteen miles. It sounded like a combination of a wild hoss neighing, a rip saw going through a oak log full of knots, and a hungry cougar screeching. I thought it come from somewhere within a mile of the camp, but I warn't sure. Alexander was shivering and whimpering he was that scairt, and stepping all over me as he tried to huddle down amongst the branches and hide his head under my shoulder. I shoved him away, but he insisted on staying as close to me as he could, and when I woke up again next morning he was sleeping with his head on my belly.

But he must of forgot about the neigh he heard, or thought it was jest a bad dream or something, because as soon as I taken the hobbles off of him he started cropping grass and wandered off amongst the thickets in his pudding-head way.

I cooked me some more b'ar steaks, and wondered if I ought to go and try to find Mister Donovan and tell him about hearing the stallion neigh, but I figgered he'd heard it. Anybody that was within a day's ride ought to of heard it. Anyway, I seen no reason why I should run errands for Donovan.

I hadn't got through eating when I heard Alexander give a horrified bray, and he come lickety-split out of a grove of trees and made for the camp, and behind him come the biggest hoss I ever seen in my life. Alexander looked like a pot-bellied bull pup beside of him. He was painted--black and white--and he r'ared up with his long mane flying agen the sunrise, and give a scornful neigh that nigh busted my ear-drums, and turned around and sa'ntered back towards the grove, cropping grass as he went, like he thunk so little of Alexander he wouldn't even bother to chase him.

Alexander come blundering into camp, blubbering and hollering, and run over the fire and scattered it every which away, and then tripped hisself over the saddle which was laying nearby, and fell on his neck braying like he figgered his life was in danger.

I catched him and threwed the saddle and bridle on to him, and by that time Cap'n Kidd was out of sight on the other side of the thicket. I onwound my lariat and headed in that direction. I figgered not even Cap'n Kidd could break that lariat. Alexander didn't want to go; he sot back on his haunches and brayed fit to deefen you, but I spoke to him sternly, and it seemed to convince him that he better face the stallion than me, so he moved out, kind of reluctantly.

We went past the grove and seen Cap'n Kidd cropping grass in the patch of rolling prairie just beyond, so I rode towards him, swinging my lariat. He looked up and snorted kinda threateningly, and he had the meanest eye I ever seen in man or beast; but he didn't move, just stood there looking contemptuous, so I threwed my rope and piled the loop right around his neck, and Alexander sot back on his haunches.

Well, it was about like roping a roaring hurricane. The instant he felt that rope Cap'n Kidd give a convulsive start, and made one mighty lunge for freedom. The lariat held, but the girths didn't. They held jest long enough for Alexander to get jerked head over heels, and naturally I went along with him. But right in the middle of the somesault we taken, both girths snapped.

Me and the saddle and Alexander landed all in a tangle, but Cap'n Kidd jerked the saddle from amongst us, because I had my rope tied fast to the horn, Texas-style, and Alexander got loose from me by the simple process of kicking me vi'lently in the ear. He also stepped on my face when he jumped up, and the next instant he was high-tailing it through the bresh in the general direction of Bear Creek. As I learned later he didn't stop till he run into pap's cabin and tried to hide under my brother John's bunk.

Meanwhile Cap'n Kidd had throwed the loop offa his head and come for me with his mouth wide open, his ears laid back and his teeth and eyes flashing. I didn't want to shoot him, so I riz up and run for the trees. But he was coming like a tornado, and I seen he was going to run me down before I could get to a tree big enough to climb, so I grabbed me a sapling about as thick as my laig and tore it up by the roots, and turned around and busted him over the head with it, just as he started to r'ar up to come down on me with his front hoofs.

Pieces of roots and bark and wood flew every which a way, and Cap'n Kidd grunted and batted his eyes and went back on to his haunches. It was a right smart lick. If I'd ever hit Alexander that hard it would have busted his skull like a egg-- and Alexander had a awful thick skull, even for a mule.

Whilst Cap'n Kidd was shaking the bark and stars out of his eyes, I run to a big oak and clumb it. He come after me instantly, and chawed chunks out of the tree as big as washtubs, and kicked most of the bark off as high up as he could rech, but it was a good substantial tree, and it held. He then tried to climb it, which amazed me most remarkable, but he didn't do much good at that. So he give up with a snort of disgust and trotted off.

I waited till he was out of sight, and then I clumb down and got my rope and saddle, and started follering him. I knowed there warn't no use trying to catch Alexander with the lead he had. I figgered he'd get back to Bear Creek safe. And Cap'n Kidd was the critter I wanted now. The minute I lammed him with that tree and he didn't fall, I knowed he was the hoss for me--a hoss which could carry my weight all day without giving out, and likewise full of spirit. I says to myself I rides him or the buzzards picks my bones.

I snuck from tree to tree, and presently seen Cap'n Kidd swaggering along and eating grass, and biting the tops off of young sapling, and occasionally tearing down a good sized tree to get the leaves off. Sometimes he'd neigh like a steamboat whistle, and let his heels fly in all directions just out of pure cussedness. When he done this the air was full of flying bark and dirt and rocks till it looked like he was in the middle of a twisting cyclone. I never seen such a critter in my life. He was as full of pizen and rambunctiousness as a drunk Apache on the warpath.

I thought at first I'd rope him and tie the other end of the rope to a big tree, but I was a-feared he'd chawed the lariat apart. Then I seen something that changed my mind. We was close to the rocky cliffs which jutted up above the trees, and Cap'n Kidd was passing a canyon mouth that looked like a big knife cut. He looked in and snorted, like he hoped they was a mountain lion hiding in there, but they warn't, so he went on. The wind was blowing from him towards me and he didn't smell me.

After he was out of sight amongst the trees I come out of cover and looked into the cleft. It was kinda like a short blind canyon. It warn't but about thirty foot wide at the mouth, but it widened quick till it made a kind of bowl a hundred yards acrost, and then narrowed to a crack again. Rock walls five hundred foot high was on all sides except at the mouth.

"And here," says I to myself, "is a ready-made corral!"

Then I lay to and started to build a wall to close the mouth of the canyon. Later on I heard that a scientific expedition (whatever the hell that might be) was all excited over finding evidences of a ancient race up in the mountains. They said they found a wall that could of been built only by giants. They was crazy; that there was the wall I built for Cap'n Kidd.

I knowed it would have to be high and solid if I didn't want Cap'n Kidd to jump it or knock it down. They was plenty of boulders laying at the foot of the cliffs which had weathered off, and I didn't use a single rock which weighed less'n three hundred pounds, and most of 'em was a lot heavier than that. It taken me most all morning, but when I quit I had me a wall higher'n the average man could reach, and so thick and heavy I knowed it would hold even Cap'n Kidd.

I left a narrer gap in it, and piled some boulders close to it on the outside, ready to shove 'em into the gap. Then I stood outside the wall and squalled like a cougar. They ain't even a cougar hisself can tell the difference when I squalls like one. Purty soon I heard Cap'n Kidd give his war-neigh off yonder, and then they was a thunder of hoofs and a snapping and crackling of bresh, and he come busting into the open with his ears laid back and his teeth bare and his eyes as red as a Comanche's war-paint. He sure hated cougars. But he didn't seem to like me much neither. When he seen me he give a roar of rage, and come for me lickety-split. I run through the gap and hugged the wall inside, and he come thundering after me going so fast he run clean across the bowl before he checked hisself. Before he could get back to the gap I'd run outside and was piling rocks in it. I had a good big one about the size of a fat hawg and I jammed it in the gap first and piled t'others on top of it.

Cap'n Kidd arriv at the gap all hoofs and teeth and fury, but it was already filled too high for him to jump and too solid for him to tear down. He done his best, but all he done was to knock some chunks offa the rocks with his heels. He sure was mad. He was the maddest hoss I ever seen, and when I got up on the wall and he seen me, he nearly busted with rage.

He went tearing around the bowl, kicking up dust and neighing like a steamboat on the rampage, and then he come back and tried to kick the wall down again. When he turned to gallop off I jumped offa the wall and landed square on his back, but before I could so much as grab his mane he throwed me clean over the wall and I landed in a cluster of boulders and cactus and skun my shin. This made me mad so I got the lariat and the saddle and clumb back on the wall and roped him, but he jerked the rope out of my hand before I could get any kind of a purchase, and went bucking and pitching around all over the bowl trying to get shet of the rope. So purty soon he pitched right into the cliff-wall and he lammed it so hard with his hind hoofs that a whole section of overhanging rock was jolted loose and hit him right between the ears. That was too much even for Cap'n Kidd.

It knocked him down and stunned him, and I jumped down into the bowl and before he could come to I had my saddle on to him, and a hackamore I'd fixed out of a piece of my lariat. I'd also mended the girths with pieces of the lariat, too, before I built the wall.

Well, when Cap'n Kidd recovered his senses and riz up, snorting and war-like, I was on his back. He stood still for a instant like he was trying to figger out jest what the hell was the matter, and then he turned his head and seen me on his back.

The next instant I felt like I was astraddle of a ring-tailed cyclone.

I dunno what all he done. He done so many things all at onst I couldn't keep track. I clawed leather. The man which could have stayed onto him without clawing leather ain't born yet, or else he's a cussed liar. Sometimes my feet was in the stirrups and sometimes they warn't, and sometimes they was in the wrong stirrups. I cain't figger out how that could be, but it was so. Part of the time I was in the saddle and part of the time I was behind it on his rump, or on his neck in front of it. He kept reching back trying to snap my laig and onst he got my thigh between his teeth and would ondoubtedly of tore the muscle out if I hadn't shook him loose by beating him over the head with my fist.

One instant he'd have his head betwixt his feet and I'd be setting on a hump so high in the air I'd get dizzy, and the next thing he'd come down stiff-laiged and I could feel my spine telescoping. He changed ends so fast I got sick at my stummick and he nigh unjointed my neck with his sunfishing. I calls it sunfishing because it was more like that than anything. He occasionally rolled over and over on the ground, too, which was very uncomfortable for me, but I hung on, because I was afeared if I let go I'd never get on him again. I also knowed that if he ever shaken me loose I'd had to shoot him to keep him from stomping my guts out. So I stuck, though I'll admit that they is few sensations more onpleasant than having a hoss as big as Cap'n Kidd roll on you nine or ten times.

He tried to scrape me off agen the walls, too, but all he done was scrape off some hide and most of my pants, though it was when he lurched agen that outjut of rock that I got them ribs cracked, I reckon.

He looked like he was able to go on forever, and aimed to, but I hadn't never met nothing which could outlast me, and I stayed with him, even after I started bleeding at the nose and mouth and ears, and got blind, and then all to onst he was standing stock still in the middle of the bowl, with his tongue hanging out about three foot, and his sweat-soaked sides heaving, and the sun was just setting over the mountains. He'd bucked nearly all afternoon!

But he was licked. I knowed it and he knowed it. I shaken the stars and sweat and blood out of my eyes and dismounted by the simple process of pulling my feet out of the stirrups and falling off. I laid there for maybe a hour, and was most amazing sick, but so was Cap'n Kidd. When I was able to stand on my feet I taken the saddle and the hackamore off and he didn't kick me nor nothing. He jest made a half- hearted attempt to bite me but all he done was to bite the buckle offa my gunbelt. They was a little spring back in the cleft where the bowl narrered in the cliff, and plenty of grass, so I figgered he'd be all right when he was able to stop blowing and panting long enough to eat and drink.

I made a fire outside the bowl and cooked me what was left of the b'ar meat, and then I lay down on the ground and slept till sunup.

When I riz up and seen how late it was, I jumped up and run and looked over the wall, and there was Cap'n Kidd mowing the grass down as ca'm as you please. He give me a mean look, but didn't say nothing. I was so eager to see if he was going to let me ride him without no more foolishness that I didn't stop for breakfast, nor to fix the buckle onto my gunbelt. I left it hanging on a spruce limb, and clumb into the bowl. Cap'n Kidd laid back his ears but didn't do nothing as I approached outside of making a swipe at me with his left hoof. I dodged and give him a good hearty kick in the belly and he grunted and doubled up, and I clapped the saddle on him. He showed his teeth at that, but he let me cinch it up, and put on the hackamore, and when I got on him he didn't pitch but about ten jumps and make but one snap at my laig.

Well, I was plumb tickled as you can imagine. I clumb down and opened the gap in the wall and led him out, and when he found he was outside the bowl he bolted and dragged me for a hundred yards before I managed to get the rope around a tree. After I tied him up though, he didn't try to bust loose.

I started back towards the tree where I left my gunbelt when I heard hosses running, and the next thing I knowed Donovan and his five men busted into the open and pulled up with their mouths wide open. Cap'n Kidd snorted warlike when he seen 'em, but didn't cut up no other way.

"Blast my soul!" says Donovan. "Can I believe my eyes? If there ain't Cap'n Kidd hisself, saddled and tied to that tree! Did _you_ do that?"

"Yeah," I said.

He looked me over and said: "I believes it. You looked like you been through a sausage-grinder. Air you still alive?"

"My ribs is kind of sore," I said.

"--!" says Donovan. "To think that a blame half-naked hillbilly should do what the best hossmen of the West has attempted in vain! I don't aim to stand for it! I knows my rights! That there is my hoss by rights! I've trailed him nigh a thousand miles, and combed this cussed plateau in a circle. He's my hoss!"

"He ain't, nuther," I says. "He come from the Humbolts original, jest like me. You said so yoreself. Anyway, I caught him and broke him, and he's mine."

"He's right, Bill," one of the men says to Donovan.

"You shet up!" roared Donovan. "What Wild Bill Donovan wants, he gits!"

I reched for my gun and then remembered in despair that it was hanging on a limb a hundred yards away. Donovan covered me with the sawed-off shotgun he jerked out of his saddle-holster as he swung down.

"Stand where you be," he advised me. "I ought to shoot you for not comin' and tellin' me when you seen the hoss, but after all you've saved me the trouble of breakin' him in."

"So yo're a hoss-thief!" I said wrathfully.

"You be keerful what you calls me!" he roared. "I ain't no hoss thief. We gambles for that hoss. Set down!"

I sot and he sot on his heels in front of me, with his sawed-off still covering me. If it'd been a pistol I would of took it away from him and shoved the barrel down his throat. But I was quite young in them days and bashful about shotguns. The others squatted around us, and Donovan says: "Smoky, haul out yore deck--the special one. Smoky deals, hillbilly, and the high hand wins the hoss."

"I'm puttin' up my hoss, it looks like," I says fiercely. "What _you_ puttin' up?"

"My Stetson hat!" says he. "Haw! haw! haw!"

"Haw! haw! haw!" chortles the other hoss-thieves.

Smoky started dealing and I said: "Hey! Yo're dealin' Donovan's hand offa the bottom of the deck!"

"Shet up!" roared Donovan, poking me in the belly with his shotgun. "You be keerful how you slings them insults around! This here is a fair and square game, and I just happen to be lucky. Can you beat four aces?"

"How you know you got four aces?" I says fiercely. "You ain't looked at yore hand yet."

"Oh," says he, and picked it up and spread it out on the grass, and they was four aces and a king. "By golly!" says he. "I shore called that shot right!"

"Remarkable foresight!" I said bitterly, throwing down my hand which was a three, five and seven of hearts, a ten of clubs and a jack of diamonds.

"Then I wins!" gloated Donovan, jumping up. I riz too, quick and sudden, but Donovan had me covered with that cussed shotgun.

"Git on that hoss and ride him over to our camp, Red," says Donovan, to a big red-headed _hombre_ which was shorter than him but jest about as big. "See if he's properly broke. I wants to keep my eye on this hillbilly myself."

So Red went over to Cap'n Kidd which stood there saying nothing, and my heart sunk right down to the tops of my spiked shoes. Red ontied him and clumb on him and Cap'n Kidd didn't so much as snap at him. Red says: "Git goin', cuss you!" Cap'n Kidd turnt his head and looked at Red and then he opened his mouth like a alligator and started laughing. I never seen a hoss laugh before, but now I know what they mean by a hoss-laugh. Cap'n Kidd didn't neigh nor nicker. He jest laughed. He laughed till the acorns come rattling down outa the trees and the echoes rolled through the cliffs like thunder. And then he reched his head around and grabbed Red's laig and dragged him out of the saddle, and held him upside down with guns and things spilling out of his scabbards and pockets, and Red yelling blue murder. Cap'n Kidd shaken him till he looked like a rag and swung him around his head three or four times, and then let go and throwed him clean through a alder thicket.

Them fellers all stood gaping, and Donovan had forgot about me, so I grabbed the shotgun away from him and hit him under the ear with my left fist and he bit the dust. I then swung the gun on the others and roared: "Onbuckle them gun-belts, cuss ye!" They was bashfuller about buckshot at close range than I was. They didn't argy. Them four gunbelts was on the grass before I stopped yelling.

"All right," I said. "Now go catch Cap'n Kidd."

Because he had gone over to where their hosses was tied and was chawing and kicking the tar out of them and they was hollering something fierce.

"He'll kill us!" squalled the men.

"Well, what of it?" I snarled. "Gwan!"

So they made a desperate foray onto Cap'n Kidd and the way he kicked 'em in the belly and bit the seat out of their britches was beautiful to behold. But whilst he was stomping them I come up and grabbed his hackamore and when he seen who it was he stopped fighting, so I tied him to a tree away from the other hosses. Then I throwed Donovan's shotgun onto the men and made 'em get up and come over to where Donovan was laying, and they was a bruised and battered gang. The way they taken on you'd of thought somebody had mistreated 'em.

I made 'em take Donovan's gunbelt offa him and about that time he come to and sot up, muttering something about a tree falling on him.

"Don't you remember me?" I says. "I'm Breckinridge Elkins."

"It all comes back," he muttered. "We gambled for Cap'n Kidd."

"Yeah," I says, "and you won, so now we gambles for him again. You sot the stakes before. This time I sets 'em. I matches these here britches I got on agen Cap'n Kidd, and yore saddle, bridle, gunbelt, pistol, pants, shirt, boots, spurs and Stetson."

"Robbery!" he bellered. "Yo're a cussed bandit!"

"Shet up," I says, poking him in the midriff with his shotgun. "Squat! The rest of you, too."

"Ain't you goin' to let us do somethin' for Red?" they said. Red was laying on the other side of the thicket Cap'n Kidd had throwed him through, groaning loud and fervent.

"Let him lay for a spell," I says. "If he's dyin' they ain't nothin' we can do for him, and if he ain't, he'll keep till this game's over. Deal, Smoky, and deal from the top of the deck this time."

So Smoky dealt in fear and trembling, and I says to Donovan: "What you got?"

"A royal flush of diamonds, by God!" he says. "You cain't beat that!"

"A royal flush of hearts'll beat it, won't it, Smoky?" I says, and Smoky says: "Yuh--yuh--yeah! Yeah! Oh, yeah!"

"Well," I said, "I ain't looked at my hand yet, but I bet that's jest what I got. What you think?" I says, p'inting the shotgun at Donovan's upper teeth. "Don't you reckon I've got a royal flush in hearts?"

"It wouldn't surprise me a bit," says Donovan, turning pale.

"Then everybody's satisfied and they ain't no use in me showin' my hand," I says, throwing the cards back into the pack. "Shed them duds!"

He shed 'em without a word, and I let 'em take up Red, which had seven busted ribs, a dislocated arm and a busted laig, and they kinda folded him acrost his I saddle and tied him in place. Then they pulled out without saying a word or looking back. They all looked purty wilted, and Donovan particularly looked very pecooliar in the blanket he had wrapped around his middle. If he'd had a feather in his hair he'd of made a lovely Piute, as I told him. But he didn't seem to appreciate the remark. Some men just naturally ain't got no sense of humor.

They headed east, and as soon as they was out of sight, I put the saddle and bridle I'd won onto Cap'n Kidd and getting the bit in his mouth was about like rassling a mountain tornado. But I done it, and then I put on the riggins I'd won. The boots was too small and the shirt fit a mite too snug in the shoulders, but I sure felt elegant, nevertheless, and stalked up and down admiring myself and wishing Glory McGraw could see me then.

I cached my old saddle, belt and pistol in a holler tree, aiming to send my younger brother Bill back after 'em. He could have 'em, along with Alexander. I was going back to Bear Creek in style, by golly!

With a joyful whoop I swung onto Cap'n Kidd, headed him west and tickled his flanks with my spurs--them trappers in the mountains which later reported having seen a blue streak traveling westwardly so fast they didn't have time to tell what it was, and was laughed at and accused of being drunk, was did a injustice. What they seen was me and Cap'n Kidd going to Bear Creek. He run fifty miles before he even pulled up for breath.

I ain't going to tell how long it took Cap'n Kidd to cover the distance to Bear Creek. Nobody wouldn't believe me. But as I come up the trail a few miles from my home cabin, I heard a hoss galloping and Glory McGraw bust into view. She looked pale and scairt, and when she seen me she give a kind of a holler and pulled up her hoss so quick it went back onto its haunches.

"Breckinridge!" she gasped. "I jest heard from yore folks that yore mule come home without you, and I was just startin' out to look for--oh!" says she, noticing my hoss and elegant riggings for the first time. She kind of froze up, and said stiffly: "Well, _Mister_ Elkins, I see yo're back home again."

"And you sees me rigged up in store-bought clothes and ridin' the best hoss in the Humbolts, too, I reckon," I said. "I hope you'll excuse me, Miss McGraw. I'm callin' on Ellen Reynolds as soon as I've let my folks know I'm home safe. Good day!"

"Don't let me detain you!" she flared, but after I'd rode on past she hollered: "Breckinridge Elkins, I hate you!"

"I know that," I said bitterly, "they warn't no use in tellin' me again--"

But she was gone, riding lickety-split off through the woods towards her home-cabin and I rode on for mine, thinking to myself what curious critters gals was anyway.

CHAPTER IV

GUNS OF THE MOUNTAINS

THINGS RUN purty smooth for maybe a month after I got back to Bear Creek. Folks come from miles around to see Cap'n Kidd and hear me tell about licking Wild Bill Donovan, and them fancy clothes sure had a pleasing effeck on Ellen Reynolds. The only flies in the 'intment was Joel Braxton's brother Jim, Ellen's old man, and my Uncle Garfield Elkins; but of him anon as the French says.

Old Man Braxton didn't like me much, but I had learnt my lesson in dealing with Old Man McGraw. I taken no foolishness offa him, and Ellen warn't nigh as sensitive about it as Glory had been. But I warn't sure about Jim Braxton. I discouraged him from calling on Ellen, and I done it purty vi'lent, but I warn't sure he warn't sneaking around and sparking her on the sly, and I couldn't tell just what she thought about him. But I was making progress, when the third fly fell into the 'intment.

Pap's Uncle Garfield Elkins come up from Texas to visit us.

That was bad enough by itself, but between Grizzly Run and Chawed Ear the stage got held up by some masked bandits, and Uncle Garfield, never being able to forget that he was a gunfighting fool thirty or forty years ago, pulled his old cap-and-ball instead of reching for the clouds like he was advised to. For some reason, instead of blowing out his light, they merely busted him over the head with a .45 barrel, and when he come to he was rattling on his way towards Chawed Ear with the other passengers, minus his money and watch.

It was his watch what caused the trouble. That there timepiece had been his grandpap's, back in Kentucky, and Uncle Garfield sot more store by it than he did all his kin folks.

When he arriv onto Bear Creek he imejitly let into howling his woes to the stars like a wolf with the belly-ache. And from then on we heered nothing but that watch. I'd saw it and thunk very little of it. It was big as my fist, and wound up with a key which Uncle Garfield was always losing and looking for. But it was solid gold, and he called it a hairloom, whatever them things is. And he nigh driv the family crazy.

"A passle of big hulks like you-all settin' around and lettin' a old man git robbed of all his property," he would say bitterly. "When _I_ was a young buck, if'n _my_ uncle had been abused that way, I'd of took the trail and never slept nor et till I brung back his watch and the sculp of the skunk which hived it. Men now days--" And so on and so on, till I felt like drownding the old jassack in a barrel of corn licker.

Finally pap says to me, combing his beard with his fingers; "Breckinridge," says he, "I've endured Uncle Garfield's belly-achin' all I aim to. I wants you to go look for his cussed watch, and don't come back without it."

"How'm I goin' to know where to look?" I protested. "The feller which got it may be in Californy or Mexico by now."

"I realizes the difficulties," says pap. "But warn't you eager for farin's which would make you a name in the world?"

"They is times for everything," I said. "Right now I'm interested in sparkin' a gal, which I ain't willin' to leave for no wild goose chase."

"Well," says pap, "I've done made up our mind. If Uncle Garfield knows somebody is out lookin' for his cussed timepiece, maybe he'll give the rest of us some peace. You git goin', and if you cain't find that watch, don't come back till after Uncle Garfield has went home."

"How long does he aim to stay?" I demanded.

"Well," says pap, "Uncle Garfield's visits generally last a year, at least."

At this I bust into earnest profanity.

I says: "I got to stay away from home a _year?_ Dang it, Pap, Jim Braxton'll steal Ellen Reynolds away from me whilst I'm gone. I been courtin' that gal till I'm ready to fall dead. I done licked her old man three times, and now, jest when I got her goin', you tells me I got to up and leave her for a year with that dern Jim Braxton to have no competition with."

"You got to choose between Ellen Reynolds and yore own flesh and blood," says pap. "I'm derned if I'll listen to Uncle Garfield's squawks any longer. You make yore own choice--but if you don't choose to do what I asks you to, I'll fill yore hide with buckshot every time I see you from now on."

Well, the result was that I was presently riding morosely away from home and Ellen Reynolds, and in the general direction of where Uncle Garfield's blasted watch might possibly be.

I rode by the Braxton cabin with the intention of dropping Jim a warning about his actions whilst I was gone, but I didn't see his saddle on the corral fence, so I knowed he warn't there. So I issued a general defiance to the family by sling- ing a .45 slug through the winder which knocked a corn cob pipe outa old man Braxton's mouth. That soothed me a little, but I knowed very well that Jim would make a bee-line for the Reynolds cabin the second I was out of sight. I could just see him gorging on Ellen's b'ar meat and honey, and bragging on hisself. I hoped Ellen would notice the difference between a loud- mouthed boaster like him, and a quiet modest young man like me, which never bragged, though admittedly the biggest man and the best fighter in the Humbolts.

I hoped to meet Jim somewhere in the woods as I rode down the trail, because

I was intending to do something to kinda impede his courting whilst I was gone, like breaking his laig or something, but luck wasn't with me.

I headed in the general direction of Chawed Ear, and a few days later seen me riding in gloomy grandeur through a country quite some distance from Ellen Reynolds. Nobody'd been able to tell me anything in Chawed Ear, so I thought I might as well comb the country between there and Grizzly Run. Probably wouldn't never find them dern bandits anyway.

Pap always said my curiosity would be the ruination of me some day, but I never could listen to guns popping up in the mountains without wanting to find out who was killing who. So that morning, when I heard the rifles talking off amongst the trees, I turned Cap'n Kidd aside and left the trail and rode in the direction of the noise.

A dim path wound up through the big boulders and bushes, and the shooting kept getting louder. Purty soon I come out into a glade, and just as I did, _bam!_ somebody let go at me from the bresh and a .45- 70 slug cut both my bridle reins nearly in half. I instantly returned the shot with my .45, getting jest a glimpse of something in the bresh, and a man let out a squall and jumped out into the open, wringing his hands. My bullet had hit the lock of his Winchester and mighty nigh jarred his hands offa him.

"Cease that ungodly noise," I said sternly, p'inting my .45 at his bay-winder, "and explain how come you waylays innercent travellers."

He quit working his fingers and moaning, and he said: "I thought you was Joel Cairn, the outlaw. Yo're about his size."

"Well, I ain't," I said. "I'm Breckinridge Elkins, from Bear Creek. I was jest ridin' over to find out what all the shootin' was about."

The guns was banging in the trees behind the feller, and somebody yelled what was the matter.

"Ain't nothin' the matter," he hollered back. "Just a misunderstandin'." And he says to me: "I'm glad to see you, Elkins. We need a man like you. I'm Sheriff Dick Hopkins, from Grizzly Run."

"Where at's yore star?" I inquired.

"I lost it in the bresh," he said. "Me and my deputies have been chasin' Tarantula Bixby and his gang for a day and a night, and we got 'em cornered over there in a old deserted cabin in a holler. The boys is shootin' at 'em now. I heered you comin' up the trail and snuck over to see who it was. Just as I said, I thought you was Cairn. Come on with me. You can help us."

"I ain't no deperty," I said. "I got nothin' against Tranchler Bixby."

"Well, you want to uphold the law, don't you?" he said.

"Naw," I said.

"Well, gee whiz!" he wailed. "If you ain't a hell of a citizen! The country's goin' to the dogs. What chance has a honest man got?"

"Aw, shet up," I said. "I'll go over and see the fun, anyhow."

So he picked up his gun, and I tied Cap'n Kidd, and follered the sheriff through the trees till we come to some rocks, and there was four men laying behind them rocks and shooting down into a hollow. The hill sloped away mighty steep into a small basin that was jest like a bowl, with a rim of slopes all around. In the middle, of this bowl they was a cabin and puffs of smoke was coming from the cracks between the logs.

The men behind the rocks looked at me in surprise, and one of 'em said: "What the hell?"

The sheriff scowled at them and said, "Boys, this here is Breck Elkins. I done already told him about us bein' a posse from Grizzly Run, and about how we got Tarantula Bixby and two of his cutthroats trapped in that there cabin."

One of the deputies bust into a loud guffaw and Hopkins glared at him and said: "What _you_ laughin' about, you spotted hyener?"

"I swallered my terbaccer and that allus gives me the hystericals," mumbled the deputy, looking the other way.

"Hold up yore right hand, Elkins," requested Hopkins, so I done so, wondering what for, and he said: "Does you swear to tell the truth, the whole truth and nothing but the truth, e pluribus unum, anno dominecker, to wit in status quo?"

"What the hell are you talkin' about?" I demanded.

"Them which God has j'ined asunder let no man put together," said Hopkins. "Whatever you say will be used agen you and the Lord have mercy on yore soul. That means yo're a deputy. I just swore you in."

"Go set on a prickly pear," I snorted disgustedly. "Go catch yore own thieves. And don't look at me like that. I might bend a gun over yore skull."

"But Elkins," pleaded Hopkins, "with yore help we can catch them rats easy. All you got to do is lay up here behind this big rock and shoot at the cabin and keep 'em occupied till we can sneak around and rush 'em from the rear. See, the bresh comes down purty close to the foot of the slope on the other side, and gives us cover. We can do it easy, with somebody keepin' their attention over here. I'll give you part of the reward."

"I don't want no derned blood-money," I said, backing away, "And besides--_ ow!"_

I'd absent-mindedly backed out from behind the big rock where I'd been standing, and a .30-30 slug burned its way acrost the seat of my britches.

"Dern them murderers!" I bellered, seeing red. "Gimme a rifle! I'll learn 'em to shoot a man behind his back! Gwan, and git 'em from behind whilst I attracts their attention with a serenade of hot lead!"

"Good boy!" says Hopkins. "You'll git plenty for this!"

It sounded like somebody was snickering to theirselves as they snuck away, but I give no heed. I squinted cautiously around the big boulder and begun sniping at the cabin. All I could see to shoot at was the puffs of smoke which marked the cracks they was shooting through, but from the cussing and yelling which begun to float up from the shack, I must of throwed some lead mighty close to them.

They kept shooting back, and the bullets splashed and buzzed on the rocks, and I kept looking at the further slope for some sign of Sheriff Hopkins and the posse. But all I heard was a sound of hosses galloping away towards the west. I wondered who it was, and I kept expecting the posse to rush down the oppersite slope and take them desperadoes in the rear, and whilst I was craning my neck around a corner of the boulder--_whang!_ A bullet smashed into the rock a few inches from my face and a sliver of stone taken a notch out of my ear. I don't know of nothing that makes me madder'n getting shot in the ear.

I seen red and didn't even shoot back. A ordinary rifle was too paltry to satisfy me. Suddenly I realized that the big boulder in front of me was jest poised on the slope, its underside partly embedded in the earth. I throwed down my rifle and bent my knees and spread my arms and gripped it.

I shook the sweat and blood outa my eyes, and bellered so them in the hollow could hear me: "I'm givin' you-all a chance to surrender! Come out with yore hands up!"

They give loud and sarcastic jeers, and I yelled: "All right, you ring-tailed jackasses! If you gits squashed like a pancake, it's yore own fault. _Here she comes!"_

And I heaved with all I had. The veins stood out onto my temples, and my feet sunk into the ground, but the earth bulged and cracked all around the big rock, rivulets of dirt began to trickle down, and the big boulder groaned, give way and lurched over.

A dumbfounded yell riz from the cabin. I lept behind a bush, but the outlaws was too surprised to shoot at me. That enormous boulder was tumbling down the hill, crushing bushes flat and gathering speed as it rolled. And the cabin was right in its path.

Wild yells bust the air, the door was throwed vi'lently open, and a man hove into view. Jest as he started out of the door I let _bam_ at him and he howled and ducked back jest like anybody will when a .45-90 slug knocks their hat off. The next instant that thundering boulder hit the cabin. _Smash!_ It knocked it sidewise like a ten pin and caved in the wall, and the whole structure collapsed in a cloud of dust and bark and splinters.

I run down the slope, and from the yells which issued from under the ruins, I knowed they warn't all kilt.

"Does you-all surrender?" I roared.

"Yes, dern it!" they squalled. "Git us out from under this landslide!"

"Throw out yore guns," I ordered.

"How in hell can we throw anything?" they hollered wrathfully. "We're pinned down by a ton of rocks and boards and we're bein' squoze to death. Help, murder!"

"Aw, shet up," I said. "You all don't hear _me_ carryin' on in no such hysterical way, does you?"

Well, they moaned and complained, and I sot to work dragging the ruins offa them, which warn't no great task. Purty soon I seen a booted laig and I laid hold of it and dragged out the critter it was fastened to, and he looked more done up than what my brother Buckner did that time he rassled a mountain lion for a bet. I taken his pistol out of his belt, and laid him down on the ground and got the others out. They was three, altogether, and I taken their arms and laid 'em out in a row.

Their clothes was nearly tore off, and they was bruised and scratched and had splinters in their hair, but they warn't hurt permanent. They sot up and felt of theirselves, and one of 'em said: "This here's the first earthquake I ever seen in this country."

"'Twarn't no earthquake," said another'n. "It was a avalanche."

"Lissen here, Joe Partland," said the first'n, grinding his teeth. "I says it was a earthquake, and I ain't the man to be called a liar-- "

"Oh, you ain't, hey?" says the other'n, bristling up. "Well, lemme tell you somethin', Frank Jackson--"

"This ain't no time for sech argyments," I admonished 'em sternly. "As for that there rock, I rolled that at you-all myself."

They gaped at me, and one of 'em says: "Who are you?" he says, mopping the blood offa his ear.

"Never mind that," I says. "You see this here Winchester? Well, you-all set still and rest yorselves. Soon as the sheriff gits here I'm goin' to hand you over to him."

His mouth fell open. "Sheriff?" he said, dumb-like. "What sheriff?"

"Dick Hopkins, from Grizzly Run," I said.

"Why, you demed fool!" he screamed, scrambling up.

"Set down!" I roared, shoving my rifle barrel at him, and he sank back, all white and shaking. He couldn't hardly talk.

"Lissen to me!" he gasped. "_I'm_ Dick Hopkins! _I'm_ sheriff of Grizzly Run! These men are my deputies."

"Yeah?" I said sarcastically. "And who was the fellers shootin' at you from the bresh?"

"Tarantula Bixby and his gang," he says. "We was follerin' 'em when they jumped us, and bein' outnumbered and surprised, we taken cover in that old hut. They robbed the Grizzly Run bank day before yesterday. And now they'll be gittin' further away every minute! Oh, Judas J. Iscariot! Of all the dumb, bone-headed jackasses--"

"Heh! heh! heh!" I said cynically. "You must think I ain't got no sense. If yo're the sheriff, where at's yore star?"

"It was on my suspenders," he said despairingly. "When you hauled me out by the laig my suspenders caught on somethin' and tore off. If you'll lemme look amongst them rooins--"

"You set still," I commanded. "You cain't fool me. Yo're Tranchler Bixby yore-self. Sheriff Hopkins told me so. Him and the posse'll be here directly. Set still and shet up."

We stayed there, and the feller which claimed to be the sheriff moaned and pulled his hair and shed a few tears, and the other fellers tried to convince me they was deputies till I got tired of their gab and told 'em to shet up or I'd bend my Winchester over their heads. I wondered why Hopkins and them didn't come, and I begun to get nervous, and all to onst the feller which said he was the sheriff give a yell that startled me so I jumped and nearly shot him. He had something in his hand and was waving it around.

"See here?" he hollered so loud his voice cracked. "I found it! It must of fell down into my shirt when my suspenders busted! Look at it, you derned mountain grizzly!"

I looked and my flesh crawled. It was a shiny silver star.

"Hopkins said he lost his'n," I said weakly. "Maybe you found it in the bresh."

"You know better!" he bellered. "Yo're one of Bixby's men. You was left here to hold us whilst Tarantula and the rest made their gitaway. You'll git ninety years for this!"

I turned cold all over as I remembered them hosses I heard galloping. I'd been fooled! This _was_ the sheriff! That pot-bellied thug which shot at me had been Bixby hisself! And whilst I held up the real sheriff and his posse, them outlaws was riding out of the country! I was the prize sucker.

"You better gimme that gun and surrender," opined Hopkins. "Maybe if you do they won't hang you."

"Set still!" I snarled. "I'm the biggest fool that ever straddled a mustang, but even idjits has their feelin's. Pap said never resist a officer, but this here is a special case. You ain't goin' to put me behind no bars, jest because I made a mistake. I'm goin' up that there slope, but I'll be watchin' you. I've throwed yore guns over there in the bresh. If anybody makes a move towards 'em, I'll shove a harp right into his hand."

They set up a chant of hate as I backed away, but they sot still. I went up the slope backwards till I hit the rim, and then I turned and ducked into the bresh and run. I heard 'em cussing something awful down in the hollow, but I didn't pause. I come to where I'd left Cap'n Kidd and forked him and pulled out, being thankful them outlaws had been in too big a hurry to steal him. But I doubt if he'd a-let 'em. I throwed away the rifle they give me and headed west.

I aimed to cross Thunder River at Ghost Canyon, and head into the wild mountain region beyond there. I figgered I could dodge a posse indefinite onst I got there. I let Cap'n Kidd out into a long lope, cussing my reins which had been notched deep by Bixby's bullet. I didn't have time to fix 'em, and Cap'n Kidd was a iron-jawed outlaw.

He was sweating plenty when I finally hove in sight of the place I was heading for. As I topped the canyon's crest before I dipped down to the crossing, I looked back. They was a high notch in the hills a few miles behind me, and as I looked three hossmen was etched in that notch, lined agen the sky behind 'em. I cussed free and fervent. Why hadn't I had sense enough to know Hopkins and his men was bound to have hosses tied somewheres near? They got their mounts and follered me, figgering I'd aim for the country beyond Thunder River. It was about the only place I could go.

Not wanting no running fight with no sheriff's posse, I raced recklessly down the sloping canyon wall, busted out of the bushes--and stopped short. Thunder River was on the rampage--bank-full in the narrow channel and boiling and foaming. Been a cloud-bust somewhere away up on the head, and the hoss warn't never foaled which could swum it. Not even Cap'n Kidd, though he snorted warlike and was game to try it.

They wasn't but one thing to do, and I done it. I wheeled Cap'n Kidd and headed up the canyon. Five miles up the river they was another crossing, with a bridge--if it hadn't been washed away. Like as not it had been, with the luck I was having. A nice pickle Uncle Garfield's cussed watch had got me in, I reflected bitterly. Jest when I was all sot to squelch Glory McGraw onst and for all by marrying Ellen Reynolds, here I was throwed into circumstances which made me a fugitive from justice. I could just imagine Glory laughing at me, and it nigh locoed me.

I was so absorbed in these thoughts I paid little attention to my imejit surroundings, but all of a sudden I heard a noise ahead, above the roar of the river and the thunder of Cap'n Kidd's hoofs on the rocky canyon floor. We was approaching a bend in the gorge where a low ridge run out from the canyon wall, and beyond that ridge I heard guns banging. I heaved back on the reins--and both of 'em snapped in two!

Cap'n Kidd instantly clamped his teeth on the bit and bolted, like he always does when he gits the chance. He headed straight for the bushes at the end of the ridge, and I leaned forward and tried to get hold of the bit rings with my fingers. But all I done was swerve him from his course. Instead of follering the canyon bed on around the end of the ridge, he went right over the rise, which sloped on that side. It didn't slope on t'other side; it fell away abrupt. I had a fleeting glimpse of five men crouching amongst the bushes on the canyon floor with guns in their hands. They looked up--and Cap'n Kidd braced his laigs and slid to a halt at the lip of the blow bluff, and simultaneous bogged his head and throwed me heels over head down amongst 'em.

My boot heel landed on somebody's head, and the spur knocked him cold and blame near sculped him. That partly bust my fall, and it was further cushioned by another feller which I lit on in a setting position, and which taken no further interest in the proceedings. But the other three fell on me with loud brutal yells, and I reched for my .45 and found to my humiliation that it had fell out of my scabbard when I was throwed.

So I riz up with a rock in my hand and bounced it offa the head of a feller which was fixing to shoot me, and he dropped his pistol and fell on top of it. At this juncture one of the survivors put a buffalo gun to his shoulder and sighted, then evidently fearing he would hit his companion which was carving at me on the other side with a bowie knife, he reversed it and run in swinging it like a club.

The man with the knife got in a slash across my ribs and I then hit him on the chin which was how his jawbone got broke in four places. Meanwhile the other'n swung at me with his rifle, but missed my head and broke the stock off across my shoulder. Irritated at his persistency in trying to brain me with the barrel, I laid hands on him and throwed him head-on agen the bluff, which is when he got his fractured skull and concussion of the brain, I reckon.

I then shaken the sweat outa my eyes, and glaring down, rekernized the remains as Bixby and his gang. I might have knew they'd head for the wild country across the river, same as me. Only place they could go.

Just then, however, a clump of bushes parted, nigh, the river bank, and a big black-bearded man riz up from behind a dead hoss. He had a six-shooter in his hand and he approached me cautiously.

"Who're you?" he demanded suspiciously. "Whar'd you come from?"

"I'm Breckinridge Elkins," I answered, wringing the blood outa my shirt. "What is this here business, anyway?"

"I was settin' here peaceable waitin' for the river to go down so I could cross," he says, "when up rode these yeggs and started shootin'. I'm a honest citizen--"

"Yo're a liar," I said with my usual diplomacy. "Yo're Joel Cairn, the wust outlaw in these hills. I seen yore picher in the post office at Chawed Ear."

With that he p'inted his .45 at me and his beard bristled like the whiskers of a old timber wolf.

"So you know me, hey?" he said. "Well, what you goin' to do about it, hey? Want to colleck the reward money, hey?"

"Naw, I don't," I says. "I'm a outlaw myself, now. I just run foul of the law account of these skunks. They's a posse right behind me."

"They is?" he snarled. "Why'nt you say so? Here, le's catch these fellers' hosses and light out. Cheapskates! They claims I double- crossed 'em in the matter of a stagecoach hold-up we pulled together recent. I been avoidin' 'em 'cause I'm a peaceful man by nater, but they rode onto me onexpected awhile ago. They shot down my hoss first crack; we been tradin' lead for more'n a hour, without doin' much damage, but they'd got me eventually, I reckon. Come on. We'll pull out together.

"No, we won't," I said. "I'm a outlaw by force of circumstances, but I ain't no murderin' bandit."

"Purty particular of yore comperny, ain'tcha?" he sneered. "Well, anyway, help me catch me a hoss. Yore's is still up thar on that bluff. The day's still young--"

He pulled out a big gold watch and looked at it; it was one which wound with a key.

I jumped like I was shot. "Where'd you git that watch?" I hollered.

He jerked up his head kinda startled, and said: "My grandpap gimme it. Why?"

"You're a liar!" I bellered. "You taken that off'n my Uncle Garfield. _Gimme that watch!_"

"Air you crazy?" he yelled, going white under his whiskers. I plunged for him, seeing red, and he let _bang!_ and I got it in the left thigh. Before he could shoot again I was on top of him and knocked the gun up. It banged but the bullet went singing up over the bluff and Cap'n Kidd squealed with rage and started changing ends. The pistol flew outa Cairn's hand and he hit hit me vi'lently on the nose which made me see stars. So I hit him in the belly and he grunted and doubled up; and come up with a knife out of his boot which he cut me acrost the boozum with, also in the arm and shoulder and kicked me in the groin. So I swung him clear of the ground and throwed him down headfirst and jumped on him with both boots. And that settled his hash.

I picked up the watch where it had fell, and staggered over to the cliff, spurting blood at every step like a stuck hawg.

"At last my search is at a end!" I panted. "I can go back to Ellen Reynolds who patiently awaits the return of her hero--"

It was at this instant that Cap'n Kidd, which had been stung by Cairn's wild shot and was trying to buck off his saddle, bucked hisself off the bluff. He fell on me....

The first thing I heard was bells ringing, and then they turned to hosses galloping. I sot up and wiped off the blood which was running into my eyes from where Cap'n Kidd's left hind shoe had split my sculp. And I seen Sheriff Hopkins, Jackson and Partland come tearing around the ridge. I tried to get up and run, but my right laig wouldn't work. I reched for my gun and it still wasn't there. I was trapped.

"Look there!" yelled Hopkins, plumb wild-eyed. "That's Bixby on the ground--and all his gang! And ye gods, there's Joel Cairn! What is this, anyway? It looks like a battle-field! What's that settin' there? He's so bloody I cain't rekernize him!"

"It's the hillbilly!" yelped Jackson. "Don't move or I'll shoot'cha!"

"I already been shot," I snarled. "Gwan--do yore wust. Fate is agen me."

They dismounted and stared in awe.

"Count the dead, boys," said Hopkins in a still, small voice.

"Aw," said Partland, "ain't none of 'em dead, but they'll never be the same men again. Look! Bixby's comin' to! Who done this, Bixby?"

Bixby cast a wabbly eye about till he spied me, and then he moaned and shrivelled up. "He tried to sculp me!" he wailed. "He ain't human!"

They all looked at me, and all taken their hats off.

"Elkins," says Hopkins in a tone of reverence, "I see it all now. They fooled you into thinkin' they was the posse and we was the outlaws, didn't they? And when you realized the truth, you hunted 'em down, didn't you? And cleaned 'em out single-handed, and Joel Cairn, too, didn't you?"

"Well," I said groggily, "the truth is--"

"We understand," Hopkins soothed. "You mount tain men is all modest. Hey, boys, tie up them outlaws whilst I look at Elkins' wounds."

"If you'll catch my hoss," I said, "I got to be ridin' back--"

"Gee whiz, man!" he said, "you ain't in no shape to ride a hoss! Do you know you got five busted ribs and a fractured arm, and one laig broke and a bullet in the other'n, to say nothin' of bein' slashed to ribbons? We'll rig up a litter for you. What's that you got in yore good hand?"

I suddenly remembered Uncle Garfield's watch which I'd kept clutched in a death grip. I stared at what I held in my hand; and I fell back with a low moan. All I had in my hand was a bunch of busted metal and broken wheels and springs, bent and smashed plumb beyond recognition.

"Grab him!" yelled Hopkins. "He's fainted!"

"Plant me under a pine tree, boys," I murmured weakly. "Just kyarve onto my tombstone: 'He fit a good fight but Fate dealt him the joker.'"

A few days later a melancholy procession wound its way up the trail to Bear Creek. I was being toted on a litter. I told 'em I wanted to see Ellen Reynolds before I died, and to show Uncle Garfield the rooins of the watch so he'd know I done my duty as I seen it.

When we'd got to within a few miles of my home cabin, who should meet us but Jim Braxton, which tried to conceal his pleasure when I told him in a weak voice that I was a dying man. He was all dressed up in new buckskins and his exuberance was plumb disgustful to a man in my condition.

"Too bad," says he. "Too bad, Breckinridge. I hoped to meet you, but not like this, of course. Yore pap told me to tell you about yore Uncle Garfield's watch if I seen you. He thought I might run into you on my way to Chawed Ear to git a licence--"

"Hey?" I said, pricking up my ears.

"Yeah, me and Ellen Reynolds is goin' to git married," he says. "Well, as I started to say, seems like one of them bandits which robbed the stage was a feller whose dad was a friend of yore Uncle Garfield's back in Texas. He rekernized the name in the watch and sent it back, and it got here the day after you left--"

They say it was jealousy which made me rise up on my litter and fracture Jim Braxton's jawbone. I denies that. I stoops to no sech petty practices. What impelled me was family conventions. I couldn't hit Uncle Garfield; I had to hit somebody; and Jim Braxton jest happened to be the only man in rech.

CHAPTER V

A GENT FROM BEAR CREEK

"YOU," says my sister Ouachita, p'inting a accusing finger at me, "ought a be shot for the way you treat Glory McGraw!"

"Don't mention that gal's name to me," I says bitterly. "I don't want to hear nothin' about her. Don't talk to me about her--why you think I ain't treated her right?"

"Well," says Ouachita, "after they brung you back from Chawed Ear lookin' like you'd been through a sorghum mill, Glory come right over when she heered you was hurt. And what did you do when she come through the door?"

"I didn't do nothin'," I says. "What'd I do?"

"You turnt over towards the wall," says Ouachita, "and you says, says you: 'Git that woman outa here; she's come to t'ant me in my helpless condition!'"

"Well, she did!" I said fiercely.

"She didn't!" says Ouachita. "When she heered you say them words, she turnt pale, and she turnt around and walked outa the cabin with her head up in the air, not sayin' a word. And she ain't been back since."

"Well, I don't want her to," I says. "She come over here jest to gloat on my misery."

"I don't believe no such," says Ouachita. "First thing she says, was: 'Is Breckinridge hurt bad?' And she didn't say it in no gloatin' way. She come over here to help you, I bet, and you talked to her like that! You ought to be ashamed."

"You mind yore own business," I advised her, and got up and got outa the cabin to get some peace and quiet.

I went towards the creek aiming to do a little fishing. My laig had knit proper and quick, and that had been the only thing which had kept me laid up. On my way to the creek I got to thinking over what Ouachita had said, and I thought, well, maybe I was a mite hasty. Maybe Glory did repent of her treatment of me when I was laying wounded. Maybe I ought not to of spoke so bitterly.

I thought, it's no more'n my neighborly duty to go over and thank Glory for coming over to see me, and tell her I didn't mean what I said. I'd tell her I was delirious and thought it was Ellen Reynolds. After all, I was a man with a great, big, generous, forgiving heart, and if forgiving Glory McGraw was going to brighten her life, why, I warn't one to begrudge it. So I headed for the McGraw cabin--a trail I hadn't took since the day I shot up Mister Wilkinson.

I went afoot because I wanted to give my laig plenty of exercise now it was healed. And I hadn't gone more'n halfway when I met the gal I was looking for. She was riding her bay mare, and we met face to face right spang in the middle of the trail. I taken off my Stetson and says: "Howdy, Glory. You warn't by any chance headin' for my cabin?"

"And why should I be headin' for yore cabin, Mister Elkins?" she said as stiff and cold as a frozen bowie knife.

"Well," I said, kinda abashed, "well--uh--that is, Glory, I jest want to thank you for droppin' in to see about me when I was laid up, and--"

"I didn't," she snapped. "I jest come to borrer some salt. I didn't even know you'd been hurt."

"What you want to talk like that for, Glory?" I protested. "I didn't aim to hurt yore feelin's. Fact is, I war delirious, and thought you was somebody else--"

"Ellen Reynolds, maybe?" says she sneeringly. "Or was she already there, holdin' yore hand? Oh, no! I'd plumb forgot! She was gittin' married to Jim Braxton about that time! Too bad, Breckinridge! But cheer up! Ellen's got a little sister which'll be growed up in a few years. Maybe you can git her--if some Braxton don't beat you to her."

"To hell with the Braxtons and the Reynolds too!" I roared, seeing red again. "And you can go along with 'em, far's I'm consarned! I was right! Ouachita's a fool, sayin' you was sorry for me. You jest come over there to gloat over me when I was laid up!"

"I didn't!" she says, in a changed voice.

"You did, too!" I says bitterly. "You go yore way and I'll go mine. You think I cain't git me no woman, just because you and Ellen Reynolds turned me down. Well, you-all ain't the only women they is! I ain't goin' to marry no gal on Bear Creek! I'm goin' to git me a town- gal!"

"A town-gal wouldn't look at a hillbilly like you!" she sneered.

"Oh, is that so?" I bellered, convulsively jerking some saplings up by the roots in my agitation. "Well, lemme tell you somethin', Miss McGraw, I'm pullin' out right now, this very day, for the settlements, where purty gals is thick as flies in watermelon time, and I aim to bring back the purtiest one of the whole kaboodle! You wait and see!"

And I went storming away from there so blind mad that I fell into the creek before I knowed it, and made a most amazing splash. I thought I heard Glory call me to come back, jest before I fell, but I was so mad I didn't pay no attention. I'd had about all the badgering I could stand for one day. I clumb out on t'other side, dripping like a muskrat, and headed for the tall timber. I could hear her laughing behind me, and she must of been kinda hysterical, because it sounded like she was crying instead of laughing, but I didn't stop to see. All I wanted was to put plenty of distance between me and Glory McGraw, and I headed for home as fast as I could laig it.

It was my fullest intention to saddle Cap'n Kidd and pull out for Chawed Ear or somewheres as quick as I could. I meant what I said about getting me a town-gal. But right then I was fogging head-on into the cussedest mix-up I'd ever saw, up to that time, and didn't know it. I didn't even get a inkling of it when I almost stumbled over a couple of figures locked in mortal combat on the bank of the creek.

I was surprised when I seen who it was. The folks on Bear Creek ain't exactly what you'd call peaceable by nature, but Erath Elkins and his brother-in-law Joel Gordon had always got along well together, even when they was full of corn juice. But there they was, so tangled up they couldn't use their bowies to no advantage, and their cussin' was scandalous to hear.

Remonstrances being useless, I kicked their knives out of their hands and throwed 'em bodily into the creek. That broke their holds and they come swarming out with blood-thirsty shrieks and dripping whiskers, and attacked me. Seeing they was too blind mad to have any sense, I bashed their heads together till they was too dizzy to do anything but holler.

"Is this any way for relatives to ack?" I ast disgustedly.

"Lemme at him!" howled Joel, gnashing his teeth whilst blood streamed down his whiskers. "He's broke three of my fangs and I'll have his life!"

"Stand aside, Breckinridge!" raved Erath. "No man can chaw a ear offa me and live to tell the tale."

"Aw, shet up," I snorted. "Ca'm down, before I sees is yore fool heads harder'n this." I brandished a large fist under their noses and they subsided sulkily. "What's all this about?" I demanded.

"I jest discovered my brother-in-law is a thief," said Joel bitterly. At that Erath give a howl and a vi'lent plunge to get at his relative, but I kind of pushed him backwards, and he fell over a willer stump.

"The facks is, Breckinridge," says Joel, "me and this here polecat found a buckskin poke full of gold nuggets in a holler oak over on Apache Ridge yesterday, right nigh the place whar yore brother Garfield fit them seven wildcats last year. We didn't know whether somebody in these parts had jest hid it thar for safe-keepin', or whether some old prospector had left it thar a long time ago and maybe got sculped by the Injuns and never come back to git it. We agreed to leave it alone for a month, and if it was still thar when we come back, we'd feel purty shore that the original owner was dead, and we'd split the gold between us. Well, last night I got to worryin' lest somebody'd find it which warn't as honest as me, so this mornin' I thought I better go see if it was still thar..."

At this p'int Erath laughed bitterly.

Joel glared at him ominously and continued: "Well, no sooner I hove in sight of the holler tree than this skunk let go at me from the bresh with a rifle-gun--"

"That's a lie!" yelped Erath. "It war jest the other way around!"

"Not bein' armed, Breckinridge," Joel said with dignity, "and realizin' that this coyote was tryin' to murder me so he could claim all the gold, I laigged it for home and my weppin's. And presently I sighted him sprintin' through the bresh after me."

Erath begun to foam slightly at the mouth. "I warn't chasin' you!" he howled. "I war goin' home after my rifle-gun."

"What's yore story, Erath?" I inquired.

"Last night I drempt somebody had stole the gold," he answered sullenly. "This mornin' I went to see if it was safe. Jest as I got to the tree, this murderer begun shootin' at me with a Winchester. I run for my life, and by some chance I finally run right into him. Likely he thought he'd hived me and was comin' for the sculp."

"Did either one of you see t'other'n shoot at you?" I ast.

"How could I, with him hid in the bresh?" snapped Joel. "But who else could it been?"

"I didn't have to see him," growled Erath. "I felt the wind of his lead."

"But each one of you says he didn't have no rifle," I said.

"He's a cussed liar," they accused simultaneous, and would have fell onto each other tooth and nail if they could have got past my bulk. "I'm convinced they'd been a mistake," I said. "Git home and cool off."

"Yo're too big for me to lick, Breckinridge," said Erath. "But I warn you, if you cain't prove to me that it warn't Joel which tried to murder me, I ain't goin' to rest nor sleep nor eat till I've nailed his mangy sculp to the highest pine on Apache Ridge."

"That goes for me, too," says Joel, grinding his teeth. "I'm declarin' truce till tomorrer mornin'. If Breckinridge cain't show me by then that you didn't shoot at me, either my wife or yore'n'll be a widder before midnight."

So saying they stalked off in oppersite directions, whilst I stared helplessly after 'em, slightly dazed at the responsibility which had been dumped onto me. That's the drawback of being the biggest man in yore settlement. All the relatives piles their trouble onto you. Here it was up to me to stop what looked like the beginnings of a regular family feud which was bound to reduce the population awful. I couldn't go sparking me no town-gal with all this hell brewing.

The more I thought of the gold them idjits had found, the more I felt like I ought to go and take a look at it myself, so I went back to the corral and saddled Cap'n Kidd and lit out for Apache Ridge. From the remarks they'd let fall whilst cussing each other, I had a purty good idee where the holler oak was at, and sure enough I found it without much trouble. I tied Cap'n Kidd and clumb up onto the trunk till I reched the holler. And then as I was craning my neck to look in, I heard a voice say: "Another dern thief!"

I looked around and seen Uncle Jeppard Grimes p'inting a gun at me.

"Bear Creek is goin' to hell," says Uncle Jeppard. "First it was Erath and Joel, and now it's you. I aim to throw a bullet through yore hind laig jest to teach you a little honesty. Hold still whilst I draws my bead."

With that he started sighting along the barrel of his Winchester, and I says: "You better save yore lead for that Injun over there."

Him being a old Injun fighter he jest naturally jerked his head around quick, and I pulled my .45 and shot the rifle out of his hands. I jumped down and put my foot on it, and he pulled a knife out of his leggin', and I taken it away from him and shaken him till he was so addled when I let him go he run in a circle and fell down cussing something terrible.

"Is everybody on Bear Creek gone crazy?" I demanded. "Cain't a man look into a holler tree without gittin' assassinated?"

"You was after my gold!" swore Uncle Jeppard.

"So it's yore gold, hey?" I said. "Well, a holler tree ain't no bank."

"I know it," he growled, combing the pine-needles out of his whiskers. "When I come here early this mornin' to see if it was safe, like I frequent does, I seen right off somebody'd been handlin' it. Whilst I was meditatin' over this, I seen Joel Gordon sneakin' towards the tree. I fired a shot acrost his bows in warnin' and he run off. But a few minutes later here come Erath Elkins slitherin' through the pines. I was mad by this time, so I combed his whiskers with a chunk of lead and _he_ high-tailed it. And now, by golly, here you come--"

"You shet up!" I roared. "Don't you accuse me of wantin' yore blame gold. I jest wanted to see if it was safe, and so did Joel and Erath. If them men was thieves, they'd have took it when they found it yesterday. Where'd you git it, anyway?"

"I panned it, up in the hills," he said sullenly. "I ain't had time to take it to Chawed Ear and git it changed into cash money. I figgered this here tree was as good a place as any. But I done put it elsewhar now."

"Well," I said, "you got to go tell Erath and Joel it war you which shot at 'em, so they won't kill each other. They'll be mad at you, but I'll restrain 'em, with a hickery club, if necessary."

"All right," he said. "I'm sorry I misjedged you, Breckinridge. Jest to show I trusts you, I'll show you whar I hid it after I taken it outa the tree."

He led me through the trees till he come to a big rock jutting out from the side of a cliff, and p'inted at a smaller rock wedged beneath it.

"I pulled out that there rock," he said, "and dug a hole and stuck the poke in. Look!"

He heaved the rock out and bent down. And then he went straight up in the air with a yell that made me jump and pull my gun with cold sweat busting out all over me.

"What's the matter?" I demanded. "Air you snake-bit!"

"Yeah, by human snakes!" he hollered. "_It's gone!_ I been robbed!"

I looked and seen the impressions the wrinkles in the buckskin poke had made in the soft earth. But there warn't nothing there now.

Uncle Jeppard was doing a scalp dance with a gun in one hand and a bowie knife in the other'n. "I'll fringe my leggin's with their mangy sculps! I'll pickle their hearts in a barr'l of brine! I'll feed their gizzards to my houn' dawgs!" he yelled.

"Whose gizzards?" I inquired.

"Whose, you idjit?" he howled. "Joe Gordon and Erath Elkins, dern it! They didn't run off. They snuck back and seen me move the gold! War-paint and rattle-snakes! I've kilt better men than them for less'n half that much!"

"Aw," I said, "t'ain't possible they stole yore gold--"

"Then whar is it?" he demanded bitterly. "Who else knowed about it?"

"Look here!" I said, p'inting to a belt of soft loam nigh the rocks. "There's a hoss's tracks."

"Well, what of it?" he demanded. "Maybe they had hosses tied in the bresh."

"Aw, no," I said. "Look how the calks is sot. They ain't no hosses on Bear Creek shod like that. These is the tracks of a stranger--I bet the feller I seen ride past my cabin jest about daybreak. A black- whiskered man with one ear missin'. That hard ground by the big rock don't show where he got off and stomped around, but the man which rode this hoss stole yore gold, I'll bet my guns."

"I ain't convinced," says Uncle Jeppard. "I'm goin' home and ile my rifle-gun, and then I'm goin' to go over and kill Joel and Erath."

"Now you lissen," I said forcibly, taking hold of the front of his buckskin shirt and h'isting him off the ground by way of emphasis, "I know what a stubborn old jassack you are, Uncle Jeppard, but this time you got to lissen to reason, or I'll forgit myself to the extent of kickin' the seat out of yore britches. I'm goin' to foller this feller and take yore gold away from him, because I know it war him that stole it. And don't you dare to kill nobody till I git back."

"I'll give you till tomorrer mornin'," he compromised. "I won't pull a trigger till then. But," said Uncle Jeppard waxing poetical, "if my gold ain't in my hands by the time the mornin' sun h'ists itself over the shinin' peaks of the Jackass Mountains, the buzzards will rassle their hash on the carcasses of Joel Gordon and Erath Elkins."

I went away from there, and mounted Cap'n Kidd and headed west on the stranger's trail. A hell of a chance _I_ had to go sparking a town-gal, with my lunatickal relatives thirsting for each other's gore.

It was still tolerably early in the morning, and one of them long summer days ahead of me. They warn't a hoss in the Humbolts which could equal Cap'n Kidd for endurance. I've rode him a hundred miles between sundown and sunup. But the hoss the stranger was riding must have been some chunk of hoss-meat hisself, and of course he had a long start of me. The day wore on, and still I hadn't come up with my man. I'd covered a lot of distance and was getting into country I warn't familiar with, but I didn't have no trouble follering his trail, and finally, late in the evening, I come out on a narrer dusty path where the calk-marks of his hoss's shoes was very plain.

The sun sunk lower and my hopes dwindled. Even if I got the thief and got the gold, it'd be a awful push to get back to Bear Creek in time to prevent mayhem. But I urged on Cap'n Kidd, and presently we come out into a road, and the tracks I was follering merged with a lot of others. I went on, expecting to come to some settlement, and wondering jest where I was.

Jest at sundown I rounded a bend in the road and I seen something hanging to a tree, and it was a man. They was another man in the act of pinning something to the corpse's shirt, and when he heard me he wheeled and jerked his gun--the man, I mean, not the corpse. He was a mean looking cuss, but he warn't Black Whiskers. Seeing I made no hostile motion, he put up his gun and grinned.

"That feller's still kickin'?" I said.

"We just strung him up," he said. "The other boys has rode back to town, but I stayed to put this warnin' on his buzzum. Can you read?"

"No," I said.

"Well," says he, "this here paper says: 'Warnin' to all outlaws and specially them on Grizzly Mountain--Keep away from Wampum.'"

"How far's Wampum from here?" I ast.

"Half a mile down the road," he said. "I'm Al Jackson, one of Bill Ormond's deputies. We aim to clean up Wampum. This is one of them outlaws which has denned up on Grizzly Mountain."

Before I could say anything more, I heard somebody breathing quick and gaspy, and they was a patter of bare feet in the bresh, and a kid gal about fourteen years old bust into the road.

"You've killed Uncle Joab!" she shrieked. "You murderers! A boy told me they was fixin' to hang him! I run as fast as I could--"

"Git away from that corpse!" roared Jackson, hitting at her with his quirt.

"You stop that!" I ordered. "Don't you hit that young 'un."

"Oh, please, Mister!" she wept, wringing her hands. "You ain't one of Ormond's men. Please help me! He ain't dead--I seen him move!"

Waiting for no more I spurred alongside the body and drawed my knife.

"Don't you cut that rope!" squawked the deputy, jerking his gun. So I hit him under the jaw and knocked him out of his saddle and into the bresh beside the road where he lay groaning. I then cut the rope and eased the hanged man down onto my saddle and got the noose offa his neck. He was purple in the face and his eyes was closed and his tongue lolled out, but he still had some life in him. Evidently they didn't drop him, but jest hauled him up to strangle to death.

I laid him on the ground and worked over him till some of his life begun to come back to him, but I knowed he ought to have medical attention, so I said: "Where's the nearest doctor?"

"Doc Richards in Wampum," whimpered the kid. "But if we take him there Ormond'll git him again. Won't you please take him home?"

"Where you-all live?" I inquired.

"We been livin' in a cabin on Grizzly Mountain every since Ormond run us out of Wampum," she whimpered.

"Well," I said, "I'm goin' to put yore uncle onto Cap'n Kidd and you can set behind the saddle and help hold him on, and tell me which way to go."

I done this and Cap'n Kidd didn't like it none, but after I busted him between the ears with the butt of my six-shooter he subsided and come along sulkily as I led him. As we went I seen that deputy Jackson drag hisself out of the bresh and go limping down the road holding onto his jaw.

I was losing a awful lot of time, but I couldn't leave this feller to die, even if he was a outlaw, because probably the little gal didn't have nobody else to take care of her but him.

It was well after dark when we come up a narrer trail that wound up a thickly timbered mountain side, and purty soon somebody in a thicket ahead of us hollered: "Halt whar you be or I'll shoot!"

"Don't shoot, Jim!" called the gal. "This is Betty, and we're bringin' Uncle Joab home."

A tall hard-looking young feller stepped out into the open, p'inting his Winchester at me. He cussed when he seen our load.

"He ain't dead," I said. "But we oughta git him to his cabin."

So Jim led the way through the thickets till we come into a clearing where they was a cabin and a woman come running out and screamed like a catamount when she seen Joab. Me and Jim lifted him off and toted him in and laid him on a bunk, and the women begun to work over him, and I went out to my hoss, because I was in a hurry to get gone. Jim follered me.

"This is the kind of stuff we've been havin' ever since Ormond come to Wampum," he says bitterly. "We been livin' up here like rats, afeared to stir in the open. I warned Joab agen slippin' down into the village to-day, but he was sot on it, and wouldn't let none of the boys go with him. Said he'd sneak in and git what he wanted and sneak out again."

"Well," I says, "what's yore business ain't none of mine. But this here life is hard lines on the women and chillern."

"You must be a friend of Joab's," he said. "He sent a man east some days ago, but we was afraid one of Ormond's men trailed him and killed him. But maybe he got through. Air you the man Joab sent for?"

"Meanin' am I some gunman come in to clean up the town?" I snorted. "Naw,

I ain't. I never seen this feller Joab before."

"Well," says Jim, "cutting him down like you done has already got you in bad with Ormond. Whyn't you help us run them fellers out of the country? They's still a good many of us in these hills, even if we have been run out of Wampum. This hangin' is the last straw. I'll round up the boys tonight, and we'll have a show-down with Ormond's men. We're outnumbered, and we been licked bad onst before, but we'll try it again. Why don't you throw in with us?"

"Lissen," I says, climbing into the saddle, "jest because I cut down a outlaw ain't no sign I'm ready to be one myself. I done it jest because I couldn't stand to see the little gal take on so. Anyway, I'm lookin' for a feller with black whiskers and one ear missin' which rides a roan with a big Lazy-A brand."

Jim fell back from me and lifted his rifle. "You better ride on, then," he said sombrely. "I'm obleeged to you for what you've did--but a friend of Wolf Ashley cain't be no friend of our'n."

I give him a snort of defiance and rode off down the mountains and headed for Wampum, because it was reasonable to suppose that maybe I'd find Black Whiskers there.

Wampum warn't much of a town, but they was one big saloon and gambling hall where sounds of hilarity was coming from, and not many people on the streets and them which was mostly went in a hurry. I stopped one of them and ast him where a doctor lived, and he p'inted out a house where he said Doc Richards lived, so I rode up to the door and hollered, and somebody inside said: "What do you want? I got you covered."

"Air you Doc Richards?" I said, and he said: "Yes, keep your hands away from your belt or I'll salivate you."

"This is a nice, friendly town!" I snorted. "I ain't figgerin' on doin' you no harm. They's a man up in the hills which needs yore attention."

At that the door opened and a man with red whiskers and a shotgun stuck his head out and said: "Who do you mean?"

"They call him Joab," I said. "He's on Grizzly Mountain."

"Hmmmmm!" said Doc Richards, looking at me very sharp where I sot Cap'n Kidd in the starlight. "I set a man's jaw tonight, and he had a good deal to say about a certain party who cut down a man that was hanged. If you happen to be that party, my advice to you is to hit the trail before Ormond catches you."

"I'm hungry and thirsty and I'm lookin' for a man," I said. "I aim to leave Wampum when I'm good and ready."

"I never argue with a man as big as you," said Doc Richards. "I'll ride to Grizzly Mountain as quick as I can get my horse saddled. If I never see you alive again, which is very probable, I'll always remember you as the biggest man I ever saw, and the biggest fool. Good night!"

I thought the folks in Wampum is the queerest acting I ever seen. I taken Cap'n

Kidd to the barn which served as a livery stable and seen that he was properly fixed in a stall to hisself, as far away from the other hosses as I could get him, because I knowed if he got to 'em he'd chaw the ears off 'em. The barn didn't look strong enough to hold him, but I told the livery stable man to keep him occupied with fodder, and to run for me if he got rambunctious. Then I went into the big saloon which was called the Golden Eagle. I was low in my spirits because I seemed to have lost Black Whiskers' trail entirely, and even if I found him in Wampum, which I hoped, I never could make it back to Bear Creek by sunup. But I hoped to recover that derned gold yet, and get back in time to save a few lives, anyway.

They was a lot of tough looking fellers in the Golden Eagle drinking and gambling and talking loud and cussing, and they all stopped their noise as I come in, and looked at me very fishy. But I give 'em no heed and went up to the bar, and purty soon they kinda forgot about me, and the racket started up again.

Whilst I was drinking me a few fingers of whisky, somebody shouldered up to me and said: "Hey!" I turnt around and seen a big, broad-built man with a black beard and blood-shot eyes and a pot-belly and two guns on.

I says: "Well?"

"Who air you?" he demanded.

"Who air you?" I come back at him.

"I'm Bill Ormond, sheriff of Wampum," he says. "That's who!" And he showed me a star onto his shirt.

"Oh," I says. "Well, I'm Breckinridge Elkins, from Bear Creek."

I noticed a kind of quiet come over the place, and fellers was laying down their glasses and their billiard sticks, and hitching up their belts and kinda gathering around me. Ormond scowled and combed his beard with his fingers, and rocked on his heels and said: "I got to 'rest you!"

I sot down my glass quick and he jumped back and hollered: "Don't you dast pull no gun on the law!" And they was a kind of movement amongst the men around me.

"What you arrestin' me for?" I demanded. "I ain't busted no law."

"You assaulted one of my deperties," he said, and then I seen that feller Jackson standing behind the sheriff with his jaw all bandaged up. He couldn't work his chin to talk. All he could do was p'int his finger at me and shake his fists.

"You likewise cut down a outlaw we had just hunged," says Ormond. "Yo're under arrest!"

"But I'm lookin' for a man!" I protested. "I ain't got time to be arrested!"

"You should of thunk about that when you busted the law," opined Ormond. "Gimme yore gun and come along peaceable."

A dozen men had their hands on their guns, but it warn't that which made me give in. Pap had always told me not to resist no officer of the law. It was kind of instinctive for me to hand over my gun to this feller with the star on his shirt.

Somehow it didn't seem right, but I was kind of bewildered and my thoughts was addled. I ain't one of these fast thinking sharps. So I jest done what pap always told me to do.

Ormond taken me down the street a-ways, with a whole bunch of men follering us, and stopped at a log building with barred winders which was next to a board shack. A man come out of this shack with a big bunch of keys, and Ormond said he was the jailer. So they put me in the log jail and Ormond went off with everybody but the jailer, who sot down on the step outside his shack and rolled hisself a cigaret.

They warn't no light in the jail, but I found the bunk and tried to lay down on it, but it warn't built for a man six and a half foot tall. I sot down on it and at last realized what a infernal mess I was in. Here I ought to be hunting Black Whiskers and getting the gold to take back to Bear Creek and save the lives of a swarm of my kin-folks, but instead of that I was in jail, and no way of getting out without killing a officer of the law. With daybreak Joel and Erath would be at each others' throats, and Uncle Jeppard would be gunning for both of 'em. It was too much to hope that the other relatives would let them three fight it out amongst theirselves. I never seen sech a clan for buttin' into each others' business. The guns would be talking all up and down Bear Creek, and the population would be decreasing with every volley. I thunk about it till I got dizzy and then the jailer stuck his head up to the winder and said if I'd give him five dollars he'd go get me something to eat.

I had five dollars I won in a poker game a few days before and I give it to him, and he went off and was gone quite a spell, and at last he come back and give me a ham sandwich. I ast him was that all he could get for five dollars, and he said grub was awful high in Wampum. I et the sandwich with one bite, and he said if I'd give him some more money he'd get me another sandwich. But I didn't have no more and told him so.

"What!" he said, breathing licker fumes in my face through the winder bars. "No money? And you expect us to feed you for nothin'?" So he cussed me, and went off, and purty soon the sheriff come and looked in at me, and said: "What's this I hear about you not havin' no money?"

"I ain't got none left," I said, and he cussed something fierce.

"How you expeck to pay yore fine?" he demanded. "You think you can lay up in our jail and eat us out of house and home? What kind of a critter are you, anyway?"

Just then the jailer chipped in and said somebody told him I had a hoss down at the livery stable.

"Good," said the sheriff. "We'll sell his hoss for his fine."

"You won't neither," I says, beginning to get mad. "You try to sell Cap'n Kidd, and I'll forgit what pap told me about law-officers, and take you plumb apart."

I riz up and glared at him through the winder, and he fell back and put his hand on his gun. But jest about that time I seen a man going into the Golden Eagle which was in easy sight of the jail, and lit up so the light streamed out into the street. I give a yell that made Ormond jump about a foot. It was Black Whiskers!

"Arrest that man, Sheriff!" I hollered. "He's a thief!"

Ormond whirled and looked, and then he said: "Air you plumb crazy? That's Wolf Ashley, my deperty."

"I don't give a dern," I said. "He stole a poke of gold from my Uncle Jeppard Grimes up in the Humbolts, and I've trailed him clean from Bear Creek. Do yore duty and arrest him."

"You shet up!" roared Ormond. "You cain't tell me my business! I ain't goin' to arrest my best gunman--my star deperty, I mean. What you mean tryin' to start trouble this way? One more yap outa you and I'll throwa chunk of lead through you."

And he turned around and stalked off muttering: "Poke of gold, huh? Holdin' out on me, is he? I'll see about that!"

"I sot down and held my head in bewilderment. What kind of a sheriff was this which wouldn't arrest a derned thief? My thoughts run in circles till my wits was addled. The jailer had gone off and I wondered if he had went to sell Cap'n Kidd. I wondered what was going on back on Bear Creek, and I shivered to think what would bust loose at daybreak. And here I was in jail, with them fellers fixing to sell my hoss, whilst that dern thief swaggered around at large. I looked help-lessly out a the winder.

It was getting late, but the Golden Eagle was going full blast. I could hear the music blaring away, and the fellers yipping and shooting their pistols in the air, and their boot heels stomping on the board walk. I felt like busting down and bawling, and then I begun to get mad. I get mad slow, generally, and before I was plumb mad, I heard a noise at the winder.

I seen a pale face staring in at me, and a couple of small white hands on the bars.

"Mister!" a voice whispered. "Oh, Mister!"

I stepped over and looked out and it was the kid gal Betty.

"What you doin' here, gal?" I ast.

"Doc Richards said you was in Wampum," she whispered. "He said he was afraid Ormond would do for you because you helped us, so I slipped away on his hoss and rode here as hard as I could. Jim was out tryin' to round up the boys for a last stand, and Aunt Rachel and the other women was busy with Uncle Joab. They wasn't nobody but me to come, but I had to! You saved Uncle Joab, and I don't care if Jim does say yo're a outlaw because yo're a friend of Wolf Ashley. Oh, I wish't I wasn't jest a gal! I wisht I could shoot a gun, so's I could kill Bill Ormond!"

"That ain't no way for a gal to talk," I says. "Leave the killin' to the men. But I appreciates you goin' to all this trouble. I got some kid sisters myself--in fact I got seven or eight, as near as I remember. Don't you worry none about me. Lots of men gits throwed in jail."

"But that ain't it!" she wept, wringing her hands. "I listened outside the winder of the back room in the Golden Eagle and heard Ormond and Ashley talkin' about you. I dunno what you wanted with Ashley when you ast Jim about him, but he ain't yo're friend. Ormond accused him of stealin' a poke of gold and holdin' out on him, and Ashley said it was a lie. Then Ormond said you told him about it, and he said he'd give Ashley till midnight to perjuice that gold, and if he didn't Wampum would be too small for both of 'em."

"Then he went out to the bar, and I heered Ashley talkin' to a pal of his'n, and Ashley said he'd have to raise some gold somehow, or Ormond would have him killed, but that he was goin' to fix _you,_ Mister, for lyin' about him. Mister, Ashley and his bunch air over in the back of the Golden Eagle right now plottin' to bust into jail before daylight and hang you!"

"Aw," I says, "the sheriff wouldn't let 'em do that."

"But Ormond ain't the sheriff!" she cried. "Him and his gunmen come into Wampum and killed all the people that tried to oppose him, or run 'em up into the hills. They got us penned up there like rats, nigh starvin' and afeared to come to town. Uncle Joab come into Wampum this mornin' to git some salt, and you seen what they done to him. _He's_ the real sheriff. Ormond is jest a bloody outlaw. Him and his gang is usin' Wampum for a hang-out whilst they rob and steal and kill all over the country."

"Then that's what yore friend Jim meant," I said slowly. "And me, like a dumb damn' fool, I thought him and Joab and the rest of you-all was jest outlaws, like that fake deperty said."

"Ormond took Uncle Joab's badge and called hisself the sheriff to fool strangers," she whimpered. "What honest people is left in Wampum air afeared to say anything. Him and his gunmen air rulin' this whole part of the country. Uncle Joab sent a man east to git us some help in the settlements on Buffalo River, but none never come, and from what I overheard tonight, I believe Wolf Ashley follered him and killed him over east of the Humbolts somewheres. What air we goin' to do?" she sobbed.

"Git on Doc Richards' hoss and ride for Grizzly Mountain," I said. "When you git there, tell the Doc to light a shuck for Wampum, because there's goin' to be plenty of work for him time he gits here."

"But what about you?" she cried. "I cain't go off and leave you to git hanged!"

"Don't worry about me, gal," I said. "I'm Breckinridge Elkins of the Humbolt Mountains, and I'm preparin' for to shake my mane! Hustle!"

I reckon something about me convinced her, because she glided away into the shadders, whimpering, and presently I heard the clack of hoss' hoofs dwindling in the distance. I then riz and laid hold of the winder bars and tore 'em out by the roots. Then I sunk my fingers into the sill log and tore it out, and three or four more along with it, and the wall give way and the roof fell down on me, but I shaken aside the rooins and heaved up out of the wreckage like a b'ar out of a deadfall.

About this time the jailer come running up, and when he seen what I had did he was so surprised he forgot to shoot with his pistol. So I taken it away from him and knocked down the door of his shack with him and left him laying in its rooins.

I then strode up the street towards the Golden Eagle and here come a feller galloping down the street, and who should it be but that derned fake deputy, Jackson. He couldn't holler with his bandaged jaw, but when he seen me he jerked loose his lariat and piled it around my neck, and sot spurs to his cayuse aiming for to drag me to death. But I seen he had his rope tied fast to his horn, Texas style, so I laid hold onto it with both hands and braced my laigs, and when the hoss got to the end of the rope, the girths busted and the hoss went out from under the saddle, and Jackson come down on his head in the street and laid still.

I throwed the rope off my neck and went onto the Golden Eagle with the jailer's .45 in my scabbard. I looked in and seen the same crowd there, and Ormond r'ared back at the bar with his belly stuck out, roaring and bragging.

I stepped in and hollered: "Look this way, Bill Ormond, and pull iron, you dirty thief!"

He wheeled, paled, and went for his gun, and I slammed six bullets into him before he could hit the floor. I then throwed the empty gun at the dazed crowd and give one deafening roar and tore into 'em like a mountain cyclone. They begun to holler and surge onto me and I throwed 'em and knocked 'em right and left like ten pins. Some was knocked over the bar and some under the tables and some I knocked down stacks of beer kegs with. I ripped the roulette wheel loose and mowed down a whole row of 'em with it, and I throwed a billiard table through the mirror behind the bar jest for good measure. Three or four fellers got pinned under it and yelled bloody murder.

Meanwhile they was hacking at me with bowies and hitting me with chairs and brass knuckles and trying to shoot me, but all they done with their guns was shoot each other because they was so many they got in each other's way, and the other things just made me madder. I laid hands on as many as I could hug at onst, and the thud of their heads banging together was music to me. I also done good work heaving 'em head-on agen the walls, and I further slammed several of 'em heartily agen the floor and busted all the tables with their carcasses. In the melee the whole bar collapsed, and the shelves behind the bar fell down when I slang a feller into 'em, and bottles rained all over the floor. One of the lamps also fell off the ceiling which was beginning to crack and cave in, and everybody begun to yell: "Fire!" and run out through the doors and jump out the winders.

In a second I was alone in the blazing building except for them which was past running. I'd started for a door myself when I seen a buckskin pouch on the floor along with a lot of other belongings which had fell out of men's pockets as they will when the men gets swung by the feet and smashed agen the wall.

I picked it up and jerked the tie-string, and a trickle of gold dust spilt into my hand. I begun to look on the floor for Ashley, but he warn't there. But he was watching me from outside, because I looked and seen him jest as he let _bam_ at me with a .45 from the back room which warn't on fire much yet. I plunged after him, ignoring his next slug which took me in the shoulder, and then I grabbed him and taken the gun away from him. He pulled a bowie and tried to stab me in the groin, but only sliced my thigh, so I throwed him the full length of the room and he hit the wall so hard his head went through the boards.

Meantime the main part of the saloon was burning so I couldn't go out that way. I started to go out the back door of the room I was in, but got a glimpse of some fellers which was crouching jest outside the door waiting to shoot me as I come out. So I knocked out a section of the wall on another side of the room, and about that time the roof fell in so loud them fellers didn't hear me coming, so I fell on 'em from the rear and beat their heads together till the blood ran out of their ears, and stomped 'em and taken their shotguns away from 'em.

Then I was aware that people was shooting at me in the light of the burning saloon, and I seen that a bunch was ganged up on the other side of the street, so I begun to loose my shotguns into the thick of them, and they broke and run yelling blue murder.

And as they went out one side of the town, another gang rushed in from the other, yelling and shooting, and I snapped a empty shell at 'em before one yelled: "Don't shoot, Elkins! We're friends!" And I seen it was Jim and Doc Richards, and a lot of other fellers I hadn't never seen before then.

They went tearing after Ormond's gang, whooping and yelling, and the way them outlaws took to the tall timber was a caution. They warn't no fight left in 'em at all.

Jim pulled up, and looked at the wreckage of the jail, and the remnants of the Golden Eagle, and he shook his head like he couldn't believe it.

"We was on our way to make a last effort to take the town back from that gang," says he. "Betty met us as we come down the trail and told us you was a friend and a honest man. We hoped to git here in time to save you from gittin' hanged." Again he shaken his head with a kind of bewildered look. Then he says "Oh, say, I'd about forgot. On our way here we run onto a man on the road who said he was lookin' for you. Not knowin' who he was, we roped him and brung him along with us. Bring the prisoner, boys!"

They brung him, tied to his saddle, and it was Jack Gordon, Joel's youngest brother and the fastest gunslinger on Bear Creek.

"What you doin' houndin' me?" I demanded bitterly. "Has the feud begun already and has Joel sot you on _my_ trail? Well, I got what I come after, and I'm headin' back for Bear Creek. I cain't git there by daylight, but maybe I'll git there in time to keep everybody from gittin' kilt. Here's Uncle Jeppard's cussed gold!" And I waved the poke in front of him.

"But that cain't be it!" says he. "I been trailin' you all the way from Bear Creek, tryin' to catch you and tell you the gold had been found! Uncle Jeppard and Joel and Erath got together and everything was explained and is all right. Where'd you git that gold?"

"I dunno whether Ashley's pals got it together so he could give it to Ormond and not git kilt for holdin' out on his boss, or what," I says. "But I know the owner ain't got no more use for it now, and probably stole it in the first place. I'm givin' this gold to Betty," I says. "She shore deserves a reward. And giving it to her makes me feel like maybe _some_ good come outa this wild goose chase, after all."

Jim looked around at the ruins of the outlaw hangout, and murmured something I didn't catch. I says to Jack: "You said Uncle Jeppard's gold was found. Where was it, anyway?"

"Well," said Jack, "little General William Harrison Grimes, Joash Grimes's youngest boy, he seen his grand-pap put the gold under the rock, and he got it out to play with it. He was usin' the nuggets for slugs in his nigger-shooter," Jack said, "and it's plumb cute the way he pops a rattlesnake with 'em. What did you say?"

"Nothin'," I said between my teeth. "Nothin' that'd be fit to repeat, anyway."

"Well," he said, "if you've had yore fun, I reckon yo're ready to start back to Bear Creek with me."

_"I_ reckon I ain't," I said. "I'm goin' to 'tend to my own private affairs for a change. I told Glory McGraw early this mornin' I was goin' to git me a town-gal, and by golly, I meant it. Gwan on back to Bear Creek, and if you see Glory, tell her I'm headin' for Chawed Ear where the purty gals is as thick as honey bees around a apple tree."

CHAPTER VI

THE FEUD BUSTER

I PULLED out of Wampum before sunup. The folks, wanted me to stay and be a deputy sheriff, but I taken a good look at the female population and seen that the only single woman in town was a Piute squaw. So I headed acrost the mountains for Chawed Ear, swinging wide to avoid coming anywheres nigh to the Humbolts. I didn't want to chance running into Glory McGraw before I had me a town-gal.

But I didn't get to Chawed Ear nigh as soon as I'd figgered to. As I passed through the hills along the head-waters of Mustang River, I run into a camp of cowpunchers from the Triple L which was up there rounding up strays. The foreman needed some hands, and I happened to think maybe I'd cut a better figger before the Chawed Ear belles if'n I had some money in my pocket, so I taken on with them. After he seen me and Cap'n Kidd do one day's work the foreman 'lowed that they warn't no use in hiring the six or seven other men he aimed; he said I filled the bill perfect.

So I worked with 'em three weeks, and then collected my pay and pulled for Chawed Ear.

I was all primed for the purty settlement-gals, little suspected the jamboree I was riding into blind, the echoes of which ain't yet quit circulating through the mountain country. And that reminds me to remark that I'm sick and tired of the slanders which has been noised abroad about that there affair, and if they don't stop, I'll liable to lose my temper, and anybody in the Humbolts can tell you when I loses my temper the effect on the population is wuss'n fire, earthquake and cyclone.

First-off, it's a lie that I rode a hundred miles to mix into a feud which wasn't none of my business. I never heard of the Warren- Barlow war before I come into the Mezquital country. I hear tell the Barlows is talking about suing me for destroying their property. Well, they ought to build their cabins solider if they don't want 'em tore down. And they're all liars when they says the Warrens hired me to exterminate 'em at five dollars a sculp. I don't believe even a Warren would pay five dollars for one of their mangy sculps. Anyway, I don't fight for hire for nobody, And the Warrens needn't belly-ache about me turnin' on 'em and trying to massacre the entire clan. All I wanted to do was kind of disable 'em so they couldn't interfere with my business. And my business, from first to last, was defending the family honor. If I had to wipe up the earth with a couple of feuding clans whilst so doing, I cain't help it. Folks which is particular of their hides ought to stay out of the way of tornadoes, wild bulls, devastating torrents and a insulted Elkins.

This is the way it was: I was dry and hot and thirsty when I hit Chawed Ear, so I went into a saloon and had me a few drinks. Then I was going out and start looking for a gal, when I spied a friendly game of kyards going on between a hoss-thief and three train-robbers, and I decided I'd set in for a hand or so. And whilst we was playing, who should come in but Uncle Jeppard Grimes. I should of knew my day was spoilt the minute he hove in sight. Dern near all the calamities which takes place in southern Nevada can be traced back to that old lobo. He's got a in-grown disposition and a natural talent for pestering his feller man. Specially his relatives.

He didn't say a word about that wild goose chase I went on to get back the gold I thought Wolf Ashley had stole from him. He come over and scowled down on me like I was the missing lynx or something, and purty soon, jest as I was all sot to make a killing, he says: "How can you set there so free and keerless, with four aces into yore hand, when yore family name is bein' besmirched?"

I flang down my hand in annoyance, and said: "Now look what you done! What you mean blattin' out information of sech a private nature? What you talkin' about, anyhow?"

"Well," he says, "durin' the time you been away from home roisterin' and wastin' yore substance in riotous livin'--"

"I been punchin' cows!" I said fiercely. "And before that I was chasin' a man to git back the gold I thought he'd stole from you. I ain't squandered nothin' no-wheres. Shet up and tell me whatever yo're a-talkin' about."

"Well," says he, "whilst you been gone young Dick Blanton of Grizzly Run has been courtin' yore sister Elinor, and the family's been expectin' 'em to set the day, any time now. But now I hear he's been braggin' all over Grizzly Run about how he done jilted her. Air you goin' to set there and let yore sister become the laughin' stock of the country? When I was a young man--"

"When you was a young man Dan'l Boone warn't whelped yet!" I bellered, so mad I included him and everybody else in my irritation. They ain't nothing upsets me like injustice done to some of my close kin. "Git out of my way! I'm headin' for Grizzly Run--what _you_ grinnin' at, you spotted hyener?" This last was ad-dressed to the hoss- thief in which I seemed to detect signs of amusement.

"I warn't grinnin'," he said.

"So I'm a liar, I reckon!" I said, impulsively shattering a demi- john over his head, and he fell under the table hollering bloody murder, and all the fellers drink-ing at the bar abandoned their licker and stampeded for the street hollering: "Take cover, boys! Breckinridge Elkins is on the rampage!"

So I kicked all the slats out of the bar to relieve my feelings, and stormed out of the saloon and forked Cap'n Kidd. Even he seen it was no time to take liberties with me; he didn't pitch but seven jumps, and then he settled down to a dead run, and we headed for Grizzly Run.

Everything kind of floàted in a red haze all the way, but them folks which claims I tried to murder' em in cold blood on the road between Chawed Ear and Grizzly Run is jest narrer-minded and super- sensitive. The reason I shot off everybody's hats that I met was jest to kind of ca'm my nerves, because I was afeared if I didn't cool off some by the time I hit Grizzly Run I might hurt somebody. I'm that mild-mannered and retiring by nature that I wouldn't willing hurt man, beast, nor Injun unless maddened beyond all endurance.

That's why I acted with so much self-possession and dignity when I got to Grizzly Run and entered the saloon where Dick Blanton generally hung out.

"Where's Dick Blanton?" I demanded, and everybody must of been nervous, because when I boomed out they all jumped and looked around, and the bartender dropped a glass and turned pale.

"Well," I hollered, beginning to lose patience. "Where is the coyote?"

"G-gimme time, will ya?" stuttered the bar-keep. "I--uh--he--uh--"

"Evadin' the question, hey?" I said, kicking the foot-rail loose. "Friend of his'n, hey? Tryin' to pertect him, hey?" I was so overcome by this perfidy that I lunged for him and he ducked down behind the bar and I crashed into it bodily with all my lunge and weight, and it collapsed on top of him, and all the customers run out of the saloon hollering: "Help, murder, Elkins is killin' the bartender!"

That individual stuck his head up from amongst the rooins of the bar and begged: "For God's sake, lemme alone! Blanton headed south for the Mezquital Mountains yesterday."

I throwed down the chair I was fixing to bust all the ceiling lamps with, and run out and jumped on Cap'n Kidd and headed south, whilst behind me folks emerged from their cyclone cellars and sent a rider up in the hills to tell the sheriff and his deputies they could come on back now.

I knowed where the Mezquitals was, though I hadn't never been there. I crossed the Californy line about sundown, and shortly after dark I seen Mezquital Peak looming ahead of me. Having ca'med down somewhat, I decided to stop and rest Cap'n Kidd. He warn't tired, because that hoss has got alligator blood in his veins, but I knowed I might have to trail Blanton clean to The Angels, and they warn't no use in running Cap'n Kidd's laigs off on the first lap of the chase.

It warn't a very thick settled country I'd come into, very mountainous and thick timbered, but purty soon I come to a cabin beside the trail and I pulled up and hollered: "Hello!"

The candle inside was instantly blowed out, and somebody pushed a rifle barrel through the winder and bawled: "Who be you?"

"I'm Breckinridge Elkins from Bear Creek, Nevada," I said. "I'd like to stay all night, and git some feed for my hoss."

"Stand still," warned the voice. "We can see you agen the stars, and they's four rifle-guns a-kiverin' you."

"Well, make up yore minds," I said, because I could could hear 'em discussin' me. I reckon they thought they was whispering. One of 'em said: "Aw, he cain't be a Barlow. Ain't none of 'em that big." T'other'n said: "Well, maybe he's a derned gunfighter they've sent for to help 'em. Old jake's nephew's been up in Nevady."

"Le's let him in," says a third. "We can mighty quick tell what he is."

So one of 'em come out and 'lowed it would be all right for me to stay the night, and he showed me a corral to put Cap'n Kidd in, and hauled out some hay for him.

"We got to be keerful," he said. "We got lots of enemies in these hills."

We went into the cabin, and they lit the candle again, and sot some corn pone and sow-belly and beans on the table and a jug of corn licker. They was four men, and they said their names was Warren-- George, Ezra, Elisha, and Joshua, and they was brothers. I'd always heard tell the Mezquital country was famed for big men, but these fellers warn't so big--not much over six foot high apiece. On Bear Creek they'd been considered kind of puny and undersized, so to speak.

They warn't very talkative. Mostly they sot with their rifles acrost their knees and looked at me without no expression onto their faces, but that didn't stop me from eating a hearty supper, and would of et a lot more only the grub give out; and I hoped they had more licker somewheres else because I was purty dry. When I turned up the jug to take a snort it was brim-full, but before I'd more'n dampened my gullet the dern thing was plumb empty.

When I got through I went over and sot down on a raw-hide bottomed chair in front of the fire-place where they warn't no fire because it was summer time, and they said: "What's yore business, stranger?"

"Well," I said, not knowing I was going to get the surprise of my life, "I'm lookin' for a feller named Dick Blanton--"

By golly, the words warn't clean out of my mouth when they was four men onto my neck like catamounts!

"He's a spy!" they hollered. "He's a cussed Barlow! Shoot him! Stab him! Hit him on the head!"

All of which they was endeavoring to do with such passion they was getting in each other's way, and it was only his over-eagerness which caused George to miss me with his bowie and sink it into the table instead, but Joshua busted a chair over my head and Elisha would of shot me if I hadn't jerked back my head so he jest singed my eyebrows. This lack of hospitality so irritated me that I riz up amongst 'em like a b'ar with a pack of wolves hanging onto him, and commenced committing mayhem on my hosts, because I seen right off they was critters which couldn't be persuaded to respect a guest no other way.

Well, the dust of battle hadn't settled, the casualities was groaning all over the place, and I was jest relighting the candle when I heard a hoss galloping up the trail from the south. I wheeled and drawed my guns as it stopped before the cabin. But I didn't shoot, because the next instant they was a bare-footed gal standing in the door. When she seen the rooins she let out a screech like a catamount.

"You've kilt 'em!" she screamed. "You murderer!"

"Aw, I ain't, neither," I said. "They ain't hurt much--jest a few cracked ribs and dislocated shoulders and busted laigs and sech-like trifles. Joshua's ear'll grow back on all right, if you take a few stitches into it."

"You cussed Barlow!" she squalled, jumping up and down with the hystericals. "I'll kill you! You damned Barlow!"

"I ain't no Barlow, dern it," I said. "I'm Breckinridge Elkins, of Bear Creek. I ain't never even heard of no Barlows."

At that George stopped his groaning long enough to snarl: "If you ain't a friend of the Barlows, how come you askin' for Dick Blanton? He's one of 'em."

"He jilted my sister!" I roared. "I aim to drag him back and make him marry her."

"Well, it was all a mistake," groaned George. "But the damage is done now."

"It's wuss'n you think," said the gal fiercely. "The Warrens has all forted theirselves over at pap's cabin, and they sent me to git you boys. We got to make a stand. The Barlows is gatherin' over to Jake Barlow's cabin, and they aims to make a foray onto us tonight. We was outnumbered to begin with, and now here's our best fightin' men laid out! Our goose is cooked plumb to hell!"

"Lift me onto my hoss," moaned George. "I cain't walk, but I can still shoot." He tried to rise up, and fell back cussing and groaning.

"You got to help us!" said the gal desperately, turning to me. "You done laid out our four best fightin' men, and you owes it to us. It's yore duty! Anyway, you says Dick Blanton's yore enemy--well, he's Jake Barlow's nephew, and he come back here to help 'em clean out us Warrens. He's over to Jake's cabin right now. My brother Bill snuck over and spied on 'em, and he says every fightin' man of the clan is gatherin' there. All we can do is hold the fort, and you got to come help us hold it! Yo're nigh as big as all four of these boys put together."

Well, I figgered I owed the Warrens something, so, after setting some bones and bandaging some wounds and abrasions of which they was a goodly lot, I saddled Cap'n Kidd and we sot out.

As we rode along she said: "That there is the biggest, wildest, meanest-lookin' critter I ever seen. Is he actually a hoss, or some kind of a varmint?"

"He's a hoss," I said. "But he's got painter's blood and a shark's disposition. What's this here feud about?"

"I dunno," she said. "It's been goin' on so long everybody's done forgot what started it. Somebody accused somebody else of stealin' a cow, I think. What's the difference?"

"They ain't none," I assured her. "If folks wants to have feuds it's their own business."

We was follering a winding path, and purty soon we heard dogs barking and about that time the gal turned aside and got off her hoss, and showed me a pen hid in the bresh. It was full of hosses.

"We keep our mounts here so's the Barlows ain't so likely to find 'em and run 'em off," she said, and she turnt her hoss into the pen, and I put Cap'n Kidd in, but I tied him over in one corner by hisself--otherwise he would of started fighting all the other hosses and kicked the fence down.

Then we went on along the path and the dogs barked louder and purty soon we come to a big two-story cabin which had heavy board- shutters over the winders. They was jest a dim streak of candle light come through the cracks. It was dark, because the moon hadn't come up. We stopped in the shadders of the trees, and the gal whistled like a whippoorwill three times, and somebody answered from up on the roof. A door opened a crack in a room which didn't have no light at all, and somebody said: "That you, Elizerbeth? Air the boys with you?"

"It's me," says she, starting towards the door. "But the boys ain't with me."

Then all to onst he throwed open the door and hollered: "Run, gal! They's a grizzly b'ar standin' up on his hind laigs right behind you!"

"Aw, that ain't no b'ar," says she. "That there's Breckinridge Elkins, from up in Nevady. He's goin' to help us fight the Barlows."

We went on into a room where they was a candle on the table, and they was nine or ten men there and thirty-odd women and chillern. They all looked kinda pale and scairt, and the men was loaded down with pistols and Winchesters.

They all looked at me kind of dumb-like, and the old man kept staring at me like he warn't any too sure he hadn't let a grizzly in the house, after all. He mumbled something about making a natural mistake, in the dark, and turnt to the gal, and demanded: "Whar's the boys I sent you after?"

And she says: "This gent mussed 'em up so's they ain't fitten for to fight. Now, don't git rambunctious, Pap. It war jest a honest mistake all around. He's our friend, and he's gunnin' for Dick Blanton."

"Ha! Dick Blanton!" snarled one of the men, lifting his Winchester. "Jest lemme line my sights on him! I'll cook his goose!"

"You won't, neither," I said. "He's got to go back to Bear Creek and marry my sister Elinor. Well," I says, "what's the campaign?"

"I don't figger they'll git here till well after midnight," said Old Man Warren. "All we can do is wait for 'em."

"You means you all sets here and waits till they comes and lays siege?" I says.

"What else?" says he. "Lissen here, young man, don't start tellin' me how to conduck a feud. I growed up in this here'n. It war in full swing when I was born, and I done spent my whole life carryin' it on."

"That's jest it," I snorted. "You lets these dern wars drag on for generations. Up in the Humbolts we bring sech things to a quick conclusion. Mighty nigh everybody up there come from Texas, original, and we fights our feuds Texas style, which is short and sweet--a feud which lasts ten years in Texas is a humdinger. We winds 'em up quick and in style. Where-at is this here cabin where the Barlows is gatherin'?"

"'Bout three mile over the ridge," says a young feller they called Bill.

"How many is they?" I ast.

"I counted seventeen," says he.

"Jest a fair-sized mouthful for a Elkins," I said. "Bill, you guide me to that there cabin. The rest of you can come or stay, it don't make no difference to me."

Well, they started jawing with each other then. Some was for going and some for staying. Some wanted to go with me, and try to take the Barlows by surprise, but the others said it couldn't be done--they'd git ambushed theirselves, and the only sensible thing to be did was to stay forted and wait for the Barlows to come. They given me no more heed--jest sot there and augered.

But that was all right with me. Right in the middle of the dispute, when it looked like maybe the Warrens would get to fighting among theirselves and finish each other before the Barlows could get there, I lit out with the boy Bill, which seemed to have considerable sense for a Warren.

He got him a hoss out of the hidden corral, and I got Cap'n Kidd, which was a good thing. He'd somehow got a mule by the neck, and the critter was almost at its last gasp when I rescued it. Then me and Bill lit out.

We follered winding paths over thick-timbered mountainsides till at last we come to a clearing and they was a cabin there, with light and profanity pouring out of the winders. We'd been hearing the last mentioned for half a mile before we sighted the cabin.

We left our hosses back in the woods a ways, and snuck up on foot and stopped amongst the trees back of the cabin.

"They're in there tankin' up on corn licker to whet their appertites for Warren blood!" whispered Bill, all in a shiver. "Lissen to 'em! Them fellers ain't hardly human! What you goin' to do? They got a man standin' guard out in front of the door at the other end of the cabin. You see they ain't no doors nor winders at the back. They's winders on each side, but if we try to rush it from the front or either side, they'll see us and fill us full of lead before we could git in a shot. Look! The moon's comin' up. They'll be startin' on their raid before long."

I'll admit that cabin looked like it was going to be harder to storm than I'd figgered. I hadn't had no idee in mind when I sot out for the place. All I wanted was to get in amongst them Barlows--I does my best fighting at close quarters. But at the moment I couldn't think of no way that wouldn't get me shot up. Of course I could jest rush the cabin, but the thought of seventeen Winchesters blazing away at me from close range was a little stiff even for me, though I was game to try it, if they warn't no other way.

Whilst I was studying over the matter, all to onst the hosses tied out in front of the cabin snorted, and back up in the hills something went _Oooaaaw-w-w!_ And a idee hit me.

"Git back in the woods and wait for me," I told Bill, as I headed for the thicket where we'd left the hosses.

I rode up in the hills towards where the howl had come from, and purty soon I lit and throwed Cap'n Kidd's reins over his head, and walked on into the deep bresh, from time to time giving a long squall like a cougar. They ain't a catamount in the world can tell the difference when a Bear Creek man imitates one. After awhile one answered, from a ledge jest a few hundred feet away.

I went to the ledge and clumb up on it, and there was a small cave behind it, and a big mountain lion in there. He give a grunt of surprise when he seen I was a human, and made a swipe at me, but I give him a bat on the head with my fist, and whilst he was still dizzy I grabbed him by the scruff of the neck and hauled him out of the cave and lugged him down to where I left my hoss.

Cap'n Kidd snorted when he seen the cougar and wanted to kick his brains out, but I give him a good kick in the stummick hisself, which is the only kind of reasoning Cap'n Kidd understands, and got on him and headed for the Barlow hangout.

I can think of a lot more pleasant jobs than totin' a full-growed mountain lion down a thick-timbered mountainside on the back of a iron-jawed outlaw at midnight. I had the cat by the back of the neck with one hand, so hard he couldn't squall, and I held him out at arm's length as far from me and the hoss as I could, but every now and then he'd twist around so he could claw Cap'n Kidd with his hind laigs, and when this would happen Cap'n Kidd would squall with rage and start bucking all over the place. Sometimes he would buck the derned cougar onto me, and pulling him loose from my hide was wuss'll pulling cockle-burrs out of a cow's tail.

But presently I arriv close behind the cabin. I whistled like a whippoorwill for Bill, but he didn't answer and warn't nowheres to be seen, so I decided he'd got scairt and pulled out for home. But that was all right with me. I'd come to fight the Barlows, and I aimed to fight 'em, with or without assistance. Bill would jest of been in the way.

I got off in the trees back of the cabin and throwed the reins over Cap'n Kidd's head, and went up to the back of the cabin on foot, walking soft and easy. The moon was well up, by now, and what wind they was, was blowing towards me, which pleased me, because I didn't want the hosses tied out in front to scent the cat and start cutting up before I was ready.

The fellers inside was still cussing and talking loud as I approached one of the winders on the side, and one hollered out: "Come on! Le's git started! I craves Warren gore!" And about that time I give the cougar a heave and throwed him through the winder.

He let out a awful squall as he hit, and the fellers in the cabin hollered louder'n he did. Instantly a most awful bustle broke loose in there and of all the whooping and bellering and shooting I ever heard, and the lion squalling amongst it all, and clothes and hides tearing so you could hear it all over the clearing, and the hosses busting loose and tearing out through the bresh.

As soon as I hove the cat I run around to the door and a man was standing there with his mouth open, too surprised at the racket to do anything. So I taken his rifle away from him and broke the stock off on his head, and stood there at the door with the barrel intending to brain them Barlows as they run out. I was plumb certain they _would_ run out, because I have noticed that the average man is funny that way, and hates to be shet up in a cabin with a mad cougar as bad as the cougar would hate to be shet up in a cabin with a infuriated settler of Bear Creek.

But them scoundrels fooled me. 'Pears like they had a secret door in the back wall, and whilst I was waiting for them to storm out through the front door and get their skulls cracked, they knocked the secret door open and went piling out that way.

By the time I realized what was happening and run around to the other end of the cabin, they was all out and streaking for the trees, yelling blue murder, with their clothes all tore to shreds and them bleeding like stuck hawgs.

That there catamount sure improved the shining hours whilst he was corralled with them Barlows. He come out after 'em with his mouth full of the seats of their britches, and when he seen me he give a kind of despairing yelp and taken out up the mountain with his tail betwixt his laigs like the devil was after him with a red-hot branding iron.

I taken after the Barlows, sot on scuttling at least a few of 'em, and I was on the p'int of letting _bam_ at 'em with my six-shooters as they run, when, jest as they reched the trees, all the Warren men riz out of the bresh and fell on 'em with piercing howls.

That fray was kind of pecooliar. I don't remember a single shot being fired. The Barlows had all dropped their guns in their flight, and the Warrens seemed bent on wiping out their wrongs with their bare fists and gun butts. For a few seconds they was a hell of a scramble-- men cussing and howling and bellering, and rifle-stocks cracking over heads, and the bresh crashing underfoot, and then before I could get into it, the Barlows broke every which-way and took out through the woods like jack-rabbits squalling Jedgment Day.

Old Man Warren come prancing out of the bresh waving his Winchester and his beard flying in the moonlight and he hollered: "The sins of the wicked shall return onto 'em! Elkins, we have hit a powerful lick for righteousness this here night!"

"Where'd you all come from?" I ast. "I thought you was still back in yore cabin chawin' the rag."

"Well," he says, "after you pulled out we decided to trail along and see how you come out with whatever you planned. As we come through the woods expectin' to git ambushed every second, we met Bill here who told us he believed you had a idee of circumventin' them devils, though he didn't know what it war. So we come on and hid ourselves at the aidge of the trees to see what'd happen. I see we been too timid in our dealin's with these heathens. We been lettin' 'em force the fightin' too long. You was right. A good offence is the best defence."

"We didn't kill any of the varmints, wuss luck, but we give 'em a prime lickin'. Hey, look there!" he hollered. "The boys has caught one of the critters! Lug him into the cabin, boys!"

They done so, and by the time me and the old man got there, they had the candles lit, and a rope around the Barlow's neck and one end throwed on a rafter.

That cabin was a sight, all littered with broke guns and splintered chairs and tables, and pieces of clothes and strips of hide. It looked jest about like a cabin ought to look where they has jest been a fight between seventeen polecats and a mountain lion. It was a dirt floor, and some of the poles which helped hold up the roof was splintered, so most of the weight was resting on a big post in the centre of the hut.

All the Warrens was crowding around their prisoner, and when I looked over their heads and seen the feller's pale face in the light of the candle I give a yell: "Dick Blanton!"

"So it is!" said Old Man Warren, rubbing his hands with glee. "So it is! Well, young feller, you got any last words to orate?"

"Naw," said Blanton sullenly. "But if it hadn't been for that derned lion spilin' our plans we'd of had you derned Warrens like so much pork. I never heard of a cougar jumpin' through a winder before."

"That there cougar didn't jump," I said, shouldering through the mob. "He was hev. I done the heavin'."

His mouth fell open and he looked at me like he'd saw the ghost of Sitting Bull. "Breckinridge Elkins!" says he. "I'm cooked now, for sure!"

"I'll say you air!" gritted the feller who'd yearned to shoot Blanton earlier in the night. "What we waitin' for? Le's string him up."

"Hold on," I said. "You all cain't hang him. I'm goin' to take him back to Bear Creek."

"You ain't neither," says Old Man Warren. "We're much obleeged to you for the help you've give us tonight, but this here is the first chance we've had to hang a Barlow in fifteen year, and we aims to make the most of it. String him, boys!"

"Stop!" I roared, stepping for'ard.

In a second I was covered by seven rifles, whilst three men laid hold of the rope and started to heave Blanton's feet off the floor. Them seven Winchesters didn't stop me. I'd of taken them guns away and wiped up the floor with them ongrateful mavericks, but I was afeared Blanton might get hit in the wild shooting that was certain to accompany it.

What I wanted to do was something which would put 'em all horse- de-combat, as the French say, without getting Blanton killed. So I laid hold on the center post and before they knowed what I was doing, I tore it loose and broke it off, and the roof caved in and the walls fell inwards on the roof.

In a second they warn't no cabin at all--jest a pile of timber with the Warrens all underneath and screaming blue murder. Of course I jest braced my laigs and when the roof fell my head busted a hole through it, and the logs of the falling walls hit my shoulders and glanced off, so when the dust settled I was standing waist-deep amongst the rooins and nothing but a few scratches to show for it.

The howls that riz from beneath the rooins was blood-curdling, but I knowed nobody was hurt permanent because if they was they wouldn't be able to howl like that. But I expect some of 'em would of been hurt if my head and shoulders hadn't kind of broke the fall of the roof and wall-logs.

I located Blanton by his voice, and pulled pieces of roof board and logs off him until I came onto his laig, and I pulled him out by it and laid him on the ground to get his wind back, because a beam had fell acrost his stummick and when he tried to holler he made the funniest noise I ever heard.

I then kind of rooted around amongst the debris and hauled Old Man Warren out, and he seemed kind of dazed and kept talking about earthquakes.

"You better git to work extricatin' yore misguided kin from under them logs," I told him sternly. "After that there display of ingratitude I got no sympathy for you. In fact, if I was a short- tempered man I'd feel inclined to vi'lence. But bein' the soul of kindness and generosity, I controls my emotions and merely remarks that if I _wasn't_ mild-mannered as a lamb, I'd hand you a boot in the pants--like this!"

I showed him how I meant.

"Owww!" wails he, sailing through the air and sticking his nose to the hilt in the dirt.

"I'll have the law on you, you derned murderer!" he wept, shaking his fists at me, and as I departed with my captive I could hear him chanting a hymn of hate as he pulled logs off of his bellering relatives.

Blanton was trying to say something, but I told him I warn't in no mood for perlite conversation and the less he said the less likely I was to lose my temper and tie his neck into a knot around a blackjack. I was thinking how the last time I seen Glory McGraw I told her I was faring forth to find me a town-gal, and now instead of bringing a wife back to Bear Creek, I was bringing back a brother-in-law. My relatives, I reflected bitterly, was sure playing hell with my matrimonial plans. Looked like I warn't never going to get started on my own affairs.

Cap'n Kidd made the hundred miles from the Mezquital Mountains to Bear Creek by noon the next day, carrying double, and never stopping to eat, sleep, nor drink. Them that don't believe that kindly keep their mouths shet. I have already licked nineteen men for acting like they didn't believe it.

I stalked into the cabin and throwed Dick Blanton down onto the floor before Elinor which looked at him and me like she thought I was crazy.

"What you finds attractive about this coyote," I said bitterly, "is beyond the grasp of my dust-coated brain. But here he is, and you can marry him right away."

She said: "Air you drunk or sunstruck? Marry that good-for- nothin', whis-ky-swiggin', kyard-shootin' loafer? Why, it ain't been a week since I run him out of the house with a broom-handle."

"Then he didn't jilt you?" I gasped.

"Him jilt me?" she said. "I jilted him!"

I turned to Dick Blanton more in sorrer than in anger.

"Why," said I, "did you boast all over Grizzly Run about jiltin' Elinor Elkins?"

"I didn't want folks to know she turned me down," he said sullenly. "Us Blantons is proud. The only reason I ever thought about marryin' her was I was ready to settle down on the farm pap gave me, and I wanted to marry me a Elkins gal, so I wouldn't have to go to the expense of hirin' a couple of hands and buyin' a span of mules, and--"

They ain't no use in Dick Blanton threatening to have the law onto me. He got off light to what he'd have got if pap and my brothers hadn't all been off hunting. They've got terrible tempers. But I was always too soft-hearted for my own good. In spite of Dick Blanton's insults I held my temper. I didn't do nothing to him at all, except escort him with dignity for five or six miles down the Chawed Ear trail, kicking him in the seat of his britches.

CHAPTER VII

THE ROAD TO BEAR CREEK

AS I come back up the trail after escorting Dick Blanton down it, I got nervous as I approached the p'int where the path that run from the McGraw cabin came out into it. If they was anybody I in the world right then I didn't want to meet, it was Glory McGraw. I got past and hove a sigh of relief, and jest as I done so, I heard a hoss, and looked back and she was riding out of the path.

I taken to the bresh and to my rage she spurred her hoss and come after me. She was on a fast cayuse, but I thought if I keep my lead I'd be all right, because soon I'd be in the dense thickets where she couldn't come a-hossback. I speeded up, because I'd had about all of her rawhiding I could endure. And then, as I was looking back over my shoulder, I run right smack into a low-hanging oak limb and nearly knocked my brains out. When things stopped spinning around me, I was setting on the ground, and Glory McGraw was setting on her hoss looking down at me.

"Why, Breckinridge," she says mockingly. "Air in you scairt of me? What you want to run from me for?"

"I warn't runnin' from you," I growled, glaring up at her. "I didn't even know you was anywheres around. I seen one of pap's steers sneakin' off in the bresh, and I was tryin' to head him. Now you done scairt him I away!"

I riz and breshed the dust offa my clothes with my I hat, and she says: "I been hearin' a lot about you, Breckinridge. Seems like yo're gittin' to be quite a famous man."

"Hmmmm!" I says, suspicious.

"But where, Breckinridge," she cooed, leaning over the saddle horn towards me, "where is that there purty town-gal you was goin' to bring back to Bear Creek as yore blushin' bride?"

"We ain't sot the day yet," I muttered, looking off.

"Is she purty, Breckinridge?" she pursued.

"Purty as a pitcher," I says. "They ain't a gal on Bear Creek can hold a candle to her."

"Where's she live?" ast Glory.

"War Paint," I said, that being the first town that come into my mind.

"What's her name, Breckinridge?" ast Glory, and I couldn't think of a gal's name if I'd knowed I was going to be shot.

I stammered and floundered, and whilst I was trying my damndest to think of _some_ name to give her, she bust into laughter.

"What a lover _you_ be!" says she. "Cain't even remember the name of the gal yo're goin' to marry--you _air_ goin' to marry her, ain't you, Breckinridge?"

"Yes, I am!" I roared. "I _have_ got a gal in War Paint! I'm goin' to see her right now, soon as I can git back to my corral and saddle my hoss! What d'you think of _that_, Miss Smarty?"

"I think yo're the biggest liar on Bear Creek!" says she, with a mocking laugh, and reined around and rode off whilst I stood in helpless rage. "Give my regards to yore War Paint sweetheart, Breckinridge!" she called back over her shoulder. "Soon as you remember what her name is!"

I didn't say nothing. I was past talking. I was too full of wishing that Glory McGraw was a man for jest about five minutes. She was clean out of sight before I could even see straight, much less talk or think reasonable. I give a maddened roar and ripped a limb off a tree as big as a man's laig and started thrashing down the bresh all around, whilst chawing the bark offa all the trees I could rech, and by the time I had cooled off a little that thicket looked like a cyclone had hit it. But I felt a little better and I headed for home on the run, cussing a blue streak and the bobcats and painters taken to the high ridges as I come.

I made for the corral, and as I come out into the clearing I heard a beller like a mad bull up at the cabin, and seen my brothers Buckner and Garfield and John and Bill run out of the cabin and take to the woods, so I figgered pap must be having a touch of the rheumatiz. It makes him remarkable peevish. But I went on and saddled Cap'n Kidd. I was determined to make good on what I told Glory. I didn't have no gal in War Paint, but by golly, I aimed to, and this time I warn't to be turnt aside. I was heading for War Paint, and I was going to get me a gal if I had to lick the entire town.

Well, jest as I was leading Cap'n Kidd outa the corral, my sister Brazoria come to the door of the cabin and hollered: "Oh, Breckinridge! Come up to the shack! Pap wants you!"

"--!" says. "What the hell now?"

I went up to the cabin and tied Cap'n Kidd and went in. At first glance I seen pap had past the peevish stage and was having a remorseful spell. Rheumatism effects him that way. But the remorse is always for something that happened a long time ago. He didn't seem a bit regretful for having busted a ox-yoke over brother Garfield's head that morning.

He was laying on his b'ar-skin with a jug of corn licker at his elbow, and he says: "Breckinridge, the sins of my youth is ridin' my conscience heavy. When I was a young man I was free and keerless in my habits, as numerous tombstones on the boundless prairies testifies. I sometimes wonders if I warn't a trifle hasty in shootin' some of the gents which disagreed with my principles. Maybe I should of controlled my passion and jest chawed their ears off.

"Take Uncle Esau Grimes, for instance." And then pap hove a sigh like a bull, and said: "I ain't seen Uncle Esau for many years. Me and him parted with harsh words and gun-smoke. I've often wondered if he still holds a grudge agen me for plantin' that charge of buckshot in his hind laig."

"What about Uncle Esau?" I said.

Pap perjuiced a letter and said: "He was brung to my mind by this here letter which Jim Braxton fotched me from War Paint. It's from my sister Elizabeth, back in Devilville, Arizona, whar Uncle Esau lives. She says Uncle Esau is on his way to Californy, and is due to pass through War Paint about the tenth--that's tomorrer. She don't know whether he intends turnin' off to see me or not, but suggests that I meet him at War Paint, and make peace with him."

"Well?" I demanded, because from the way pap combed his beard with his fingers and eyed me, I knowed he was aiming to call on me to do something for him.

"Well," said pap, taking a long swig out of the jug, "I want you to meet the stage tomorrer mornin' at War Paint, and invite Uncle Esau to come up here and visit us. Don't take no for a answer. Uncle Esau is as cranky as hell, and a pecooliar old duck, but I think he'll like you. Specially if you keep yore mouth shet and don't expose yore ignorance."

"Well," I said, "for onst the job you've sot for me falls in with my own plans. I was just fixin' to light out for War Paint. But how'm I goin' to know Uncle Esau? I ain't never seen him."

"He ain't a big man," said pap. "Last time I seen him he had a right smart growth of red whiskers. You bring him home regardless. Don't pay no attention to his belly-achin'. He's awful suspicious because he's got lots of enemies. He burnt plenty of powder in his younger days, all the way from Texas to Californy. He war mixed up in more feuds and range-wars than any man I ever knowed. He's supposed to have considerable money hid away somewheres, but that ain't got nothin' to do with us. I wouldn't take his blasted money as a gift. All I want to do is talk to him, and git his forgiveness for fillin' his hide with buckshot in a moment of youthful passion.

"If he don't forgive me," says pap, taking another pull at his jug, "I'll bend my .45 over his stubborn old skull. Git goin'."

So I hit out acrost the mountains, and the next morning found me eating breakfast at the aidge of War Paint, with a old hunter and trapper by the name of old Bill Polk which was camped there temporary.

War Paint was a new town which had sprung up out of nothing on account of a gold rush right recent, and old Bill was very bitter.

"A hell of a come-off this is!" he snorted. "Clutterin' up the scenery and scarin' the animals off with their fool houses and claims. Last year I shot deer right whar that saloon yonder stands now," he said, glaring at me like it was my fault.

I said nothing but chawed my venison which we was cooking over his fire, and he said: "No good'll come of it, you mark my word. These mountains won't be fit to live in. These camps draws scum like a dead hoss draws buzzards. The outlaws is already ridin' in from Arizona and Utah and Californy, besides the native ones. Grizzly Hawkins and his thieves is hidin' up in the hills, and no tellin' how many more'll come in. I'm glad they cotched Badger Chisom and his gang after they robbed that bank at Gunstock. That's one gang which won't bedevil us, becaze they're in jail. If somebody'd jest kill Grizzly Hawkins, now-- "

"Who's that gal?" I ejaculated suddenly, forgetting to eat in my excitement.

"Who? Whar?" says old Bill, looking around. "Oh, that gal jest goin' by the Golden Queen restaurant? Aw, that's Dolly Rixby, the belle of the town."

"She's awful purty," I says.

"_You_ never seen a purtier," says he.

"I have, too," I says absent-mindedly. "Glory McGraw--" Then I kind of woke up to what I was saying and flang my breakfast into the fire in disgust. "Sure, she's the purtiest gal I ever seen!" I snorted. "Ain't a gal in the Humbolts can hold a candle to her. What you say her name was? Dolly Rixby? A right purty name, too."

"You needn't start castin' sheep's eyes at her," he opined. "They's a dozen young bucks sparkin' her already. I think Blink Wiltshaw's the favorite to put his brand onto her, though. She wouldn't look at a hillbilly like you."

"I might remove the competition," I suggested.

"You better not try no Bear Creek rough-stuff in War Paint," says he. "The town's jest reekin' with law and order. Why, I actually hear they ups and puts you in jail if you shoots a man within the city limits."

I was scandalized. Later I found out that was jest a slander started by the citizens of Chawed Ear which was jealous of War Paint, but at the time I was so upsot by this information I was almost afeared to go into town for fear I'd get arrested.

"Where's Miss Rixby goin' with that bucket?" I ast him.

"She's takin' a bucket of beer to her old man which is workin' a claim up the creek," says old Bill.

"Well, lissen," I says. "You git over there behind that thicket, and when she comes by, make a noise like a Injun."

"What kind of damfoolishness is this?" he demanded. "You want me to stampede the whole camp?"

"Don't make a loud noise," I said. "Jest make it loud enough for her to hear."

"Air you crazy?" he ast.

"No, dern it!" I said fiercely, because she was coming along stepping purty fast. "Git in there and do like I say. I'll rush up from the other side and pertend to rescue her from the Injuns and that'll make her like me. Gwan!"

"I mistrusts yo're a blasted fool," he grumbled. "But I'll do it." He snuck into the thicket which she'd have to pass on the other side, and I circled around so she wouldn't see me till I was ready to rush out and I save her from being sculped. Well, I warn't hardly in position when I heard a kind of mild war-whoop, and it sounded jest like a Blackfoot, only not so loud. But imejitly there come the crack of a pistol and another yell which warn't subdued like the first. It was lusty and energetic. I run towards the thicket, but before I could get into the open trail, old Bill come piling out of the back side of the clump with his hands to the seat of his britches.

"You planned this a-purpose, you snake in the grass!" he yelped. "Git outa my way!"

"Why, Bill," I says. "What happened?"

"I bet you knowed she had a derringer in her stockin'," he snarled as he run past me. "It's all yore fault! When I whooped, she pulled it and shot into the bresh! Don't speak to me! I'm lucky to be alive. I'll git even with you for this if it takes a hundred years!"

He headed on into the deep bresh, and I run around the thicket and seen Dolly Rixby peering into it with her gun smoking in her hand. She looked up as I come onto the trail, and I taken off my hat and said, perlite: "Howdy, miss; can I be of no assistance to you?"

"I jest shot a Injun," she said. "I heard him holler. You might go in there and git the sculp, if you don't mind. I'd like to have it for a soovenir."

"I'll be glad to, miss," I says heartily. "I'll likewise cure and tan it for you myself."

"Oh, thank you!" she says, dimpling when she smiled. "It's a pleasure to meet a real gent like you."

"The pleasure is all mine," I assured her, and went into the bresh and stomped around a little, and then come out and says: "I'm awful sorry, miss, but the critter ain't nowheres to be found. You must of jest winged him. If you want me to I'll take his trail and foller it till I catch up with him, though."

"Oh, I wouldn't think of puttin' you to no sech trouble," she says much to my relief, because I was jest thinking that if she did demand a sculp, the only thing I could do would be to catch old Bill and sculp him, and I'd hate awful bad to have to do that.

But she looked me over with admiration in her eyes, and said: "I'm Dolly Rixby. Who're you?"

"I knowed you the minute I seen you," I says. "The fame of yore beauty has reched clean into the Humbolts. I'm Breckinridge Elkins."

Her eyes kind of sparkled, and she said: "I've heard of you, too! You broke Cap'n Kidd, and it was you that cleaned up Wampum!"

"Yes'm," I says, and jest then I seen the stagecoach fogging it down the road from the east, and I says: "Say, I got to meet that there stage, but I'd like to call on you at yore convenience."

"Well," she says, "I'll be back at the cabin in about a hour. What's the matter with then? I live about ten rods north of The Red Rooster gamblin' hall."

"I'll be there," I promised, and she gimme a dimply smile and went on down the trail with her old man's bucket of beer, and I hustled back to where I left Cap'n Kidd. My head was in a whirl, and my heart was pounding. And here, thinks I, is where I show Glory McGraw what kind of stuff a Elkins is made of. Jest wait till I ride back to Bear Creek with Dolly Rixby as my bride!

I rode into War Paint just as the stage pulled up at the stand, which was also the post office and a saloon. They was three passengers, and they warn't none of 'em tenderfeet. Two was big hard- looking fellers, and t'other'n was a wiry oldish kind of a bird with red whiskers, so I knowed right off it was Uncle Esau Grimes. They was going into the saloon as I dismounted, the big men first, and the older feller follering 'em. Thinks I, I'll start him on his way to Bear Creek, and then I'll come back and start sparking Dolly Rixby.

I touched him on the shoulder, and he whirled most amazing quick with a gun in his hand, and he looked at me very suspicious, and said: "What you want?"

"I'm Breckinridge Elkins," I said. "I want you to come with me. I recognized you as soon as I seen you--"

I then got a awful surprise, but not as sudden as it would have been if pap hadn't warned me that Uncle Esau was pecooliar. He hollered: "Bill! Jim! Help!" And swung his six-shooter agen my head with all his might.

The other two fellers whirled and their hands streaked for their guns, so I knocked Uncle Esau flat to keep him from getting hit by a stray slug, and shot one of 'em through the shoulder before he could unlimber his artillery. T'other'n grazed my neck with a bullet, so I perforated him in the arm and the hind laig and he fell down acrost the other'n. I was careful not to shoot 'em in no vital parts, because I seen they was friends of Uncle Esau; but when guns is being drawn it ain't no time to argy or explain.

Men was hollering and running out of saloons, and I stooped and started to lift Uncle Esau, who was kind of groggy because he'd hit his head agen a hitching post. He was crawling around on his all-fours cussing something terrible, and trying to find his gun which he'd dropped. When I laid hold onto him he commenced biting and kicking and hollering, and I said: "Don't ack like that, Uncle Esau. Here comes a lot of fellers, and the sheriff may be here any minute and 'rest me for shootin' them idjits. We got to git goin'. Pap's waitin' for you, up on Bear Creek."

But he jest fit that much harder and hollered that much louder, so I scooped him up bodily and jumped onto Cap'n Kidd and throwed Uncle Esau face down acrost the saddle-bow, and headed for the hills. A lot of men yelled at me to stop, and some of 'em started shooting at me, but I give no heed.

I give Cap'n Kidd the rein and we went tearing down the road and around the first bend, and I didn't even take time to change Uncle Esau's position, because I didn't want to get arrested. A fat chance I had of keeping my date with Dolly Rixby. I wonder if anybody ever had sech cussed relatives as me.

Jest before we reched the p'int where the Bear Creek trail runs into the road, I seen a man on the road ahead of me, and he must have heard the shooting and Uncle Esau yelling because he whirled his hoss and blocked the road. He was a wiry old cuss with grey whiskers.

"Where you goin' with that man?" he yelled as I approached at a thundering gait.

"None of yore business," I retorted. "Git outa my way."

"Help! Help!" hollered Uncle Esau. "I'm bein' kidnapped and murdered!"

"Drop that man, you derned outlaw!" roared the stranger, suiting his actions to his words.

Him and me drawed simultaneous, but my shot was a split-second quicker'n his'n. His slug fanned my ear, but his hat flew off and he pitched out of his saddle like he'd been hit with a hammer. I seen a streak of red along his temple as I thundered past him.

"Let that larn you not to interfere in family affairs!" I roared, and turned up the trail that switched off the road and up into the mountains.

"Don't never yell like that," I said irritably to Uncle Esau. "You like to got me shot. That feller thought I was a criminal."

I didn't catch what he said, but I looked back and down over the slopes and shoulders, and seen men boiling out of town full tilt, and the sun glinted on six-shooters and rifles, so I urged on Cap'n Kidd and we covered the next few miles at a fast clip.

Uncle Esau kept trying to talk, but he was bouncing up and down so all I could understand was his cuss words, which was free and fervent. At last he gasped: "For God's sake lemme git off this cussed saddle- horn; it's rubbin' a hole in my belly."

So I pulled up and seen no sign of my pursuers, so I said: "All right, you can ride in the saddle and I'll set on behind. I was goin' to hire you a hoss at the livery stable, but we had to leave so quick they warn't no time."

"Where you takin' me?" he demanded.

"To Bear Creek," I said. "Where you think?"

"I don't wanta go to Bear Creek," he said fiercely. "I _ain't_ goin' to Bear Creek."

"You are, too," I said. "Pap said not to take no for a answer. I'm goin' to slide over behind the saddle, and you can set in it."

So I pulled my feet outa the stirrups and moved over the cantle, and he slid into the seat--and the first thing I knowed he had a knife out of his boot and was trying to kyarve my gizzard.

Now I likes to humor my relatives, but they is a limit to everything. I taken the knife away from him, but in the struggle, me being handicapped by not wanting to hurt him, I lost hold of the reins and Cap'n Kidd bolted and run for several miles through the pines and bresh. What with me trying to grab the reins and keep Uncle Esau from killing me at the same time, and neither one of us in the stirrups, finally we both fell off, and if I hadn't managed to catch hold of the bridle as I went off, we'd had a long walk ahead of us.

I got Cap'n Kidd stopped, after being drug for about seventy-five yards, and then I went back to where Uncle Esau was laying on the ground trying to get his wind back, because I had kind of fell on him.

"Is that any way to ack, tryin' to stick a knife in a man which is doin' his best to make you comfortable?" I said reproachfully. All he done was gasp, so I said: "Well, pap told me you was a cranky old duck, so I reckon the only thing to do is to jest not notice yore pecooliarities."

I looked around to get my bearings, because Cap'n Kidd had got away off the trail. We was west of it, in very wild country, but I seen a cabin off through the trees, and I said: "We'll go over there and see can I buy or hire a hoss for you to ride. That'll be more convenient for both of us."

I h'isted him back into the saddle, and he said kind of dizzily: "This here's a free country. I don't have to go to Bear Creek if'n I don't want to."

"Well," I said severely, "you oughta want to, after all the trouble I've went to, comin' and invitin' you, and passin' up a date with the purtiest gal in War Paint on account of you. Set still now. I'm settin' on behind but I'm holdin' the reins."

"I'll have yore life for this," he promised blood-thirstily, but I ignored it, because pap had said Uncle Esau was pecooliar.

Purty soon we hove up to the cabm I'd glimpsed through the trees. Nobody was in sight, but I seen a hoss tied to a tree in front of the cabin. I rode up to the door and knocked, but nobody answered. But I seen smoke coming out of the chimney, so I decided I'd go in.

I dismounted and lifted Uncle Esau off, because I seen from the gleam in his eye that he was intending to run off on Cap'n Kidd if I give him half a chance. I got a firm grip onto his collar, because I was determined that he was going to visit us up on Bear Creek if I had to tote him on my shoulder all the way, and I went into the cabin with him.

They warn't nobody in there, though a big pot of beans was simmering over some coals in the fireplace, and I seen some rifles in racks on the wall and a belt with two pistols hanging on a peg.

Then I heard somebody walking behind the cabin, and the back door opened and there stood a big, black-whiskered man with a bucket of water in his hand and a astonished glare on his face. He didn't have no guns on.

"Who the hell are you?" he demanded, but Uncle Esau give a kind of gurgle, and said: "Grizzly Hawkins!"

The big man jumped and glared at Uncle Esau, and then his black whiskers bristled in a ferocious grin, and he said: "Oh, it's you, is it? Who'd of thunk I'd ever meet you _here?"_

"Grizzly Hawkins, hey?" I said, realizing that I'd stumbled onto the hideout of the wust outlaw in them mountains. "So you-all know each other?"

"I'll say we do!" rumbled Hawkins, looking at Uncle Esau like a wolf looks at a fat yearling.

"I'd heard you was from Arizona," I said, being naturally tactful. "Looks to me like they's enough cow-thieves in these hills already without outsiders buttin' in. But yore morals ain't none of my business. I want to buy or hire or borrer a hoss for this here gent to ride."

"Oh, no, you ain't!" said Grizzly. "You think I'm goin' to let a fortune slip through my fingers like that? Tell you what I'll do, though: I'll split with you. My gang had business over towards Chawed Ear this momin', but they're due back soon. Me and you will work him over before they gits back, and we'll nab all the loot ourselves."

"What you mean?" I ast. "My uncle and me is on our way to Bear Creek--"

"Aw, don't ack innercent with me!" he snorted disgustedly. "Uncle! Hell! You think I'm a plumb fool? Cain't I see he's yore prisoner, the way you got him by the neck? Think I don't know what yo're up to? Be reasonable. Two can work this job better'n one. I know lots of ways to make a man talk. I betcha if we kinda massage his hinder parts with a red-hot brandin' iron he'll tell us quick enough where the money is hid."

Uncle Esau turnt pale under his whiskers, and I said indignantly: "Why, you low-lifed polecat! You got the crust to pertend to think I'm kidnappin' my own uncle for his dough? I got a good mind to shoot you."

"So yo're greedy, hey?" he snarled, showing his teeth. "Want all the loot yore-self, hey? I'll show you!" And quick as a cat he swung that water bucket over his head and let it go at me. I ducked and it hit Uncle Esau in the head and stretched him out all drenched with water, and Hawkins give a roar and dived for a .45-90 on the wall. He wheeled with it and I shot it out of his hands. He then come for me wild-eyed with a bowie out of his boot, and my next cartridge snapped, and he was on top of me before I could cock my gun again.

I dropped it and grappled with him, and we fit all over the cabin and every now and then we would tromple on Uncle Esau which was trying to crawl towards the door, and the way he would holler was pitiful to hear.

Hawkins lost his knife in the melee, but he was as big as me, and a bear-cat at rough-and-tumble. We would stand up and whale away with both fists, and then clinch and roll around the floor, biting and gouging and slugging, and onst we rolled clean over Uncle Esau and kind of flattened him out like a pancake.

Finally Hawkins got hold of the table which he lifted like it was a board and splintered over my head, and this made me mad, so I grabbed the pot off the fire and hit him in the head with it, and about a gallon of red-hot beans went down his back and he fell into a corner so hard he jolted the shelves loose from the logs, and all the guns fell off the walls.

He come up with a gun in his hand, but his eyes was so full of blood and hot beans that he missed me the first shot, and before he could shoot again I hit him on the chin so hard it fractured his jaw bone and sprained both his ankles and laid him out cold.

Then I looked around for Uncle Esau, and he was gone and the front door was open. I rushed out of the cabin and there he was jest climbing aboard Cap'n Kidd. I hollered for him to wait, but he kicked Cap'n Kidd in the ribs and went tearing off through the trees. Only he didn't head north back towards War Paint. He was p'inted south-east, in the general direction of Hideout Mountain. I grabbed my gun up off the floor and lit out after him, though I didn't have much hope of catching him. Grizzly's cayuse was a good hoss, but he couldn't hold a candle to Cap'n Kidd.

I wouldn't have caught him, neither, if it hadn't been for Cap'n Kidd's determination not to be rode by nobody but me. Uncle Esau was a crack hossman to stay on as long as he did.

But finally Cap'n Kidd got tired of sech foolishness, and about the time he crossed the trail we'd been follerin' when he first bolted, he bogged his head and started busting hisself in two, with his snoot rubbing the grass and his heels scraping the clouds offa the sky.

I could see mountain peaks between Uncle Esau and the saddle, and when Cap'n Kidd start sunfishing it looked like the wrath of Jedgment Day, but somehow Uncle Esau managed to stay with him till Cap'n Kidd plumb left the earth like he aimed to aviate from then on, and Uncle Esau left the saddle with a shriek of despair and sailed head-on into a blackjack thicket.

Cap'n Kidd give a snort of contempt and trotted off to a patch of grass and started grazing, and I dismounted and went and ontangled Uncle Esau from amongst the branches. His clothes was tore and he was scratched so he looked like he'd been fighting with a drove of wildcats, and he left a right smart bunch of his whiskers amongst the bresh.

But he was full of pizen and hostility.

"I understand this here treatment," he said bitterly, like he blamed me for Cap'n Kidd pitching him into the thicket, "but you'll never git a penny. Nobody but me knows whar the dough is, and you can pull my toe nails out by the roots before I tells you."

"I know you got money hid away," I said, deeply offended, "but I don't want it."

He snorted skeptical and said sarcastic: "Then what're you draggin' me over these cussed hills for?"

"'Cause pap wants to see you," I said. "But they ain't no use in askin' me a lot of fool questions. Pap said for me to keep my mouth shet."

I looked around for Grizzly's hoss, and seen he had wandered off. He sure hadn't been trained proper.

"Now I got to go look for him," I said disgustedly. "Will you stay here till I git back?"

"Sure," he said. "Sure. Go on and look for the hoss. I'll wait here."

But I give him a searching look, and shook my head.

"I don't want to seem like I mistrusts you," I said, "but I see a gleam in yore eye which makes me believe that you intends to run off the minute my back's turned. I hate to do this, but I got to bring you safe to Bear Creek; so I'll just kinda hawg-tie you with my lariat till I git back."

Well, he put up a awful holler, but I was firm, and when I rode off on Cap'n Kidd I was satisfied that he couldn't untie them knots by hisself. I left him laying in the grass beside the trail, and his language was painful to listen to.

That derned hoss had wandered farther'n I thought. He'd moved north along the trail for a short way, and then turned off and headed in a westerly direction, and after a while I heard hosses galloping somewheres behind me, and I got nervous, thinking what if Hawkins's gang had got back to their hangout and he'd told 'em about us, and sent 'em after us, to capture pore Uncle Esau and torture him to make him tell where his savings was hid. I wished I'd had sense enough to shove Uncle Esau back in the thicket so he wouldn't be seen by anybody riding along the trail, and I'd just decided to let the hoss go and turn back, when I seen him grazing amongst the trees ahead of me.

I caught him and headed back for the trail, aiming to hit it a short piece north of where I'd left Uncle Esau, and before I got in sight of it, I heard hosses and saddles creaking ahead of me.

I pulled up on the crest of a slope, and looked down onto the trail, and there I seen a gang of men riding north, and they had Uncle Esau amongst 'em. Two of the men was ridin' double, and they had him on a hoss in the middle of 'em. They'd took the ropes off'n him, but he didn't look happy. Instantly I realized that my premonishuns was correct. The Hawkins gang had follered us, and now pore Uncle Esau was in their clutches.

I let go of Hawkins's hoss and reched for my gun, but I didn't dare fire for fear of hitting Uncle Esau, they was clustered so clost about him. I reched up and tore a limb off a oak tree as big as my arm, and I charged down the slope yelling: "I'll save you, Uncle Esau!"

I come so sudden and onexpected them fellers didn't have time to do nothing but holler before I hit 'em. Cap'n Kidd ploughed through their hosses like a avalanche through saplings, and he was going so hard I couldn't check him in time to keep him from knocking Uncle Esau's hoss sprawling. Uncle Esau hit the turf with a shriek.

All around me men was yelling and surging and pulling guns and I riz in my stirrups and laid about me right and left, and pieces of bark and oak leaves and blood flew in showers and in a second the ground was littered with writhing figgers, and the hollering and cussing was awful to hear. Knives was flashing and pistols was banging, but them outlaws' eyes was too full of bark and stars and blood for them to aim, and right in the middle of the brawl, when the guns was roaring and hosses was neighing and men yelling and my oak- limb going _crack! crack! crack!_ on their skulls, down from the north swooped _another_ gang, howling like hyeners!

"There he is!" one of 'em yelled. "I see him crawlin' around under them hosses! After him, boys! We got as much right to his dough as anybody!"

The next minute they'd dashed in amongst us and embraced the members of the other gang and started hammering 'em over the heads with their pistols, and in a second there was the damndest three- cornered war you ever seen, men fighting on the ground and on the hosses, all mixed and tangled up, two gangs trying to exterminate each other, and me whaling hell out of both of 'em.

Meanwhile Uncle Esau was on the ground under us, yelling bloody murder and being stepped on by the hosses, but finally I cleared me a space with a devastating sweep of my club, and leaned down and scooped him up with one hand and hung him over my saddle horn and started battering my way clear.

But a big feller which was one of the second gang come charging through the melee yelling like a Injun, with blood running down his face from a cut in his scalp. He snapped a empty ca'tridge at me, and then leaned out from his saddle and grabbed Uncle Esau by the foot.

"Leggo!" he howled. "He's my meat!"

"Release Uncle Esau before I does you a injury!" I roared, trying to jerk Uncle Esau loose, but the outlaw hung on, and Uncle Esau squalled like a catamount in a wolf-trap. So I lifted what was left of my club and splintered it over the outlaw's head, and he give up the ghost with a gurgle. I then wheeled Cap'n Kidd and rode off like the wind. Them fellers was too busy fighting each other to notice my flight. Somebody did let _bam_ at me with a Winchester, but all it done was to nick Uncle Esau's ear.

The sounds of carnage faded out behind us as I headed south along the trail. Uncle Esau was belly-aching about something. I never seen sech a cuss for finding fault, but I felt they was no time to be lost, so I didn't slow up for some miles. Then I pulled Cap'n Kidd down and said: "What did you say, Uncle Esau?"

"I'm a broken man!" he gasped. "Take my secret, and lemme go back to the posse. All I want now is a good, safe prison term."

"What posse?" I ast, thinking he must be drunk, though I couldn't figger where he could of got any booze.

"The posse you took me away from," he said. "Anything's better'n bein' dragged through these hellish mountains by a homicidal maneyack."

"Posse?" I gasped wildly. "But who was the second gang?"

"Grizzly Hawkins's outlaws," he said, and added bitterly: "Even they'd be preferable to what I been goin' through. I give up. I know when I'm licked. The dough's hid in a holler oak three miles west of Gunstock."

I didn't pay no attention to his remarks, because my head was in a whirl. A posse! Of course; the sheriff and his men had follered us from War Paint, along the Bear Creek trail, and finding Uncle Esau tied up, had thought he'd been kidnapped by a outlaw instead of merely being invited to visit his relatives. Probably he was too cussed ornery to tell 'em any different. I hadn't rescued him from no bandits; I'd took him away from a posse which thought _they_ was rescuing him.

Meanwhile Uncle Esau was clamoring: "Well, why'n't you lemme go? I've told you whar the dough is. What else you want?"

"You got to go on to Bear Creek with me--" I begun; and Uncle Esau give a shriek and went into a kind of convulsion, and the first thing I knowed he'd twisted around and jerked my gun out of its scabbard and let _bam!_ right in my face so close it singed my hair. I grabbed his wrist and Cap'n Kidd bolted like he always does whenever he gets the chance.

"They's a limit to everything!" I roared. "A hell of a relative you be, you old maneyack!"

We was tearing over slopes and ridges at breakneck speed and fighting all over Cap'n Kidd's back--me to get the gun away from him, and him to commit murder. "If you warn't kin to me, Uncle Esau," I said wrathfully, "I'd plumb lose my temper!"

"What you keep callin' me that fool name for?" he yelled, frothing at the mouth. "What you want to add insult to injury--" Cap'n Kidd swerved sudden and Uncle Esau tumbled over his neck. I had him by the shirt and tried to hold him on, but the shirt tore. He hit the ground on his head and Cap'n Kidd run right over him. I pulled up as quick as I could and hove a sigh of relief to see how close to home I was.

"We're nearly there, Uncle Esau," I said, but he made no comment. He was out cold.

A short time later I rode up to the cabin with my eccentric relative slung over my saddle-bow, and I taken him off and stalked into where pap was laying on his b'ar-skin, and slung my burden down on the floor in disgust. "Well, here he is," I said.

Pap stared and said: "Who's this?"

"When you wipe the blood off," I said, "you'll find it's yore Uncle Esau Grimes. And," I added bitterly, "the next time you wants to invite him to visit us, you can do it yoreself. A more ungrateful cuss I never seen. Pecooliar ain't no name for him; he's as crazy as a locoed jackass."

"But _that_ ain't Uncle Esau!" said pap.

"What you mean?" I said irritably. "I know most of his clothes is tore off, and his face is kinda scratched and skint and stomped outa shape, but you can see his whiskers is red, in spite of the blood."

"Red whiskers turn grey, in time," said a voice, and I wheeled and pulled my gun as a man loomed in the door.

It was the grey-whiskered old feller I'd traded shots with on the edge of War Paint. He didn't go for his gun, but stood twisting his moustache and glaring at me like I was a curiosity or something.

"Uncle Esau!" said pap.

"What?" I hollered. "Air _you_ Uncle Esau?"

"Certainly I am!" he snapped.

"But you warn't on the stagecoach--" I begun.

"Stagecoach!" he snorted, taking pap's jug and beginning to pour licker down the man on the floor. "Them things is for wimmen and childern. I travel hoss-back. I spent last night in War Paint, and aimed to ride on up to Bear Creek this mornin'. In fact, Bill," he addressed pap, "I was on the way here when this young maneyack creased me." He indicated a bandage on his head.

"You mean Breckinridge shot you?" ejaculated pap.

"It seems to run in the family," grunted Uncle Esau.

"But who's this?" I hollered wildly, pointing at the man I'd thought was Uncle Esau, and who was jest coming to.

"I'm Badger Chisom," he said, grabbing the jug with both hands. "I demands to be pertected from this lunatick and turned over to the sheriff."

"Him and Bill Reynolds and Jim Hopkins robbed a bank over at Gunstock three weeks ago," said Uncle Esau; the real one, I mean. "A posse captured them, but they'd hid the loot somewhere and wouldn't say where. They escaped several days ago, and not only the sheriffs was lookin' for 'em, but all the outlaw gangs too, to find out where they'd hid their plunder. It was a awful big haul. They must of figgered that escapin' out of the country by stagecoach would be the last thing folks would expect 'em to do, and they warn't known around War Paint.

"But I recognized Billy Reynolds when I went back to War Paint to have my head dressed, after you shot me, Breckinridge. The doctor was patchin' him and Hopkins up, too. I knowed Reynolds back in Arizona. The sheriff and a posse lit out after you, and I follered 'em when I'd got my head fixed. 'Course, I didn't know who you was. I come up while the posse was fightin' with the Hawkins gang, and with my help we corralled the whole bunch. Then I took up yore trail again. Purty good day's work, wipin' out two of the wust gangs in the West. One of Hawkins's men said Grizzly was laid up in his cabin, and the posse was going to drop by for him."

"What you goin' to do about me?" clamored Chisom.

"Well," said pap, "we'll bandage you up good, and then I'll let Breckinridge here take you back to War Paint--hey, what's the matter with him?"

Badger Chisom had fainted.

CHAPTER VIII

THE SCALP HUNTER

MY RETURN to War Paint with Badger Chisom was plumb uneventful. He was awful nervous all the way and every time I spoke to him he jumped and ducked like he expected to be shot at, and he hove a distinct sigh of relief when the sheriff taken charge of him. He said something like, "Safe at last, thank God!" and seemed in a sweat to get into a good, strong cell. Criminals is pecooliar people.

Well, to my surprise I found that I had become a kind of personage in War Paint account of shooting Chisom's pards and bringing him in. It warn't a narrer-minded town at all, like the folks over to Chawed Ear had led me to believe. Things was free and easy, big gambling games running all the time, bars open all day and all night, and pistols popping every hour of the day. They had a sheriff but he was a sensible man which didn't interfere with the business of honest citizens. He 'lowed it was his job to see that the town warn't overrun by thieving, murdering outlaws, not to go butting into folks' affairs. He told me that if I had occasion to shoot another gent he'd take it as a personal favor if I'd be careful not to hit no innercent bystander by mistake, and when I said I would, he said I was a credit to the community, and we had a drink.

I was about half scairt to go see Dolly Rixby, but I screwed up my courage by thinking of what Glory McGraw would say if I didn't get me a gal soon, and called on her. She warn't as peeved as I thought, though she did say: "Well, yo're a mite late, ain't you? About two days, I believe! But better late than never, I reckon."

She was broad-minded enough to understand my position, and we got along fine. Well, we did after I persuaded them young bucks which was mooning around her that I wasn't going to stand for no claim-jumping. I had to be kind of subtle about this, because it always made Dolly mad for me to disable any of her admirers. She liked me, but she also seemed to like a lot of other fellers, especially young Blink Wiltshaw, which was a good-looking young miner. Sometimes I wondered whether Dolly's interest in me was really for myself, or on account of the glory which was reflected onto her by me calling on her regular. Because by this time I'd made quite a name for myself around over the country, jest like I told Glory McGraw I would. But it didn't make much difference to me, as long as Dolly let me spark her, and I figgered that in a little time more I'd have her roped and hawgtied and branded, and I drempt of the day when I'd take her back to Bear Creek and interjuice her to everybody as my wife. I plumb gloated over how Glory McGraw'd look then, and got to feeling kind of sorry for her, and decided I wouldn't rub it in on her too raw. I'd jest be dignified and tolerant, as become a man of my importance.

And then my money give out. Things had run remarkable smooth since I come back to War Paint, and my luck had suited it. The first night I was there I sot into a poker game in The Rebel Captain saloon with ten dollars and run it up to five hundred before I riz--more money than I'd ever knowed they was in the world. I had a remarkable run of luck at gambling for maybe three weeks, and lived high, wide and handsome, and spent money on Dolly right and left. Then my streak broke, and the first thing I knowed, I was busted.

Well, it taken money to live in a fast-stepping town like War Paint, and go with a gal like Dolly Rixby, so I cast about for something to do to get me some dough. About the time I was about ready to start working somebody's claim for day-wages, I got wind of a big jamboree which was going to be staged in Yavapai, a cowcountry town about a hundred miles north of War Paint. They was going to be hoss- races and roping and bull-dogging and I seen where it was a good chance to pick up me some easy prize money. I knowed, of course, that all them young bucks which I'd cut out could be counted on to start shining up to Dolly the minute my back was turnt, but I didn't look for no serious competition from them, and Blink Wiltshaw had pulled out for Teton Gulch a week before. I figgered he'd de-cided I was too much for him.

So I went and told Dolly that I was heading for Yavapai, and urged her not to pine away in my absence, because I'd be back before many days with plenty of dough. She 'lowed she could bear up under it till I got back, so I kissed her hearti-ly, and sallied forth into the starlit evening where I got a onpleasant surprise. I run into Blink Wiltshaw jest coming up onto the stoop. I was so overcome by irritation that I started to sweep the street with him, when Dolly come out and stopped me and made us shake hands. Blink swore that he was going back to Teton Gulch next morning, and had jest stopped by to say hello, so I was mollified and pulled out for Yavapai without no more delay.

Well, a couple of days later I pulled into Yavapai, which was plumb full of wild cowboys and drunk Injuns, and everybody was full of licker and rambunctious-ness, so it taken 'em a whole day to get things into shape enough and everybody sober enough to get the races started. I started entering Cap'n Kidd in every race that was run, me riding him, of course, and he won the first three races, one after another, and everybody cussed something terrible, and then the jedges said they'd have to bar me from entering any more races. So I said all right I will now lick the jedges and they turnt pale and gimme fifty dollars to agree not to run Cap'n Kidd in any more of their races.

What with that, and the prizes, and betting on Cap'n Kidd myself, I had about a thousand dollars, so I decided I wouldn't stay for the roping and bull-dogging contests next day, but would hustle back to War Paint. I'd been gone three days and was beginning to worry about them young bucks which was sweet on Dolly. I warn't scairt of 'em, but they warn't no use givin' 'em too much chance.

But I thought I'd have a little hand of poker before I pulled out, and that was a mistake. My luck warn't holding. When I ariz at midnight I had exactly five dollars in my pants. But I thinks, to hell with it; I ain't going to stay away from Dolly no longer. Blink Wiltshaw might not have went back to Teton Gulch after all. They is plenty of dough in the world, but not many gals like Dolly.

So I headed back for War Paint without waiting for morning. After all, I was five bucks to the good, and by playing clost to my shirt I might run them up to several hundred, when I got back amongst men whose style of play I knowed.

About the middle of the next morning I run head-on into a snag on the path of progress in the shape of Tunk Willoughby.

And right here lemme say that I'm sick and tired of these lies which is being circulated about me terrorizing the town of Grizzly Claw. They is always more'n one side to anything. These folks which is going around telling about me knocking the mayor of Grizzly Claw down a flight of steps with a kitchen stove ain't yet added that the mayor was trying to blast me with a sawed-off shotgun. If I was a hot-headed man like some I know, I could easy lose my temper over them there slanders, but being shy and retiring by nature, I keeps my dignity and merely remarks that these gossipers is blamed liars which I'll kick the ears off of if I catch 'em.

I didn't have no intention whatever of going to Grizzly Claw, in the first place. It lay a way off my road.

But as I passed the place where the trail from Grizzly Claw comes into the road that runs from War Paint to Yavapai, I seen Tunk Willoughby setting on a log in the fork of the trails. I knowed him at War Paint. Tunk ain't got no more sense'n the law allows anyway, and now he looked plumb discouraged. He had a mangled ear, a couple of black eyes, and a lump onto his head so big his hat wouldn't fit. From time to time he spit out a tooth.

I pulled up Cap'n Kidd and said: "What kind of a brawl have you been into?"

"I been to Grizzly Claw," he said, jest like that explained it. But I didn't get the drift, because I hadn't never been to Grizzly Claw.

"That's the meanest town in these mountains," he says. "They ain't got no real law there, but they got a feller which claims to be a officer, and if you so much as spit, he says you busted a law and has got to pay a fine. If you puts up a holler, the citizens comes to his assistance. You see what happened to me. I never found out jest what law I was supposed to have broke," Tunk said, "but it must of been one they was particular fond of. I give 'em a good fight as long as they confined theirselves to rocks and gun butts, but when they interjuiced fence rails and wagon-tongues into the fray, I give up the ghost."

"What you go there for, anyhow?" I ast.

"Well," he said, mopping off some dried blood, "I was lookin' for you. Three days ago I met yore cousin Jack Gordon, and he told me somethin' to tell you."

Him showing no signs of going on, I says: "Well, what was it?"

"I cain't remember," he said. "That lammin' they give me in Grizzly Claw has plumb addled my brains. Jack told me to tell you to keep a sharp look-out for somebody, but I cain't remember who, or why. But somebody had did somethin' awful to somebody on Bear Creek--seems like it was yore Uncle Jeppard Grimes."

"But what did you go to Grizzly Claw for?" I demanded. "I warn't there."

"I dunno," he said. "Seems like the feller which Jack wanted you to git was from Grizzly Claw, or was supposed to go there, or somethin'."

"A great help you be!" I said in disgust. "Here somebody has went and wronged one of my kinfolks, maybe, and you forgits the details. Try to remember the name of the feller, anyway. If I knew who he was, I could lay him out, and then find out what he done later on. Think, cain't you?"

"Did you ever have a wagon-tongue busted over yore head?" he said. "I tell you, it's jest right recent that I remembered my own name. It was all I could do to rekernize you jest now. If you'll come back in a couple of days, maybe by then I'll remember what all Jack told me."

I give a snort of disgust and turned off the road and headed up the trail for Grizzly Claw. I thought maybe I could learn something there. Anyway, it was up to me to try. Us Bear Creek folks may fight amongst ourselves, but we stands for no stranger to impose on anyone of us. Uncle Jeppard was about as old as the Humbolt Mountains, and he'd fit Injuns for a living in his younger days. He was still a tough old knot. Anybody that could do him a wrong and get away with it sure wasn't no ordinary man, so it warn't no wonder that word had been sent out for me to get on his trail. And now I hadn't no idee who to look for, or why, jest because of Tunk Willoughby's weak skull. I despise these here egg-headed weaklings.

I arrove in Grizzly Claw late in the afternoon and went first to the wagon-yard and seen that Cap'n Kidd was put in a good stall and fed proper, and warned the feller there to keep away from him if he didn't want his brains kicked out. Cap'n Kidd has got a disposition like a shark and he don't like strangers. There was only five other hosses in the wagon-yard, besides me and Cap'n Kidd--a pinto, a bay, a piebald, and a couple of pack-hosses.

I then went back into the business part of the village, which was one dusty street with stores and saloons on each side, and I didn't pay much attention to the town, because I was trying to figger out how I could go about trying to find out what I wanted to know, and couldn't think of no questions to ask nobody about nothing.

Well, I was approaching a saloon called the Apache Queen, and was looking at the ground in meditation, when I seen a silver dollar laying in the dust clost to a hitching rack. I immejitly stooped down and picked it up, not noticing how clost it was to the hind laigs of a mean-looking mule. When I stooped over he hauled off and kicked me in the head. Then he let out a awful bray and commenced jumping around holding up his hind hoof, and some men come running out of the saloon, and one of 'em hollered: "He's tryin' to kill my mule! Call the law!"

Quite a crowd gathered and the feller which owned the mule hollered like a catamount. He was a mean-looking cuss with mournful whiskers and a cock-eye. He yelled like somebody was stabbing him, and I couldn't get in a word aidge-ways. Then a feller with a long skmny neck and two guns come up and said: "I'm the sheriff. What's goin' on here? Who is this giant? What's he did?"

The whiskered cuss hollered: "He kicked hisself in the head with my mule and crippled the pore critter for life! I demands my rights! He's got to pay me three hundred and fifty dollars for my mule!"

"Aw, heck," I said, "that mule ain't hurt none; his laig's jest kinda numbed. Anyway, I ain't got but six bucks, and whoever gets them will take 'em offa my dead corpse." I then hitched my six-shooters for'ards, and the crowd kinda fell away.

"I demands that you 'rest him!" howled Drooping-whiskers. "He tried to 'ssassinate my mule!"

"You ain't got no star," I told the feller which said he was the law. "You ain't goin' to arrest me."

"Does you dast resist arrest?" he says, fidgeting with his belt.

"Who said anything about resistin' arrest?" I retorted. "All I aim to do is see how far yore neck will stretch before it breaks."

"Don't you dast lay hands onto a officer of the law!" he squawked, backing away in a hurry.

I was tired of talking, and thirsty, so I merely give a snort and turned away through the crowd towards a saloon pushing 'em right and left out of my way. I seen 'em gang up in the street behind me, talking low and mean, but I give no heed.

They warn't nobody in the saloon except the barman and a gangling cow-puncher which had draped hisself over the bar. I ordered whisky, and when I had drunk a few fingers of the rottenest muck I believe I ever tasted, I give it up in disgust and throwed the dollar on the bar which I had found, and was starting out when the bartender hollered: "Hey!"

I turned around and said courteously: "Don't you yell at me like that, you bat-eared buzzard! What you want?"

"This here dollar ain't no good!" says he, banging it on the bar.

"Well, neither is yore whisky!" I snarled, because I was getting mad. "So that makes us even!"

I am a long-suffering man, but it looked like everybody in Grizzly Claw was out to gyp the stranger in their midst.

"You cain't run no blazer over me!" he hollered. "You gimme a real dollar, or else--"

He ducked down behind the bar and come up with a shotgun so I taken it away from him and bent the barrel double acrost my knee and throwed it after him as he run out the back door hollering help, murder.

The cowpuncher had picked up the dollar and bit on it, and then he looked at me very sharp, and said: "Where did you get this?"

"I found it, if it's any of yore derned business," I snapped, and strode out the door, and the minute I hit the street somebody let _bam!_ at me from behind a rain-barrel acrost the street and shot my hat off. So I slammed a bullet back through the barrel and the feller hollered and fell out in the open yelling blue murder. It was the feller which called hisself the sheriff and he was drilled through the hind laig. I noticed a lot of heads sticking up over winder sills and around doors, so I roared: "Let that be a warnin' to you Grizzly Claw coyotes! I'm Breckinridge Elkins from Bear Creek up in the Humbolts, and I shoot better in my sleep than most men does wide awake!"

I then lent emphasis to my remarks by punctuating a few signboards and knocking out a few winder panes and everybody hollered and ducked. So I shoved my guns back in their scabbards and went into a restaurant. The citizens come out from their hiding-places and carried off my victim, and he made more noise over a broke laig than I thought was possible for a grown man.

They was some folks in the restaurant but they stampeded out the back door as I come in at the front, all except the cook which tried to take refuge somewheres else.

"Come outa there and fry me some bacon!" I commanded, kicking a few slats out of the counter to add p'int to my request. It disgusts me to see a grown man trying to hide under a stove. I am a very patient and mild-mannered human, but Grizzly Claw was getting under my hide. So the cook come out and fried me a mess of bacon and ham and aigs and pertaters and sourdough bread and beans and coffee, and I et three cans of cling peaches. Nobody come into the restaurant whilst I was eating but I thought I heard somebody sneaking around outside.

When I got through I ast the feller how much, and he told me, and I planked down the cash, and he commenced to bite it. This lack of faith in his feller humans so enraged me that I drawed my bowie knife and said: "They is a limit to any man's patience! I been insulted onst tonight and that's enough! You jest dast to say that coin's phoney and I'll slice off yore whiskers plumb at the roots!"

I brandished my bowie under his nose, and he hollered and stampeded back into the stove and upsot it and fell over it, and the coals went down the back of his shirt, so he riz up and run for the creek yelling bloody murder. And that's how the story got started that I tried to burn a cook alive, Injun-style, because he fried my bacon too crisp. Matter of fact, I kept his shack from catching fire and burning down, because I stomped out the coals before they done no more than burn a big hole through the floor, and I throwed the stove out the back door.

It ain't my fault if the mayor of Grizzly Claw was sneaking up the back steps with a shotgun jest at that moment. Anyway, I hear he was able to walk with a couple of crutches after a few months.

I emerged suddenly from the front door, hearing a suspicious noise, and I seen a feller crouching clost to a side winder peeking through a hole in the wall. It was the cowboy I seen in the Apache Queen. He whirled when I come out, but I had him covered.

"Air you spyin' on me?" I demanded. "'Cause if you air--"

"No, no!" he says in a hurry. "I was jest leanin' up agen that wall restin'."

"You Grizzly Claw folks is all crazy," I said disgustedly, and looked around to see if anybody else tried to shoot me, but they wam't nobody in sight, which was suspicious, but I give no heed. It was dark by that time so I went to the wagon-yard, and they warn't nobody there. I reckon the man which run it was off somewheres drunk, because that seemed to be the main occupation of most of them Grizzly Claw devils.

The only place for folks to sleep was a kind of double log-cabin. That is, it had two rooms, but they warn't no door between 'em; and in each room they wasn't nothing but a fireplace and a bunk, and jest one outside door. I seen Cap'n Kidd was fixed for the night, and then I went into the cabin and brought in my saddle and bridle and saddle blanket because I didn't trust the people thereabouts. I taken off my boots and hat and hung 'em on the wall, and hung my guns and bowie on the end of the bunk, and then spread my saddle-blanket on the bunk and laid down glumly.

I dunno why they don't build them dern things for ordinary sized humans. A man six and a half foot tall like me can't never find one comfortable for him. You'd think nobody but pigmies ever expected to use one. I laid there and was disgusted at the bunk, and at myself too, because I hadn't learnt who it was done something to Uncle Jeppard, or what he done. It looked like I'd have to go clean to Bear Creek to find out, and then maybe have to come clean back to Grizzly Claw again to get the critter. By that time Dolly Rixby would be plumb wore out of patience with me, and I wouldn't blame her none.

Well, as I lay there contemplating, I heard a man come into the wagon-yard, and purty soon I heard him come towards the cabin, but I thought nothing of it. Then the door begun to open, and I riz up with a gun in each hand and said: "Who's there? Make yoreself knowed before I blasts you down!"

Whoever it was mumbled some excuse about being on the wrong side, and the door closed. But the voice sounded kind of familiar, and the feller didn't go into the other room. I heard his footsteps sneaking off, and I riz and went to the door, and looked over towards the row of stalls. So purty soon a man led the pinto out of his stall, and swung aboard him and rode off. It was purty dark, but if us folks on Bear Creek didn't have eyes like a hawk, we'd never live to get grown. I seen it was the cowboy I'd seen in the Apache Queen and outside the restaurant. Onst he got clear of the wagon-yard, he slapped in the spurs and went racing through the village like they was a red war- party on his trail. I could hear the beat of his hoss's hoofs fading south down the rocky trail after he was out of sight.

I knowed he must of follered me to the wagon-yard, but I couldn't make no sense out of it, so I went and laid down on the bunk again. I was jest about to go to sleep when I was woke by the sounds of somebody coming into the other room of the cabin, and I heard somebody strike a match. The bunk was built agen the partition wall, so they was only a few feet from me, though with the log wall betwixt us.

They was two of them, from the sounds of their talking.

"I tell you," one of them was saying, "I don't like his looks. I don't believe he's what he pertends to be. We better take no chances, and clear out. After all, we cain't stay here forever. These people air beginning to git suspicious, and if they find out for shore, they'll be demandin' a cut in the profits, to pertect us. The stuff's all packed and ready to jump at a second's notice. Let's run for it tonight. It's a wonder nobody ain't never stumbled onto that hide-out before now."

"Aw," said the other'n, "these Grizzly Claw yaps don't do nothin' but swill licker and gamble and think up swindles to work on sech strangers as is unlucky enough to wander in here. They don't never go into the hills southwest of the village whar our cave is. Most of 'em don't even know there's a path past that big rock to the west."

"Well, Bill," said t'other'n, "we've done purty well, countin' that job up in the Bear Creek country."

At that I was wide awake and listening with both ears.

Bill laughed. "That was kind of funny, warn't it, Jim?" says he.

"You ain't never told me the particulars," says Jim. "Did you have any trouble?"

"Well," said Bill. "T'warn't to say easy. That old Jeppard Grimes was a hard old nut. If all Injun fighters was like him, I feel plumb sorry for the Injuns."

"If any of them Bear Creek devils ever catches you--" begun Jim.

Bill laughed again.

"Them hillbillies never strays more'n ten miles from Bear Creek," says he. "I had the sculp and was gone before they knowed what was up. I've collected bounties for wolves and b'ars, but that's the first time I ever got money for a human sculp!"

A icy chill run down my spine. Now I knowed what had happened to pore old Uncle Jeppard! Scalped! After all the Injun sculps he'd lifted! And them cold-blooded murderers could set there and talk about it like it was the ears of a coyote or a rabbit!

"I told him he'd had the use of that there sculp long enough," Bill was saying. "A old cuss like him--"

I waited for no more. Everything was red around me. I didn't stop for my boots, guns nor nothing. I was too crazy mad even to know sech things existed. I riz up from that bunk and put my head down and rammed that partition wall like a bull going through a rail fence.

The dried mud poured out of the chinks and some of the logs give way, and a howl went up from the other side.

"What's that?" hollered one, and t'other'n yelled: "Lookout! It's a b'ar!"·

I drawed back and rammed the wall again. It caved inwards and I crashed headlong through it in a shower of dry mud and splinters, and somebody shot at me and missed. They was a lighted lantern setting on a hand-hewn table, and two men about six feet tall each that hollered and let _bam_ at me with their six-shooters. But they was too dumbfounded to shoot straight. I gathered 'em to my bosom and we went backwards over the table, taking it and the lantern with us, and you ought to of heard them critters howl when the burning ile splashed down their necks.

It was a dirt floor so nothing caught on fire, and we was fighting in the dark, and they was hollering: "Help! Murder! We are bein' 'sassinated! Ow! Release go my ear!" And then one of 'em got his boot heel wedged in my mouth, and whilst I was twisting it out with one hand, the other'n tore out of his shirt which I was gripping with t'other hand, and run out the door. I had hold of the other feller's foot and commenced trying to twist it off, when he wrenched his laig outa the boot, and took it on the run. When I started to foller him I fell over the table in the dark and got all tangled up in it.

I broke off a laig for a club and rushed to the door, and jest as I got to it a whole mob of folks come surging into the wagon-yard with torches and guns and dogs and a rope, and they hollered: "There he is, the murderer, the outlaw, the counterfeiter, the house-burner, the mule-killer!"

I seen the man that owned the mule, and the restaurant feller, and the barkeep, and a lot of others. They come roaring and bellering up to the door, hollering: "Hang him! Hang him! String up the murderer!" And they begun shooting at me, so I fell amongst 'em with my table- laig and laid right and left till it busted. They was packed so clost together I laid out three or four at a lick, and they hollered something awful. The torches was all knocked down and trompled out except them which was held by fellers which danced around on the aidge of the mill, hollering: "Lay hold on him! Don't be scairt of the big hillbilly! Shoot him! Knife him! Knock him in the head!" The dogs having more sense than the men, they all run off except one big mongrel that looked like a wolf, and he bit the mob often'ern he did me.

They was a lot of wild shooting and men hollering: "Oh, I'm shot! I'm kilt! I'm dyin'!" and some of them bullets burnt my hide they come so clost, and the flashes singed my eye-lashes, and somebody broke a knife agen my belt buckle. Then I seen the torches was all gone except one, and my club was broke, so I bust right through the mob, swinging right and left with my fists and stomping on them that tried to drag me down. I got clear of everybody except the man with the torch who was so excited he was jumping up and down trying to shoot me without cocking his gun. That blame dog was snapping at my heels, so I swung him by the tail and hit the man over the head with him. They went down in a heap and the torch went out, and the dog clamped onto the feller's ear, and he let out a squall like a steam-whistle.

They was milling in the dark behind me, and I run straight to Cap'n Kidd's stall and jumped on him bareback with nothing but a hackamore on him. Jest as the mob located where I went, we come storming out of the stall like a hurricane and knocked some of 'em galley-west and run over some more, and headed for the gate. Somebody shet the gate but Cap'n Kidd took it in his stride, and we was gone into the darkness before they knowed what hit 'em.

Cap'n Kidd decided then was a good time to run away, like he usually does, so he taken to the hills and run through bushes and clumps of trees trying to scrape me off. When I finally pulled him up we was maybe a mile south of the village, with Cap'n Kidd no bridle nor saddle nor blanket, and me with no guns, knife, boots nor hat. And what was wuss, them devils which sculped Uncle Jeppard had got away from me, and I didn't know where to look for 'em.

I sot meditating whether to go back and fight the whole town of Grizzly Claw for my boots and guns, or what to do, when all to onst I remembered what Bill and Jim had said about a cave and a path running to it. I thought I bet them fellers will go back and get their hosses and pull out, jest like they was planning, and they had stuff in the cave, so that's the place to look for 'em. I hoped they hadn't already got the stuff, whatever it was, and gone.

I knowed where that rock was, because I'd saw it when I come into town that afternoon--a big rock that jutted up above the trees about a mile to the west of Grizzly Claw. So I started out through the bresh, and before long I seen it looming up agen the stars, and I made straight for it. Sure enough, they was a narrer trail winding around the base and leading off to the southwest. I follered it, and when I'd went nearly a mile, I come to a steep mountainside, all clustered with bresh.

When I seen that I slipped off and led Cap'n Kidd off the trail and tied him back amongst the trees. Then I crope up to the cave which was purty well masked with bushes. I listened, but everything was dark and still, but all to onst, away down the trail, I heard a burst of shots, and what sounded like hosses running. Then everything was still again, and I quick ducked into the cave, and struck a match.

They was a narrer entrance that broadened out after a few feet, and the cave run straight like a tunnel for maybe thirty steps, about fifteen foot wide, and then it made a bend. After that it widened out and got purty big--about fifty feet wide, and I couldn't tell how far back into the mountain it run. To the left the wall was very broken and notched with ledges, mighty nigh like stair-steps, and when the match went out, away up above me I seen some stars which meant that they was a cleft in the wall or roof away up on the mountain somewheres.

Before the match went out, I seen a lot of junk over in a corner covered up with a tarpaulin, and when I was fixing to strike another match I heard men coming up the trail outside. So I quick clumb up the broken wall and laid on a ledge about ten feet up and listened.

From the sounds as they arriv at the cave mouth, I knowed it was two men on foot, running hard and panting loud. They rushed into the cave and made the turn, and I heard 'em fumbling around. Then a light flared up and I seen a lantern being lit and hung up on a spur of rock.

In the light I seen them two murderers, Bill and Jim, and they looked plumb dilapidated. Bill didn't have no shirt on and the other'n was wearing jest one boot and limped. Bill didn't have no gun in his belt neither, and both was mauled and bruised, and scratched, too, like they'd been running through briars.

"Look here," said Jim, holding his head which had a welt on it which was likely made by my fist. "I ain't sartain in my mind as to jest what all _has_ happened. Somebody must of hit me with a club some time tonight, and things is happened too fast for my addled wits. Seems like we been fightin' and runnin' all night. Listen, _was_ we settin' in the wagon-yard shack talkin' peaceable, and _did_ a grizzly b'ar bust through the wall and nigh slaughter us?"

"That's plumb correct," said Bill. "Only it warn't no b'ar. It was some kind of a human critter--maybe a escaped maneyack. We ought to of stopped for hosses--"

"I warn't thinkin' 'bout no hosses," broke in Jim. "When I found myself outside that shack my only thought was to kiver ground, and I done my best, considerin' that I'd lost a boot, and that critter had nigh onhinged my hind laig. I'd lost you in the dark, so I made for the cave knowin' you'd come there eventual, if you was still alive, and it seemed like I was forever gittin' through the woods, crippled like I was. I hadn't no more'n hit the path when you come up it on the run."

"Well," says Bill, "as I went over the wagon-yard wall a lot of people come whoopin' through the gate, and I thought they was after us, but it must of been the feller we fit, because as I run I seen him layin' into 'em right and left. After I'd got over my panic, I went back after our hosses, but I run right into a gang of men on hossback, and one of 'em was that derned feller which passed hisself off as a cowboy. I didn't need no more. I taken out through the woods as hard as I could pelt, and they hollered, 'There he goes!' and hot-foot after me."

"And was them the fellers I shot at back down the trail?" ast Jim.

"Yeah," says Bill. "I thought I'd shooken 'em off, but jest as I seen you on the path, I heard hosses comin' behind us, so I hollered to let 'em have it, and you did."

"Well, I didn't know who it was," said Jim. "I tell you, my head's buzzin' like a circle-saw."

"Well," said Bill, "we stopped 'em and scattered 'em. I dunno if you hit anybody in the dark, but they'll be mighty keerful about comin' up the trail. Let's clear out."

"On foot?" says Jim. "And me with jest one boot?"

"How else?" says Bill. "We'll have to hoof it till we can steal us some cayuses. We'll have to leave all this stuff here. We don't dare go back to Grizzly Claw after our hosses. I _told_ that derned cowboy would do to watch. He ain't no cowpoke at all. He's a blame detective."

"What's that?" broke in Jim.

"Hosses' hoofs!" exclaimed Bill, turning pale. "Here, blow out that lantern! We'll climb the ledges and git out through the cleft, and take out over the mountain whar they cain't foller with hosses, and then--"

It was at that instant that I launched myself offa the ledge on top of 'em. I landed with all my two hundred and ninety pounds square on jim's shoulders and when he hit the ground under me he kind of spread out like a toad when you tromp on him. Bill give a scream of astonishment and tore off a hunk of rock about the size of a man's head and lammed me over the ear with it as I riz. This irritated me, so I taken him by the neck, and also taken away a knife which he was trying to hamstring me with, and begun sweeping the floor with his carcass.

Presently I paused and kneeling on him, I strangled him till his tongue lolled out, whilst hammering his head fervently agen the rocky floor.

"You murderin' devil!" I gritted betwixt my teeth. "Before I varnishes this here rock with yore brains, tell me why you taken my Uncle jeppard's sculp!"

"Let up!" he gurgled, being purple in the face where he warn't bloody. "They was a dude travellin' through the country and collectin' souvenirs, and he heard about that sculp and wanted it. He hired me to go git it for him."

I was so shocked at that cold-bloodedness that I forgot what I was doing and choked Bill nigh to death before I remembered to ease up on him.

"Who was he?" I demanded. "Who is the skunk which hires old men mur-dered so's he can colleck their sculps? My God, these Eastern dudes is wuss'n Apaches! Hurry up and tell me, so I can finish killin' you."

But he was unconscious; I'd squoze his neck too hard. I riz up and looked around for some water or whisky or something to bring him to so he could tell who hired him to sculp Uncle Jeppard, before I twisted his head off, which was my earnest intention of doing, when somebody said: "Han's up!"

I whirled and there at the crook of the cave stood that there cowboy which had spied on me in Grizzly Claw, and ten other men. They all had their Winchesters p'inted at me, and the cowboy had a star on his buzum.

"Don't move!" he said. "I'm a Federal detective, and I'm arrestin' you for man-ufactorin' counterfeit money!"

"What you mean?" I snarled, backing up to the wall.

"You know," he said, kicking the tarpaulin off the junk in the corner. "Look here, men! All the stamps and dyes he used to make phoney coins and bills! All packed up, ready to light out. I been hangin' around Grizzly Claw for days, know-in' that whoever was passin' this stuff made his, or their headquarters here some-wheres. Today I spotted that dollar you give the barkeep, and I went _pronto_ for my men which was camped back in the hills a few miles. I thought you was settled in the wagon-yard for the night, but it seems you give us the slip. Put the cuffs on him, men!"

"No, you don't!" I snarled, bounding back. "Not till I've finished these devils on the floor--and maybe not then! I dunno what yo're talkin' about, but--"

"Here's a couple of corpses!" hollered one of the men. "He's kilt a couple of fellers!"

One of them stooped over Bill, but he had recovered his senses, and now he riz up on his elbows and give a howl. "Save me!" he bellered. "I confesses! I'm a counterfeiter, and so is Jim there on the floor! We surrenders, and you got to pertect us!"

"_Yo're_ the counterfeiters?" ejaculated the detective, took aback as it were. "Why, I was follerin' this giant! I seen him pass fake money myself. We got to the wagon-yard awhile after he'd run off, but we seen him duck in the woods not far from there, and we been chasin' him. He shot at us down the trail while ago--"

"That was us," said Bill. "It was me you was chasin'. If he was passin' fake stuff, he musta found it somewheres. I tell you, we're the men you're after, and you got to pertect us! I demands to be put in the strongest jail in this state, which even this here devil cain't bust into!"

"And he ain't no counterfeiter?" said the detective.

"He ain't nothin' but a man-eater," said Bill. "Arrest us and take us outa his rech."

"_No!"_ I roared, clean beside myself. "They belongs to me! They sculped my uncle! Give 'em knives or guns or somethin', and let us fight it out."

"Cain't do that," said the detective. "They're Federal prisoners. If you got any charge agen 'em, they'll have to be indicted in the proper form."

His men hauled 'em up and handcuffed 'em and started to lead 'em out.

"Blast yore cussed souls!" I raved. "You low-down, mangy, egg- suckin' coyotes! Does you mean to perteck a couple of dirty sculpers? I'll--"

I started for 'em and they all p'inted their Winchesters at me.

"Keep back!" said the detective. "I'm grateful for you leadin' us into this den, and layin' out these criminals for us, but I don't hanker after no battle in a cave with a human grizzly like you."

Well, what could I do? If I'd had my guns, or even my knife, I'd of took a chance with the whole eleven men, officers or not, but even I can't fight eleven .45-90's with my bare hands. I stood speechless with rage whilst they filed out, and then I went for Cap'n Kidd in a kind of a daze. I felt wuss'n a hoss-thief. Them fellers would be put in the pen safe out of my rech, and Uncle Jeppard's sculp was unavenged! It was awful. I felt like bawling.

Time I got my hoss back onto the trail, the posse with their prisoners was out of sight and hearing. I seen the only thing to do was to go back to Grizzly Claw and get my outfit, and then foller 'em and try to take their prisoners away from 'em some way.

Well, the wagon-yard was dark and still. The wounded had been carried away to have their injuries bandaged, and from the groaning that was still coming from the shacks and cabins along the street, the casualities had been plenteous. The citizens of Grizzly Claw must have been shook up something terrible, because they hadn't even stole my guns and saddle and things yet; everything was in the cabin jest like I'd left 'em.

I put on my boots, hat and belt, saddled and bridled Cap'n Kidd and sot out on the road I knowed the posse had took. But they had a long start on me, and when daylight come I hadn't overtook 'em, though I knowed they couldn't be far ahead of me. But I did meet somebody else. It was Tunk Willoughby riding up the trail, and when he seen me he grinned all over his battered features.

"Hey, Breck!" he hailed me. "After you left I sot on that there log and thunk, and thunk, and I finally remembered what Jack Gordon told me, and I started out to find you again and tell you. It was this: he said to keep a close lookout for a feller from Grizzly Claw named Bill Croghan, because he'd gypped yore Uncle Jeppard in a deal."

"What?" I said.

"Yeah," said Tunk. "He bought somethin' from Jeppard and paid him in counterfeit money. Jeppard didn't know it was phoney till after the feller had got plumb away," said Tunk, "and bein' as he was too busy kyorin' some b'ar meat to go after him, he sent word for you to git him."

"But the sculp--" I said wildly.

"Oh," said Tunk, "that was what Jeppard sold the feller. It was the sculp Jeppard taken offa old Yeller Eagle, the Comanche war-chief forty years ago, and been keepin' for a souvenear. Seems like a Eastern dude heard about it and wanted to buy it, but this Croghan feller must of kept the money he give him to git it with, and give Jeppard phoney cash. So you see everything's all right, even if I did forgit a little, and no harm did--"

And that's why Tunk Willoughby is going around saying I'm a homicidal maneyack, and run him five miles down a mountain and tried to kill him--which is a exaggeration, of course. I wouldn't of kilt him if I could of caught him--which I couldn't when he taken to the thick bresh. I would merely of raised a few knots on his head and tied his hind laigs in a bow-knot around his fool neck, and did a few other little things that might of improved his memory.

CHAPTER IX

CUPID FROM BEAR CREEK

WHEN I reined my hoss towards War Paint again, I didn't go back the way I'd come. I was so far off my route that I knowed it would be nearer to go through the mountains by the way of Teton Gulch than it would be to go clean back to the Yavapai-War Paint road. So I headed out.

I aimed to pass right through Teton Gulch without stopping, because I was in a hurry to get back to War Paint and Dolly Rixby, but my thirst got the best of me, and I stopped in the camp. It was one of them new mining towns that springs up overnight like mushrooms. I was drinking me a dram at the bar of the Yaller Dawg Saloon and Hotel, when the barkeep says, after studying me a spell, he says: "You must be Breckinridge Elkins, of Bear Creek."

I give the matter due consideration, and 'lowed as how I was.

"How come you knowed me?" I inquired suspiciously, because I hadn't never been in Teton Gulch before, and he says: "Well, I've heard tell of Breckinridge Elkins, and when I seen you, I figgered you must be him, because I don't see how they can be two men in the world that big. By the way, there's a friend of yore'n upstairs--Blink Wiltshaw, from War Paint. I've heered him brag about knowin' you personal. He's upstairs now, fourth door from the stair-head, on the left."

So Blink had come back to Teton, after all. Well, that suited me fine, so I thought I'd go up and pass the time of day with him, and find out if he had any news from War Paint, which I'd been gone from for about a week. A lot of things can happen in a week in a fast- moving town like War Paint.

I went upstairs and knocked on the door, and _bam!_ went a gun inside and a .45 slug ripped through the door and taken a nick out of my off-ear. Getting shot in the ear always did irritate me, so without waiting for no more exhibitions of hospitality, I give voice to my displeasure in a deafening beller and knocked the door off'n its hinges and busted into the room over its rooins.

For a second I didn't see nobody, but then I heard a kind of gurgle going on, and happened to remember that the door seemed kind of squishy underfoot when I tromped over it, so I knowed that whoever was in the room had got pinned under the door when I knocked it down.

So I reched under it and got him by the collar and hauled him out, and sure enough it was Blink Wiltshaw. He was limp as a lariat, and glassy-eyed and pale, and was still trying to shoot me with his six- shooter when I taken it away from him.

"What the hell's the matter with you?" I demanded sternly, dangling him by the collar with one hand, whilst shaking him till his teeth rattled. "Didn't Dolly make us shake hands? What you mean by tryin' to 'sasserinate me through a hotel door?"

"Lemme down, Breck," he gasped. "I didn't know it was you. I thought it was Rattlesnake Harrison comin' after my gold."

So I sot him down. He grabbed a jug of licker and taken him a swig, and his hand shook so he spilt half of it down his neck.

"Well?" I demanded. "Ain't you goin' to offer me a snort, dern it?"

"Excuse me, Breckinridge," he apolergized. "I'm so derned jumpy I dunno what I'm doin'. You see them buckskin pokes?" says he, p'inting at some bags on the bed. "Them is plumb full of nuggets. I got a claim up the Gulch, and the day I got back from War Paint I hit a regular bonanza. But it ain't doin' me no good."

"What you mean?" I ast.

"The mountains around Teton is full of outlaws," says he. "They robs and murders every man which makes a strike. The stagecoach has been stuck up so often nobody sends their dust out on it no more. When a man makes a pile he sneaks out through the mountains at night, with his gold on pack-mules. I aimed to do that last night. But them outlaws has got spies all over the camp, and I know they got me spotted. Rattlesnake Harrison's their chief, and he's a ring-tailed he-devil. I been squattin' over this here gold with my pistol in fear and tremblin', expectin' 'em to come right into camp after me. I'm dern nigh loco!"

And he shivered and cussed kind of whimpery, and taken another dram, and cocked his pistol and sot there shaking like he'd saw a ghost or two.

"You got to help me, Breckinridge," he said desperately. "You take this here gold out for me, willya? The outlaws don't know you. _You_ could hit the old Injun path south of the camp and foller it to Hell- Wind Pass. The Chawed Ear-Wahpeton stage goes there about sundown. You could put the gold on the stage there, and they'd take it on to Wahpeton. Harrison wouldn't never think of holdin' it up _after_ it left Hell-Wind. They always holds it up this side of the Pass."

"What I want to risk my neck for you for?" I demanded bitterly, memories of Dolly Rixby rising up before me. "If you ain't got the guts to tote out yore own gold--"

"'Tain't altogether the gold, Breck," says he. "I'm tryin' to git married, and--"

"_Married?_" says I. "Here? In Teton Gulch? To a gal in Teton Gulch?"

"Maried to a gal in Teton Gulch," he avowed. "I was aimin' to git hitched tomorrer, but they ain't a preacher or a justice of the peace in camp to tie the knot. But her uncle the Reverant Rembrandt Brockton is a circuit rider, and he's due to pass through Hell-Wind Pass on his way to Wahpeton today. I was aimin' to sneak out last night, hide in the hills till the stage come through, and then put the gold on it and bring Brother Rembrandt back with me. But yesterday I learnt Harrison's spies was watchin' me, and I'm scairt to go. Now Brother Rembrandt will go on to Wahpeton, not knowin' he's needed here, and no tellin' when I'll be able to git married--"

"Hold on," I said hurriedly, doing some quick thinking. I didn't want this here wedding to fall through. The more Blink was married to some gal in Teton, the less he could marry Dolly Rixby.

"Blink," I said, grasping his hand warmly, "never let it be said that a Elkins ever turned down a friend in distress. I'll take yore gold to Hell-Wind Pass and bring back Brother Rembrandt."

Blink fell onto my neck and wept with joy. "I'll never forgit this, Breckinridge," says he, "and I bet you won't neither! My hoss and pack-mule are in the stables behind the saloon."

"I don't need no pack-mule," I says. "Cap'n Kidd can pack the dust easy."

Cap'n Kidd was getting fed out in the corral next to the hotel. I went out there and got my saddle-bags, which is a lot bigger'n most saddle-bags, because all my plunder has to be made to fit my size. They're made outa three-ply elkskin, stitched with rawhide thongs, and a wildcat couldn't claw his way out of 'em.

I noticed quite a bunch of men standing around the corral looking at Cap'n Kidd, but thunk nothing of it, because he is a hoss which naturally attracks attention. But whilst I was getting my saddle-bags, a long lanky cuss with long yaller whiskers come up and said, says he: "Is that yore hoss in the corral?"

I says: "If he ain't he ain't nobody's."

"Well, he looks a whole lot like a hoss that was stole off my ranch six months ago," he said, and I seen ten or fifteen hard-looking _hombres_ gathering around me. I laid down my saddle-bags sudden-like and reched for my guns, when it occurred to me that if I had a fight I there I might get arrested and it would interfere with me bringing Brother Rembrandt in for the wedding.

"If that there is yore hoss," I said, "you ought to be able to lead him out of that there corral."

"Shore I can," he says with a oath. "And what's more, I aim'ta."

"That's right, Jake," says another feller. "Stand up for yore rights. Us boys is right behind you."

"Go ahead," I says. "If he's yore hoss, prove it. Go git him!"

He looked at me suspiciously, but he taken up a rope and clumb the fence and started towards Cap'n Kidd which was chawing on a block of hay in the middle of the corral. Cap'n Kidd throwed up his head and laid back his ears and showed his teeth, and Jake stopped sudden and turned pale.

"I--I don't believe that there _is_ my hoss, after all!" says he.

"Put that lasso on him!" I roared, pulling my right-hand gun. "You say he's yore'n; I say he's mine. One of us is a liar and a hoss-thief and I aim to prove which. Gwan, before I festoons yore system with lead polka-dots!"

"He looked at me and he looked at Cap'n Kidd, and he turned bright green all over. He looked again at my .45 which I now had cocked and p'inted at his long neck, which his adam's apple was going up and down like a monkey on a pole, and he begun to aidge towards Cap'n Kidd again, holding the rope behind him and sticking out one hand.

"Whoa, boy," he says, kind of shudderingly. "Whoa--good old feller--nice hossie--whoa, boy--_ow!"_

He let out a awful howl as Cap'n Kidd made a snap and bit a chunk out of his hide. He turned to run but Cap'n Kidd wheeled and let fly both heels which catched Jake in the seat of the britches, and his shriek of despair was horrible to hear as he went head-first through the corral-fence into a hoss-trough on the other side. From this he ariz dripping water, blood and profanity, and he shook a quivering fist at me and croaked: "You derned murderer! I'll have yore life for this!"

"I don't hold no conversation with hoss-thieves," I snorted, and picked up my saddle-bags and stalked through the crowd which give back in a hurry and take care to cuss under their breath when I tromped on their fool toes.

I taken the saddle-bags up to Blink's room, and told him about Jake, thinking he'd be amoosed, but he got a case of the aggers again, and said: "That was one of Harrison's men! He aimed to take yore hoss. It's a old trick, and honest folks don't dare interfere. Now they got you spotted! What'll you do?"

"Time, tide and a Elkins waits for no man!" I snorted, dumping the gold into the saddle-bags. "If that yaller-whiskered coyote wants any trouble, he can git a bellyfull! Don't worry, yore gold will be safe in my saddle-bags. It's as good as in the Wahpeton stage right now. And by midnight I'll be back with Brother Rembrandt Brockton to hitch you up with his niece."

"Don't yell so loud," begged Blink. "The cussed camp's full of spies. Some of 'em may be downstairs right now, lissenin'."

"I warn't speakin' above a whisper," I said indignantly.

"That bull's beller may pass for a whisper on Bear Creek," says he, wipin' off the sweat, "but I bet they can hear it from one end of the Gulch to the other'n, at least."

It's a pitable sight to see a man with a case of the scairts. I shook hands with him and left him pouring red licker down his gullet like it was water, and I swung the saddle-bags over my shoulder and went downstairs, and the barkeep leaned over the bar and whispered to me: "Look out for Jake Roman! He was in here a minute ago, lookin' for trouble. He pulled out jest before you come down, but he won't be forgittin' what yore hoss done to him."

"Not when he tries to set down, he won't," I agreed, and went out to the corral, and they was a crowd of men watching Cap'n Kidd eat his hay, and one of 'em seen me and hollered: "Hey, boys, here comes the giant! He's goin' to saddle that man-eatin' monster! Hey, Bill! Tell the boys at the bar."

And here come a whole passel of fellers running out of all the saloons, and they lined the corral fence solid, and started laying bets whether I'd get the saddle onto Cap'n Kidd, or get my brains kicked out. I thought miners must all be crazy. They ought've knowed I was able to saddle my own hoss.

Well, I saddled him and throwed on the saddle-bags and clumb aboard, and he pitched about ten jumps like he always does when I first fork him--'twarn't nothing, but them miners hollered like wild Injuns. And when he accidentally bucked hisself and me through the fence and knocked down a section of it along with fifteen men which was setting on the top rail, the way they howled you'd of thought something terrible had happened. Me and Cap'n Kidd don't bother about gates. We usually makes our own through whatever happens to be in front of us. But them miners is a weakly breed. As I rode out of town I seen the crowd dipping nine or ten of 'em into a hoss-trough to bring 'em to, on account of Cap'n Kidd having accidentally tromped on 'em.

Well, I rode out of the Gulch and up the ravine to the south and come out into the high-timbered country, and hit the old Injun trail Blink had told me about. It warn't traveled much. I didn't meet nobody after I left the Gulch. I figgered to hit Hell-Wind Pass at least a hour before sundown which would give me plenty of time. Blink said the stage passed through there about sundown. I'd have to bring back Brother Rembrandt on Cap'n Kidd, I reckoned, but that there hoss can carry double and still out-run and out-last any other hoss in the State of Nevada. I figgered on getting back to Teton about midnight or maybe a little later.

After I'd went several miles I come to Apache Canyon, which was a deep, narrer gorge, with a river at the bottom which went roaring and foaming along betwixt rock walls a hundred and fifty feet high. The old trail hit the rim at a place where the canyon warn't only about seventy foot wide, and somebody had felled a whopping big pine tree on one side so it fell acrost and made a foot-bridge, where a man could walk acrost. They'd onst been a gold strike in Apache Canyon, and a big camp there, but now it was plumb abandoned and nobody lives anywheres near it.

I turned east and follered the rim for about half a mile. Here I come into a old wagon road which was jest about growed up with saplings now, but it run down into a ravine into the bed of the canyon, and they was a bridge acrost the river which had been built during the days of the gold rush. Most of it had done been washed away by head-rises, but a man could still ride a hoss acrost what was left. So I done so, and rode up a ravine on the other side, and come out on high ground again.

I'd rode a few hundred yards past the mouth of the ravine when somebody said: "Hey!" and I wheeled with both guns in my hands. Out of the bresh sa'ntered a tall gent in a long frock tail coat and broad- brimmed hat.

"Who air you and what the hell you mean by hollerin' 'Hey!' at me?" I demanded courteously, p'inting my guns at him. A Elkins is always perlite.

"I am the Reverant Rembrandt Brockton, my good man," says he. "I am on my way to Teton Gulch to unite my niece and a young man of that camp in the bonds of holy matrimony."

"The he--you don't say!" I says. "Afoot?"

"I alit from the stagecoach at--ah--Hades-Wind Pass," says he. "Some very agreeable cowboys happened to be awaiting the stage there, and they offered to escort me to Teton."

"How come you knowed yore niece was wantin' to be united in acrimony?" I ast.

"The cowpersons informed me that such was the case," says he.

"Where-at are they now?" I next inquore.

"The mount with which they supplied me went lame a little while ago," says he. "They left me here while they went to procure another from a nearby ranch-house."

"I dunno who'd have a ranch anywheres around near here," I muttered. "They ain't got much sense leavin' you here by yore high lonesome."

"You mean to imply there is danger?" says he, blinking mildly at me.

"These here mountains is lousy with outlaws which would as soon kyarve a preacher's gullet as anybody's," I said, and then I thought of something else. "Hey!" I says. "I thought the stage didn't come through the Pass till sundown?"

"Such was the case," says he. "But the schedule has been altered."

"Heck!" I says. "I was aimin' to put this here gold on it which my saddle-bags is full of. Now I'll have to take it back to Teton with me. Well, I'll bring it out tomorrer and catch the stage then. Brother Rembrandt, I'm Breckinridge Elkins of Bear Creek, and I come out here to meet you and escort you back to the Gulch, so's you can unite yore niece and Blink Wiltshaw in the holy bounds of alimony. Come on. We'll ride double."

"But I must await my cowboy friends!" he said. "Ah, here they come now!"

I looked over to the east, and seen about fifteen men ride into sight and move towards us. One was leading a hoss without no saddle onto it.

"Ah, my good friends!" beamed Brother Rembrandt. "They have procured a mount for me, even as they promised."

He hauled a saddle out of the bresh, and says: "Would you please saddle my horse for me when they get here? I should be delighted to hold your rifle while you did so."

I started to hand him my Winchester, when the snap of a twig under a hoss's hoof made me whirl quick. A feller had jest rode out of a thicket about a hundred yards south of me, and he was raising a Winchester to his shoulder. I recognized him instantly. If us Bear Creek folks didn't have eyes like a hawk, we'd never live to get growed. It was Jake Roman!

Our Winchesters banged together. His lead fanned my ear and mine knocked him end-ways out of his saddle.

"Cowboys, hell!" I roared. "Them's Harrison's outlaws! I'll save you, Brother Rembrandt!"

I swooped him up with one arm and gouged Cap'n Kidd with the spurs and he went from there like a thunderbolt with its tail on fire. Them outlaws come on with wild yells. I ain't in the habit of running from people, but I was afeared they might do the Reverant harm if it come to a close fight, and if he stopped a chunk of lead, Blink might not get to marry his niece, and might get disgusted and go back to War Paint and start sparking Dolly Rixby again.

I was heading for the canyon, aiming to make a stand in the ravine if I had to, and them outlaws was killing their hosses trying to get to the bend of the trail ahead of me, and cut me off. Cap'n Kidd was running with his belly to the ground, but I'll admit Brother Rembrandt warn't helping me much. He was laying acrost my saddle with his arms and laigs waving wildly because I hadn't had time to set him comfortable, and when the horn jobbed him in the belly he uttered some words I wouldn't of expected to hear spoke by a minister of the gospel.

Guns begun to crack and lead hummed past us, and Brother Rembrandt twisted his head around and screamed: "Stop that--shootin', you--sons of--! You'll hit me!"

I thought it was kind of selfish from Brother Rembrandt not to mention me, too, but I said: "'Tain't no use to remonstrate with them skunks, Reverant. They ain't got no respeck for a preacher even."

But to my amazement, the shooting did stop, though them bandits yelled louder'n ever and flogged their cayuses harder. But about that time I seen they had me cut off from the lower canyon crossing, so I wrenched Cap'n Kidd into the old Injun track and headed straight for the canyon rim as hard as he could hammer, with the bresh lashing and snapping around us, and slapping Brother Rembrandt in the face when it whipped back. Them outlaws yelled and wheeled in behind us, but Cap'n Kidd drawed away from them with every stride, and the canyon rim loomed jest ahead of us.

"Pull up, you jack-eared son of Baliol!" howled Brother Rembrandt. "You'll go over the edge!"

"Be at ease, Reverant," I reassured him. "We're goin' over the log."

"Lord have mercy on my soul!" he squalled, and shet his eyes and grabbed a stirrup leather with both hands, and then Cap'n Kidd went over that log like thunder rolling on Jedgment Day.

I doubt if they is another hoss west of the Pecos, or east of it either, which would bolt out onto a log foot-bridge acrost a canyon a hundred and fifty foot deep like that, but they ain't nothing in this world Cap'n Kidd's scairt of except maybe me. He didn't slacken his speed none. He streaked acrost that log like it was a quarter-track, with the bark and splinters flying from under his hoofs, and if one foot had slipped a inch, it would of been Sally bar the door. But he didn't slip, and we was over and on the other side almost before you could catch yore breath.

"You can open yore eyes now, Brother Rembrandt," I said kindly, but he didn't say nothing. He'd fainted. I shaken him to wake him up, and in a flash he come to and give a shriek and grabbed my laig like a b'ar trap. I reckon he thought we was still on the log. I was trying to pry him loose when Cap'n Kidd chose that moment to run under a low- hanging oak tree limb. That's his idee of a joke. That there hoss has got a great sense of humor.

I looked up jest in time to see the limb coming, but not in time to dodge it. It was as big around as my thigh, and it took me smack acrost the wish-bone. We was going full-speed, and something had to give way. It was the girths--both of 'em. Cap'n Kidd went out from under me, and me and Brother Rembrandt and the saddle hit the ground together.

I jumped up but Brother Rembrandt laid there going: "Wug wug wug!" like water running out of a busted jug. And then I seen them cussed outlaws had dismounted off of their hosses and was coming acrost the bridge single file on foot, with their Winchesters in their hands.

I didn't waste no time shooting them misguided idjits. I run to the end of the foot-bridge, ignoring the slugs they slung at me. It was purty pore shooting, because they warn't shore of their footing, and didn't aim good. So I only got one bullet in the hind laig and was creased three or four other unimportant places--not enough to bother about.

I bent my knees and got hold of the end of the tree and heaved up with it, and them outlaws hollered and fell along it like ten pins, and dropped their Winchesters and grabbed holt of the log. I given it a shake and shook some of 'em off like persimmons off a limb after a frost, and then I swung the butt around clear of the rim and let go, and it went down end over end into the river a hundred and fifty feet below, with a dozen men still hanging onto it and yelling blue murder.

A regular geyser of water splashed up when they hit, and the last I seen of 'em they was all swirling down the river together in a thrashing tangle of arms and laigs and heads.

I remembered Brother Rembrandt and run back to where he'd fell, but he was already on his feet. He was kind of pale and wild-eyed and his laigs kept bending under him, but he had hold of the saddle-bags, and was trying to drag 'em into a thicket, mumbling kind of dizzily to hisself.

"It's all right now, Brother Rembrandt," I said kindly. "Them outlaws is all horse-de-combat now, as the French say. Blink's gold is safe."

"--" says Brother Rembrandt, pulling two guns from under his coat tails, and if I hadn't grabbed him, he would of ondoubtedly shot me. We rassled around and I protested: "Hold on, Brother Rembrandt! I ain't no outlaw. I'm yore friend, Breckinridge Elkins. Don't you remember?"

His only reply was a promise to eat my heart without no seasoning, and he then sunk his teeth into my ear and started to chaw it off, whilst gouging for my eyes with both thumbs, and spurring me severely in the hind laigs. I seen he was out of his head from fright and the fall he got, so I said sorrerfully: "Brother Rembrandt, I hates to do this. It hurts me more'n it does you, but we cain't waste time like this. Blink is waitin' to git married." And with a sigh I busted him over the head with the butt of my six-shooter, and he fell over and twitched a few times and then lay limp.

"Pore Brother Rembrandt," I sighed sadly. "All I hope is I ain't addled yore brains so's you've forgot the weddin' ceremony."

So as not to have no more trouble with him when, and if, he come to, I tied his arms and laigs with pieces of my lariat, and taken his weppins which was most surprising arms for a circuit rider. His pistols had the triggers out of 'em, and they was three notches on the butt of one, and four on t'other'n. Moreover he had a bowie knife in his boot, and a deck of marked kyards and a pair of loaded dice in his hip-pocket. But that warn't none of my business.

About the time I finished tying him up, Cap'n Kidd come back to see if he'd kilt me or jest crippled me for life. To show him I could take a joke too, I give him a kick in the belly, and when he could get his breath again, and ondouble hisself, I throwed the saddle on him. I spliced the girths with the rest of my lariat, and put Brother Rembrandt in the saddle and clumb on behind and we headed for Teton Gulch.

After a hour or so Brother Rembrandt come to and says kind of dizzily: "Was anybody saved from the typhoon?"

"Yo're all right, Brother Rembrandt," I assured him. "I'm takin' you to Teton Gulch."

"I remember," he muttered. "It all comes back to me. Damn Jake Roman! I thought it was a good idea, but it seems I was mistaken. I thought we had an ordinary human being to deal with. I know when I'm licked. I'll give you a thousand dollars to let me go."

"Take it easy, Brother Rembrandt," I soothed, seeing he was still delirious. "We'll be to Teton in no time."

"I don't want to go to Teton!" he hollered.

"You got to," I told him. "You got to unite yore niece and Blink Wiltshaw in the holy bums of parsimony."

"To hell with Blink Wiltshaw and my--niece!" he yelled.

"You ought to be ashamed usin' sech langwidge, and you a minister of the gospel," I reproved him sternly. His reply would of curled a Piute's hair.

I was so scandalized I made no reply. I was jest fixing to untie him, so's he could ride more comfortable, but I thought if he was that crazy, I better not. So I give no heed to his ravings which growed more and more unbearable as we progressed. In all my born days I never seen sech a preacher.

It was sure a relief to me to sight Teton at last. It was night when we rode down the ravine into the Gulch, and the dance halls and saloons was going full blast. I rode up behind the Yaller Dawg Saloon and hauled Brother Rembrandt off with me and sot him onto his feet, and he said, kind of despairingly: "For the last time, listen to reason. I've got fifty thousand dollars cached up in the hills. I'll give you every cent if you'll untie me."

"I don't want no money," I said. "All I want is for you to marry yore niece and Blink Wiltshaw. I'll untie you then."

"All right," he said. "All right! But untie me now!"

I was jest fixing to do it, when the bar-keep come out with a lantern, and he shone it on our faces and said in a startled tone: "Who the hell is that with you, Elkins?"

"You wouldn't never suspect it from his langwidge," I says, "but it's the Reverant Rembrandt Brockton."

"Are you crazy?" says the bar-keep. "That's Rattle snake Harrison!"

"I give up," said my prisoner. "I'm Harrison. I'm licked. Lock me up somewhere away from this lunatic!"

I was standing in a kind of daze, with my mouth open, but now I woke up and bellered: "_What?_ Yo're Harrison? I see it all now! Jake Roman overheard me talkin' to Blink Wiltshaw, and rode off and fixed it with you to fool me like you done, so's to git Blink's gold! That's why you wanted to hold my Winchester whilst I saddled yore cayuse."

"How'd you ever guess it?" he sneered. "We ought to have shot you from ambush like I wanted to, but Jake wanted to catch you alive and torture you to death account of your horse bitin' him. The fool must have lost his head at the last minute and decided to shoot you after all. If you hadn't recognized him we'd had you surrounded and stuck up before you knew what was happening."

"But now the real preacher's gone on to Wahpeton!" I hollered. "I got to foller him and bring him back--"

"Why, he's here," said one of the men which was gathering around us. "He come in with his niece a hour ago on the stage from War Paint."

"War Paint?" I howled, hit in the belly by a premonishun. I run into the saloon, where they was a lot of people, and there was Blink and a gal holding hands in front of a old man with a long white beard, and he had a book in his hand, and the other'n lifted in the air. He was saying: "--And I now pernounces you-all man and wife. Them which God has j'ined togither let no snake-hunter put asunder."

"Dolly!" I yelled. Both of 'em jumped about four foot and whirled, and Dolly jumped in front of Blink and spread her arms like she was shooing chickens.

"Don't you tech him, Breckinridge!" she hollered. "I jest married him and I don't aim for no Humbolt grizzly to spile him!"

"But I don't _sabe_ all this--" I said dizzily, nervously fumbling with my guns which is a habit of mine when upsot.

Everybody in the wedding party started ducking out of line, and Blink said hurriedly: "It's this way, Breck. When I made my pile so onexpectedly quick, I sent for Dolly to come and marry me, like she'd promised that night, jest after you pulled out for Yavapai. I _was_ aimin' to take my gold out today, like I told you, so me and Dolly could go to San Francisco on our honeymoon, but I learnt Harrison's gang was watchin' me, jest like I told you. I wanted to git my gold out, and I wanted to git you out of the way before Dolly and her uncle got here on the War Paint stage, so I told you that there lie about Brother Rembrandt bein' on the Wahpeton stage. It was the only lie."

"You said you was marryin' a gal in Teton," I accused fiercely.

"Well," says he, "I did marry her in Teton. You know, Breck, all's fair in love and war."

"Now, now, boys," says Brother Rembrandt--the real one, I mean. "The gal's married, yore rivalry is over, and they's no use holdin' grudges. Shake hands and be friends."

"All right," I said heavily. No man can't say I ain't a good loser. I was cut deep, but I concealed my busted heart.

Leastways I concealed it all I was able to. Them folks which says I crippled Blink Wiltshaw with malice aforethought is liars which I'll sweep the road with when I catches 'em. I didn't aim to break his cussed arm when we shaken hands. It was jest the convulsive start I give when I suddenly thought of what Glory Mc-Graw would say when she heard about this mess. And they ain't no use in folks saying that what imejitly follered was done in revenge for Dolly busting me in the head with that cuspidor. When I thought of the rawhiding I'd likely get from Glory McGraw I kind of lost my head and stampeded like a loco bull. When something got in my way I removed it without stopping to see what it was. How was I to know it was Dolly's Uncle Rembrandt which I absent-mindedly throwed through a winder. And as for them fellers which claims they was knocked down and trompled on, they ought to of got outa my way, dern 'em.

As I headed down the trail on Cap'n Kidd I wondered if I ever really loved Dolly, after all, because I was less upsot over her marrying another feller than I was about what Glory McGraw would say.

CHAPTER X

THE HAUNTED MOUNTAIN

THEY SAY when a critter is mortally wounded he generally heads for his den, so maybe that's why I headed for Bear Creek when I rode out of Teton Gulch that night; I'd had about as much civilization as I could stand for awhile.

But the closer I got to Bear Creek the more I thought about Glory McGraw and I bust into profuse sweat every time I thought about what she'd say to me, because I'd sent her word by one of the Braxton boys that I aimed to bring Dolly Rixby to Bear Creek as Miz Breckinridge Elkins.

I thought about this so much that when I cut the Chawed Ear road I turned aside and headed up it. I'd met a feller a few miles back which told me about a rodeo which was going to take place at Chawed Ear, so I thought it was a good way to pick up some easy money whilst avoiding Glory at the same time. But I forgot I had to pass by the cabin of one of my relatives.

The reason I detests tarantulas, stinging lizards, and hydrophobia skunks is because they reminds me so much of Aunt Lavaca Grimes, which my Uncle Jacob Grimes married in a absent-minded moment, when he was old enough to know better.

That there woman's voice plumb puts my teeth on aidge, and it has the same effect on Cap'n Kidd, which don't otherwise shy at nothing less'n a cyclone. So when she stuck her head out of her cabin as I was riding by and yelled: "Breck-in-ri-i-idge!" Cap'n Kidd jumped like he was shot, and then tried to buck me off.

"Stop tormentin' that pore animal and come here," commanded Aunt Lavaca, whilst I was fighting for my life agen Cap'n Kidd's spine- twisting sunfishing. "Always showin' off! I never see such a inconsiderate, worthless, no-good--"

She kept on yapping away till I had wore him down and reined up alongside the cabin-stoop, and said: "What you want, Aunt Lavaca?"

She give me a scornful stare, and put her hands onto her hips and glared at me like I was something she didn't like the smell of.

"I want you to go git yore Uncle Jacob and bring him home," she said at last. "He's off on one of his idjiotic prospectin' sprees again. He snuck out before daylight with the bay mare and a pack mule--I wisht I'd woke up and caught him. I'd of fixed him! If you hustle you can catch him this side of Haunted Mountain Gap. You bring him back if you have to lasso him and tie him to his saddle. Old fool! Off huntin' gold when they's work to be did in the alfalfa fields. Says he ain't no farmer. Huh! I 'low I'll make a farmer outa him yet. You git goin'."

"But I ain't got time to go chasin' Uncle Jacob all over Haunted Mountain," I protested. "I'm headin' for the rodeo over to Chawed Ear. I'm goin' to winme a prize bull-doggin' some steers--"

"Bull-doggin'!" she snapped. "A fine ockerpashun! Gwan, you worthless loafer! I ain't goin' to stand here all day argyin' with a big ninny like you be. Of all the good-for-nothin', triflin', lunk- headed--"

When Aunt Lavaca starts in like that you might as well travel. She can talk steady for three days and nights without repeating herself, with her voice getting louder and shriller all the time till it nigh splits a body's ear drums. She was still yelling at me as I rode up the trail towards Haunted Mountain Gap, and I could hear her long after I couldn't see her no more.

Pore Uncle Jacob! He never had much luck prospecting, but trailing around with a jackass is a lot better'n listening to Aunt Lavaca. A jackass's voice is mild and soothing alongside of her'n.

Some hours later I was climbing the long rise that led up to the gap and I realized I had overtook the old coot when something went _ping!_ up on the slope, and my hat flew off. I quick reined Cap'n Kidd behind a clump of bresh, and looked up towards the Gap, and seen a pack-mule's rear end sticking out of a cluster of boulders.

"You quit that shootin' at me, Uncle Jacob!" I roared.

"You stay whar you be," his voice come back rambunctious and warlike. "I know Lavacky sent you after me, but I ain't goin' home. I'm onto somethin' big at last, and I don't aim to be interfered with."

"What you mean?" I demanded.

"Keep back or I'll ventilate you," he promised. "I'm goin' after the Lost Haunted Mine."

"You been huntin' that thing for fifty years," I snorted.

"This time I finds it," he says. "I bought a map off'n a drunk Mexican down to Perdition. One of his ancestors was a Injun which helped pile up the rocks to hide the mouth of the cave whar it is."

"Why didn't he go find it and git the gold?" I ast.

"He's scairt of ghosts," said Uncle Jacob. "All Mexes is awful superstitious. This 'un'd ruther set and drink, anyhow. They's millions in gold in that there mine. I'll shoot you before I'll go home. Now will you go on back peacable, or will you throw in with me? I might need you, in case the pack-mule plays out."

"I'll come with you," I said, impressed. "Maybe you have got somethin', at that. Put up yore Winchester, I'm comin'."

He emerged from his rocks, a skinny, leathery old cuss, and he said: "What about Lavacky? If you don't come back with me, she'll foller us herself, she's that strong-minded."

"You can write, cain't you, Uncle Jacob?" I said, and he said, "Yeah, I always carries me a pencil-stub in my saddle-bags. Why?"

"We'll write her a note," I said. "Joe Hopkins always comes down through the Gap onst a week on his way to Chawed Ear. He's due through here today. We'll stick the note on a tree, where he'll see it and take it to her."

So I tore a piece of wrapping paper off'n a can of tomatoes Uncle Jacob had in his pack, and he got out his pencil stub, and writ as I told him, as follers:

"Dere Ant Lavaca: I am takin uncle Jacob way up in the mountins don't try to foler us it wont do no good gold is what Im after. Breckinridge."

We folded it and I told Uncle Jacob to write on the outside:

"Dere Joe: pleeze take this here note to Miz Lavaca Grimes on the Chawed Ear rode."

It was lucky Joe knowed how to read. I made Uncle Jacob read me what he had writ to be sure he had got it right. Education is a good thing in its place, but it never taken the place of common hoss-sense.

But he had got it right for a wonder, so I stuck the note on a spruce limb, and me and Uncle Jacob sot out for the higher ranges. He started telling me all about the Lost Haunted Mine again, like he'd already did about forty times before. Seems like they was onst a old prospector which stumbled onto a cave about sixty years before then, which the walls was solid gold and nuggets all over the floor till a body couldn't walk, as big as mushmelons. But the Injuns jumped him and run him out and he got lost and nearly starved in the desert, and went crazy. When he come to a settlement and finally got his mind back, he tried to lead a party back to it, but never could find it. Uncle Jacob said the Injuns had took rocks and bresh and hid the mouth of the cave so nobody could tell it was there. I ast him how he knowed the Injuns done that, and he said it was common knowledge. He said any fool ought a know that's jest what they done.

"This here mine," says Uncle Jacob, "is located in a hidden valley which lies away up amongst the high ranges. I ain't never seen it, and I thought I'd explored these mountains plenty. Ain't nobody more familiar with 'em than me, except old Joshua Braxton. But it stands to reason that the cave is awful hard to find, or somebody'd already found it. Accordin' to this here map, that lost valley must lie jest beyond Wildcat Canyon. Ain't many white men know whar that is, even. We're headin' there."

We had left the Gap far behind us, and was moving along the slanting side of a sharp-angled crag whilst he was talking. As we passed it we seen two figgers with hosses emerge from the other side, heading in the same direction we was, so our trails converged. Uncle Jacob glared and reched for his Winchester.

"Who's that?" he snarled.

"The big 'un's Bill Glanton," I said. "I never seen t'other'n."

"And nobody else, outside of a freak show," growled Uncle Jacob.

The other feller was a funny-looking little maverick, with laced boots and a cork sun-helmet and big spectacles. He sot his hoss like he thought it was a rocking-chair, and held his reins like he was trying to fish with 'em. Glanton hailed us. He was from Texas, original, and was rough in his speech and free with his weppins, but me and him had always got along together very well.

"Where you-all goin'?" demanded Uncle Jacob.

"I am Professor Van Brock, of New York," said the tenderfoot, whilst Bill was getting rid of his terbaccer wad. "I have employed Mr. Glanton, here, to guide me up into the mountains. I am on the track of a tribe of aborigines, which according to fairly well substantiated rumor, have inhabited the haunted Mountains since time immemorial."

"Lissen here, you four-eyed runt," said Uncle Jacob in wrath, "air you givin' me the hoss-laugh?"

"I assure yon that equine levity is the furthest thing from my thoughts," says Van Brock. "Whilst touring the country in the interests of science, I heard the rumors to which I have referred. In a village possessing the singular appellation of Chawed Ear, I met an aged prospector who told me that he had seen one of the aborigines, clad in the skin of a wild animal and armed with a bludgeon. The wild man, he said, emitted a most peculiar and piercing cry when sighted, and fled into the recesses of the hills. I am confident that it is some survivor of a pre-Indian race, and I am determined to investigate."

"They ain't no sech critter in these hills," snorted Uncle Jacob. "I've roamed all over 'em for fifty year, and I ain't seen no wild man."

"Well," says Glanton, "they's _somethin'_ onnatural up there, because I been hearin' some funny yarns myself. I never thought I'd be huntin' wild men," he says, "but since that hash-slinger in Perdition turned me down to elope with a travelin' salesman, I welcomes the chance to lose myself in the mountains and forgit the perfidy of women-kind. What you-all doin' up here? Prospectin'?" he said, glancing at the tools on the mule.

"Not in earnest," said Uncle Jacob hurriedly. "We're jest whilin' away our time. They ain't no gold in these mountains."

"Folks says that Lost Haunted Mine is up here somewheres," said Glanton.

"A pack of lies," snorted Uncle Jacob, busting into a sweat. "Ain't no sech mine. Well, Breckinridge, le's be shovin'. Got to make Antelope Peak before sundown."

"I thought we was goin' to Wildcat Canyon," I says, and he give me a awful glare, and said: "Yes, Breckinridge, that's right, Antelope Peak, jest like you said. So long, gents."

"So long," says Glanton.

So we turned off the trail almost at right angles to our course, me follering Uncle Jacob bewilderedly. When we was out of sight of the others, he reined around again.

"When Nature give you the body of a giant, Breckinridge," he said, "she plumb forgot to give you any brains to go along with yore muscles. You want everybody to know what we're lookin' for, and whar?"

"Aw," I said, "them fellers is jest lookin' for wild men."

"Wild men!" he snorted. "They don't have to go no further'n Chawed Ear on payday night to find more wild men than they could handle. I ain't swallerin' no sech tripe. Gold is what they're after, I tell you. I seen Glanton talkin' to that Mex in Perdition the day I bought that map from him. I believe they either got wind of that mine, or know I got that map, or both."

"What you goin' to do?" I ast him.

"Head for Wildcat Canyon by another trail," he said.

So we done so and arriv there after night, him not willing to stop till we got there. It was deep, with big high cliffs cut with ravines and gulches here and there, and very wild in appearance. We didn't descend into the canyon that night, but camped on a plateau above it. Uncle Jacob 'lowed we'd begin exploring next morning. He said they was lots of caves in the canyon, and he'd been in all of 'em. He said he hadn't never found nothing except b'ars and painters and rattlesnakes, but he believed one of them caves went on through into another hidden canyon, and that was where the gold was at.

Next morning I was awoke by Uncle Jacob shaking me, and his whiskers was curling with rage.

"What's the matter?" I demanded, setting up and pulling my guns.

"They're here!" he squalled. "Dawgone it, I suspected 'em all the time! Git up, you big lunk! Don't set there gawpin' with a gun in each hand like a idjit! They're here, I tell you!"

"Who's here?" I ast.

"That dern tenderfoot and his cussed Texas gunfighter," snarled Uncle Jacob. "I was up jest at daylight, and purty soon I seen a wisp of smoke curlin' up from behind a big rock t'other side of the flat. I snuck over there, and there was Glanton fryin' bacon, and Van Brock was pertendin' to be lookin' at some flowers with a magnifyin' glass-- the blame fake. He ain't no perfessor. I bet he's a derned crook. They're follerin' us. They aim to murder us and take my map."

"Aw, Glanton wouldn't do that," I said, and Uncle Jacob said: "You shet up! A man will do anything whar gold's consarned. Dang it all, git up and do somethin'! Air you goin' to set there, you big lummox, and let us git murdered in our sleep?"

That's the trouble of being the biggest man in yore clan; the rest of the family always dumps all the onpleasant jobs onto yore shoulders. I pulled on my boots and headed acrost the flat with Uncle Jacob's war-songs ringing in my ears, and I didn't notice whether he was bringing up the rear with his Winchester or not.

They was a scattering of trees on the flat, and about halfway acrost a figger emerged from amongst it and headed my direction with fire in his eye. It was

Glanton.

"So, you big mountain grizzly," he greeted me rambunctiously, "you was goin' to Antelope Peak, hey? Kinda got off the road, didn't you? Oh, we're on to you, we air!"

"What you mean?" I demanded. He was acting like he was the one which ought a feel righteously indignant instead of me.

"You know what I mean!" he says, frothing slightly at the mouth. "I didn't believe it when Van Brock first said he suspicioned you, even though you _hombres_ did act funny yesterday when he met you on the trail. But this mornin' when I glimpsed yore fool Uncle Jacob spyin' on our camp, and then seen him sneakin' off through the bresh, I knowed Van Brock was right. Yo're after what we're after, and you- all resorts to dirty, onderhanded tactics. Does you deny yo're after the same thing we air?"

"Naw, I don't," I said. "Uncle Jacob's got more right to it than you-all has. And when you says we uses onderhanded tricks, yo're a liar."

"That settles it!" gnashed he. "Go for yore gun!"

"I don't want to perforate you," I growled.

"I ain't hankerin' to conclude yore mortal career," he admitted. "But Haunted Mountain ain't big enough, for both of us. Take off yore guns, and I'll maul the livin' daylights out you, big as you be."

I unbuckled my gun-belt, and hung it on a limb, and he laid off his'n, and hit me in the stummick and on the ear and in the nose, and then he busted me in the jaw and knocked out a tooth. This made me mad, so I taken him by the neck and throwed him agen the ground so hard it jolted all the wind outa him. I then sot on him and started banging his head agen a convenient boulder, and his cussing was terrible to hear.

"If you-all had acted like white men," I gritted, "we'd of _give_ you a share in that there mine."

"What the hell air you talkin' about?" he gurgled, trying to haul his bowie out of his boot which I had my knee on.

"The Lost Haunted Mine, what you think?" I snarled, getting a fresh grip on his ears.

"Hold on!" he protested. "You mean you-all air jest lookin' for gold? Is that on the level?"

I was so astonished I quit hammering his skull agen the rock.

"Why, what else?" I demanded. "Ain't you-all follerin' us to steal Uncle jacob's map which shows where at the mine is hid?"

"Git offa me!" he snorted disgustfully, taking advantage of my surprise to push me off. "Hell!" says he, starting to knock the dust offa his britches. "I might of knowed that tenderfoot was wool- gatherin'. After we seen you-all yesterday, and he heard you mention Wildcat Canyon, he told me he believed you was follerin' us. He said that yarn about prospectin' was jest a blind. He said he believed you was workin' for a rival scientific society to git ahead of us and capture that there wild man yoreselves."

"What?" I said. "You mean that wild man yarn is straight goods?"

"Far as we're consarned," said Bill. "Prospectors is been tellin' some onusual stories about Wildcat Canyon. Well, I laughed at him at first, but he kept on usin' so many .45 calibre words that he got me to believin' it might be so. 'Cause, after all, here was me guidin' a tenderfoot on the trail of a wild man, and they warn't no reason to think that you and Jacob Grimes was any more sensible than me.

"Then, this mornin' when I seen Jacob peekin' at me from the bresh, I decided Van Brock must be right. You-all hadn't never went to Antelope Peak. The more I thought it over, the more sartain I was that you was follerin' us to steal our wild man, so I started over to have a show-down."

"Well," I said, "we've reched a understandin'. You don't want our mine, and we sure don't want yore wild man. They's plenty of them amongst my relatives on Bear Creek. Le's git Van Brock and lug him over to our camp and explain things to him and my weak-minded uncle."

"All right," said Glanton, buckling on his guns. "Hey, what's that?"

From down in the canyon come a yell: "Help! Aid! Assistance!"

"It's Van Brock!" yelped Glanton. "He's wandered down into the canyon by hisself! Come on!"

Right nigh their camp they was a ravine leading down to the floor of the canyon. We pelted down that at full speed and emerged nigh the wall of the cliffs. They was the black mouth of a cave showing nearby, in a kind of cleft, and jest outside this cleft Van Brock was staggering around, yowling like a hound-dawg with his tail caught in the door.

His cork helmet was laying on the ground all bashed outa shape, and his specs was lying nigh it. He had a knot on his head as big as a turnip and he was doing a kind of ghost-dance or something all over the place.

He couldn't see very good without his specs, 'cause when he sighted us he give a shriek and started legging it up the canyon, seeming to think we was more enemies. Not wanting to indulge in no sprinting in that heat, Bill shot a heel offa his boot, and that brung him down squalling blue murder.

"Help!" he shrieked. "Mr. Glanton! Help! I am being attacked! Help!"

"Aw, shet up," snorted Bill. "I'm Glanton. Yo're all right. Give him his specs, Breck. Now, what's the matter?"

He put 'em on, gasping for breath, and staggered up, wild-eyed, and p'inted at the cave, and hollered: "The wild man! I saw him, as I descended into the canyon on a private exploring expedition! A giant with a panther's skin about his waist, and a club in his hand. When I sought to apprehend him he dealt me a murderous blow with the bludgeon and fled into that cavern. He should be arrested!"

I looked into the cave. It was too dark to see anything except for a hoot-owl.

"He must of saw somethin', Breck," said Glanton, hitching his gun-harness. "_Somethin'_ shore cracked him on the conk. I've been hearin' some queer tales about this canyon, myself. Maybe I better sling some lead in there--"

"No, no, no!" broke in Van Brock. "We must capture him alive!"

"What's goin' on here?" said a voice, and we turned to see Uncle Jacob approaching with his Winchester in his hands.

"Everything's all right, Uncle Jacob," I said. "They don't want yore mine. They're after the wild man, like they said, and we got him cornered in that there cave."

"All right, huh?" he snorted. "I reckon you thinks it's all right for you to waste yore time with sech dern foolishness when you oughta be helpin' me look for my mine. A big help you be!"

"Where was you whilst I was argyin' with Bill here?" I demanded.

"I knowed you could handle the situation, so I started explorin' the canyon," he said. "Come on, we got work to do."

"But the wild man!" cried Van Brock. "Your nephew would be invaluable in securing the specimen. Think of science! Think of progress! Think of--"

"Think of a striped skunk!" snorted Uncle Jacob. "Breckinridge, air you comin'?"

"Aw, shet up," I said disgustedly. "You both make me tired. I'm goin' in there and run that wild man out, and Bill, you shoot him in the hind-laig as he comes out, so's we can catch him and tie him up."

"But you left yore guns hangin' onto that limb up on the plateau," objected Glanton.

"I don't need 'em," I said. "Didn't you hear Van Brock say we was to catch him alive? If I started shootin' in the dark I might rooin him."

"All right," says Bill, cocking his six-shooters. "Go ahead. I figger yo're a match for any wild man that ever come down the pike."

So I went into the cleft and entered the cave and it was dark as all get-out. I groped my way along and discovered the main tunnel split in two, so I taken the biggest one. It seemed to get darker the further I went, and purty soon I bumped into something big and hairy and it went "Wump!" and grabbed me.

Thinks I, it's the wild man, and he's on the war-path. So I waded into him and he waded into me, and we tumbled around on the rocky floor in the dark, biting and mauling and tearing. Bear Creek is famed far and wide for its ring-tailed scrappers, and I don't have to repeat I'm the fightin'est of 'em all, but that cussed wild man sure give me my hands full. He was the biggest, hairiest critter I ever laid hands on, and he had more teeth and talons than I thought a human could possibly have. He chawed me with vigor and enthusiasm, and he walzed up and down my frame free and hearty, and swept the floor with me till I was groggy.

For a while I thought I was going to give up the ghost, and I thought with despair of how humiliated my relatives on Bear Creek would be to hear their champeen battler had been clawed to death by a wild man in a cave.

This thought maddened me so I redoubled my onslaughts, and the socks I give him ought to of laid out any man, wild or tame, to say nothing of the pile-driver kicks in his belly, and butting him with my head so he gasped. I got what felt like a ear in my mouth and commenced chawing on it, and presently, what with this and other mayhem I committed on him, he give a most inhuman squall and bust away and went lickety-split for the outside world.

I riz up and staggered after him, hearing a wild chorus of yells break forth, but no shots. I bust out into the open, bloody all over, and my clothes hanging in tatters.

"Where is he?" I hollered. "Did you let him git away?"

"Who?" said Glanton, coming out from behind a boulder, whilst Van Brock and Uncle Jacob dropped down out of a tree nearby.

"The wild man, damn it!" I roared.

"We ain't seen no wild man," said Glanton.

"Well, what was that thing I jest run outa the cave?" I hollered.

"That was a grizzly b'ar," said Glanton.

"Yeah," sneered Uncle Jacob, "and that was Van Brock's 'wild man'! And now, Breckinridge, if yo're through playin', we'll--"

"No, no!" hollered Van Brock, jumping up and down. "It was indubitably a human being which smote me and fled into the cavern. Not a bear! It is still in there somewhere, unless there is another exit to the cavern."

"Well, he ain't in there now," said Uncle Jacob, peering into the mouth of the cave. "Not even a wild man would run into a grizzly's cave, or if he did, he wouldn't stay long--_ooomp!"_

A rock come whizzing out of the cave and hit Uncle Jacob in the belly, and he doubled up on the ground.

"Aha!" I roared, knocking up Glanton's ready six-shooter. "I know! They's two tunnels in there. He's in that smaller cave. I went into the wrong one! Stay here, you-all, and gimme room! This time I gits him!"

With that I rushed into the cave mouth again, disregarding some more rocks which emerged, and plunged into the smaller opening. It was dark as pitch, but I seemed to be running along a narrer tunnel, and ahead of me I heard bare feet pattering on the rock. I follered 'em at full lope, and presently seen a faint hint of light. The next minute I rounded a turn and come out into a wide place, which was lit by a shaft of light coming in through a cleft in the wall, some yards up. In the light I seen a fantastic figger climbing up on a ledge, trying to rech that cleft.

"Come down offa that!" I thundered, and give a leap and grabbed the ledge by one hand and hung on, and reched for his laigs with t'other hand. He give a squall as I grabbed his ankle and splintered his club over my head. The force of the lick broke off the lip of the rock ledge I was holding on to, and we crashed to the floor together, because I didn't let loose of him. Fortunately, I hit the rock floor headfirst which broke my fall and kept me from fracturing any of my important limbs, and his head hit my jaw, which rendered him unconscious.

I riz up and picked up my limp captive and carried him out into the daylight where the others was waiting. I dumped him on the ground and they stared at him like they couldn't believe it. He was a ga'nt old cuss with whiskers about a foot long and matted hair, and he had a mountain lion's hide tied around his waist.

"A white man!" enthused Van Brock, dancing up and down. "An unmistakable Caucasian! This is stupendous! A pre-historic survivor of a pre-Indian epoch! What an aid to anthropology! A wild man! A veritable wild man!"

"Wild man, hell!" snorted Uncle Jacob. "That there's old Joshua Braxton, which was trying to marry that old maid schoolteacher down at Chawed Ear all last winter."

"_I_ was tryin' to marry her!" said Joshua bitterly, setting up suddenly and glaring at all of us. "That there is good, that there is! And me all the time fightin' for my life agen it. Her and all her relations was tryin' to marry _her_ to me. They made my life a curse. They was finally all set to kidnap me and marry me by force. That's why I come away off up here, and put on this rig to scare folks away. All I crave is peace and quiet and no dern women."

Van Brock begun to cry because they warn't no wild man, and Uncle Jacob said: "Well, now that this dern foolishness is settled, maybe I can git to somethin' important. Joshua, you know these mountains even better'n I do. I want ya to help me find the Lost Haunted Mine."

"There ain't no sech mine," said Joshua. "That old prospector imagined all that stuff whilst he was wanderin' around over the desert crazy."

"But I got a map I bought from a Mexican in Perdition!" hollered Uncle Jacob.

"Lemme see that map," said Glanton. "Why, hell," he said, "that there is a fake. I seen that Mexican drawin' it, and he said he was goin' to try to sell it to some old jassack for the price of a drunk."

Uncle Jacob sot down on a rock and pulled his whiskers. "My dreams is bust. I'm goin' to go home to my wife," he said weakly.

"You must be desperate if it's come to that," said old Joshua acidly. "You better stay up here. If they ain't no gold, they ain't no women to torment a body, neither."

"Women is a snare and a delusion," agreed Glanton. "Van Brock can go back with these fellers. I'm stayin' with Joshua."

"You all oughta be ashamed talkin' about women that way," I reproached 'em. "I've suffered from the fickleness of certain women more'n either of you snake-hunters, but I ain't let it sour me on the sex. What," I says, waxing oratorical, "in this lousy and troubled world of six-shooters and centipedes, what, I asts you-all, can compare to women's gentle sweetness--"

"There the scoundrel is!" screeched a familiar voice like a rusty buzzsaw. "Don't let him git away! Shoot him if he tries to run!"

We turned sudden. We'd been argying so loud amongst ourselves we hadn't noticed a gang of folks coming down the ravine. There was Aunt Lavaca and the sheriff of Chawed Ear with ten men, and they all p'inted sawed-off shotguns at me.

"Don't git rough, Elkins," warned the sheriff nervously. "They're loaded with buckshot and ten-penny nails. I knows yore repertation and I takes no chances. I arrests you for the kidnappin' of Jacob Grimes."

"Air you plumb crazy?" I demanded.

"Kidnappin'!" hollered Aunt Lavaca, waving a piece of paper. "Abductin' yore pore old uncle! Aimin' to hold him for ransom! It's all writ down over yore name right here on this here paper! Sayin' yo're takin' Jacob away off into the mountains--warnin' me not to try to foller! Same as threatenin' me! I never heered of sech doin's! Soon as that good-for-nothin' Joe Hopkins brung me that there impertent letter, I went right after the sheriff.... Joshua Braxton, what _air_ you doin' in them ondecent togs? My land, I dunno what we're a-comin' to! Well, sheriff, what you standin' there for like a ninny? Why'n't you put some handcuffs and chains and shackles onto him? Air you scairt of the big lunkhead?"

"Aw, heck," I said. "This is all a mistake. I warn't threatenin' nobody in that there letter--"

"Then where's Jacob?" she demanded. "Perjuice him imejitly, or--"

"He ducked into the cave," said Glanton.

I stuck my head in and roared: "Uncle Jacob! You come outa there and explain before I come in after you!"

He snuck out looking meek and down-trodden, and I says: "You tell these idjits that I ain't no kidnapper."

"That's right," he said. "I brung him along with me."

"Hell!" said the sheriff disgustedly. "Have we come all this way on a wild goose chase? I should of knew better'n to lissen to a woman--"

"You shet yore fool mouth!" squalled Aunt Lavaca. "A fine sheriff you be. Anyway--what was Breckinridge doin' up here with you, Jacob?"

"He was helpin' me look for a mine, Lavacky," he said.

"_Helpin'_ you?" she screeched. "Why, I sent him to fetch you back! Breckinridge Elkins, I'll tell yore pap about this, you big, lazy, good-for-nothin', low-down, ornery--"

"Aw, SHET UP!" I roared, exasperated beyond endurance. I seldom lets my voice go its full blast. Echoes rolled through the canyon like thunder, the trees shook and pine cones fell like hail, and rocks tumbled down the mountain sides.

Aunt Lavaca staggered backwards with a outraged squall.

"Jacob!" she hollered. "Air you goin' to 'low that ruffian to use that there tone of voice to me? I demands that you flail the livin' daylights outa the scoundrel right now!"

"Now, now, Lavacky," he started soothing her, and she give him a clip under the ear that changed ends with him, and the sheriff and his posse and Van Brock took out up the ravine like the devil was after 'em.

Glanton bit hisself off a chaw of terbaccer and says to me, he says: "Well, what was you fixin' to say about women's gentle sweetness?"

"Nothin'," I snarled. "Come on, let's git goin'. I yearns to find a more quiet and secluded spot than this here'n. I'm stayin' with Joshua and you and the grizzly."

CHAPTER XI

EDUCATE OR BUST

Me and Bill Glanton and Joshua Braxton stood on the canyon rim and listened to the orations of Aunt Lavaca Grimes fading in the distance as she herded Uncle Jacob for the home range.

"There," says Joshua sourly, "goes the most hen-pecked pore critter in the Humbolts. For sech I has only pity and contempt. He's that scairt of a woman he don't dast call his soul his own."

"And what air we, I'd like to know?" says Glanton, slamming his hat down on the ground. "What right has we to criticize Jacob, when it's on account of women that we're hidin' in these cussed mountains? Yo're here, Joshua, because yo're scairt of that old maid schoolteacher. Breck's here because a gal in War Paint give him the gate. And I'm here sourin' my life because a hash-slinger done me wrong!"

"I'm tellin' you gents," says Bill, "no woman is goin' to rooin my life! Lookin' at Jacob Grimes has teached me a lesson. I ain't goin' to eat my heart out up here in the mountains in the company of a soured old hermit and a love-lorn human grizzly. I'm goin' to War Paint, and bust the bank at the Yaller Dawg's Tail gamblin' hall, and then I'm goin' to head for San Francisco and a high-heeled old time! The bright lights calls me, gents, and I heeds the summons! You-all better take heart and return to yore respective corrals."

"Not me," I says. "If I go back to Bear Creek without no gal, Glory McGraw will rawhide the life outa me."

"As for me returnin' to Chawed Ear," snarls old Joshua, "whilst that old she-mudhen is anywhere in the vicinity, I haunts the wilds and solitudes, if it takes all the rest of my life. You 'tend to yore own business, Bill Glanton."

"Oh, I forgot to tell you," says Bill. "So dern many things is been happenin' I ain't had time to tell you. But that old maid schoolteacher ain't to Chawed Ear no more. She pulled out for Arizona three weeks ago."

"That's news!" says Joshua, straightening up and throwing away his busted club. "Now I can return and take my place among men--Hold on!" says he, reching for his club again. "Likely they'll be gittin' some other old harridan to take her place! That new-fangled schoolhouse they got at Chawed Ear is a curse and a blight. We'll never be rid of female school-shooters. I better stay up here, after all."

"Don't worry," says Bill. "I seen a pitcher of the gal that's comin' to take Miss Stark's place, and I can assure you right now, that a gal as young and purty as her wouldn't never try to sot her brand on no old buzzard like you."

I come alive suddenly.

"Young and purty, you says?" I says.

"As a pitcher," he says. "First time I ever knowed a schoolteacher could be less'n forty and have a face that didn't look like the beginnin's of a long drought. She's due into Chawed Ear tomorrer, on the stage from the East, and the whole town's goin' to turn out to welcome her. The mayor aims to make a speech, if he's sober enough, and they've got together a band to play."

"Damn foolishness!" snorted Joshua. "I don't take no stock in eddication."

"I dunno," I said. "They's times when I wish I could read and write."

"What would you read outside of the labels on whisky bottles?" snorted old Joshua.

"Everybody ought to know how," I said defiantly. "We ain't never had no school on Bear Creek."

"Funny how a purty face changes a man's views," says Bill. "I remember onst Miss Stark ast you how you folks up on Bear Creek would like for her to come up there and teach yore chillern, and you taken one look at her face, and told her that it was agen the principles of Bear Creek to have their peaceful innercence invaded by the corruptin' influences of education, and the folks was all banded together to resist sech corruption."

I ignored him and says: "It's my duty to Bear Creek to pervide culture for the risin' generation. We ain't never had a school, but by golly, we're goin' to, if I have to lick every old moss-back in the Humbolts. I'll build the cabin for the school-house myself."

"And where'll you git a teacher?" ast old Joshua. "This gal that's comin' to teach at Chawed Ear is the only one in the county. Chawed Ear ain't goin' to let you have her."

"Chawed Ear is, too," I says. "If they won't give her up peaceful, I resorts to vi'lence. Bear Creek is goin' to have education and culture, if I have to wade an-kle-deep in gore to pervide it. Come on, le's go! I'm r'arin' to start the ball for arts and letters. Air you all with me?"

"Till hell freezes!" acclaimed Bill. "My shattered nerves needs a little excite-ment, and I can always count on you to pervide sech. How about it, Joshua?"

"Yo're both crazy," growls old Joshua. "But I've lived up here eatin' nuts and wearin' a painter-hide till I ain't shore of my own sanity. Anyway, I know the only way to disagree successfully with Elkins is to kill him, and I got strong doubts of bein' able to do that, even if I wanted to. Lead on! I'll do anything in reason to keep eddication out of Chawed Ear. 'Tain't only my own feelin's in regard to school-teachers. It's the principle of the thing."

"Git yore clothes then," I said, "and le's hustle."

"This painter hide is all I got," he said.

"You cain't go down into the settlements in that garb," I says.

"I can and will," says he. "I look about as civilized as you do, with yore clothes all tore to rags account of that b'ar. I got a hoss down in that canyon. I'll git him."

So Joshua got his hoss, and Glanton got his'n, and I got Cap'n Kidd, and then the trouble started. Cap'n Kidd evidently thought Joshua was some kind of a varmint, because every time Joshua come near him he taken in after him and run him up a tree. And every time Joshua tried to come down, Cap'n Kidd busted loose from me and run him back up again.

I didn't get no help from Bill; all he done was laugh like a spotted hyener, till Cap'n Kidd got irritated at them guffaws and kicked him in the belly and knocked him clean through a clump of spruces. Time I got him ontangled he looked about as disreputable as what I did, because his clothes was tore most off of him. We couldn't find his hat, neither, so I tore up what was left of my shirt and he tied the pieces around his head like a Apache. We was sure a wild- looking bunch.

But I was so disgusted thinking about how much time we was wasting while all the time Bear Creek was wallering in ignorance, so the next time Cap'n Kidd went for Joshua I took and busted him betwixt the ears with my six-shooter, and that had some effect on him.

So we sot out, with Joshua on a ga'nt old nag he rode bare-back with a hackamore, and a club he toted not having no gun. I had Bill to ride betwixt him and me, so's to keep that painter hide as far from Cap'n Kidd as possible, but every time the wind shifted and blowed the smell to him, Cap'n Kidd reched over and taken a bite at Joshua, and sometimes he bit Bill's hoss instead, and sometimes he bit Bill, and the langwidge Bill directed at that pore dumb animal was shocking to hear.

But between rounds, as you might say, we progressed down the trail, and early the next morning we come out onto the Chawed Ear Road, some miles west of Chawed Ear. And there we met our first human--a feller on a pinto mare, and when he seen us he give a awful squall and took out down the road towards Chawed Ear like the devil had him by the seat of the britches.

"Le's catch him and find out if the teacher's got there yet!" I hollered, and we taken out after him, yelling for him to wait a minute, but he spurred his hoss that much harder, and before we'd gone any piece, hardly, Joshua's fool hoss jostled agen Cap'n Kidd, which smelt that painter skin and got his bit betwixt his teeth and run Joshua and his hoss three miles through the bresh before I could stop him. Glanton follered us, and of, course, time we got back to the road, the feller on the pinto mare was out of sight long ago.

So we headed for Chawed Ear, but everybody that lived along the road had run into their cabins and bolted the doors, and they shot at us through their winders as we rode by. Glanton said irritably, after having his off-ear nicked by a buffalo rifle, he says: "Dern it, they must know we aim to steal their schoolteacher."

"Aw, they couldn't know that," I said. "I bet they is a war on between Chawed Ear and War Paint."

"Well, what they shootin' at _me_ for, then?" demanded old Joshua. "I don't hang out at War Paint, like you fellers. I'm a Chawed Ear man myself."

"I doubt if they rekernizes you with all them whiskers and that rig you got on," I said. "Anyway--what's that?"

Ahead of us, away down the road, we seen a cloud of dust, and here come a gang of men on hosses, waving their guns and yelling.

"Well, whatever the reason is," says Glanton, "we better not stop to find out! Them gents is out for blood!"

"Pull into the bresh," says I. "I'm goin' to Chawed Ear today in spite of hell, high water, and all the gunmen they can raise!"

So we taken to the bresh, leaving a trail a blind man could of follered, but we couldn't help it, and they lit into the bresh after us, about forty or fifty of 'em, but we dodged and circled and taken short cuts old Joshua knowed about, and when we emerged into the town of Chawed Ear, our pursuers warn't nowheres in sight. They warn't nobody in sight in the town, neither. All the doors was closed and the shutters up on the cabins and saloons and stores and everything. It was pecooliar.

As we rode into the clearing somebody let _bam_ at us with a shotgun from the nearest cabin, and the load combed old Joshua's whiskers. This made me mad, and I rode at the cabin and pulled my foot out'n the stirrup and kicked the door in, and while I was doing this, the feller inside hollered and jumped out the winder, and Glanton grabbed him by the neck and taken his gun away from him. It was Esau Barlow, one of Chawed Ear's confirmed citizens.

"What the hell does you Chawed Ear buzzards mean by this here hostility?" roared Bill.

"Is that you, Glanton?" gasped Barlow, blinking his eyes.

"Yes, it's me!" bellered Bill wrathfully. "Do I look like a Injun?"

"Yes--_ow!_ I mean, I didn't know you in that there turban," says Barlow. "Am I dreamin', or is that Joshua Braxton and Breckinridge Elkins?"

"Shore it's us!" snorted Joshua. "Who you think?"

"Well," says Esau, rubbing his neck, "I didn't know!" He stole a glance at Joshua's painter-hide and he batted his eyes again, and kind of shaken his head like he warn't sure of hisself, even then.

"Where is everybody?" Joshua demanded.

"Well," says Esau, "a little while ago Dick Lynch rode into town with his hoss all of a lather, and swore he'd jest out-run the wildest war-party that ever come down from the hills!

"'Boys,' says Dick, 'they ain't neither Injuns nor white men! They're them cussed wild men that New York perfessor was talkin' about! One of 'em's big as a grizzly b'ar, with no shirt on, and he's ridin' a hoss bigger'n a bull moose. One of the others is as ragged and ugly as him, but not so big, and wearin' a Apache head-dress. T'other'n's got nothin' on but a painter's hide, and a club, and his hair and whiskers falls to his shoulders! When they seen me,' says Dick, 'they sot up the awfullest yells I ever heard and come for me like so many wild Injuns. I fogged it for town,' says Dick, warnin' everybody along the road to fort theirselves in their cabins."

"Well," says Esau, "when he says that, sech men as was left in town got their hosses and guns--except me which cain't ride account of a risin' I got in a vital spot--and they taken out up the road to meet the war-party before it got into town."

"Well, of all the cussed fools!" I snorted. "Lissen, where-at's the new school-teacher?"

"She ain't arriv yet," says he. "She's due on the next stage, and the mayor and the band rode out to meet her at the Yaller Creek crossin' and escort her into town in honor. They pulled out before Dick Lynch brung news of the war-party."

"Well, come on!" I says to my warriors. "I aims to meet that stage too!"

So we pulled out and fogged it down the road, and purty soon we heard music blaring ahead of us, and men yipping and shooting off their pistols like they does when they're celebrating, so we jedged the stage had already arriv.

"What you goin' to do now?" ast Glanton, and about that time a noise bust out behind us, and I looked back and seen that gang of Chawed Ear maniacs which had been chasing us dusting down the road after us, waving their Winchesters. I seen it warn't no use to try to stop and argy with 'em. They'd fill us full of lead before we could get clost enough to make 'em hear what we was saying. So I hollered: "Come on! If they git her into town they'll fort theirselves agen us, and we'll never git her! We'll have to take her by force! Foller me!"

So we swept down the road and around the bend, and there was the stage-coach coming up the road with the mayor riding alongside with his hat in his hand, and a whisky bottle sticking out of each saddle-bag and his hip pocket. He was orating at the top of his voice to make hisself heard above the racket the band was making. They was blowing horns of every kind, and banging drums, and twanging on Jews harps, and the hosses was skittish and shying and jumping. But we heard the mayor say: "--And so we welcomes you, Miss Devon, to our peaceful little community, where life runs smooth and tranquil, and men's souls is overflowing with milk and honey--" And jest then we stormed around the the bend and come tearing down on 'em with the mob right behind us yelling and cussing and shooting free and fervent.

The next minute they was the damndest mix-up you ever seen, what with the hosses bucking their riders off, and men yelling and cussing, and the hosses hitched to the stage running away and knocking the mayor off his hoss. We hit 'em like a cyclone and they shot at us and hit us over the head with their derned music horns, and right in the middle of the fray the mob behind us rounded the bend and piled up amongst us before they could check theirselves, and everybody was so confused they started fighting everybody else. Old Joshua was laying right and left with his club, and Glanton was beating the band over their heads with his six-shooter, and I was trompling everybody in my rush for the stage.

Because the fool hosses had whirled around and started in the general direction of the Atlantic Ocean, and neither the driver nor the shotgun guard could stop 'em. But Cap'n Kidd overtook it in maybe a dozen strides, and I left the saddle in a flying leap and landed on it. The guard tried to shoot me with his shotgun so I throwed it into a alder clump and he didn't let go of it quick enough so he went along with it.

I then grabbed the reins out of the driver's hands and swung them fool hosses around, and the stage kind of revolved on one wheel for a dizzy instant and then settled down again and we headed back up the road lickety-split and in a instant was right amongst the melee that was going on around Bill and Joshua.

About that time I realized that the driver was trying to stab me with a butcher knife, so I kind of tossed him off the stage, and there ain't no sense in him going around saying he's going to have me arrested account of him landing headfirst in the bass horn so it take seven men to pull his head out of it. He ought to watch where he falls, when he gets throwed off a stage going at a high run.

I feels, moreover, that the mayor is prone to carry petty grudges, or he wouldn't be belly-aching about me accidentally running over him with all four wheels. And it ain't my fault he was stepped on by Cap'n Kidd, neither. Cap'n Kidd was jest follering the stage, because he knowed I was on it. And it naturally irritates any well-trained hoss to stumble over somebody, and that's why Cap'n Kidd chawed the mayor's ear.

As for them fellers which happened to get knocked down and run over by the stage, I didn't have nothing personal agen 'em. I was jest rescuing Joshua and Bill which I seen was outnumbered about twenty to one. I was doing them idjits a favor, if they only knowed it, because in about another minute Bill would of started using the front ends of his six-shooters instead of the butts, and the fight would of turnt into a massacre. Glanton has got a awful temper.

Him and Joshua had laid out a remarkable number of the enemy, but the battle was going agen 'em when I arriv on the field of carnage. As the stage crashed through the mob I reched down and got Joshua by the neck and pulled him out from under about fifteen men which was beating him to death with their gun butts and pulling out his whiskers, and I slung him up on top of the other luggage. About that time we was rushing past the melee which Bill was the center of, and I reched down and snared him as we went by, but three of the men which had hold of him wouldn't let go, so I hauled all four of 'em up into the stage. I then handled the team with one hand whilst with the other'n I pulled them idjits loose from Bill like pulling ticks off a cow's hide, and throwed 'em at the mob which was chasing us.

Men and hosses piled up in a stack on the road which was further complicated by Cap'n Kidd's actions as he come busting along after the stage, and by the time we sighted Chawed Ear again, our enemies was far behind us down the road.

We busted right through Chawed Ear in a fog of dust, and the women and chillern which had ventured out of their cabins, squalled and run back in again, though they warn't in no danger at all. But Chawed Ear folks is pecooliar that way.

When we was out of sight of Chawed Ear on the road to War Paint I give the lines to Bill and swung down on the side of the stage and stuck my head in.

They was one of the purtiest gals I ever seen in there, all huddled up in a corner as pale as she could be, and looking so scairt I thought she was going to faint, which I'd heard Eastern gals had a habit of doing.

"Oh, spare me!" she begged, clasping her hands in front of her. "Please don't scalp me! I cannot speak your language, but if you can understand English, please have mercy on me--"

"Be at ease, Miss Devon," I reassured her. "I ain't no Injun, nor wild man neither. I'm a white man, and so is my friends here. We wouldn't none of us hurt a flea. We're that refined and tender-hearted you wouldn't believe it--" About that time a wheel hit a stump and the stage jumped into the air and I bit my tongue, and roared in some irritation: "Bill, you--son of a--polecat! Stop them hosses before I comes up there and breaks yore--neck!"

"Try it and see what you git, you beefheaded lummox!" he retorted, but he pulled the hosses to a stop, and I taken off my hat and opened the stage door. Bill and Joshua clumb down and peered over my shoulder.

"Miss Devon," I says, "I begs yore pardon for this here informal welcome. But you sees before you a man whose heart bleeds for the benighted state of his native community. I'm Breckinridge Elkins from Bear Creek, where hearts is pure and motives is noble, but education is weak.

"You sees before you," I says, "a man which has growed up in ignorance. I cain't neither read nor write my own name. Joshua here, in the painter-skin, he cain't neither, and neither can Bill--"

"That's a lie," says Bill. "I can read and--_oomp!_" Because I'd kind of stuck my elbow in his stummick. I didn't want Bill Glanton to spile the effeck of my speech.

"They is some excuse for men like us," I says. "When we was cubs schools was unknown in these mountains, and keepin' a sculpin' knife from betwixt yore skull and yore hair was more important than makin' marks onto a slate.

"But times has changed. I sees the young 'uns of my home range growin' up in the same ignorance as me," I said, "and my heart bleeds for 'em. They is no sech excuse for them as they was for me. The Injuns has went, mostly, and a age of culture is due to be ushered in.

"Miss Devon," I says, "will you please come up to Bear Creek and be our schoolteacher?"

"Why," says she, bewilderedly, "I came West expecting to teach school at a place called Chawed Ear, but I haven't signed any contract--"

"How much was them snake-hunters goin' to pay you?" I ast.

"Ninety dollars a month," says she.

"We pays you a hundred on Bear Creek," I says. "Board and lodgin' free."

"But what will the people of Chawed Ear say?" she said.

"Nothin'!" I says heartily. "I done arranged that. They got the interests of Bear Creek so much at heart, that they wouldn't think of interferin' with any arrangements I make. You couldn't drag 'em up to Bear Creek with a team of oxen!"

"It seems all very strange and irregular," says she, "but I suppose--"

So I says: "Good! Fine! Great! Then it's all settled. Le's go!"

"Where?" she ast, grabbing hold of the stage as I clumb into the seat.

"To War Paint, first," I says, "where I gits me some new clothes and a good gentle hoss for you to ride--because nothin' on wheels can git over the Bear Creek road--and then we heads for home! Git up, hosses! Culture is on her way to the Humbolts!"

Well, a few days later me and the schoolteacher was riding sedately up the trail to Bear Creek, with a pack-mule carrying her plunder, and you never seen nothing so elegant--store-bought clothes and a hat with a feather into it, and slippers and everything. She rode in a side-saddle I bought for her--the first that ever come into the Humbolts. She was sure purty. My heart beat in wild enthusiasm for education ever time I looked at her.

I swung off the main trail so's to pass by the spring in the creek where Glory McGraw filled her pail every morning and evening. It was jest about time for her to be there, and sure enough she was. She straightened when she heard the hosses, and started to say something, and then her eyes got wide as she seen my elegant companion, and her purty red mouth stayed open. I pulled up my hoss and taken off my hat with a perlite sweep I learnt from a gambler in War Paint, and I says: "Miss Devon, lemme interjuice you to Miss Glory McGraw, the datter of one of Bear Creek's leadin' citizens. Miss McGraw, this here is Miss Margaret Devon, from Boston, Massachusetts, which is goin' to teach school here."

"How do you do?" says Miss Margaret, but Glory didn't say nothing. She jest stood there, staring, and the pail fell outa her hand and splashed into the creek.

"Allow me to pick up yore pail," I said, and started to lean down from my saddle to get it, but she started like she was stung, and said, in a voice which sounded kind of strained and onnatural: "Don't tech it! Don't tech nothin' I own! Git away from me!"

"What a beautiful girl!" says Miss Margaret as we rode on. "But how peculiarly she acted!"

But I said nothing, because I was telling myself, well, I reckon I showed Glory McGraw something this time. I reckon she sees now that I warn't lying when I said I'd bring a peach back to Bear Creek with me. But somehow I warn't enjoying my triumph nigh as much as I'd thought I would.

CHAPTER XII

WAR ON BEAR CREEK

PAP DUG the nineteenth buckshot out of my shoulder and said: "Pigs is more disturbin' to the peace of a community than scandal, divorce, and corn-licker put together. And," says pap, pausing to strop his bowie on my sculp where the hair was all burnt off, "when the pig is a razorback hawg, and is mixed up with a lady schoolteacher, a English tenderfoot, and a passle of blood-thirsty relatives, the result is appallin' for a peaceable man to behold. Hold still till Buckner gits yore ear sewed back on."

Pap was right. I warn't to blame for nothing that happened. Breaking Joe Gordon's laig was a mistake, and Erath Elkins is a liar when he says I caved in them five ribs of his'n on purpose. If Uncle Jeppard Grimes had been tending to his own business, he wouldn't have got the seat of his britches filled with bird-shot, and I don't figger it was my fault that cousin Bill Kirby's cabin got burned down. And I don't take no blame for Jim Gordon's ear which Jack Grimes shot off, neither. I figger everybody was more to blame than I was, and I stand ready to wipe up the road with anybody which disagrees with me.

But I'm getting ahead of myself. Lemme go back to the days when culture first reared its head amongst the simple inhabitants of Bear Creek.

Jest like I said, I was determined that education should be committed on the rising generation, and I gathered the folks in a clearing too far away for Miss Devon to be stampeded by the noise of argyment and persuasion, and I sot forth my views. Opinions differed vi'lently like they always does on Bear Creek, but when the dust settled and the smoke drifted away, it was found that a substantial majority of folks agreed to see things my way. Some was awful sot agen it, and said no good would come of book larning, but after I had swept the clearing with six or seven of them, they allowed it might be a good thing after all, and agreed to let Miss Margaret take a whack at uplifting the young 'uns.

Then they ast me how much money I'd promised her, and when I said a hundred a month they sot up a howl that they wasn't that much hard money seen on Bear Creek in a year's time. But I settled that. I said each family would contribute whatever they was able--coonskins, honey, b'ar hides, corn-licker, or what not, and I'd pack the load into War Paint each month and turn it into cash money. I added that I'd be more'n glad to call around each month to make sure nobody failed to contribute.

Then we argyed over where to build the cabin for the schoolhouse, and I wanted to build it between pap's cabin and the corral, but he riz up and said he'd be dadgasted he'd have a schoolhouse anywhere nigh his dwelling-house, with a passle of yelling kids scaring off all the eatable varmints. He said if it was built within a mile of his cabin it would be because they was somebody on Bear Creek which had a quicker trigger finger and a better shooting eye than what he did. So after some argyment in the course of which five of Bear Creek's leading citizens was knocked stiff, we decided to build the schoolhouse over nigh the settlement on Apache Mountain. That was the thickest populated spot on Bear Creek anyway. And Cousin Bill Kirby agreed to board her for his part of contributing to her wages.

Well, it would of suited me better to had the schoolhouse built closer to my home-cabin, and have Miss Margaret board with us, but I was purty well satisfied, because this way I could see her any time I wanted to. I done this every day, and she looked purtier every time I seen her. The weeks went by, and everything was going fine. I was calling on Miss Margaret every day, and she was learning me how to read and write, though it was a mighty slow process. But I was progressing a little in my education, and a whole lot--I thought--in my love affair, when peace and romance hit a snag in the shape of a razorback pig named Daniel Webster.

It begun when that there tenderfoot come riding up the trail from War Paint with Tunk Willoughby. Tunk ain't got no more sense than the law allows, but he sure showed good jedgment that time, because having delivered his charge to his destination, he didn't tarry. He merely handed me a note, and p'inted dumbly at the tenderfoot, whilst holding his hat reverently in his hand meanwhile.

"What you mean by that there gesture?" I ast him rather irritably, and he said: "I doffs my sombrero in respect to the departed. Bringin' a specimen like that onto Bear Creek is jest like heavin' a jackrabbit to a pack of starvin' loboes."

He hove a sigh and shook his head, and put his hat back on. "Rassle a cat in pieces," he said.

"What the hell air you talkin' about?" I demanded.

"That's Latin," he said. "It means rest in peace."

And with that he dusted it down the trail and left me alone with the tenderfoot which all the time was setting his cayuse and looking at me like I was a curiosity or something.

I called for my sister Ouachita to come read that there note for me, because she'd learnt how from Miss Margaret, so she did, and it run as follers:

"Dere Breckinridge: This will interjuice Mr. J. Pembroke Pemberton a English sportsman which I met in Frisco recent. He was disapinted because he hadnt found no adventures in America and was fixin to go to Aferker to shoot liuns and elerfants but I perswaded him to come with me because I knowed he would find more hell on Bear Creek in a week than he would find in a yere in Aferker or any other place. But the very day we hit War Paint I run into a old ackwaintance from Texas I will not speak no harm of the ded but I wish the son of a buzzard had shot me somewheres besides in my left laig which already had three slugs in it which I never could get cut out. Anyway I am lade up and not able to come on to Bear Creek with J. Pembroke Pemberton. I am dependin' on you to show him some good bear huntin' and other excitement and pertect him from yore relatives I know what a awful responsibility I am puttin on you but I am askin this as yore friend, William Harrison Glanton, Esqy ."

I looked J. Pembroke over. He was a medium-sized young feller and looked kinda soft in spots. He had yaller hair and very pink cheeks like a gal; and he had on whip-cord britches and tan riding boots which was the first I ever seen. And he had on a funny kinda coat with pockets and a belt which he called a shooting jacket, and a big hat like a mushroom made outa cork with a red ribbon around it. And he had a pack-hoss loaded with all kinds of plunder, and five or six different kinds of shotguns and rifles.

"So yo're J. Pembroke," I says, and he says: "Oh, rahther! And you, no doubt, are the person Mr. Glanton described to me as Breckinridge Elkins?"

"Yeah," I said. "Light and come in. We got b'ar meat and honey for supper."

"I say," he says, climbing down. "Pardon me for being a bit personal, old chap, but may I ask if your--ah--magnitude of bodily stature is not a bit unique?"

"I dunno," I says, not having the slightest idee what he was talking about. "I always votes a straight Democratic ticket, myself."

He started to say something else, but jest then pap and my brothers John and Bill and Jim and Buckner and Garfield come to the door to see what the noise was about, and he turned pale and said faintly: "I beg your pardon; giants seem to be the rule in these parts."

"Pap says men ain't what they was when he was in his prime," I said, "but we manage to git by."

Well, J. Pembroke laid into them b'ar steaks with a hearty will, and when I told him we'd go after b'ar next day, he ast me how many days travel it'd take till we got to the b'ar country.

"Heck!" I says. "You don't have to travel to git b'ar in these parts. If you forgit to bolt yore door at night yo're liable to find a grizzly sharin' yore bunk before mornin'. This here'n we're eatin' was catched by my sister Elinor there whilst tryin' to rob the pig-pen out behind the cabin last night."

"My word!" he says, looking at her pecooliarly. "And may I ask, Miss Elkins, what calibre of firearm you used?"

"I knocked him in the head with a wagon spoke," she said, and he shook his head to hisself and muttered: "Extraordinary!"

J. Pembroke slept in my bunk and I taken the floor that night; and we was up at daylight and ready to start after the b'ar. Whilst J. Pembroke was fussing over his guns, pap come out and pulled his whiskers and shook his head and said: "That there is a perlite young man, but I'm afeared he ain't as hale as he ought a be. I jest give him a pull at my jug, and he didn't gulp but one good snort and like to choked to death."

"Well," I said, buckling the cinches on Cap'n Kidd, "I've done learnt not to jedge outsiders by the way they takes their licker on Bear Creek. It takes a Bear Creek man to swig Bear Creek corn juice."

"I hopes for the best," sighed pap. "But it's a dismal sight to see a young man which cain't stand up to his licker. Whar you takin' him?"

"Over towards Apache Mountain," I said. "Erath seen a exter big grizzly over there day before yesterday."

"Hmmmmm!" says pap. "By a pecooliar coincidence the schoolhouse is over on the side of Apache Mountain, ain't it, Breckinridge?"

"Maybe it is and maybe it ain't," I replied with dignerty, and rode off with J. Pembroke ignoring pap's sourcastic comment which he hollered after me: "Maybe they is a connection betwixt book-larnin' and b'ar-huntin', but who am I to say?"

J. Pembroke was a purty good rider, but he used a funny-looking saddle without no horn nor cantle, and he had the derndest gun I ever seen. It was a double-barrel rifle, and he said it was a elerfant-gun. It was big enough to knock a hill down. He was surprised I didn't tote no rifle and ast me what would I do if we met a b'ar. I told him I was depending on him to shoot it, but I said if it was necessary for me to go into action, my six-shooters was plenty.

"My word!" says he. "You mean to say you can bring down a grizzly with a shot from a pistol?"

"Not always," I said. "Sometimes I have to bust him over the head with the barrel to finish him."

He didn't say nothing for a long time after that.

Well, we rode over on the lower slopes of Apache Mountain, and tied the hosses in a holler and went through the bresh on foot. That was a good place for b'ars, because they come there very frequently looking for Uncle Jeppard Grimes' pigs which runs loose all over the lower slopes of the mountain.

But jest like it always is when yo're looking for something special, we didn't see a cussed b'ar.

The middle of the evening found us around on the side of the mountain where they is a settlement of Kirbys and Grimeses and Gordons. Half a dozen families has their cabins within a mile or so of each other, and I dunno what in hell they want to crowd up together that way for, it would plumb smother me, but pap says they was always pecooliar that way.

We warn't in sight of the settlement, but the schoolhouse warn't far off, and I said to J. Pembroke: "You wait here a spell, and maybe a b'ar will come by. Miss Margaret Devon is teachin' me how to read and write, and it's time for my lesson."

I left J. Pembroke setting on a log hugging his elerfant-gun, and I strode through the bresh and come out at the upper end of the run which the settlement was at the other'n, and school had jest turned out and the chillern was going home, and Miss Margaret was waiting for me in the log schoolhouse.

She was setting at her hand-made desk as I come in, ducking my head so as not to bump it agen the top of the door and perlitely taking off my Stetson. She looked kinda tired and discouraged, and I said: "Has the young'uns been raisin' any hell today, Miss Margaret?"

"Oh, no," she said. "They're very polite--in fact I've noticed that Bear Creek people are always polite when they're not killing each other. I've finally gotten used to the boys wearing their pistols and bowie knives to school. But somehow it seems so futile. This is all so terribly different from everything to which I've always been accustomed. I get discouraged and feel like giving it up."

"You'll git used to it," I consoled her. "It'll be a lot different onst yo're married to some honest reliable young man."

She give me a startled look and said: "Married to someone here on Bear Creek?"

"Shore," I said, involuntarily expanding my chest. "Everybody is jest wonderin' when you'll set the day. But le's git at my readin' lesson. I done learnt the words you writ out for me yesterday."

But she warn't listenin', and she said: "Do you have any idea of why Mr. Joel Grimes and Mr. Esau Gordon quit calling on me? Until a few days ago one or the other was at Mr. Kirby's cabin where I board almost every night."

"Now don't you worry none about them," I soothed her. "Joel'll be about on crutches before the week's out, and Esau can already walk without bein' helped. I always handles my relatives as easy as possible."

"You fought with them?" she exclaimed.

"I jest convinced 'em you didn't want to be bothered with 'em," I reassured her. "I'm easy-goin', but I don't like competition."

"Competition!" Her eyes flared wide open and she looked at me like she hadn't never seen me before. "Do you mean that you--that I--that-- "

"Well," I said modestly, "everybody on Bear Creek is jest wonderin' when yo're goin' to set the day for us to git hitched. You see gals don't generally stay single very long in these parts--hey, what's the matter?"

Because she was getting paler and paler like she'd et something which didn't agree with her.

"Nothing," she said faintly. "You--you mean people are expecting me to marry you?"

"Sure," I said.

She muttered something that sounded like "My God!" and licked her lips with her tongue and looked at me like she was about ready to faint. Well, it ain't every gal which has a chance to get hitched to Breckinridge Elkins, so I didn't blame her for being excited.

"You've been very kind to me, Breckinridge," she said feebly. "But I--this is so sudden--so unexpected--I never thought--I never _dreamed_--"

"I don't want to rush you," I said. "Take yore time. Next week will be soon enough. Anyway, I got to build us a cabin, and--"

Bang! went a gun, too loud for a Winchester.

"Elkins!" It was J. Pembroke yelling for me up the slope. "Elkins! Hurry!"

"Who's that?" she exclaimed, jumping to her feet like she was working on a spring.

"Aw," I said in disgust, "it's a fool tenderfoot Bill Glanton wished on me. I reckon a b'ar is got him by the neck. I'll go see."

"I'll go with you!" she said, but from the way J. Pembroke was yelling I figgered I better not waste no time getting to him, so I couldn't wait for her, and she was some piece behind me when I mounted the lap of the slope and met him running out from amongst the trees. He was gibbering with excitement.

"I winged it!" he squawked. "I'm sure I winged the blighter! But it ran in among the underbrush and I dared not follow it, for the beast is most vicious when wounded. A friend of mine once wounded one in South Africa, and--"

"A b'ar?" I ast.

"No, no!" he said. "A wild boar! The most vicious brute I have ever seen! It ran into that brush there!"

"Aw, they ain't no wild boars in the Humbolts," I snorted. "You wait here, I'll go see jest what you did shoot."

I seen some splashes of blood on the grass, so I knowed he'd shot _something._ Well, I hadn't gone more'n a few hundred feet and was jest out of sight of J. Pembroke when I run into Uncle Jeppard Grimes.

Uncle Jeppard was one of the first white men to come into the Humbolts, in case I ain't mentioned that before, and he wears fringed buckskins and moccasins jest like he done fifty years ago. He had a bowie knife in one hand and he waved something in the other'n like a flag of revolt, and he was frothing at the mouth.

"The derned murderer!" he shrieked. "You see this? That's the proper tail of Dan'l Webster, the finest derned razorback boar which ever trod the Humbolts! That danged tenderfoot of yore'n tried to 'sassernate him! Shot his tail off, right spang up to the hilt! I'll show him he cain't muterlate my animals like this! I'll have his heart's blood!"

And he done a war-dance waving that pig-tail and his bowie and cussing in American and Spanish and Apache Injun all at onst.

"You ca'm down, Uncle Jeppard," I said sternly. "He ain't got no sense, and he thought Daniel Webster was a wild boar like they have in Aferker and England and them foreign places. He didn't mean no harm."

"No harm," said Uncle Jeppard fiercely. "And Dan'l Webster with no more tail onto him than a jackrabbit!"

"Well," I said, "here's a five dollar gold piece to pay for the dern hawg's tail, and you let J. Pembroke alone!"

"Gold cain't satisfy honor," he said bitterly, but nevertheless grabbing the coin like a starving Kiowa grabbing a beefsteak. "I'll let this here outrage pass for the time. But I'll be watchin' that maneyack to see that he don't muterlate no more of my prize livestock."

And so saying he went off muttering in his beard.

I went back to where I left J. Pembroke, and there he was talking to Miss Margaret which had jest come up. She had more color in her face than I'd saw recent.

"Fancy meeting a girl like you here!" J. Pembroke was saying.

"No more surprising than meeting a man like you!" says she with a kind of fluttery laugh.

"Oh, a sportsman wanders into all sorts of out-of-the-way places," says he, and seeing they hadn't noticed me coming up, I says: "Well, J. Pembroke, I didn't find yore wild boar, but I met the owner."

He looked at me kinda blank, and said vaguely: "Wild boar? _What_ wild boar?"

"That 'un you shot the tail off of with that there fool elerfant gun," I said. "Lissen: next time you see a hawg-critter you remember there ain't no wild boars in the Humbolts. They is critters called haverleeners in South Texas, but they ain't even none of them in Nevada. So next time you see a hawg, jest reflect that it's merely one of Uncle Jeppard Grimes' razorbacks and refrain from shootin' at it."

"Oh, quite!" he agreed absently, and started talking to Miss Margaret again.

So I picked up the elerfant gun which he'd absent-mindedly laid down, and said: "Well, it's gittin' late. Let's go. We won't go back to pap's cabin tonight, J. Pembroke. We'll stay at Uncle Saul Garfield's cabin on t'other side of the Apache Mountain settlement."

Like I said, them cabins was awful clost together. Uncle Saul's cabin was below the settlement, but it warnt much over three hundred yards from cousin Bill Kirby's cabin where Miss Margaret boarded. The other cabins was on t'other side of Bill's, mostly, strung out up the run and up and down the slopes.

I told J. Pembroke and Miss Margaret to walk on down to the settlement whilst I went back and got the hosses.

They'd got to the settlement time I catched up with 'em, and Miss Margaret had gone into the Kirby cabin, and I seen a light spring up in her room. She had one, of them new-fangled ile lamps she brung with her, the only one on Bear Creek. Taller candles and pine chunks was good enough for us folks. And she'd hanged rag-things over the winders which she called curtains. You never seen nothing like it. I tell you she was that elegant you wouldn't believe it.

We walked on towards Uncle Saul's, me leading the hosses, and after awhile J. Pembroke says: "A wonderful creature!"

"You mean Dan'l Webster?" I ast.

"No!" he said. "No, no! I mean Miss Devon."

"She sure is," I said. "She'll make me a fine wife."

He hirled like I'd stabbed him and his face looked pale in the dusk.

"You?" he said. "_You_ a fine wife?"

"Well," I said bashfully, "she ain't sot the day yet, but I've sure sot my heart on that gal."

"Oh!" he says. "_Oh!_" says he, like he had the toothache. Then he said kinda hesitatingly: "Suppose--er, just suppose, you know! Suppose a rival for her affections should appear? What would you do?"

"You mean if some dirty, low-down son of a mangy skunk was to try to steal my gal?" I said, whirling so sudden he staggered backwards.

"Steal my gal?" I roared, seeing red at the mere thought. "Why, I'd--I'd--"

Words failing me I grabbed a big sapling and tore it up by the roots and broke it acrost my knee and throwed the pieces clean through a rail fence on the other side of the road.

"That there is a faint idee!" I said, panting with passion.

"That gives me a very vivid conception," he said faintly, and he said nothing more till we reched the cabin and seen Uncle Saul Garfield standing in the light of the door combing his black beard with his fingers.

Next morning J. Pembroke seemed like he'd kinda lost interest in b'ars. He said all that walking he done over the slopes of Apache Mountain had made his laig muscles sore. I never heard of sech a thing, but nothing that gets the matter with these tenderfeet surprises me much, they is sech a effemernate race, so I ast him would he like to go fishing down the run and he said all right.

But we hadn't been fishing more'n a hour when he said he believed he'd go back to Uncle Saul's cabin and take him a nap, and he insisted on going alone, so I stayed where I was and catched me a nice string of trout.

I went back to the cabin about noon, and ast Uncle Saul if J. Pembroke had got his nap out.

"Why, heck," said Uncle Saul, "I ain't seen him since you and him started down the run this mornin'. Wait a minute--yonder he comes from the other direction."

Well, J. Pembroke didn't say where he'd been all morning, and I didn't ast him, because a tenderfoot don't generally have no reason for anything he does.

We et the trout I catched, and after dinner he perked up a right smart and got his shotgun and said he'd like to hunt some wild turkeys. I never heard of anybody hunting anything as big as a turkey with a shotgun, but I didn't say nothing, because tenderfeet is like that.

So we headed up the slopes of Apache Mountain, and I stopped by the schoolhouse to tell Miss Margaret I probably wouldn't get back in time to take my reading and writing lesson, and she said: "You know, until I met your friend, Mr. Pembroke, I didn't realize what a difference there was between men like him, and--well, like the men on Bear Creek."

"I know," I said. "But don't hold it agen him. He means well. He jest ain't got no sense. Everybody cain't be smart like me. As a special favor to me, Miss Margaret, I'd like for you to be exter nice to the poor sap, because he's a friend of my friend Bill Glanton down to War Paint."

"I will, Breckinridge," she replied heartily, and I thanked her and went away with my big manly heart pounding in my gigantic bosom.

Me and J. Pembroke headed into the heavy timber, and we hadn't went far till I was convinced that somebody was follering us. I kept hearing twigs snapping, and onst I thought I seen a shadowy figger duck behind a bush. But when I run back there, it was gone, and no track to show in the pine needles. That sort of thing would of made me nervous, anywheres else, because they is a goodly number of people which would like to get a clean shot at my back from the bresh, but I knowed none of them dast come after me in my own territory. If anybody was trailing us it was bound to be one of my relatives and to save my neck I couldn't think of no reason why anyone of 'em would be gunning for me.

But I got tired of it, and left J. Pembroke in a small glade whilst I snuck back to do some shaddering of my own. I aimed to cast a big circle around the clearing and see could I find out who it was, but I'd hardly got out of sight of J. Pembroke when I heard a gun bang.

I turned to run back and here come J. Pembroke yelling: "I got him! I got him! I winged the bally aborigine!"

He had his head down as he busted through the bresh and he run into me in his excitement and hit me in the belly with his head so hard he bounced back like a rubber ball and landed in a bush with his riding boots brandishing wildly in the air.

"Assist me, Breckinridge!" he shrieked. "Extricate me! They will be hot on our trail!"

"Who?" I demanded, hauling him out by the hind laig and setting him on his feet.

"The Indians!" he hollered, jumping up and down and waving his smoking shotgun frantically. "The bally redskins! I shot one of them! I saw him sneaking through the bushes! I saw his legs! I knew it was an Indian instantly because he had on moccasins instead of boots! Listen! That's him now!"

"A Injun couldn't cuss like that," I said. "You've shot Uncle Jeppard Grimes!"

Telling him to stay there, I run through the bresh, guided by the maddened howls which riz horribly on the air, and busting through some bushes I seen Uncle Jeppard rolling on the ground with both hands clasped to the rear bosom of his buckskin britches which was smoking freely. His langwidge was awful to hear.

"Air you in misery Uncle Jeppard?" I inquired solicitously. This evoked another ear-splitting squall.

"I'm writhin' in my death-throes," he says in horrible accents, "and you stands there and mocks my mortal agony! My own blood-kin!" he says "--!" says Uncle Jeppard with passion.

"Aw," I said, "that there bird-shot wouldn't hurt a flea. It cain't be very deep under yore thick old hide. Lie on yore belly, Uncle Jeppard," I says, stropping my bowie on my boot, "and I'll dig out them shot for you."

"Don't tech me!" he said fiercely, painfully climbing onto his feet. "Where's my rifle-gun? Gimme it! Now then, I demands that you bring that British murderer here where I can git a clean lam at him! The Grimes honor is besmirched and my new britches is rooint. Nothin' but blood can wipe out the stain on the family honor!"

"Well," I said, "you didn't have no business sneakin' around after us that-away--"

Here Uncle Jeppard give tongue to loud and painful shrieks.

"Why shouldn't I?" he howled. "Ain't a man got no right to perteck his own property? I war follerin' him to see that he didn't shoot no more tails offa my hawgs. And now he shoots me in the same place! He's a fiend in human form--a monster which stalks ravelin' through these hills bustin' for the blood of the in-nercent!"

"Aw, J. Pembroke thought you was a Injun," I said.

"He thought Dan'l Webster was a wild wart-hawg," gibbered Uncle Jeppard. "He thought I was Geronimo. I reckon he'll massacre the entire population of Bear Creek under a misapprehension, and you'll uphold and defend him! When the cabins of yore kinfolks is smoulderin' ashes, smothered in the blood of yore own relations, I hope you'll be satisfied--bringin' a foreign assassin into a peaceful com-munity!"

Here Uncle Jeppard's emotions choked him, and he chawed his whiskers and then yanked out the five-dollar gold piece I give him for Daniel Webster's tail, and throwed it at me.

"Take back yore filthy lucre," he said bitterly. "The day of retribution is nigh onto hand, Breckinridge Elkins, and the Lord of battles shall jedge betwixt them which turns agen their kinsfolks in their extremerties!"

"In their which?" I ast, but he merely snarled and went limping off through the trees, calling back over his shoulder: "They is still men on Bear Creek which will see jestice did for the aged and helpless. I'll git that English murderer if it's the last thing I do, and you'll be sorry you stood up for him, you big lunkhead!"

I went back to where J. Pembroke was waiting bewilderedly, and evidently still expecting a tribe of Injuns to bust out of the bresh and sculp him, and I said in disgust: "Let's go home. Tomorrer I'll take you so far away from Bear Creek you can shoot in any direction without hittin' a prize razorback or a antiquated gun-man with a ingrown disposition. When Uncle Jeppard Grimes gits mad enough to throw away money, it's time to ile the Winchesters and strap yore scabbard-ends to yore laigs."

"Legs?" he said mistily. "But what about the Indians?"

"They warn't no Injun, gol-dern it!" I howled. "They ain't been none on Bear Creek for four or five year. They--aw, hell! What the hell! Come on. It's gittin' late. Next time you see somethin' you don't understand, ast me before you shoot it. And remember, the more ferocious and woolly it looks, the more likely it is to be a leadin' citizen of Bear Creek."

It was dark when we approached Uncle Saul's cabin, and J. Pembroke glanced back up the road, towards the settlement, and said: "My word, is it a political rally? Look! A torchlight parade!"

I looked, and said: "Quick! Git into the cabin and stay there!"

He turned pale, but said: "If there is danger, I insist on--"

"Insist all you dern please," I said, "but git in that house and stay there. I'll handle this. Uncle Saul, see he gits in there."

Uncle Saul is a man of few words. He taken a firm grip onto his pipe stem and he grabbed J. Pembroke by the neck and the seat of the britches and throwed him bodily into the cabin, and shet the door and sot down on the stoop.

"They ain't no use in you gittin' mixed up in this, Uncle Saul," I said.

"You got yore faults, Breckinridge," he grunted. "You ain't got much sense, but yo're my favorite sister's son--and I ain't forgot that lame mule Jeppard traded me for a sound animal back in '69. Let 'em come!"

They come all right, and surged up in front of the cabin-- Jeppard's boys Jack and Buck and Esau and Joash and Polk County. And Erath Elkins, and a mob of Gordons and Buckners and Polks, all more or less kin to me, except Joel Braxton who wasn't kin to none of us, but didn't like me because he was sweet on Miss Margaret. But Uncle jeppard warn't with 'em. Some had torches and Polk County Grimes had a rope with a noose in it.

"Where at air you-all goin' with that there lariat?" I ast them sternly, planting my enormous bulk in their path.

"Perjuice the scoundrel!" commanded Polk County, waving his rope around his head. "Bring out the foreign invader which shoots hawgs and defenceless old men from the bresh!"

"What you aim to do?" I inquired.

"We aim to hang him!" they replied with hearty enthusiasm.

Uncle Saul knocked the ashes out of his pipe and stood up and stretched his arms which looked like knotted oak limbs, and he grinned in his black beard like a old timber wolf, and he says: "Whar is dear cousin Jeppard to speak for hisself?"

"Uncle Jeppard was havin' the shot picked outa his hide when we left," says Jim Gordon. "He'll be along directly. Breckinridge, we don't want no trouble with you, but we aims to have that Englishman."

"Well," I snorted, "you-all cain't. Bill Glanton is trustin' me to return him whole of body and limb, and--"

"What you want to waste time in argyment for, Breckinridge?" Uncle Saul reproved mildly. "Don't you know it's a plumb waste of time to try to reason with the off-spring of a lame-mule trader?"

"What would you sejest, old man?" sneeringly remarked Polk County.

Uncle Saul beamed on him benevolently, and said gently: "I'd try moral suasion--like this!" And he hit Polk County under the jaw and knocked him clean acrost the yard into a rain barrel amongst the rooins of which he reposed till he was rescued and revived some hours later.

But they was no stopping Uncle Saul onst he took the war-path. No sooner had he disposed of Polk County than he jumped seven foot in the air, cracked his heels together three times, give the rebel yell and come down with his arms around the necks of Esau Grimes and Joel Braxton, and started mopping up the cabin yard with 'em.

That started the fight, and they is no scrap in the world where mayhem is committed as free and fervent as in one of these here family rukuses.

Polk County had hardly crashed into the rain-barrel when Jack Grimes stuck a pistol in my face. I slapped it aside jest as he fired and the bullet missed me and taken a ear offa Jim Gordon. I was scairt Jack would hurt somebody if he kept on shooting reckless that way, so I kinda rapped him with my left fist and how was I to know it would dislocate his jaw? But Jim Gordon seemed to think I was to blame about his ear, because he give a maddened howl and jerked up his shotgun and let _bam_ with both barrels. I ducked jest in time to keep from getting my head blowed off, and catched most of the double charge in my shoulder, whilst the rest hived in the seat of Steve Kirby's britches. Being shot that way by a relative was irritating, but I controlled my temper and merely taken the gun away from Jim and splintered the stock over his head.

In the meantime Joel Gordon and Buck Grimes had grabbed one of my laigs apiece and was trying to rassle me to the earth, and Joash Grimes was trying to hold down my right arm, and cousin Pecos Buckner was beating me over the head from behind with a axe-handle, and Erath Elkins was coming at me from the front with a bowie knife. I reched down and got Buck Grimes by the neck with my left hand, and I swung my right and hit Erath with it, but I had to lift Joash clean off his feet and swing him around with the lick, because he wouldn't let go, so I only knocked Erath through the rail fence which was around Uncle Saul's garden.

About this time I found my left laig was free and discovered that Buck Grimes was unconscious, so I let go of his neck and begun to kick around with my left laig, and it ain't my fault if the spur got tangled up in Uncle Jonathan Polk's whiskers and jerked most of 'em out by the roots. I shaken Joash off and taken the axe-handle away from Pecos because I seen he was going to hurt somebody if he kept on swinging it around so reckless, and I dunno why he blames me because his skull got fractured when he hit that tree. He ought a look where he falls when he gets throwed acrost a cabin yard. And if Joel Gordon hadn't been so stubborn trying to gouge me he wouldn't of got his laig broke neither.

I was handicapped by not wanting to kill any of my kinfolks, but they was so mad they all wanted to kill me, so in spite of my carefulness the casualties was increasing at a rate which would of discouraged anybody but Bear Creek folks. But they are the stubbornest people in the world. Three or four had got me around the laigs again, refusing to be convinced that I couldn't be throwed that way, and Erath Elkins, having pulled hisself out of the rooins of the fence, come charging back with his bowie.

By this time I seen I'd have to use vi'lence in spite of myself, so I grabbed Erath Elkins and squoze him with a grizzly-hug and that was when he got them five ribs caved in, and he ain't spoke to me since. I never seen sech a cuss for taking offence over trifles.

For a matter of fact, if he hadn't been wrought up, he'd of realized how kindly and kindredly I felt towards him, even in the heat of battle. If I had dropped him underfoot he might of got fatally tromped on, for I was kicking folks right and left. So I carefully throwed Erath out of range of the melee, and he's a liar when he says I aimed him at Ozark Grimes' pitchfork; I didn't even see the cussed implement.

It was at this moment that somebody swung at me with a axe and ripped a ear offa my head, and I begun to lose my temper. Four or five other relatives was kicking and hitting and biting me all at onst, and they is a limit even to my timid manners and mild nature. I voiced my displeasure with a beller of wrath that shook the leaves offa the trees, and lashed out with both fists, and my misguided relatives fell all over the yard like persimmons after a frost. I grabbed Joash Grimes by the ankles and began to knock them ill-advised idjits in the head with him, and the way he hollered you'd of thought somebody was man-handling him. The yard was beginning to look like a battlefield when the cabin door opened and a deluge of b'iling water descended on us.

I got about a gallon down my neck, but paid very little attention to it, however the others ceased hostilities and started rolling on the ground and hollering and cussing, and Uncle Saul riz up from amongst the rooins of Esau Grimes and Joel Braxton, and bellered: "Woman! Whar air you at?"

Aunt Zavalla Garfield was standing in the doorway with a kettle in her hand, and she said: "Will you idjits stop fightin'? The Englishman's gone. He run out the back door when the fightin' started, and saddled his nag and pulled out. Now will you born fools stop, or will I give you another surge? Land save us! What's that light?"

Somebody was yelling off towards the settlement, and I was aware of a pecooliar glow which didn't come from sech torches as was still burning. And here come Medina Kirby, one of Bill's gals, yelping like a Comanche.

"Our cabin's burnin'!" she squalled. "A stray bullet went through the winder and busted Miss Margaret's ile lamp!"

With a yell of dismay I abandoned the fray and headed for Bill's cabin, follered by everybody which was able to toller me. They had been several wild shots fired during the melee and one of 'em must have hived in Miss Margaret's winder. The Kirbys had dragged most of their belongings into the yard and some was toting water from the creek, but the whole cabin was in a blaze by now.

"Where's Miss Margaret?" I roared.

"She must be still in there," shrilled Miz Kirby. "A beam fell and wedged her door so we couldn't open it, and--"

I grabbed a blanket one of the gals had rescued and plunged it into the rain barrel and run for Miss Margaret's room. They wasn't but one door in it, which led into the main part of the cabin, and was jammed like they said, and I knowed I couldn't never get my shoulders through either winder, so I jest put down my head and rammed the wall full force and knocked four or five logs outa place and made a hole big enough to go through.

The room was so full of smoke I was nigh blinded but I made out a figger fumbling at the winder on the other side. A flaming beam fell outa the roof and broke acrost my head with a loud report and about a bucketful of coals rolled down the back of my neck, but I paid no heed.

I charged through the smoke, nearly fracturing my shin on a bedstead or something, and enveloped the figger in the wet blanket and swept it up in my arms. It kicked wildly and fought and though its voice was muffled in the blanket I catched some words I never would of thought Miss Margaret would use, but I figgered she was hysterical. She seemed to be wearing spurs, too, because I felt 'em every time she kicked.

By this time the room was a perfect blaze and the roof was falling in and we'd both been roasted if I'd tried to get back to the hole I'd knocked in the oppersite wall. So I lowered my head and butted my way through the near wall, getting all my eyebrows and hair burnt off in the process, and come staggering through the rooins with my precious burden and fell into the arms of my relatives which was thronged outside.

"I've saved her!" I panted. "Pull off the blanket! Yo're safe, Miss Margaret!"

"--!" said Miss Margaret.

Uncle Saul groped under the blanket and said: "By golly, if this is the school-teacher she's growed a remarkable set of whiskers since I seen her last!"

He yanked off the blanket--to reveal the bewhiskered countenance of Uncle Jeppard Grimes!

"Hell's fire!" I bellered. "What _you_ doin' here?"

"I was comin' to jine the lynchin', you blame fool!" he snarled. "I seen Bill's cabin was afire so I clum in through the back winder to save Miss Margaret. She was gone, but they was a note she'd left. I was fixin' to climb out the winder when you grabbed me, you cussed maneyack!"

"Gimme that note!" I bellered, grabbing it. "Medina! Come here and read it for me."

That note run:

"Dear Breckinridge. I am sorry, but I can't stay on Bear Creek any longer. It was tough enough anyway, but being expected to marry you was the last straw. You've been very kind to me, but it would be too much like marrying a grizzly bear. Please forgive me. I am eloping with J. Pembroke Pemberton. We're going out the back window to avoid any trouble, and ride away on his horse. Give my love to the children. We are going to Europe on our honeymoon. With love, Margaret Devon."

"Now what you got to say?" sneered Uncle Jeppard.

"Where's my hoss?" I yelled, gomg temporarily insane. "I'll foller 'em! They cain't do me this way! I'll have his sculp if I have to foller 'em to Europe or to hell! Git outa my way!"

Uncle Saul grabbed me as I plunged through the crowd.

"Now, now, Breckinridge," he expostulated, trying to brace his laigs as he hung on and was dragged down the road. "You cain't do nothin' to him. She done this of her own free will. She made her choice, and--"

"Release go of me!" I roared, jerking loose. "I'm ridin' on their trail, and the man don't live which can stop me! Life won't be worth livin' when Glory McGraw hears about this, and I aim to take it out on that Britisher's hide! Hell hath no fury like a Elkins scorned! Git outa my way!"

CHAPTER XIII

WHEN BEAR CREEK CAME TO CHAWED EAR

I DUNNO how far I rode that night before the red haze cleared out from around me so's I could even see where I was. I knowed I was follering the trail to War Paint, but that was about all. I knowed Miss Margaret and J. Pembroke would head for War Paint, and I knowed Cap'n Kidd would run 'em down before they could get there, no matter how much start they had. And I must of rode for hours before I come to my senses.

It was like waking up from a bad dream. I pulled up on the crest of a rise and looked ahead of me where the trail dipped down into the holler and up over the next ridge. It was jest getting daylight and everything looked kinda grey and still. I looked down in the trail and seen the hoof prints of J. Pembroke's hoss fresh in the dust, and knowed they couldn't be more'n three or four miles ahead of me. I could run' em down within the next hour.

But thinks I, what the hell? Am I plumb locoed? The gal's got a right to marry whoever she wants to, and if she's idjit enough to choose him instead of me, why, 'tain't for me to stand in her way. I wouldn't hurt a hair onto her head; yet here I been aiming to hurt her the wust way I could, by shooting down her man right before her eyes. I felt so ashamed of myself I wanted to cuss--and so sorry for myself I wanted to bawl.

"Go with my blessin'," I said bitterly, shaking my fist in the direction where they'd went, and then reined Cap'n Kidd around and headed for Bear Creek. I warn't aiming to stay there and endure Glory McGraw's rawhiding, but I had to get me some clothes. Mine was burnt to rags, and I didn't have no hat, and the buckshot in my shoulder was stinging me now and then.

A mile or so on the back-trail I crossed the road that runs from Cougar Paw to Grizzly Run, and I was hungry and thirsty so I turnt up it to the tavern which had been built recent on the crossing at Mustang Creek.

The sun warn't up when I pulled at the hitch-rack and clumb off and went in. The bartender give a holler and fell backwards into a tub of water and empty beer bottles, and started yelling for help, and I seen a man come to one of the doors which opened into the bar, and look at me. They was something familiar about him, but I couldn't place him for the instant.

"Shet up and git outa that tub," I told the bar-keep petulantly. "It's me, and I want a drink."

"Excuse me, Breckinridge," says he, hauling hisself onto his feet. "I rekernize you now, but I'm a nervous man, and you got no idee what a start you gimme when you come through that door jest now, with yore hair and eye-lashes all burnt off, and most of yore clothes, and yore hide all black with soot. What the hell--"

"Cease them personal remarks and gimme some whisky," I snarled, being in no mood for airy repartee. "Likewise wake up the cook and tell him to fry me some ham and aigs."

So he sot the bottle onto the bar and stuck his head into the kitchen and hollered: "Break out a fresh ham and start bustin' aigs. Breckinridge Elkins craves fodder!"

When he come back I said: "Who was that lookin' through that door there while ago?"

"Oh, that?" says he. "Why, that was a man nigh as famous as what you be-- Wild Bill Donovan. You-all ever met?"

"I'll say we has," I grunted, pouring me a drink. "He tried to take Cap'n Kidd away from me when I was a ignorant kid. I was forced to whup him with my bare fists before he'd listen to reason."

"He's the only man I ever seen which was as big as you," said the bar-keep. "And at that he ain't quite as thick in the chest and arms as you be. I'll call him in and you-all can chin about old times."

"Save yore breath," I growled. "The thing I craves to do about chins with that coyote is to bust his'n with a pistol butt."

This seemed to kinda intimidate the bartender. He got behind the bar and started shining beer mugs whilst I et my breakfast in gloomy grandeur, halting only long enough to yell for somebody to feed Cap'n Kidd. Three or four menials went out to do it, and being afeared to try to lead Cap'n Kidd to the trough, they filled it and carried it to him, so only one of them got kicked in the belly. It's awful hard for the average man to dodge Cap'n Kidd.

Well, I finished my breakfast whilst they was dipping the stable- hand in a hoss-trough to bring him to, and I said to the bar-keep, "I ain't got no money to pay for what me and Cap'n Kidd et, but I'll be headin' for War Paint late this evenin' or tonight, and when I git the money I'll send it to you. I'm broke right now, but I ain't goin' to be broke long."

"All right," he said, eyeing my scorched skull in morbid fascination. "You got no idee how pecoolier you look, Breckinridge, with that there bald dome--"

"Shet up!" I roared wrathfully. A Elkins is sensitive about his personal appearance. "This here is merely a temporary inconvenience which I cain't help. Lemme hear no more about it. I'll shoot the next son of a polecat which calls attention to my singed condition!"

I then tied a bandanner around my head and got on Cap'n Kidd and pulled for home.

I arriv at pap's cabin about the middle of the afternoon and my family rallied around to remove the buckshot from my hide and repair other damages which had been did.

Maw made each one of my brothers lend me a garment, and she let 'em out to fit me.

"Though how much good it'll do you," said she, "I don't know. I never seen any man so hard on his clothes as you be, in my life. If it ain't fire it's bowie knives, and if it ain't bowie knives, it's buckshot."

"Boys will be boys, maw," soothed pap. "Breckinridge is jest full of life and high spirits, ain't you, Breckinridge?"

"From the whiff I got of his breath," snorted Elinor, "I'd say they is no doubt about the spirits."

"Right now I'm full of gloom and vain regrets," I says bitterly. "Culture is a flop on Bear Creek, and my confidence has been betrayed. I have tooken a sarpent with a British accent to my bosom and been bit. I stands knee-deep in the rooins of education and romance. Bear Creek lapses back into ignorance and barbarism and corn-licker, and I licks the wounds of unrequited love like a old wolf after a tussle with a pack of hound dawgs!"

"What you goin' to do?" ast pap, impressed.

"I'm headin' for War Paint," I said gloomily. "I ain't goin' to stay here and have the life rawhided outa me by Glory McGraw. It's a wonder to me she ain't been over already to gloat over my misery."

"You ain't got no money," says pap.

"I'll git me some," I said. "And I ain't particular how. I'm going now. I ain't goin' to wait for Glory McGraw to descend onto me with her derned sourcasm."

So I headed for War Paint as soon as I could wash the soot off of me. I had a Stetson I borrowed from Garfield and I jammed it down around my ears so my bald condition warn't evident, because I was awful sensitive about it.

Sundown found me some miles from the place where the trail crossed the Cougar Paw-Grizzly Run road, and jest before the sun dipped I was hailed by a pecooliar-looking gent.

He was tall and gangling--tall as me, but didn't weigh within a hundred pounds as much. His hands hung about three foot out of his sleeves, and his neck with a big adam's apple riz out of his collar like a crane's, and he had on a plug hat instead of a Stetson, and a long-tailed coat. He moreover sot his hoss like it was a see-saw, and his stirrups was so short his bony knees come up almost level with his shoulders. He wore his pants laigs down over his boots, and altogether he was the funniest-looking human I ever seen. Cap'n Kidd give a disgusted snort when he seen him and wanted to kick his bony old sorrel nag in the belly, but I wouldn't let him.

"Air you," said this apparition, p'inting a accusing finger at me, "air you

Breckinridge Elkins, the bearcat of the Humbolts?"

"I'm Breckinridge Elkins," I replied suspiciously.

"I dedooced as much," he says ominously. "I have come a long ways to meet you, Elkins. They can be only one sun in the sky, my roarin' grizzly from the high ranges. They can be only one champeen in the State of Nevada. I'm him!"

"Oh, be you?" I says, scenting battle afar. "Well, I feels the same way about one sun and one champeen. You look a mite skinny and gantlin' to be makin' sech big talk, but far be it from me to deny you a tussle after you've come so far to git it. Light down from yore hoss whilst I mangles yore frame with a free and joyful spirit! They is nothin' I'll enjoy more'n uprootin' a few acres of junipers with yore carcass and festoonin' the crags with yore innards."

"You mistakes my meanin', my bloodthirsty friend," says he. "I warn't referrin' to mortal combat. Far as I'm consarned, yo're supreme in that line. Nay, nay, B. Elkins, esquire! Reserve yore personal ferocity for the b'ars and knife-fighters of yore native mountains. I challenges you in another department entirely.

"Look well, my bowie-wieldin' orang-outang of the high peaks. Fame is shakin' her mane. I am Jugbelly Judkins, and my talent is guzzlin'. From the live-oak grown coasts of the Gulf to the sun-baked buttes of Montana," says he oratorical, "I ain't yet met the gent I couldn't drink under the table betwixt sundown and sunup. I have met the most celebrated topers of plain and mountain, and they have all went down in inglorious and rum-soaked defeat. Afar off I heard men speak of you, praisin' not only yore genius in alterin' the features of yore feller man, but also laudin' yore capacity for corn-licker. So I have come to cast the ga'nt-let at yore feet, as it were."

"Oh," I says, "you wants a drinkin' match."

"'Wants' is a weak word, my murderous friend," says he. "I demands it."

"Well, come on," I said. "Le's head for War Paint then. They'll be plenty of gents there willin' to lay heavy bets--"

"To hell with filthy lucre!" snorted Jugbelly. "My mountainous friend, I am an artist. I cares nothin' for money. My reputation is what I upholds."

"Well, then," I said, "they's a tavern on Mustang Creek--"

"Let it rot," says he. "I scorns these vulgar displays in low inns and cheap taverns, my enormous friend. I supplies the sinews of war myself. Foller me!"

So he turnt his hoss off the trail, and I follered him through the bresh for maybe a mile, till he come to a small cave in a bluff with dense thickets all around. He reched into the cave and hauled out a gallon jug of licker.

"I hid a goodly supply of the cup that cheers in that cave," says he. "This is a good secluded spot where nobody never comes. We won't be interrupted here, my brawny but feeble-minded gorilla of the high ridges!"

"But what're we bettin'?" I demanded. "I ain't got no money. I was goin' down to War Paint and git me a job workin' somebody's claim for day-wages till I got me a stake and built it up playin' poker, but--"

"You wouldn't consider wagerin' that there gigantic hoss you rides?" says he, eyeing me very sharp.

"Never in the world," I says with a oath.

"Very well," says he. "Let the bets go. We battles for honor and glory alone! Let the carnage commence!"

So we started. First he'd take a gulp, and then me, and the jug was empty about the fourth gulp I taken, so he dragged out another'n, and we emptied it, and he hauled out another. They didn't seem to be no limit to his supply. He must of brought it there on a whole train of pack mules. I never seen a man drink like that skinny cuss. I watched the liquor careful, but he lowered it every time he taken a swig, so I knowed he warn't jest pertending. His belly expanded enormous as we went along and he looked very funny, with his skinny frame, and that there enormous belly bulging out his shirt till the buttons flew off of his coat.

I ain't goin' to tell you how much we drunk, because you wouldn't believe me. But by midnight the glade was covered with empty jugs and Jugbelly's arms was so tired lifting 'em he couldn't hardly move. But the moon and the glade and everything was dancing around and around to me, and he warn't even staggerring. He looked kind of pale and wan, and onst he says, in a awed voice: "I wouldn't of believed it if I hadn't saw it myself!" But he kept on drinking and so did I, because I couldn't believe a skinny maverick like that could lick me, and his belly kept getting bigger and bigger till I was scairt it was going to bust, and things kept spinning around me faster than ever.

After awhile I heard him muttering to hisself, away off: "This is the last jug, and if it don't fix him, nothin' will. By God, he ain't human."

That didn't make no sense to me, but he passed me the jug and said: "Air you capable, my gulf-bellied friend?"

"Gimme that jug!" I muttered, bracing my laigs and getting a firm hold of myself. I taken a big gulp--and then I didn't know nothing.

When I woke up the sun was high above the trees. Cap'n Kidd was cropping grass nearby, but Jugbelly was gone. So was his hoss and all the empty jugs. There warn't no sign to show he'd ever been there, only the taste in my mouth which I cain't describe because I am a gent and there is words no gent will stoop to use. I felt like kicking myself in the pants. I was ashamed something terrible at being beat by that skinny mutt. It was the first time I'd ever drunk enough to lay me out. I don't believe in a man making a hawg out of hisself, even in a good cause.

I saddled Cap'n Kidd and pulled out for War Paint, and stopped a few rods away and drunk five or six gallons of water at a spring, and felt a lot better. I started on again, but before I come to the trail, I heard somebody bawling and pulled up, and there sot a feller on a stump, crying like his heart would bust.

"What's the trouble?" I ast, and he blinked the tears out of his eyes and looked up mournful and melancholy. He was a scrawny cuss with over-sized whiskers.

"You beholds in me," says he sobfully, "a critter tossed on the crooel tides of fate. Destiny has dealt my hand from the bottom of the deck. Whoa is me!" says he, and wept bitterly.

"Buck up," I said. "Things might well be wuss. Dammit," I said, waxing irritable, "stop that blubberin' and tell me what's the matter. I'm Breckinridge Elkins. Maybe I can help you."

He swallered some sobs, and said: "You air a man of kind impulses and a noble heart. My name is Japhet Jalatin. In my youth I made a enemy of a wealthy, powerful and unscrupulous man. He framed me and sent me to the pen for somethin' I never done. I busted free and under a assumed name, I come West. By hard workin' I accumulated a tidy sum which I aimed to send to my sorrowin' wife and baby datters. But jest last night I learnt that I had been rekernized and the bloodhounds of the law was on my trail. I have got to skip to Mexico. My loved ones won't never git the dough.

"Oh," says he, "if they was only some one I could trust to leave it with till I could write 'em a letter and tell 'em where it was so they could send a trusted man after it! But I trust nobody. The man I left it with might tell where he got it, and then the bloodhounds of the law would be onto my trail again, houndin' me day and night."

He looked at me desperate, and says: "Young man, you got a kind and honest face. Won't _you_ take this here money and hold it for my wife, till she can come after it?"

"Yeah, I'll do that," I said. He jumped up and run to his hoss which was tied nearby, and hauled out a buckskin poke, and shoved it into my hands.

"Keep it till my wife comes for it," says he. "And promise me you won't never breathe a word of how you got it, except to her!"

"A Elkins never broke his word in his life," I said. "Wild hosses couldn't drag it outa me."

"Bless you, young man!" he cries, and grabbed my hand with both of his'n and pumped it up and down like a pump-handle, and then jumped on his hoss and fogged. I thought they is some curious people in the world, as I stuffed the poke in my saddle-bags and headed for War Paint again.

I thought I'd turn off to the Mustang Creek tavern and eat me some breakfast, but I hadn't much more'n hit the trail I'd been follerin' when I met Jugbelly, than I heard hosses behind me, and somebody hollered: "Stop, in the name of the law!"

I turnt around and seen a gang of men riding towards me, from the direction of Bear Creek, and there was the sheriff leading 'em, and right beside him was pap and Uncle John Garfield and Uncle Bill Buckner and Uncle Bearfield Gordon. A tenderfoot onst called them four men the patriarchs of Bear Creek. I dunno what he meant, but they generally decides argyments which has got beyond the public control, as you might say. Behind them and the sheriff come about thirty more men, most of which I rekernized as citizens of Chawed Ear, and therefore definitely not my friends. Also, to my surprise, I rekernized Wild Bill Donovan amongst 'em, with his thick black hair falling down to his shoulders. They was four other hard-looking strangers which rode clost beside him.

All the Chawed Ear men had sawed-off shotguns and that surprised me, because that made it look like maybe they was coming to arrest me, and I hadn't done nothing, except steal their schoolteacher, several weeks before, and if they'd meant to arrest me for that, they'd of tried it before now.

"There he is!" yelped the sheriff, p'inting at me. "Han's up!"

"Don't be a damn' fool!" roared pap, knocking his shotgun out of his hands as he started to raise it. "You want to git you and yore cussed posse slaughtered? Come here, Breckinridge," he said, and I rode up to them, some bewildered. I could see pap was worried. He scowled and tugged at his beard. My uncles didn't have no more expression onto their faces than so many red Injuns.

"What the hell's all this about?" I ast.

"Take off yore hat," ordered the sheriff.

"Look here, you long-legged son of a mangy skunk," I said heatedly, "if yo're tryin' to rawhide me, lemme tell you right now--"

"'Tain't a joke," growled pap. "Take off yore sombrero."

I done so bewilderedly, and instantly four men in the gang started hollering: "That's him! That's the man! He had on a mask, but when he taken his hat off, we seen the hair was all off his head! That's shore him!"

"Elkins," said the sheriff, "I arrests you for the robbery of the Chawed Ear stage!"

I convulsively went for my guns. It was jest a instinctive move which I done without knowing it, but the sheriff hollered and ducked, and the possemen throwed up their guns, and pap spurred in between us.

"Put down them guns, everybody!" he roared, covering me with one six-shooter and the posse with the other'n. "First man that pulls a trigger, I'll salivate him!"

"I ain't aimin' to shoot nobody!" I bellered. "But what the hell is this all about?"

"As if he didn't know!" sneered one of the posse. "Tryin' to ack innercent! Heh heh heh--_glup!_"

Pap riz in his stirrups and smashed him over the head with his right-hand six-shooter barrel, and he crumpled into the trail and laid there with the blood oozing out of his sculp.

"Anybody else feel humorous?" roared pap, sweeping the posse with a terrible eye. Evidently nobody did, so he turnt around and says to me, and I seen drops of perspiration standing on his face which warn't caused altogether by the heat. Says he: "Breckinridge, early last night the Chawed Ear stage was stuck up and robbed a few miles t'other side of Chawed Ear. The feller which done it not only taken the passengers' money and watches and things, and the mail sack, but he also shot the driver, old Jim Harrigan, jest out of pure cussedness. Old Jim's layin' over in Chawed Ear now with a bullet through his laig.

"These born fools thinks you done it! They was on Bear Creek before daylight--the first time a posse ever dared to come onto Bear Creek, and it was all me and yore uncles could do to keep the boys from massacrein, 'em. Bear Creek was sure wrought up. These mavericks," pap p'inted a finger of scorn at the four men which had claimed to identify me, "was on the stage. You know Ned Ashley, Chawed Ear's leadin' merchant. The others air strangers. They say their names is Hurley, Jackson and Slade. They claim to lost considerable money."

"We done that!" clamored Jackson. "I had a buckskin poke crammed full of gold pieces the scoundrel taken. I tell you, that's the man which done it!" He p'inted at me, and pap turnt to Ned Ashley, and said: "Ned, what do you say?"

"Well, Bill," says Ashley reluctantly, "I hates to say it, but I don't see who else it could of been. The robber was Breckinridge's size, all right, and you know they ain't many men that big. He warn't ridin' Cap'n Kidd, of course; he was ridin' a big bay mare. He had on a mask, but as he rode off he taken off his hat, and we all seen his head in the moonlight. The hair was all off of it, jest like it is Breckinridge's. Not like he was naturally bald, but like it had been burnt off or shaved off recent."

"Well," says the sheriff, "unless he can prove a alibi I'll have to arrest him."

"Breckinridge," says pap, "whar was you last night?"

"I was layin' out in the woods drunk," I says.

I felt a aidge of doubt in the air.

"I didn't know you could drink enough to git drunk," says pap. "It ain't like you, anyway. What made you? Was it thinkin' about that gal?"

"Naw," I said. "I met a gent in a plug hat named Jugbelly Judkins and he challenged me to a drinkin' match."

"Did you win?" ast pap anxiously.

"Naw!" I confessed in bitter shame. "I lost."

Pap muttered disgustedly in his beard, and the sheriff says: "Can you perduice this Judkins _hombre?"_

"I dunno where he went," I said. "He'd pulled out when I woke up."

"Very inconvenient, I says!" says Wild Bill Donovan, running his fingers lovingly through his long black locks, and spitting.

"Who ast you yore opinion?" I snarled blood-thirstily. "What you doin' in the Humbolts? Come back to try to git even for Cap'n Kidd?"

"I forgot that trifle long ago," says he. "I holds no petty grudge. I jest happened to be ridin' the road this side of Chawed Ear when the posse come by and I come with 'em jest to see the fun."

"You'll see more fun than you can tote home if you fool with me," I promised.

"Enough of this," snorted pap. "Breckinridge, even I got to admit yore alibi sounds kind of fishy. A critter named Jugbelly with a plug hat! It sounds plumb crazy. Still and all, we'll look for this cussed maverick, and if we find him and he establishes whar you was last night, why--"

"He put my gold in his saddle-bags!" clamored Jackson. "I seen him! That's the same saddle! Look in them bags and I bet you'll find it!"

"Go ahead and look," I invited, and the sheriff went up to Cap'n Kidd very gingerly, whilst I restrained Cap'n Kidd from kicking his brains out. He run his hand in the bags and I'll never forget the look on pap's face when the sheriff hauled out that buckskin poke Japhet Jalatin had give me. I'd forgot all about it.

"How you explain _this_?" exclaimed the sheriff. I said nothing. A Elkins never busts his word, not even if he hangs for it.

"It's mine!" hollered Jackson. "You'll find my initials worked onto it! J.J., for Judah Jackson."

"There they air," announced the sheriff. "J.J. That's for Judah Jackson, all right."

"They don't stand for that!" I roared. "They stand for--" Then I stopped. I couldn't tell him they stood for Japhet Jalatin without breaking my word and giving away Japhet's secret.

"'Tain't his'n," I growled. "I didn't steal it from nobody."

"Then where'd you git it?" demanded the sheriff.

"None of yore business," I said sullenly.

Pap spurred forwards, and I seen beads of sweat on his face.

"Well, say somethin', damn it!" he roared. "Don't jest set there! No Elkins was ever accused of thievin' before, but if you done it, say so! I demands that you tells me whar you got that gold! If you didn't take it off'n the stage, why don't you say so?"

"I cain't tell you," I muttered.

"Hell's fire!" bellered pap. "Then you must of robbed that stage! What a black shame onto Bear Creek this here is! But these town-folks ain't goin' to haul you off to their cussed jail, even if you did turn thief! Jest come out plain and tell me you done it, and we'll lick the whole cussed posse if necessary!"

I seen my uncles behind him drawing in and cocking their Winchesters, but I was too dizzy with the way things was happening to think straight about anything.

"I never robbed the cussed stage!" I roared. "I cain't tell you where I got that gold--but I didn't rob the gol-derned stage."

"So yo're a liar as well as a thief!" says pap, drawing back from me like I was a reptile. "To think it should come to this! From this day onwards," he says, shaking his fist in my face, "you ain't no son of mine! I disowns you! When they lets you out of the pen, don't you come sneakin' back to Bear Creek! Us folks there if is rough and ready; we kyarves and shoots each other free and frequent; but no Bear Creek man ever yet stole nor lied. I could forgive the thievin', maybe, maybe even the shootin' of pore old Jim Harrigan. But I cain't forgive a lie. Come on, boys."

And him and my uncles turnt around and rode back up the trail towards Bear Creek with their eyes straight ahead of 'em and their backs straight as ramrods. I glared after 'em wildly, feeling like the world was falling to pieces. It war the first time in my life I'd ever knowed Bear Creek folks to turn their backs on a Bear Creek man.

"Well, come along," said the sheriff, and started to hand the poke to Jackson, when I come alive. I warn't going to let Japhet Jalatin's wife spend the rest of her life in poverty if I could help it. I made one swoop and grabbed the poke out of his hand and simultaneous drove in the spurs. Cap'n Kidd made one mighty lunge and knocked Jackson and his hoss sprawling and went over them and into the bresh whilst them fool posse-men was fumbling with their guns. They was a lot of cussing and yelling behind me and some shooting, but we was out of sight of them in a instant, and I went crashing on till I hit a creek I knowed was there. I jumped off and grabbed a big rock which was in the bed of the creek, with about three foot of water around it--jest the top stuck out above the water. I grabbed it and lifted it, and stuck the poke down under it, and let the rock back down again. It was safe here. Nobody'd ever suspect it was hid there, and it was a cinch nobody was going to be lifting the rock jest for fun and find the gold accidental. It weighed about as much as the average mule.

Cap'n Kidd bolted off through the woods as the posse come crashing through the bresh, yelling like Injuns, and they throwed down their shotguns on me as I clumb up the bank, dripping wet.

"Catch that hoss!" yelled the sheriff. "The gold's in the saddle- bags!"

"You'll never catch that hoss," opined Wild Bill Donovan. "I know him of old."

"Maybe Elkins is got the gold on him!" hollered Jackson. "Search him!"

I didn't make no resistance as the sheriff taken my guns and snapped a exter heavy pair of hand-cuffs onto my wrists. I was still kind of numb from having pap and my uncles walk out on me like that. All I'd been able to think of up to then was to hide the gold, and when that was hid my brain wouldn't work no further.

"Elkins ain't got it on him!" snarled the sheriff, after slapping my pockets. "Go after that hoss! Shoot him if you cain't catch him."

"No use for that," I says. "It ain't in the saddle-bags. I hid it where you won't never find it."

"Look in all the holler trees!" says Jackson, and added viciously: "We might _make_ him talk."

"Shet up," said the sheriff. "Anything _you_ could do to him would jest make him mad. He's actin' tame and gentle now. But he's got a broodin' gleam in his eye. Le's git him in jail before he gits a change of heart and starts remodellin' the landscape with the posse's carcasses."

"I'm a broken man," I says mournfully. "My own clan has went back on me, and I got no friends. Take me to jail if you wanta! All places is dreary for a man whose kin has disown him."

So we went to Chawed Ear.

One of the fellers who was riding a big strong hoss lemme have his'n, and the posse closed around me with their shotguns p'inting at me, and we headed out.

It was after dark when we got to Chawed Ear, but everybody was out in the streets to see the posse bring me in. They warn't no friendly faces in that crowd. I'd been very onpopular in Chawed Ear ever since I stole their schoolteacher. I looked for old Joshua Braxton, but somebody said he was off on a prospecting trip.

They stopped at a log-hut clost to the jail, and some men was jest getting through working onto it.

"That there," says the sheriff, "is yore private jail. We built it special for you. As soon as word come last night that you'd robbed the stage, I set fifteen men buildin' that jail, and they're jest now gittin' through."

Well, I didn't think anybody could build anything in a night and a day which could hold me, but I didn't have no thought of trying to break out. I didn't have the heart. All I could think of was the way pap and my uncles had rode off and left me disowned and arrested.

I went in like he told me, and sot down on the bunk, and heard 'em barring the door on the outside. They was fellers holding torches outside, and the light come in at the winder so I could see it was a good strong jail. They was jest one room, with a door towards the town and a winder in the other side. It had a floor made out of logs, and the roof and walls was made out of heavy logs, and they was a big log at each corner sot in concrete, which was something new in them mountains, and the concrete wasn't dry yet. The bars in the winder was thick as a man's wrist, and drove clean through the sill and lintel logs and the ends clinched, and chinks betwixt the logs was tamped in with concrete. The door was made outa sawed planks four inches thick and braced with iron, and the hinges was big iron pins working in heavy iron sockets, and they was a big lock onto the door and three big bars made outa logs sot in heavy iron brackets.

Everybody outside was jammed around the winder trying to look in at me, but I put my head in my hands and paid no attention to 'em. I was trying to think but everything kept going round and round. Then the sheriff chased everybody away except them he told off to stay there and guard the jail, and he put his head to the bars and said: "Elkins, it'll go easier with you, maybe, if you'll tell us where you hid that there gold."

"When I do," I said gloomily, "there'll be ice in hell thick enough for the devil to skate on."

"All right," he snapped. "If you want to be stubborn. You'll git twenty years for this, or I miss my guess."

"Gwan," I said, "and leave me to my misery. What's a prison term to a man which has jest been disowned by his own blood-kin?"

He pulled back from the winder and I heard him say to somebody: "It ain't no use. Them Bear Creek devils are the most uncivilized white men I ever seen in my life. You cain't do nothin' with one of 'em. I'm goin' to send some men back to look for the gold around that creek we found him climbin' out of. I got a idee he hid it in a holler tree somewheres. He's that much like a b'ar. Likely he hid it and then run and got in the creek jest to throw us off the scent. Thought he'd make us think he hid it on t'other side of the creek. I bet he hid it in a tree this side somewheres.

"I'm goin' to git some food and some sleep. I didn't git to bed at all last night. You fellers watch him clost, and if folks git too rambunctious around the jail, call me quick."

"Ain't nobody around the jail now," said a familiar voice.

"I know," says the sheriff. "They're back in town lickerin' up at all the bars. But Elkins is got plenty of enemies here, and they ain't no tellin' what might bust loose before mornin'."

I heard him leave, and then they was silence, except for some men whispering off somewheres nearby but talking too low for me to make out what they was saying. I could hear noises coming from the town, snatches of singing, and a occasional yell, but no pistol-shooting like they usually is. The jail was on the aidge of town, and the winder looked in the other direction, acrost a narrer clearing with thick woods bordering it.

Purty soon a man come and stuck his head up to the winder and I seen by the starlight that it was Wild Bill Donovan.

"Well, Elkins," says he, "you think you've finally found a jail which can hold you?"

"What you doin' hangin' around here?" I muttered.

He patted his shotgun and said: "Me and four of my friends has been app'inted special guards. But I tell you what I'll do. I hate to see a man down and out like you be, and booted out by his own family and shore to do at least fifteen years in the pen. You tell me where you hid that there gold, and give me Cap'n Kidd, and I'll contrive to let you escape before mornin'. I got a fast hoss hid out there in the thickets, right over yonder, see? You can fork that hoss and be gone outa the country before the sheriff could catch you. All you got to do is give me Cap'n Kidd, and that gold. What you say?"

"I wouldn't give you Cap'n Kidd," I said, "not if they was goin' to hang me."

"Well," he sneered, "'tain't none too shore they ain't. They's plenty of rope-law talk in town tonight. Folks are purty well wrought up over you shootin' old Jim Harrigan."

"I didn't shoot him, damn yore soul!" I said.

"You'll have a hell of a time provin' it," says he, and turnt around and walked around towards the other end of the jail with his shotgun under his arm.

Well, I dunno how long I sot there with my head in my hands and jest suffered. Noises from the town seemed dim and far off. I didn't care if they come and lynched me before morning, I was that low- spirited. I would of bawled if I could of worked up enough energy, but I was too low for that even.

Then somebody says: "Breckinridge!" and I looked up and seen Glory McGraw looking in at the winder with the rising moon behind her.

"Go ahead and t'ant me," I said numbly. "Everything else has happened to me. You might as well, too."

"I ain't goin' to t'ant you!" she said fiercely. "I come here to help you, and I aim to, no matter what you says!"

"You better not let Donovan see you talkin' to me," I says.

"I done seen him," she said. "He didn't want to let me come to the winder, but I told him I'd go to the sheriff for permission if he didn't, so he said he'd let me talk ten minutes. Listen: did he offer to help you escape if you'd do somethin' for him?"

"Yeah," I said. "Why?"

She ground her teeth slightly.

"I thought so!" says she. "The dirty rat! I come through the woods, and snuck on foot the last few hundred feet to git a look at the jail before I come out in the open. They's a hoss tied out there in the thickets and a man hidin' behind a log right nigh it with a sawed-off shotgun. Donovan's always hated you, ever since you taken Cap'n Kidd away from him. He aimed to git you shot whilst tryin' to escape. When I seen that ambush I jest figgered on somethin' like that."

"How'd you git here?" I ast, seeing she seemed to really mean what she said about helping me.

"I follered the posse and yore kinfolks when they came down from Bear Creek," she said. "I kept to the bresh on my pony, and was within hearin' when they stopped you on the trail. After everybody had left I went and caught Cap'n Kidd, and--"

"_You_ caught Cap'n Kidd!" I said in dumbfoundment.

"Certainly," says she. "Hosses has frequently got more sense than men. He'd come back to the creek where he'd saw you last and looked like he was plumb broken-hearted because he couldn't find you. I turnt the pony loose and started him home, and I come on to Chawed Ear on Cap'n Kidd."

"Well, I'm a saw-eared jackrabbit!" I said helplessly.

"Hosses knows who their friends is," says she. "Which is more'n I can say for some men. Breckinridge, pull out of this! Tear this blame jail apart and le's take to the hills! Cap'n Kidd's waitin' out there behind that big clump of oaks. They'll never catch you!"

"I ain't got the strength, Glory," I said helplessly. "My strength has oozed out of me like licker out of a busted jug. What's the use to bust jail, even if I could? I'm a marked man, and a broken man. My own kin has throwed me down. I got no friends."

"You have, too!" she said fiercely. "_I_ ain't throwed you down. I'm standin' by you till hell freezes!"

"But folks thinks I'm a thief and a liar!" I says, about ready to weep.

"What I care what they thinks?" says she. "If you _was_ all them things, I'd still stand by you! But you ain't, and I know it!"

For a second I couldn't see her because my sight got blurry, but I groped and found her hand tense on the winder bar, and I said: "Glory, I dunno what to say. I been a fool, and thought hard things about you, and--"

"Forgit it," says she. "Listen: if you won't bust out of here, we got to prove to them fools that you didn't rob that stage. And we got to do it quick, because them strangers Hurley and Jackson and Slade air in town circulatin' around through the bars and stirrin' them fool Chawed Ear folks up to lynchin' you. A mob's liable to come bustin' out of town any minute. Won't you tell me where you got that there gold they found in yore saddle-bags? _I_ know you never stole it, but if you was to tell me, it might help us."

I shaken my head helplessly.

"I cain't tell you," I said. "Not even you. I promised not to. A Elkins cain't break his word."

"Ha!" says she. "Listen: did some stranger meet you and give you that poke of gold to give to his starvin' wife and chillern, and make you promise not to tell nobody where you got it, because his life was in danger?"

"Why, how'd you know?" I exclaimed in amazement.

"So that _was_ it!" she exclaimed, jumping up and down in her excitement. "How'd I know? Because I know you, you big bone-headed mush-hearted chump! Lissen: don't you see how they worked you? This was a put-up job.

"Jugbelly got you off and made you drink so's you'd be outa the way and couldn't prove no alibi. Then somebody that looked like you robbed the stage and shot old man Harrigan in the laig jest to make the crime wuss. Then this feller what's-his-name give you the money so they'd find it onto you!"

"It looks sensible!" I said dizzily.

"It's bound to be!" says she. "Now all we got to do is find Jugbelly and the feller which give you the gold, and the bay mare the robber rode. But first we got to find a man which has got it in for you enough to frame you like that."

"That's a big order," I says. "Nevada's full of gents which would give their eye-teeth to do me a injury."

"A big man," she mused. "Big enough to be mistook for you, with his head shaved, and ridin' a big bay mare. Hmmmmm! A man which hates you enough to do anything to you, and is got sense enough to frame somethin' like this!"

And jest then Wild Bill Donovan come around the corner of the jail with his shotgun under his arm.

"You've talked to that jail-bird long enough, gal," he says. "You better pull out. The noise is gettin' louder all the time in town, and it wouldn't surprise me to see quite a bunch of folks comin' to the jail before long--with a necktie for yore friend there."

"And I bet you'll plumb risk yore life defendin' him," she sneered.

He laughed and taken off his sombrero and run his fingers through his thick black locks.

"I don't aim to git none of my valuable gore spilt over a stagecoach robber," says he. "But I like yore looks, gal. Why you want to waste yore time with a feller like that when they is a man like me around, I dunno! His head looks like a peeled onion! The hair won't never git no chance to grow out, neither, 'cause he's goin' to git strung up before it has time. Whyn't you pick out a handsome _hombre_ like me, which has got a growth of hair as is hair?"

"He got his hair burnt off tryin' to save a human life," says she. "Somethin' that ain't been said of you, you big monkey!"

"Haw haw haw!" says he. "Ain't you got the spunk, though! That's the way I like gals."

"You might not like me so much," says she suddenly, "if I told you I'd found that big bay mare you rode last night!"

He started like he was shot and blurted out: "Yo're lyin'! Nobody could find her where I hid her--"

He checked hisself sudden, but Glory give a yelp.

"_I thought so!_ It was you!" And before he could stop her she grabbed his black locks and yanked. And his sculp come off in her hands and left his head as bare as what mine was!

"A wig jest like I thought!" she shrieked. "You robbed that stage! You shaved yore head to look like Breckinridge--" He grabbed her and clapped his hand over her mouth, and yelped: "Joe! Tom! Buck!" And at the sight of Glory struggling in his grasp I snapped them handcuffs like they was rotten cords and laid hold of them winder bars and tore 'em out. The logs they was sot in split like kindling wood and I come smashing through that winder like a b'ar through a chicken coop. Donovan let go of Glory and grabbed up his shotgun to blow my head off, but she grabbed the barrel and throwed all her weight onto it, so he couldn't bring it to bear on me, and my feet hit the ground jest as three of his pals come surging around the corner of the jail.

They was so surprised to see me out, and going so fast they couldn't stop and they run right into me and I gathered 'em to my bosom and you ought to of heard the bones crack and snap. I jest hugged the three of 'em together onst and then throwed 'em in all direction like a b'ar ridding hisself of a pack of hounds. Two of 'em fractured their skulls agen the jail-house and t'other broke his laig on a stump.

Meanwhile Donovan had let loose of his shotgun and run for the woods and Glory scrambled up onto her feet with the shotgun and let _bam_ at him, but he was so far away by that time all she done was sting his hide with the shot. But he hollered tremendous jest the same. I started to run after him, but Glory grabbed me.

"He's headed for that hoss I told you about!" she panted. "Git Cap'n Kidd! We'll have to be a-hoss-back if we catch him!"

Bang! went a shotgun in the thickets, and Donovan's maddened voice yelled: "Stop that, you cussed fool! This ain't Elkins! It's me! The game's up! We got to shift!"

"Lemme ride with you!" hollered another voice, which I reckoned was the feller Donovan had planted to shoot me if I agreed to try to escape. "My hoss is on the other side of the jail!"

"Git off, blast you!" snarled Donovan. "This boss won't carry double!" _Wham!_ I jedged he'd hit his pal over the head with his six- shooter. "I owe you that for fillin' my hide with buckshot, you blame fool!" Donovan roared as he went crashing off into the bresh.

By this time we'd reched the oaks Cap'n Kidd was tied behind, and I swung up into the saddle and Glory jumped up behind me.

"I'm goin' with you!" says she. "Don't argy! Git, goin'!"

I headed for the thickets Donovan had disappeared into, and jest inside of 'em we seen a feller sprawled on the ground with a shotgun in his hand and his sculp split open. Even in the midst of my righteous wrath I had a instant of ca'm and serene joy as I reflected that Donovan had got sprinkled with buckshot by the feller who evidently mistook him for me. The deeds of the wicked sure do return onto 'em.

Donovan had took straight out through the bresh, and left gaps in the bushes a blind man could foller. We could hear his hoss crashing through the timber ahead of us, and then purty soon the smashing stopped but we could hear the hoofs lickety-split on hard ground, so I knowed he'd come out into a path, and purty soon so did we. Moonlight hit down into it, but it was winding so we couldn't see very far ahead, but the hoof-drumming warn't pulling away from us, and we knowed we was closing in onto him. He was riding a fast critter but I knowed Cap'n Kidd would run it off its fool laigs within the next mile.

Then we seen a small clearing ahead and a cabin in it with candle- light coming through the winders, and Donovan busted out of the trees and jumped off his hoss which bolted into the bresh. Donovan run to the door and yelled: "Lemme in, you damn' fools! The game's up and Elkins is right behind me!"

The door opened and he fell in onto his all-fours and yelled: "Shet the door and bolt it! I don't believe even he can bust it down!" And somebody else hollered: "Blow out the candles! There he is at the aidge of the trees."

Guns began to crack and bullets whizzed past me, so I backed Cap'n Kidd back into cover and jumped off and picked up a big log which warn't rotten yet, and run out of the clearing and made towards the door. This surprised the men in the cabin, and only one man shot at me and he hit the log. The next instant I hit the door--or rather I hit the door with the log going full clip and the door splintered and ripped offa the hinges and crashed inwards, and three or four men got pinned under it and yelled bloody murder.

I lunged into the cabin over the rooins of the door and the candles was all out, but a little moonlight streamed in and showed me three or four vague figgers before me. They was all shooting at me but it was so dark in the cabin they couldn't see to aim good and only nicked me in a few unimportant places. So I went for them and got both arms full of human beings and started sweeping the floor with 'em. I felt several fellers underfoot because they hollered when I tromped on 'em, and every now and then I felt somebody's head with my foot and give it a good rousing kick. I didn't know who I had hold of because the cabin was so full of gunpowder smoke by this time that the moon didn't do much good. But none of the fellers was big enough to be Donovan, and them I stomped on didn't holler like him, so I started clearing house by heaving 'em one by one through the door, and each time I throwed one they was a resounding _whack!_ outside that I couldn't figger out till I realized that Glory was standing outside with a club and knocking each one in the head as he come out.

Then the next thing I knowed the cabin was empty, except for me and a figger which was dodging back and forth in front of me trying to get past me to the door. So I laid hands onto it and heaved it up over my head and started to throw it through the door when it hollered: "Quarter, my titanic friend, quarter! I surrenders and demands to be treated as a prisoner of war!"

"_Jugbelly Judkins!"_ I says.

"The same," says he, "or what's left of him!"

"Come out here where I can talk to you!" I roared, and groped my way out of the door with him. As I emerged I got a awful lick over the head, and then Glory give a shriek like a stricken elk.

"Oh, Breckinridge!" she wailed. "I didn't know it war you!"

"Never mind!" I says, brandishing my victim before her. "I got my alerbi right here by the neck! _Jugbelly Judkins_," I says sternly, clapping him onto his feet and waving a enormous fist under his snoot, "if you values yore immortal soul, speak up and tell where I was all last night!"

"Drinkin' licker with me a mile off the Bear Creek trail," gasps he, staring wildly about at the figgers which littered the ground in front of the cabin. "I confesses all! Lead me to the bastile! My sins has catched up with me. I'm a broken man. Yet I am but a tool in the hands of a master mind, same as these misguided sons of crime which lays there--"

"One of 'em's tryin' to crawl off," quoth Glory, fetching the aforesaid critter a clout on the back of the neck with her club. He fell on his belly and howled in a familiar voice.

I started vi'lently and bent over to look close at him.

"Japhet Jalatin!" I hollered. "You cussed thief, you lied to me about yore wife starvin'!"

"If he told you he had a wife it was a gross understatement," says Jugbelly. "He's got three that I know of, includin' a Piute squaw, a Mexican woman, and a Chinee gal in San Francisco. But to the best of my knowledge they're all fat and hearty."

"I have been took for a cleanin' proper," I roared, gnashing my teeth. "I've been played for a sucker! My trustin' nature has been tromped on! My faith in humanity is soured! Nothin' but blood can wipe out I this here infaminy!"

"Don't take it out on us," begged Japhet. "It war all Donovan's idee."

"Where's he?" I yelled, glaring around.

"Knowin' his nature as I does," said Judkins, working his jaw to see if it was broke in more'n one place, "I would sejest that he snuck out the back door whilst the fightin' was goin' on, and is now leggin' it for the corral he's got hid in the thicket behind the cabin, where he secreted the bay mare he rode the night he held up the stagecoach."

Glory pulled a pistol out of one of 'em's belt which he'd never got a chance to use, and she says: "Go after him, Breck. I'll take care of these coyotes!"

I taken one look at the groaning rooins on the ground, and decided she could all right, so I whistled to Cap'n Kidd, and he come, for a wonder. I forked him and headed for the thicket behind the cabin and jest as I done so I seen Donovan streaking it out the other side on a big bay mare. The moon made everything as bright as day.

"Stop and fight like a man, you mangy polecat!" I thundered, but he made no reply except to shoot at me with his six-shooter, and seeing I ignored this, he spurred the mare which he was riding bareback and headed for the high hills.

She was a good mare, but she didn't have a chance agen Cap'n Kidd. We was only a few hundred feet behind and closing in fast when Donovan busted out onto a bare ridge which overlooked a valley. He looked back and seen I was going to ride him down within the next hundred yards, and he jumped offa the mare and taken cover behind a pine which stood by itself a short distance from the aidge of the bresh. They warn't no bushes around it, and to rech him I'd of had to cross a open space in the moonlight, and every time I come out of the bresh he shot at me. So I kept in the aidge of the bresh and unslung my lariat and roped the top of the pine, and sot Cap'n Kid agen it with all his lungs and weight, and tore it up by the roots.

When it fell and left Donovan without no cover he run for the rim of the valley, but I jumped down and grabbed a rock about the size of a man's head and throwed it at him, and hit him jest above the knee on the hind laig. He hit the ground rolling and throwed away both of his six-shooters and hollered: "Don't shoot! I surrenders!"

I quiled my lariat and come up to where he was laying, and says: "Cease that there disgustin' belly-achin'. You don't hear _me_ groanin' like that, do you?"

"Take me to a safe, comfortable jail," says he. "I'm a broken man. My soul is full of remorse and my hide is full of buckshot. My laig is broke and my spirit is crushed. Where'd you git the cannon you shot me with?"

"'Twarn't no cannon," I said with dignity. "I throwed a rock at you."

"But the tree fell!" he says wildly. "Don't tell me you didn't do _that_ with artillery!"

"I roped it and pulled it down," I said, and he give a loud groan and sunk back on the ground, and I said: "Pardon me if I seems to tie yore hands behind yore back and put you acrost Cap'n Kidd. Likely they'll set yore laig at Chawed Ear if you remember to remind 'em about it."

He said nothin' except to groan loud and lusty all the way back to the cabin, and when we got there Glory had tied all them scoundrels' hands behind 'em, and they'd all come to and was groaning in chorus. I found a corral near the house full of their hosses, so I saddled 'em and put them critters onto 'em, and tied their laigs to their stirrups. Then I tied the hosses head to tail, all except one I saved for Glory, and we headed for Chawed Ear.

"What you aimin' to do now, Breck?" she ast as we pulled out.

"I'm goin' to take these critters back to Chawed Ear," I said fiercely, "and make 'em make their spiel to the sheriff and the folks. But my triumph is dust and ashes into my mouth, when I think of the way my folks has did me."

There warn't nothing for her to say; she was a Bear Creek woman. She knowed how Bear Creek folks felt.

"This here night's work," I said bitterly, "has learnt me who my friends is--and ain't. If it warn't for you these thieves would be laughin' up their sleeves at me whilst I rotted in jail."

"I wouldn't never go back on you when you was in trouble, Breck," she says, and I says: "I know that now. I had you all wrong."

We was nearing the town with our groaning caravan strung out behind us, when through the trees ahead of us, we seen a blaze of torches in the clearing around the jail, and men on hosses, and a dark mass of humanity swaying back and forth. Glory pulled up.

"It's the mob, Breck!" says she, with a catch in her throat. "They'll never listen to you. They're crazy mad like mobs always is. They'll shoot you down before you can tell 'em anything. Wait--"

"I waits for nothin'," I said bitterly. "I takes these coyotes in and crams them down the mob's throat! I makes them cussed fools listen to my exoneration. And then I shakes the dust of the Humbolts offa my boots and heads for foreign parts. When a man's kin lets him down, it's time for him to travel."

"_Look there!"_ exclaimed Glory.

We had come out of the trees, and we stopped short at the aidge of the clearing, in the shadder of some oaks.

The mob was there, all right, with torches and guns and ropes-- backed up agen the jail with their faces as pale as dough and their knees plumb knocking together. And facing 'em, on hosses, with guns in their hands, I seen pap and every fighting man on Bear Creek! Some of 'em had torches, and they shone on the faces of more Elkinses, Garfields, Gordons, Kirbys, Grimeses, Buckners, and Polks than them Chawed Ear misfits ever seen together at one time. Some of them men hadn't never been that far away from Bear Creek before in their lives. But they was all there now. Bear Creek had sure come to Chawed Ear.

"Whar is he, you mangy coyotes?" roared pap, brandishing his rifle. "What you done with him? I war a fool and a dog, desertin' my own flesh and blood to you polecats! I don't care if he's a thief or a liar, or what! A Bear Creek man ain't made to rot in a blasted town- folks jail! I come after him and I aim to take him back, alive or dead! And if you've kilt him, I aim to burn Chawed Ear to the ground and kill every able-bodied man in her! _Whar is he, damn yore souls?_"

"I swear we don't know!" panted the sheriff, pale and shaking. "When I heard the mob was formin' I come as quick as I could, and got here by the time they did, but all we found was the jail winder tore out like you see, and three men layin' senseless here and another'n out there in the thicket. They was the guards, but they ain't come to yet to tell us what happened. We was jest startin' to look for Elkins when you come, and--"

"Don't look no farther!" I roared, riding into the torch-light. "Here I be!"

"Breckinridge!" says pap. "Whar you been? Who's that with you?"

"Some gents which has got a few words to say to the assemblage," I says, drawing my string of captives into the light of the torches. Everybody gaped at 'em, and I says: "I interjuices you to Mister Jugbelly Judkins. He's the slickest word-slingin' sharp I ever seen, so I reckon it oughta be him which does the spielin'. He ain't got on his plug-hat jest now, but he ain't gagged. Speak yore piece, Jugbelly."

"Honest confession is good for the soul," says he. "Lemme have the attention of the crowd, whilst I talks myself right into the penitentiary." You could of heard a pin drop when he commenced.

"Donovan had brooded a long time about failin' to take Cap'n Kidd away from Elkins," says he. "He laid his plans careful and long to git even with Elkins without no risk to hisself. This was a job which taken plenty of caution and preparation. He got a gang of versatile performers together--the cream of the illegal crop, if I do say so myself.

"Most of us kept hid in that cabin back up in the hills, from which Elkins recently routed us. From there he worked out over the whole country--Donovan, I mean. One mornin' he run into Elkins at the Mustang Creek tavern. He overheard Elkins say he was broke, also that he was goin' back to Bear Creek and was aimin' to return to War Paint late that evenin'. All this, and Elkins' singed sculp, give him a idee how to work what he'd been plannin'.

"He sent me to meet Elkins and git him drunk and keep him out in the hills all night. Then I was to disappear, so Elkins couldn't prove no alibi. Whilst we was drinkin' up there, Donovan went and robbed the stage. He had his head shaved so's to make him look like Elkins, of course, and he shot old Jim Harrigan jest to inflame the citizens.

"Hurley and Jackson and Slade was his men. The gold Jackson had on him really belonged to Donovan. Donovan, as soon as he'd robbed the stage, he give the gold to Jalatin who lit out for the place where me and Elkins was boozin'. Then Donovan beat it for the cabin and hid the bay mare and put on his wig to hide his shaved head, and got on another hoss, and started sa'ntering along the Cougar Paw-Grizzly Run road--knowin' a posse would soon be headin' for Bear Creek.

"Which it was, as soon as the stage got in. Hurley and Jackson and Slade swore they'd knowed Elkins in Yavapai, and rekernized him as the man which robbed the stage. Ashley and Harrigan warn't ready to say for sure, but thought the robber looked like him. But you Chawed Ear gents know about that--as soon as you heard about the robbery you started buildin' yore special jail, and sent a posse to Bear Creek, along with Ashley and them three fakes that claimed to of rekernized Elkins. On the way you met Donovan, jest like he planned, and he jined you.

"But meanwhile, all the time, me and Elkins was engaged in alcoholic combat, till he passed out, long after midnight. Then I taken the jugs and hid 'em, and pulled out for the cabin to hide till I could sneak outa the country. Jalatin got there jest as I was leavin', and he waited till Elkins sobered up the next momin', and told him a sob story about havin' a wife in poverty, and give him the gold to give to her, and made him promise not to tell nobody where he got it. Donovan knowed the big grizzly wouldn't bust his word, if it was to save his neck even.

"Well, as you all know, the posse didn't find Elkins on Bear Creek. So they started out lookin' for him, with his pap and some of his uncles, and met him jest comin' out into the trail from the place where me and him had our famous boozin' bout. Imejitly Slade, Hurley and Jackson begun yellin' he was the man, and they was backed by Ashley which is a honest man but really thought Elkins was the robber, when he seen that nude skull. Donovan planned to git Elkins shot while attemptin' to escape. And the rest is now history--war-history, I might say."

"Well spoke, Jugbelly," I says, dumping Donovan off my hoss at the sheriff's feet. "That's the story, and you-all air stuck with it. My part of the game's done did, and I washes my hands of it."

"We done you a big injestice, Elkins," says the sheriff. "But how was we to know--"

"Forget it," I says, and then pap rode up. Us Bear Creek folks don't talk much, but we says plenty in a few words.

"I was wrong, Breckinridge," he says gruffly, and that said more'n most folks could mean in a long-winded speech. "For the first time in my life," he says, "I admits I made a mistake. But," says he, "the only fly in the 'intment is the fack that a Elkins was drunk off'n his feet by a specimen like that!" And he p'inted a accusing finger at Jugbelly Judkins.

"I alone have come through the adventure with credit," admitted Jugbelly modestly. "A triumph of mind over muscle, my law-shootin' friends!"

"Mind, hell!" says Jalatin viciously. "That coyote didn't drink none of that licker! He was a sleight-of-hand performer in a vaudeville show when Donovan picked him up. He had a rubber stummick inside his shirt and he poured the licker into that. He couldn't outdrink Breckinridge Elkins if he was a whole corporation, the derned thief!"

"I admits the charge," sighed Jugbelly. "I bows my head in shame."

"Well," I says, "I've saw worse men than you, at that, and if they's anything I can do, you'll git off light, you derned wind-bag, you!"

"Thank you, my generous friend," says he, and pap reined his hoss around and said: "You comin' home, Breckinridge?"

"Go ahead," I said. "I'll come on with Glory."

So pap and the men of Bear Creek turnt and headed up the trail, riding single file, with their rifles gleaming in the flare of the torches, and nobody saying nothing, jest saddles creaking and hoofs clinking softly, like Bear Creek men generally ride.

And as they went the citizens of Chawed Ear hove a loud sigh of relief, and grabbed Donovan and his gang with enthusiasm and lugged 'em off to the jail--the one I hadn't busted, I mean.

"And that," said Glory, throwing her club away, "is that. You ain't goin' off to foreign parts now, be you, Breckinridge?"

"Naw," I said. "My misguided relatives has redeemed theirselves."

We stood there a minute looking at each other, and she said: "You--you ain't got nothin' to say to me, Breckinridge?"

"Why, sure I has," I responded. "I'm mighty much obliged for what you done."

"Is that all?" she ast, gritting her teeth slightly.

"What else you want me to say?" I ast, puzzled. "Ain't I jest thanked you? They was a time when I would of said more, and likely made you mad, Glory, but knowin' how you feel towards me, I--"

"--!" says Glory, and before I knowed what she was up to, she grabbed up a rock the size of a watermelon and busted it over my head. I was so tooken by surprise I stumbled backwards and fell sprawling and as I looked up at her, a great light bust onto me.

"She loves me!" I exclaimed.

"I been wonderin' how long it was goin' to take you to find out!" says she.

"But what made you treat me like you done?" I demanded presently. "I thought you plumb hated me!"

"You ought to of knowed better," says she, snuggling in my arms. "You made me mad that time you licked pap and them fool brothers of mine. I didn't mean most of them things I said. But you got mad and said some things which made me madder, and after that I was too proud to act any way but like I done. I never loved nobody but you, but I wouldn't admit it as long as you was at the top of the ladder, struttin' around with money in yore pocket, and goin' with purty gals, and everybody eager to be friends with you. I was lovin' you then so's it nearly busted me, but I wouldn't let on. I wouldn't humble myself to no blamed man! But you seen how quick I come to you when you needed a friend, you big lunkhead!"

"Then I'm glad all this happened," I says. "It made me see things straight. I never loved no other gal but you. I was jest tryin' to forgit you and make you jealous when I was goin' with them other gals. I thought I'd lost you, and was jest tryin' to git the next best. I know that now, and I admits it. I never seen a gal which could come within a hundred miles of you in looks and nerve and everything."

"I'm glad you've come to yore senses, Breckinridge," says she.

I swung up on Cap'n Kidd and lifted her up before me, and the sky was jest getting pink and the birds was beginning to cut loose as we started up the road towards Bear Creek.

THE END

Lector House believes that a society develops through a two-fold approach of continuous learning and adaptation, which is derived from the study of classic literary works spread across the historic timeline of literature records. Therefore, we aim at reviving, repairing and redeveloping all those inaccessible or damaged but historically as well as culturally important literature across subjects so that the future generations may have an opportunity to study and learn from past works to embark upon a journey of creating a better future.

This book is a result of an effort made by Lector House towards making a contribution to the preservation and repair of original ancient works which might hold historical significance to the approach of continuous learning across subjects.

HAPPY READING & LEARNING!

LECTOR HOUSE LLP
E-MAIL: lectorpublishing@gmail.com